T0077924

ATM and J-LO

DONNELL HARRIS

authorHOUSE®

AuthorHouse™
1663 Liberty Drive
Bloomington, IN 47403
www.authorhouse.com
Phone: 833-262-8899

© 2022 Donnell Harris. All rights reserved.

No part of this book may be reproduced, stored in a retrieval system, or
transmitted by any means without the written permission of the author.

Published by AuthorHouse 06/10/2022

ISBN: 978-1-6655-6237-9 (sc)
ISBN: 978-1-6655-6236-2 (e)

Print information available on the last page.

Any people depicted in stock imagery provided by Getty Images are models,
and such images are being used for illustrative purposes only.
Certain stock imagery © Getty Images.

This book is printed on acid-free paper.

Because of the dynamic nature of the Internet, any web addresses or links contained in
this book may have changed since publication and may no longer be valid. The views
expressed in this work are solely those of the author and do not necessarily reflect the
views of the publisher, and the publisher hereby disclaims any responsibility for them.

INTRODUCTION

Ashanti "J-Lo" Taylor and Akeem "ATM" Anderson couldn't be more different than the sun to the moon. J-Lo was the product of a perfect home. Her mother and father raised her in a safe and secure environment. Her single-family home in the Gwynn Oaks section of Baltimore was consider an up-and-coming community. With mature trees lining the streets, Gwynn Oaks might be consider in another country even though the violence associated with city life was less than five miles away. You might see five-o five times during an entire week. Still playing with dolls at the age of ten with her two best friends Lisa and Chi-Town, they could be seen in front of her house playing house or having a tea party. Riding their bicycles up and down the streets or shouting, these pre-teen young ladies could be seen almost anywhere. If one of them got into a confrontation, you had to deal with them all. J-Lo with her light mocha complexion, full lips, locs extending down to her shoulders on a petite frame was considered the semi-quiet one of the three. Lisa with her light honey complexion, grayish eyes, long natural hair on a medium frame could be consider the brash one of the three while Chi-Town had those alluring bedroom eyes on a deep mocha complexion and a medium frame. She started wearing locs when J started growing hers in the second grade was consider Ms. Intellect. Although different in dispositions, you really didn't want to fuck with these young ladies.

J-Lo was so ecstatic to be attending Forest Park Middle School with her two best friends. You had to possess a strong academic to be able to walk through their doors. All of her arduous work and countless hours in the libraries since fourth grade was starting to produce fruit. A straight "A" student now, the many times she told her girlfriends that she couldn't hangout because she had to study made her parents proud and she never wanted to disappoint them. She was admiring herself in the full-length mirror. With her locs in one of the many fashions she learned to do over the years, she smiled at the reflection staring back at her. With her acid wash jeans, white blouse, and flat shoes, they had started wearing jeans or some form of pants on the first couple days of school because of knucklehead girls even a school that advocate academics. Hearing the doorbell ringing, she grabbed her leather book bag then exit her bedroom and dash down the stairs. She bid her mother goodbye before pulling open the front door and stepping outside.

"Hey, ladies" she greeted them with her broad smile.

"Hey, J" they chimed together.

"Don't yawl look cute" she complimented coming down the steps.

"Yeah, we know" they replied giggling as they proceeded down the street.

As they stood on the corner waiting for the number 91 bus, they couldn't contain their excitement. Most of the whores that walked the strip on Garrison Avenue were still out while others were just coming out to get the money the needed for their gate shot to ease the monkey that was on their backs. Most of them looked like the walking dead and the thought of washing their nasty assess never enter their thought process. Most of their tricks wanted their dick sucks while trying to ignore the funk escaping them. Their greatest aspiration was to find a trick stupid enough to put their cheating dicks inside of them for forty dollars and take the ride of death considering the high rate of HIV amongst them.

Staring back down Garrison, they spotted the bus turning from the Junction and position themselves by the bus stop sign to assure themselves of a seat. Although their ride was only about twelve blocks, neither of them wanted to stand up. As the bus came to a stop slightly ahead of Lisa and when the door swung open, she slightly bump a girl pout of position allowing J and Chi to climb aboard before her.

"Damn, bitch! You could at least say excuse me" a dark complexion girl shouted staring sat her coldly.

"Excuse me" she replied looking over her shoulder and smiling.

"Back here, Lisa!" called J-Lo moving over to allow her the window seat.

"One day, somebody is going to get with you" Chi mention staring at the girl sitting three rows ahead of them with three of her three girlfriends.

"I said excuse me" she replied giggling while staring at the girl. "So, you rather stand then sit?"

"No, I'm not saying that" she replied.

"Yeah, I didn't think so" she replied returning her stare. "If somebody does step out of their lane, they better come correct."

"Why do you always got to take on that thuggish disposition?" Chi asked returning her stare.

"Thuggish? I'm no thug" she replied not appreciating the descriptive. "I'm a young lady."

"Then act like one" interjected J-Lo slightly hardening her eyes. "Your people might be from Lexington Terrance but you're not. I swear, every time you go and spend a month with them during the summer, you come back acting more brash than when you went."

"No, I don't!"

"I just don't get you sometimes" she shared.

"All of this because of her" she said peeking t the girl. "I was just having fun. Yawl need to chill more."

3

"No, you need to chill more" counter Chi. "Every time that we get into something it's because of your mouth."

"I can say whatever I want out of my mouth" she snapped slightly snarling and hardening her eyes.

"Yes, you can but you really need to know when" she said returning her stare and slight snarl.

"Whatever" she replied turning her head to stare out the window. All she was doing was having a little fun. Why did they always have to get with her because of her little antics? Even her mother got up in her personal space recently when she returned from her summer vacation into the city, she also didn't like the influence that the city was having on her or her shitty attitude. She did had to check her mouth sometimes or catch another beat down from her mother. Her tongue had taken on the city's disposition and her alleged subtle change in her style of dress also reflect it.

As the stop across the street in front of their new school, J had to tap her to make her aware that they had reach their destination. Stepping off the bus from the back door, the bus pulled away and stared at the school that they will attend for the next three years. They spotted a few students from their previous school, but the majority of the students were unknown to them. As they carefully cross Garrison, they spotted the girl that Lisa has bump into talking to a group of girls. They peeked at one another as they continued across the street. As step on the side walk and started walking pass them, they exchanged stares.

"What the fuck you looking at bitch!" a heavy-set girl asked staring directly at Lisa while the girl that Lisa had bump was smiling.

"If you see a bitch, step to her" she stated pausing while exchanging cold stares.

"Bitch, don't get fucked up on the first day of school."

"I wish your donut face, jelly rolling ass would put your peanut butter stain stubby fingers on me. Don't let this cute face fool you.

I'll beat you down like you stole my chocolate bar you fat ass hippo" revealing that she wasn't the usual light skin girl. She didn't show no intimidation or apprehension to fight.

"Hold this" she said giving her book bag to one of her friends.

"Hold this" Lisa said giving her book bag to Chi while never averting her eyes from the girl.

"You got a slick tongue for a light skin bitch."

"Are you sure you can trust your girl with your lunch box" counter Lisa causing a few giggles among the spectators.

As the two girls got closer, Lisa surprised the hell out of her. Not another word was exchanged as she started setting fire to the heavy-set girl then got some distance while staring over at her.

"Get her Big Cheryl!" one of her girlfriends shouted encouragement.

"Bitch!" she snorted wiping the blood from her nose.

"Stop talking fat ass and come get your dessert."

As Big Cheryl came for seconds, Lisa lit fire to her again except this time she knocked her on her ass. As she scurry to her feet embarrass, she got knock back down by a barrage of vicious punches. One of her girlfriend started to make a move, J caught her eyes specifically.

"I wouldn't suggest that" she warned the girl staring in her eyes.

Looking at J-Lo's petite frame, she proceeded with her intentions to assist her friend. J hit the girl with a simple right hand, and you wouldn't have thought she hit her that hard the way she crumble to the ground. All the little boys swear that she possess heavy hands when she touch them for tapping her ass and running. She didn't understand their meaning then until this moment. The girl mouth and nose was bleeding as she stared up at her from the ground. Although the girl was taller and heavier, the look on her face revealed she thought she was hit by a teenager or woman. Her girlfriends assisted her to her feet, but she never approached her assailant only stared at her still in shock.

"Five-o!" someone shouted from the crowd as Lisa slam a final right into her mouth then accepted her book bag from Chi and step off. As the crowd disburse, Big Cheryl was struggling to get to her feet.

"Alright! Alright! Break it up!" demanded the two school police officers searching the eyes for those that might have been fighting. Lisa and them, walked right pass them as them as they focus on Big Cheryl and her girlfriend spitting blood from the mouths.

"I hope this isn't how our school year is going to be" mention J peeking over her shoulder at five-o interviewing them.

"It better not or my knuckles will look like a junky's hand" Lisa snicker as they climbed the steps to the main entrance.

"If it is, I'm transferring out" Chi threaten.

"No, you won't" replied Lisa giggling. "You won't abandon us."

"Don't be so sure" she replied as they step through the security scanners then paused at the bulletin board to locate where their homeroom was located.

"Oh, we're sure" they replied giggling as they headed towards the stairway to take it to the second floor. Entering room 224, they stared over at their homeroom teacher Mr. Smith then took a seat in the middle of the class.

"Find a seat and please be quiet" he order in his 70ish style suite.

"Look at that fake wanna be Billy D. Williams" whisper Lisa.

"I thought Jerri Swirl played out" mention J smiling.

"He has juice running down to his collar now" Chi notice smiling. "I wonder do her wear a plastic cap at night."

"If he don't, his pillow cases have to be funky as hell" describe Lisa causing them to giggle louder than anticipated causing Mr. Smith to stare in their direction.

For the next half hour, he took roll call and spoke briefly about himself. He would be the sixth period history teacher to a couple of the students but J and them wasn't included. As he wish for their experience at forest park to be memorable, the three young ladies peek at one another then started snickering.

"Is there a problem, young ladies?" he asked staring back at them.

"We are already building memories" Lisa replied smiling at him.

Akeem (judge) was born, raised, and educated in the city's most notorious high rise of Murphy Homes. His mother was a dedicated junky while his father was doing life for a double homicide. His uncles on both side of his family tree was hell raisers and very well known by the Baltimore City Police Department. Considered the most violent clan in the city, they thrive to maintain the family reputation alive and flourishing. By the time he was eight years old, he was able to assemble and disassemble a Glock 40 while know how much baby laxative to mix in a key of dope. The technic used to convert cocaine into crack was also a part of his education while learning the rules associated with the streets. Just about all of his uncles and cousins were affiliated with the drug game one way or another. Getting incarcerated was consider a badge of honor and a form of rite of passage into manhood. As psychotic as it might sound, the men with Anderson blood running through their veins was expected to take and make that nonproductive path of self-destruction or be consider a punk.

With his mother constant nagging for him to step up and be the man of the house, he would sometimes be a mule for his older cousins and uncles. Carrying well over ten-thousand vials of dope on him to distribute to their corner boys, he earned five-hundred-dollars a week. Force to give his mother half, he usually grind four days a week. With the money he had left over, he would take his two younger brothers to the second-hand store to buy clothes. Although they weren't wearing the latest fashion, nobody couldn't say they didn't dress well or that they were shy when it came to soap and water. He took them to the barber shop every two weeks to tighten up their fades. He forbid them to walk down the stairway after dark in their building even if they were going just one floor below. Taking the elevator was safer. The drug dealers that controlled the building also controlled the stairway. Stick-up crews were always hoping to catch them sleeping but they were the ones usually going to sleep, permanently. Akeem had two activities that kept him off the streets. Going to the library up at Penn-North with his two little brothers for a minimum of three hours and playing basketball. If you couldn't find him at the Penn-North, search the basketball courts especially at Chadwick and Dru Hill Park working on his game.

On the first day of school, he made sure his brothers attire was presentable then sat down to have breakfast with them. He had to leave twenty minutes ahead of them because his trip was further. He didn't have to check to make sure that their beds were made anymore. The ass kicking, he administered to them put them on point after that incident. Just before he open the front door, he stared into the front room at his mother entertaining another stranger. Although he saw the man often, he was still a stranger and wanted to keep it that way. Looking out into the morning sun, he squinch his eyes and step out while closing the door. He walked over towards the elevator and push the button. He could hear the outdated elevator struggling to make it to the nineth floor. He initially started to take the stairway, but he didn't want to see his friends parents coping their morning gate shot. Although consider functioning addicts, he had more respect for them than those that went out to steal for their money. As it finally rattled to a stop, he was glad that nobody was on it and hope that he could reach the first floor on one breath of air as the scent of urine invaded his nostrils. He step aboard and press the lobby button then the door slowly closed. 8,7,6,5,4, TING! "Shit!" As the door struggled to open, several people got aboard.

"Good morning, Akeem."

"Morning Sunshine" he replied inhaling the fresh air before the door closed again.

"How are you doing Akeem?"

"Just fine, Ms. Mabel."

"Is your mother up?"

"Yes, ma'am."

"What is she doing?"

"Besides, minding her business, she's listen to 95.9."

"Is she alone?"

"No." Ding! "She's getting ready to turn a trick" he informed her ignoring the surprise expression that came to her face as the elevator door finally open. He step out then walked casually through the lobby and exit the front door. Looking towards the court yard, several teenagers were smoking blunts and sharing a forty ounce of brew.

"Why do you have to be so vulgar?" Sunshine asked poking him in his ribs.

"Why do your mother have to ask so many damn questions?" he asked staring down into her hazel eyes.

"You know how she is?"

"And she know how I am also" he counter. "She is going to go up there anyway so why ask her business after she knew she was woke?"

"I can't dispute that" she agreed slightly smiling. "Why don't you wait to walk with me and my girls?"

"Is Biggie coming with them?"

"Yes."

"Then walk with him, he is your boyfriend, right?" he asked staring into her eyes.

"Yes."

"Then wait on him" he said stepping off and heading towards Pennsylvania Avenue.

As she stood there watching him walking away, all she could do was shake her head and remanence. Why did she take Doll's dare to kiss Biggie? She was supposed to be Akeem's girlfriend and enjoyed the times they spent together. Everybody complimented them and boasted

9

that they look extremely sexy together. Several girls in their building were always pressing up on his fine deep mocha complexion, but he politely discarded their advances especially Ecstasy fast ass. That girl was like a 7-11 Store, always open for service. She would kick that thing out to just about anybody, but she had the audacity to be attracted to Akeem.

When they were in Dru Hill Park chilling, they stumble upon Biggie with his little crew. Although he was three years older than her, he wasn't no way as cute as Akeem. His thuggish disposition did intrigued her but that was it. He didn't possess the intellect that Akeem possesses or the sexy swag he has in his walk. During their interaction, one thing led to another, and the dare was made. Before she knew it, she was in his arms kissing. After they had finish kissing, she stared around smiling at her girlfriends, but they weren't smiling back. They were staring at intensely at something or someone. Turning to see what, Akeem was standing in the distance staring at her. As she started to approach him, he put up his one hand warning her to stop, and she did. The look of hurt and anger that filled his eyes will permanently remained engraved into her consciousness. She never consider him being at the basketball court and that was asinine. She had jump out of character trying to be slick and got fucked displaying an unfaithful disposition. As hard as she tried to talk to him, her words of forgiveness was falling on deaf ears. He didn't acknowledge her for almost ten months. He broke his silence on her birthday with a birthday card.

As he was walking up Pennsylvania Avenue, he ran into Monk and Twin standing on Fayette Street.

"What's up, Akeem?" they greeted him tapping knuckles.

"Not too much" he replied looking around. "What's up with yawl?"

"Today is Monday" replied Monk. "We are waiting on the Tasty Cake truck" he shared smiling.

"Don't yawl get tire of hitting that man's truck?"

"Nope" they replied together tapping knuckles and laughing.

"Well, I'm going tom leave yawl to yawl mission."

"Why don't you wait for us?" suggested Twin.

"Na, I'm not being implicated in stealing some cakes and pies" he smiled at them.

"Aahhh, come on man."

"Na."

"Why not" insisted Twin.

"Because I don't have to" he replied tapping their knuckles. "Yawl are going to share it with me anyway."

"We might not this time" Monk counter.

"Yes, you will but I don't know about Twin" he replied laughing as he headed up Fayette Street. He wanted to include them in his private endeavors, but they showed him repeatedly that they weren't ready to explore and make the money he could offer them. They were still enjoying their childhood and he wasn't going to deny them what was denied to him. He would include them when they were ready but not before hand. Nom used growing up faster than you have to. As he was approaching McMechin Street, he spotted a small crowd forming. He was about to go and investigate but his family always told him. "If it didn't pertain to you, keep it moving." So, he kept it moving. It was almost seven-forty-five when he enter Harlem Park Junior High for the first time. There were a lot of fresh faces blessing the school especially the vibrant and blossoming young ladies. Guys that were in the eight and nineth grade were pressing straight up on them like they were fish in barrel waiting to be pluck. The scene was straight out of a movie.

"Yo, Akeem! Akeem!"

Hearing his name being called, he looked around to see who was calling him. Suddenly, he spotted who was calling him coming out of a small crowd. "Hey Cross. I didn't know you went here" he said tapping his knuckles.

"Shit, I didn't know you went here."

"My first year."

"My second" he replied smiling. "Listen man, how would you like to play ball for the school? I got something brewing" he shared.

"Sure, I'm down."

"Great, what time do you have lunch?"

"I got the early lunch."

"What a beautiful coincident. So, do I" he burst out laughing. "Things couldn't have fallen in place any more than if I set it up myself. How about meeting me here right here at lunch time. I got somebody that I want you to meet."

"No, problem. I'll be here" he assured him.

"Alright, partner. I'll holla at you later" he said tapping his knuckles then rejoining his little group. As they started up the hallway, he said something to them that had them all turned and stare at him before continuing up the hallway.

He had met Cross up at Chadwick one Saturday morning during the summer when he was originally heading to Dru Hill basketball courts. His crossover was as wick as Allen Iverson. He had broken many of guys ankles reaching for his baby. He had a glitch in his jumper, but he was somewhat consistent as he would pull up at the foul line taking that fifteen-foot jumper before the big guys could reject it. They had played on several teams against older competition and won more than they lost. They genuinely complimented one another game.

By the time lunch came around at Forrest park, word had spread around the school about the fight. When J, Lisa and Chi walked inside the cafeteria, a slight pause occurred that didn't go unnoticed by them. As they got in line to buy their lunch, they could feel the eyes of the other students following them. They brought their lunch then stood scanning the place for a seat. They eventually spotted one on the far side of the cafeteria and proceeded in that direction. Placing their trays down, they took a brief peek around before taking their seat.

"Damn, did a famous artist walked in or what?" Lisa asked taking a scoop of salad on her fork then shoving it in her mouth.

"You would think so" Chi stated taking a bite out of her tuna fish sandwich while peeking around.

"Na, word is out about us" J counter taking a sip from her apple juice and catching a young lady eyes as she walked pass.

"I hope it is" Lisa replied staring around as she crew her vegetables. "Maybe these little bitches will leave us alone."

"Time will tell" Chi replied catching a girl eye then they exchanged smiles.

"Oh, hell" J-Lo stated staring at the cafeteria door. "Here comes those girls from this morning" she informed them as they turned and stared at the door also. Big Cheryl scanned the room until she found them, but she didn't come in their direction.

"I would hate to hit that fat bitch in the face with this tray, but I surely will if she come over here with her bullshit" she promise staring at her as she put another fork load of vegetables into her mouth.

"She don't want nothing to do with you girl" Chi assured her giggling. "The ass kicking you administer to her this morning should last all year."

"I hope so" she replied peeking over at her as she moved in the opposite direction that they were sitting.

"Excuse me, ladies" a boy voice caught their attention. "My name is D.J" he introduced himself displaying a perfect set of white teeth. With natural wavy hair and light complexion, his light brown eyes stared directly at Lisa. "These are my friends D.C and Slim."

"Glad to meet yawl. I'm Lisa and these are my girls J-Lo and Chi-Town."

"We wanted to welcome yawl to our school" he informed them still smiling.

"We were welcome earlier" Lisa informed him. "What grades are yawl in?"

"The eighth."

"So, what's up?"

"We just want to get to know yawl that's all."

"That's all, huh?" she replied with a coy smile.

"Yeah" he tried to convince her.

"Right now, we are having lunch and eating in front of guys that we don't know isn't happening" she stared up at him.

"I can respect that" he told her. "So, can we hook up after school?"

"Ladies, what do yawl say" she asked staring over at them.

"That's cool" they replied together.

"So, where do yawl want to hook up?"

"How about the park on Woodlawn Drive" she suggested.

"Which one?"

"The one across the street from the apartment complex."

"Sure, what time?"

"What's good for you?"

"Four o'clock, ladies?"

"Yeah" they replied while exchanging stares with his partners.

"Cool" he replied smiling broadly at Lisa.

"Four o'clock, D.J" she said in a tone that caused his smile to slightly dissipate.

"We'll be there Lisa" he tried to assure her. "Enjoy the rest of yawl lunch."

"Oh, we will" she told him slightly smiling as he turned and led his boys away. "Damn, he's cute."

"Slim isn't bad looking" commented J.

"I don't do light skin guys and D.C is definitely light skin" Chi slightly snarled.

"Girl, you don't do anything with any guy" Lisa mention snickering.

"And it's gonna remain that way until I graduate high school" she said with conviction. "Don't forget about the oath we made."

"I don't remember it being an oath" J stated smiling. "We have a hundred-dollar bet."

"I'm damn sure not gonna break it and give yawl a hundred dollars" Chi said staring over at them.

"Neither am I" cosigned Lisa.

"Yeah, right" J and Chi said then burst out laughing.

At Harlem Middle, when Akeem arrived at the designated location, Cross was already there with three other guys.

"Fellas, this is Akeem. After today, you will know why I call him ATM" he snicker. "Let's bounce" he said leading the way towards the gym. When they enter, there was five guys down court working on a nice sweat while the gym teacher was in the bleachers. "Are they ready Mr. Cooper?" he asked starting to remove his shirt.

"Oh, they are ready and highly motivated" he replied smiling.

"The let the lessons begin" he said as the others removed their shirts then approached center court while staring at their opponents.

"Yawl sure yawl don't want to warm up first?"

"Na, we'll warm up by lighting them up" Cross replied with a serious stare.

"Okay, the game is to sixteen. Yawl switch at eight and call yawl own fouls" he instructed them then walked towards the bleacher and took a seat.

"Since yawl are the visitors, yawl can have the ball first" their main man offer.

"Thank you" replied Cross as they headed down court. "Byrd is at center while Ice play power forward. Akeem you are the three while me and Dink do our thing. Have fun but kick their asses" he slightly snarled.

As the game unfolded, Byrd earned his nickname. He had an unbelievable vertical while Ice was as strong as his young body portrayed. Cross was breaking his man's ankles repeatedly forcing Dink and Akeem's man to help. While Dink was making the nets snap, Akeem was banking shots from both baselines. Feeding the horses inside, they beat them 16-9.

"Run it back!" the main guy insisted.

"Can't" replied Cross heading towards the bleacher. "If you want the lesson to continue, meet us up at Chadwick around four."

"Na, it has to be later" interjected ATM.

"Make it at five instead" Cross smiled at him.

"We'll be there" he snarled as they gather their clothes and walked out the gym.

"Do you see what you can have?" Cross asked staring at Mr. Cooper.

"Very impressive, I must admit" he smiled staring at them. "Are yawl coming out for the basketball team this year?" he asked staring directly at Cross.

"Only if we are the starting five" he replied. "We just audition by whipping the brakes off of your previous starting five. If they come to Chadwick later today, I'll give you the results" he told him smiling.

"Come out and we'll see" he replied but his mind was already made up and there wasn't nothing that Tito could say. "What's his name?" he asked staring at Akeem.

"ATM!" they chime together then burst out laughing.

"As you saw, his bank is always open" Cross said laughing as they headed out the gym.

"Damn, ATM. You work the hell out of that backboard" Ice complimented.

"Thanks man."

"Who taught you?"

"My father favorite player was Elvin Hayes. So, I started emulating his shot as I grew up."

"Growing up?" Byrd chuckled. "You won't grow up as you say until you grow into those cruise ships that you call feet" he crack slick as they burst out laughing.

"How tall is your father?" inquired Dink.

"Six-six."

"If you get near that height, you are going to be a beast" Cross said staring in his eyes.

"I'm a beast now" he boasted slightly smiling.

"Not yet, grasshopper" Byrd told him staring in his eyes. "But you damn sure could be if you keep a level head."

"You don't have to worry about that" Cross told him. "Once we start playing against the older guys, they will humble him and us."

"That's for sure" Ice cosigned. "We might be above our peers, but those old guys is gonna toughen us up especially me and Byrd when it comes to hitting the boards."

"We have got to get our bodies stronger" mention Dink. "We need to get memberships at the Y.M.C.A."

"Now that is a terrific suggestion" Cross admitted smiling. "I know yawl are down so when do yawl want to get them?"

"Saturday" replied Byrd. "Let's hook up at ten o'clock."

"Sounds good" replied Cross. "But let's not forget what we have on our plates for later today."

"No way" replied Byrd. "I want to continue terrorizing Tito" he shared with a coy smile.

The bell suddenly ringing cease their conversation.

"Let's hook up at Penn-North at four-thirty" Cross told them.

"Alright" Byrd said starting to tap their knuckles. "Beautiful touch on that backboard."

"Way to bang those boards" he counter smiling as they tap knuckles then the squad disburse in separate directions.

At four-thirty, the ladies were still in Woodlawn Park waiting on D.J and his partners. They all decided to wear shorts and a tight-fitting T-shirt to display their young budding bodies. Chi had the most develop out of the group. She had went to sleep one night and somebody blew up her titties. While J and Lisa's were taking their good ole damn time, Chi would thrust them out at the salivating teenage boys and enjoyed witnessing their lust consume their eyes. To say she didn't appreciate the attention would be a lie. She used what she had to get what she wanted from the teenage boys. Getting them to buy her and her girlfriends snow cones or snowballs was nothing. She would lay those things on their lustful backs, and they were like puddy in her hands. Her girls would have tears in their eyes laughing that them, drooling over her while staring in her bedroom eyes.

"Let's bounce" Lisa announced getting to her feet.

"It's about time" Chi said joining her while wiping off the seat of her pants.

"So, what do yawl want to do now" inquired J as they headed towards the entrance of the park. "I really don't want to go home."

"How about going to Chadwick?" Lisa suggested with an impish grin.

"Chadwick? Where in the hell is Chadwick?" J asked not liking that grin on her face.

"Not far from Dru Hill Park" she replied avoiding their eyes.

"In the city!"

"Yes, Chi" she replied staring in her eyes. "We can catch the speedline to Mondawmin then transfer to the number 5."

"Oh, you have the route map out already" J-Lo said staring at her.

"Girl, I'm not feeling this" Chi voice her apprehension.

"Nobody is going to mess with us" she replied to assured them.

"You don't know that for sure" Chi counter exchanging stares.

"No, I don't" she admitted. "As much as we get around, we could get our asses kicked anywhere."

"True" stated J. "But we wouldn't have to run five miles to get home."

"Stop sounding like yawl are some punks, as bitches" she said hardening her eyes. "Are yawl down with me or not?"

"So, you are going with or without us?" J asked staring at her.

"Yeah, are you down or what?" he asked staring in their eyes individually.

"You know we are" Chi slightly snarled at her. "I just want it written down that I'm not feeling this."

"Okay, I'm writing it down" she replied slightly smiling. "Come on, I see the bus."

The bus was just pulling away from Woodlawn Library as they cross the street. The bus pulled up in front of them then they climbed aboard swiping their all-day pass while greeting several people that they knew as they found seats in the back. Just as they got settle, they spotted their dates walking like they were on a Sunday stroll with no place to go. Checking their watches, they were extremely late. They exit the bus five minutes later at Rogers Station then started casually walking up the ramp. Looking down the track towards Reistertown Plaza, they spotted the train coming then they started sprinting while giggling. Inserting their cards in the turnstile, they briskly walked up the escalator and paused on the platform with the others was the train came to a stop. He walked aboard and took seats near the middle. Two stops later, they were getting to their feet then following the people off the train and taking the escalator up. Coming out the station, the number five bus was sitting there just like she said. Walking towards the middle of the bus, they found seats and exhaled. This was the first time that J and Chi have ever been in the city and so close to Mondawmin Mall without at least one of their parents. They secretly hope that they weren't making an unwise decision as the five pulled off.

The ride was much quicker than both young ladies had anticipated. Their destination appeared so close that they could have walked the distance. Since they didn't know it, but Lisa did, she wanted them to feel safe and they appreciated her consideration. The bus actually stop directly across the street from their destination. There were people everywhere. As they cross the street, both full courts were occupied and so was the half courts. Guys on the courts were wearing their expensive sneakers as if they would make them a better player. As they enter the courts, they spotted seats opening up in the bleachers under the tree and near the building. Someone had their boom box plugged into the electrical socket and playing the latest tunes. The environment was more like a party atmosphere that anything else. Girls would peek at them then get back to doing what they were doing initially. In the far corner, some older teenagers and early twenties were smoking blunts with some girls. There was a small group among them dancing very provocative. They have never experience such an alluring environment.

"Is this how they get down?" inquired J smiling from ear to ear.

"Every day" Lisa replied checking out some girls checking them out as they walked pass.

"Girl, they are partying" Chi admitted amazed at the erotic scene. "You come here with your cousins?"

"Sometimes but we don't have to travel this far up to get our groove on" she told them smiling. "Are you feeling this now Chi?"

"Definitely" she admitted checking out a guy checking her out.

At five-fifteen, the man that ran the building and courts told the winners on court A to move their game over to court B.

"Why Chubby?" one of the guys asked while gather his stuff.

"Because I said so" he gave as a reason watching them move their game over. "Cross! Cross!"

"Yeah, Unc!" a bronze complexion guy answer getting to his feet.

"Get your squad on the court." As Cross squad took the court, their opponent also took it.

"Damn, those guys are much older than the other team" mention J.

"It isn't the size of the dog but the fight up in him" Lisa quoted smiling. "That's Cross, he got mad handles. I've seen the other guys before except the guy with the fade.

"He's a kindda handsome" complimented J smiling. "Mmmmm."

"Yes, he is" cosigned Chi.

As the game got started, J-Lo couldn't keep her eyes off the stranger. She watched every movement that he made. With that little swag that she never notice on a guy before, she became mesmerize by him. Sitting down on defense and taking hard elbows to the chest without complaining. When he came off a pick on either side of the court, somebody needed to get him before he elevated because he was killing them with his bank shot. The crowd was in a frizzle watching the younger squad taking the older squad to school.

"That little nigger is dangerous with that bank shot" a man stated.

"When Cross breaks his man's ankle and attacked the rim, take your poison. Dink or ATM" another guy asked smiling.

"Neither I'm staying with my man" a woman replied causing them to burst out laughing.

"His name is ATM?" inquired a teenage girl staring at him closely.

"Yup and it fits" the guy replied smiling.

As more and more people focus on the game, everybody was wondering who was ATM and where the fuck he live? Through all the speculations, no one seem to know him personally. Several girls had said they have seen him with two little boys going into Penn-North Library. Where does he hang out and with whom illuded them all? One thing they all complimented was that sexy walk he possess. He had a swag that a boy his age shouldn't possess. He was the mystery guy that everybody wanted to get to know. What was he so confident about? He was the mystery guy that everybody There was no doubt that he was handsome and didn't waste his mother's money by purchasing expensive sneakers. He wore a specific pair of sneakers designed for black tops called And 1.

"Girl, I'm going to give him my number" an extremely attractive chocolate complexion girl said to her girlfriends.

"He probably already got a girlfriend" one of her girls said.

"Then he'll have two" she replied giggling.

On the left side baseline, ATM got a pick from Ice stretching his man out. As he came across the baseline, Cross hit him on time with a perfect pass. As he took flight, the center came over to challenge him, but he was one second too late. As the ball rolled off his fingertips, the ball floated over his out stretch arm. The ball hit the sweet spot on the backboard then zip through the net.

"Ooooo!" the crowd shouted.

"Damn! In your face!"

"That little nigger can shoot!"

"You wanna run it back?" inquired Cross staring at the main guy.

"Na, yawl got it" he surrender tapping his knuckles.

"Next up!" Cross called for the next challengers.

The thing that J admired about the stranger was how cool he remained. Barely smiling especially on the basketball court but he acknowledge the praises he rightfully deserved. She watch several girls around her age or slightly older approach him and his teammates to introduce themselves especially the girl that was sitting in front of her. She wish she had the heart to boldly walk up to a guy and introduce herself. First of all, she didn't know what to say after introducing herself. The last thing she wanted was to embarrass herself or sound immature. He was handsome as hell, but she was a punk bitch.

"Yawl wanna bounce?" Lisa asked already knowing the answer.

"Not yet" replied Chi staring at a bronze complexion guy in a pair of black and white Jordans with a black playboy T-shirt.

"Na, I'm okay too" replied J never averting her eyes from ATM.

As the second game commenced, the guy that was exchanging stares with Chi finally got his heart up and came over to introduce himself. The guy that was sitting next to him eventually got up and came to sit next to Lisa. Several guys tried their hands with J, but she made it perfectly clear that she wasn't interested in anything that they may be chirping. Her full attention was on ATM. Although the second squad that played them was older, taller and play physical as hell, they also fell by a double screen set for Dink at the top of the key. As they headed towards the bleachers to rest, ATM suddenly made eye contact with J. He pause for a moment then smiled at her before heading to the bleachers.

"Damn, J. He smiled at you" teased Lisa nudging her. "He haven't smile all day until he saw you."

"Yeah, I saw that" she admitted still staring at him.

"What are you going to do?"

"What do you mean?" she asked staring in her eyes.

"Girl you better het that boy number" she urged her.

"I can't do that" she whisper embarrass.

"You want me to get it for you?"

"No, Lisa" she said adamantly. "How would that look you getting his number for me?"

"Like somebody helping their shy girlfriend out" she replied smiling.

"No, don't" she insisted hardening her eyes.

"Alright but it's your lost. Look at those little hookers trying to get up in his head.

"Let them" she replied staring back over at him. "All they are doing are making themselves look foolish."

"Maybe so but they are at least trying to get what they want" she said before continuing her conversation with her new acquaintance.

The next team was much too much for them. As hard as they tried, a maturity factor with their physical play eventually worn them down losing sixteen to eleven. As they removed their shirts to put on a dry one, J took notice of his body. Most guys his age still possess baby fat especially around the mid-section, but his body was taking on definition. She would love to see how his body have develop by the time he was fifteen or older. How was she to know that it would be three years before their eyes connected again?

At Harlem Park, the basketball team was tearing the fur off of their competitors. With their steady increase in wins, other schools started sending out scouts to view that horror show that will star them next. With the Sun Papers continuously congratulating them on winning their region, high school coaches started coming to their games in their final year. Since they will be taking their talent to Dunbar High after graduating, coaches needed to see for themselves what they will be facing next year and try to construct a defensive plan for the exceptional young talents.

ATM mother didn't show any interest in his or his two younger brothers academics. Her main conversation with him was joining the family business. She wanted him to accept her younger brother's invitation to create his own crew and maintain a corner somewhere. In the last three years, his body had gotten stronger, and he was standing six-two. Incorporating Pop's Boxing Gym on North Avenue and the Y.M.C.A in his schedule, his body had gotten stronger while the library nourish his intellect. In his neighborhood that included Lexington Terrence, everybody knew who he was including people living in Gilmore and McCullen Homes. Only two OG's on the East Side actually knew his identity and swear he was the reincarnation of his father. While trying to fly under the radar, the inevitable occurred. He had gotten into several fights for someone being disrespectful because of his nonchalant disposition or trying to impede his movement. The so-called tough guys and gangsters in training foolishly forgot rule 124. "Never judge a book by its cover."

One of the reasons why he travel around the city is to get a peace of mind and escape his popularity. No matter how far he escape, he had things he had to do for his family at eight o'clock.

"Here" his uncle T.C said extending a leather bag to him. "I need you to take this to my people up on Edmondson and Monroe."

"Edmondson and Monroe?" he repeated staring at him. "When did you set up shop there?"

"As soon as you get there" he said with a smirk on his face.

"You know those guys down at Appleton won't lay down" he informed him returning his stare as he grabbed the bag and felt the weight. "What's inside?"

"That's not your concern!" he snapped exchanging stares.

"It's my concern when I'm the one being the mule" he corrected him.

"And as far as those guys not laying down, they better be ready to get down" he replied ignoring his statement.

He understood the terminology of "getting down." Either throw your lead or move, it was just that simple. Fuck making the corner hot and the revenue that would be lost until five-o surrender the corner back. "Who is opening up shop?"

"Monk and Twin. Do you know them?"

"Yeah" he unconsciously smiled. "When did they get back?"

"Almost two months ago. They said yawl used to hang out together."

"Yeah, we did until they got caught up three years ago."

"What did they do?"

His instantly harden from the question as he stared into his eyes. "You have to ask them."

"I'm asking you!" he snarled returning his stare.

"I don't remember" he flatly said.

"Yes, you do. What did they do?"

"I got to go" he said grabbing the bag and heading towards the door. "If there is something that you want to know about another man, go ask that man" he threw his words over his shoulder just like when he asked him about his father. He open the door and step outside. He took the elevator down and minutes later he was walking through the court yard heading towards Pennsylvania Avenue. He stood on the corner of Dolphin Street signaling that he needed a hack. A minute later an old model Honda pulled over.

"Where are you going soldier?" the driver asked.

"Edmondson and Fulton."

"Five dollars."

"We can do that" he replied opening the passenger's door and climbing inside then fastening his seatbelt. He extended the five dollars to him then lean back and got comfortable. Scanning inside his car, he notice that the driver had forgot to discard a vial that was in his ashtray. He thought about the last time he saw them. They were trying to convince him to hit the Tasty Cake truck with them but as usual, he declined. When he didn't see them in school later, he knew something went wrong. It was later that night that he found out what had transpired. They had played their hand like they usually did, but this time it had an unsuspecting twist. When the driver went inside to confirm his order, they used the flat head screwdriver to pop the cheap lock. While Twin kept his eyes on the guy inside, Monk climbed inside. Hearing banging and the truck rocking, Twin race to the back and staring inside. Monk was gaffling with a white man. So, he leap inside to assist him. As they struggled with the man, Twin suddenly kicked him in the face causing him to stagger backward and falling out the open door. How ironic it was that five-o was just coming up the street. Seeing them, they leap from the truck and sprinted up Mosher

Street. Nobody have ever been able to outrun communication. Before they realize what was happening, the area was saturated with patrol cars, and they were caught minutes later then placed in handcuffs. The only reason why the white judge gave them three years in juvie was to send a message loud and clear. Assaulting a white man was the essence of their conviction not the trying to steal some cakes and pies.

"Here you are" the driver said breaking his concentration.

"Thanks" replied opening the door and stepping out. He stood on the corner surveying the area to make sure five-o wasn't monitoring the area. He eventually casually strolled down Edmondson towards Monroe. Sitting in the shadows, he spotted Monk. He could recognize the shape of his head from any distance. They had tried naming him Head Quarters, but he wasn't having that. Spotting a shadowy figure walking in the shadows, he instinctively got to his feet and stared in his direction. A broad smile suddenly came to his face.

"Man, I'll know your walk anywhere" he snicker giving him a hug then staring in his eyes.

"I said the same thing about your head" he counter blocking his punch to his ribs.

"Much love, Akeem."

"One love brother."

"What's up Twin? No love for me" he asked slightly smiling.

"Always" he replied tapping his knuckles.

"We appreciated what you did for us over the years" Monk stress.

"Man, we are family" then included. "Yawl would have done the same thing for me."

"Don't ever doubt that" Monk said with conviction in his eyes. "What are you doing up this far?"

"I'm who you are waiting for" he announced.

"What? You?" Twin burst out laughing.

"Yeah, me negro" he assured him passing him the bag.

"How do you know T.C?" inquired Monk.

"He's my uncle, man" he informed them.

"Your uncle. So, that's why he hired us after mentioning that we knew you" Twin shared snickering. "Talking about a small world."

"Where is your corner boys?"

"Exactually where they should be, out of sight but they see us" Twin replied inspecting the contents of the bag then pulling out two Glocks and several magazines. He pass one to Monk and they place them in the small of their backs before pulling out a large quality of vials containing dope. Every bundle contained fifty vials. He whistle then guys he have seen around the set materialized.

"Where re your competitors?"

"Down on Pulaski" Twin said giving two bundles to the three guys with him.

"Why don't yawl hit up at Fulton? From that location, you can monitor things in all directions. At this location, once they turn off of Fulton, your movement is limited."

"T.C wants this corner" Twin replied returning his stare.

"T.C isn't out here placing his freedom on the line. You are" he replied hardening his eyes.

"Supposed he cruise pass and don't see us?" asked Monk.

"Tell him I told yawl to move" he told him slightly hardening his eyes. "Turn around, what do you see?" he asked as they stared up towards Fulton.

"Nothing" they both replied.

"And that is why you have to move" he told them. "Yawl are out here to get that money not a criminal record for distribution. Look how dark the bus stop is, the only way somebody would know that you are there is if they were turning off Fulton and their headlights illuminate the area. Five-o know about those boys down at Pulaski and would monitor them from this location. Understand?"

"Smart move Akeem" admitted Monk smiling up at him. "Are you bouncing?"

"Na, man. I haven't seen yawl knuckleheads in a minute. Send one of your boys to the bar to pass out ten vials and informed them where they will be located."

"Turk, jump on that."

"On my way" he said walking towards the bar.

"Yawl go and post up" Twin instructed them, and they cross the street then walked up to Fulton Street and took a seat at the bus stop.

For the next three hours, he watched their business slowly take roots. As more and more junkies spread the word about the "joint" in the area, they started flocking to them like bees to honey. Eventually, just like they expected the boys at Pulaski got wind of the new crew and sent three guys to do recon.

"Yo, ATM!"

"Whoa! What's up Beanie?" he replied getting to his feet and tapping knuckles.

He looked at Monk and Twin then asked. "Are these your boys?"

"Na, they are my cousins Monk and Twin" he replied peeking at his partners. "Is there going to be a problem?"

"Na, man. As long as they stay where they are and not here everything will be good" he assured him.

"You don't have to worry about that. Right Cuz?" he asked staring in their eyes.

"Right" they replied assuring him.

"When is your next game?" Beanie asked.

"Saturday, some place in Woodlawn."

"Leave a message at Chadwick for me and I'll get it."

"Bet" he replied tapping his knuckles.

"I'll holla at you later."

"Later, Beanie" he replied watching him turning with his two associates then proceeding back down the street.

"So, you have a little clout huh?" smiled Twin.

"Na, I just know people."

"Yeah, we heard that you perfected that Bankshot down to an art" mention Monk grinning. "What are they calling you now? ATM?"

"Yeah" he admitted smiling.

"Your shit, is always on huh?"

"Not always" he admitted. "Sometimes I make an over-draft, or she might take an unannounced vacation on the other side of town, and I have to go to bring her ass back home" he shared causing them to snicker.

"So, what's on your agenda for the rest of the night?" Monk asked.

"Now that our competition know who we are and set the boundaries for us, I got to bounce.

"When can we hook up?" Monk wanted to know wishing that he didn't have to leave.

"The last day of school is tomorrow. We can patch up after that until yawl have to relieve those brothers at eight" he told him seeing the disappointment in his eyes.

"You're heading to the tenth grade, right?"

"Yup, three more years of school."

"What high school are you going to attend?" Twin wanted to know.

"Not Walbrook, that's for sure."

"I don't blame you because those fool are tripping up there."

"I'm contemplating on Western or Lake Clifton."

"You are going to run into drama from those boys around the Alameda if you attend Lake" Monk informed him.

"No, they are gonna find that the drama that they bring me will turn into a nightmare on them" he said with conviction in his voice and eyes.

"I personally don't doubt that" he replied laughing. "You know we got your back."

"Yawl always will" he assured him smiling. "I'll holla at yawl tomorrow. I'll tell T.C where yawl are grinding."

"We appreciate that" Monk smiled.

He stood on the corner talking to them while searching for a hack to take him home. It was almost eleven-thirty when he walked into his mother's apartment, she was entertaining as usual, and Ms. Mable was there also as usual.

Maintaining an "A" average gave J-Lo her wish. She will be attending Northwestern starting in the fall. It appears like the summer months bring on physical changes to a person body. Although only five-four, her body finally started maturing. Her breast finally develop even though they weren't as large as Lisa and definitely not as large as Chi, but they were hers and she was proud of them. There were a slight flare to her hips, but her legs was unusually develop for her size, but she wasn't complaining. She had despised those chicken legs she once possess. When she stare into her full-length mirror now, she stared at an incredibly attractive young lady and not the tomboy that everyone once called her.

With her development came unwanted attention, everywhere she went men not teenage boys, but men were constantly pressing up on her. Although Lisa and Chi found that flattering, she thought it was a little creepy and perverted. Although she might appear to be eighteen, she was only fifteen and illegal. When men knowing this fact and still try to holla at her, they turned her off tremendously and she might get out the gate on them for being persistent.

For the past two years, she had been dating Lamont. He was cool and everything, but he had a jealousy spot that she didn't appreciate. Sure, every girl or woman desire to know that the man or boy that they are dating desire them exclusively, but when it becomes possessive, a form of unhealthy love can materialize. Interrogating the one that you claim to love like they have did something behind your back and trying to make them feel guilty for being independent isn't attractive. For any relationship to flourish, this thing called "Me Time" must be respected. If her "me time" consisted of her hanging out with her girls doing what girls do, challenging or implying what they do together isn't cool. In fact, she would get low on him for a couple of days because of his accusations and innuendos. When she resurface, he seem to calm his jealous ass down, but he's right back doing the same dumb shit two weeks later. Sooner or later, she was going to step off from him. There were rumors that he assaulted his previous girlfriend several times. If he ever touch her in an abusive way, she had a baseball bat waiting on him then her girls will stomp the living shit out of his bitch ass.

"Hey, girl. What's on your mind?" Lisa asked seeing the distance in her eyes.

"Lamont."

"Enough said" she replied giggling.

"Not funny, Lisa" she stated catching her eyes.

"Yes, it is" replied Chi. "You know you need to drop his childish ass. You know that Doc is feeling you."

"That dog already has two children. I don't have time for no baby momma drama."

"I hear you on that" cosigned Lisa. "All he is searching for is some pantie pudding."

"Well, he won't find it here" she said pulling open the door.

As they made their way towards the bleachers on the left-hand side, Lamont suddenly materialized with three of his friends.

"Hey, where have you been the last couple of days?"

"With my girls or do you think I was with some guy?" she asked staring up into his eyes before starting to climb the bleachers.

Just as they were about to take their seats, both teams sprinted on the court. As the crowd applauded their team, Lisa nudged J. Getting her attention, she nodded towards the far court. As she stared at the players individually, she could see what Lisa wanted her to see.

"Number twelve" she whisper.

As she search and located number twelve, she stared at him. His shoulders and arms were muscular. He had a tight looking butt and very muscular calves. As he caught the ball, he took and made a fifteen-foot bank shot. As he went to the other line, she could see his face but didn't recognize him initially. When she unconsciously started leaning forward, Lisa had to nudge her back into her seat. She peeked over at Lamont who was entertaining his friends as usual and haven't peeked her. It was ATM, he grew a pencil mustache, but it was definitely him. His body had mature a lot. He was standing a good six-three and easily weighting a hundred and eighty pounds. She couldn't keep her eyes off of him or the impish smile that engulfed her face.

As the game commence, he came out banging that bank shot of his. Before the other team knew what was happening, he had eight of their first twelve points. As the game unfolded, he wasn't just a threat on the outside. He was posting his man up and elevating over him. Even she they jump together he seem to pause in mid-air to allow his defender to descend before releasing his shot. Between Cross breaking motherfuckers ankles and Ding banging out deep threes, the team decided to play a zone. They fed their big men so much they stop to enjoy the work they were putting in on the inside. By half time, they were up by twenty. As both teams walked back to their respected locker rooms, the audience got to their feet to mingle or go to the concession stand.

"Girl, did you see him?" J asked unable to contain her excitement and smile.

"Everybody did" she snicker. "When the fans started chanting ATM, he hit another gear."

"And so did all their bitches" Chi included smiling.

"Those whores sounded like they were catching an orgasm" Lisa said.

"And so did J" teased Chi giggling.

"Ah shut up" she snap.

"He look good. Don't he J?" inquired Lisa with a slight smirk.

"No, doubt" she admitted giggling while leaning against her.

"So, what are you going to do?"

"What do you mean?" she asked staring at her perplex.

"You know what she mean" interjected Chi. "What are you going to do?"

"I can't do shit. I'm here with Lamont" she used as her reason.

"Yes, you can" replied Chi staring in her eyes.

"No, I can't" she insisted.

"Yes, you can" cosigned Lisa. "You don't know when the next time you might see him again."

"Don't Lamont always say that she was a friend? Well, he could be a friend of yours."

"Yawl do know that it's been three years since our eyes connected. He probably forgot all about me."

"Don't play yourself short, Lo" Chi insisted. "You got his attention then and you might do it again."

"I'm not as sure as you are girlfriend" she admitted.

"Well, the game is gonna start soon and I want my same seat" mention Lisa. "I'm gonna pull him up after the game."

"Don't Lisa!" she insisted.

"It's a done deal J, you don't have to acknowledge him. All you have to do is hold onto Lamont's arm and walk right pass him like he don't exist."

"You're cold."

"So" she replied smiling as she led the way back into the gym.

Both teams were already back on the floor warming up when they walked through the door. ATM was in the middle of preparing to take a shot when their eyes met. He drop the ball and methodically walked in her direction. She never averted her eyes as he approached.

"Oh, shit" whisper Lisa with a light giggle.

"Excuse me" he apologized impeding their movement.

"Yes" replied Chi staring up at him.

"No, her sweetheart" he said staring deep into J-Lo's eyes causing her to blush. "I do mean to be forward. I've been searching for your eyes for three years. Where have you been?"

"Right here" she replied staring up into his eyes.

"Where is here? You live in Gwynn Oaks?"

"Yeah."

"No wonder I couldn't find you" he shared flashing his radiant smile. "What is your name?"

"J-Lo."

"No, I want your government name if you don't mind."

"Ashanti."

"I'm Akeem" he introduced himself extending his hand and shaking hers. "I would love to explore the possibility of us becoming friends. I would like to call you."

"Damn" interjected Lisa smiling. "Some real Romeo shit."

"I am not a Romeo, but I would love to explore your mind. Can we exchange numbers after the game?"

"Sure, that's innocent enough."

"I am" he replied flashing his smile again as the buzzer sounded. "Don't disappear Ashanti because I will find you."

"I won't" she replied as he suddenly turned and dash back across the court.

"Girl, Lamont have fire coming out of his eyes" mention Chi not trying to contain her giggling.

"Fuck him" she express not just surprising them but herself. She usually never use such vulgar language, but it seem so appropriate.

As they proceeded towards their seat, she could feel the eyes of the spectators on her. She felt like she had just met a celebrity, and everybody was in awe over her.

"Who the fuck was that?" snap Lamont.

"You heard his fans chanting his name. ATM" she replied staring at the anger that had consumed his eyes.

"What the fuck did he want?"

"To introduce himself."

"Why? You know him?"

"No and as far as why. He wanted to know if we can be friends" she openly confess surprising her girls.

"You appeared to be interested in him also."

"He's charming."

"Charming?"

"Yeah" she replied then turned her head as the second half commenced.

Gripping her arm firmly, he whisper. "This shit isn't over."

"You better take your hands off me like that" she order coldly staring at him.

He released her arm then said, "This isn't over."

"Whatever" she said turning her back slightly to him and seeing ATM making his first shot of the second half.

It appeared that he dedicated the second half to J-Lo, every time he would make a shot, he would stare in her direction then smile. With ten minutes to go, he requested to come out of the game. While sitting on the bench, he removed his wet shirt revealing his muscular body then put on a dry shirt. He grabbed a bottle of water and drain it then lean back in his seat. His eyes stayed focus on J while ignoring the glare from the guy sitting to her left. With five minutes to go, Cross took himself out and came to sit next to him.

"Who is the girl?" he asked grabbing a bottle of water and draining it.

"Ashanti" he replied smiling then focus back on her.

"Like the singer?" he asked removing his shirt and grabbing a dry one.

"I guess" he replied never averting his eyes from her.

"What's up with her?"

"I plan on seeing" he replied grinning.

"What about the guy that sitting next to her?"

"You can have him" he replied causing him to burst out laughing. "As far as the guy is concern, what about him?"

"I guess nothing" he replied staring over at the guy shooting daggers at him.

Seconds before the horn was to sound, ATM got to his feet and went to the score table. He requested a pen and piece of paper. He wrote his cell number now then went back to his seat to collect his property. When the horn finally sounded, he casually walked towards the gym door and posted up. Cross was giving the fellas the 4-1-1 and they stared across the court then joined him at the door still smiling at the scenario that was about to unfold. Spotting ATM at the door, Lamont tapped his partners and nodded at him as he tried to slip his arm around her waist and grip her fingers, but she wasn't having it. She wasn't going to deceive all the spectators and especially ATM like it was something that they did every day. She had tried to get him to show some form of affection when they were out together, but that made him appear soft, as he explained to her. So, trying to show any form affection because he was being threaten by another guy wasn't happening.

"Excuse me" he apologized staring in Lamont eyes then down at J-Lo. "Here's my number" he said extending it to her.

37

"Whoa player" Lamont insisted trying to manifest some fear in him. "This is my woman. You need to step off."

"I will" he replied. "Here Ashanti. Give me a call" he reiterated still extending his number to her.

Lamont suddenly slap his hand away and caused an instant transformation in ATM, especially his eyes.

"If you put your hands on me again, I'm going to embarrass you not just in front of this crowd but your woman also tough guy" he promise staring in his eyes to show his conviction. "You can play the tough guy role with these brothers out here, but I'll put your dumb ass on "fuck up street" without a map to get out. Now touch me again tough guy" he invited him staring deep into his eyes. One thing Lamont saw that was absent in his eyes was fear and apprehension. He wasn't threatening him. He was promising him. "Here Ashanti, call me" he requested extending his number back to her again. This time Lamont stayed in his lane and watch what unfolded.

She looked at Lamont then up at ATM. "What kind of young lady would I be if I accepted your number while I have a boyfriend?"

"Are you saying that having a boyfriend or girlfriend prevents a person from being sociable?"

"No, I'm not saying that" she replied confusing herself.

"What are you saying? I comprehend quickly" he replied.

"I have a boyfriend, ATM."

"Call me Akeem, please."

"Wouldn't you think it was disrespectful if your girlfriend accepted another guys number?"

"Me?" he suddenly flash that sexy smile he possess. "Na, I would find it flattering men would desire to get to explore my woman."

"You wouldn't be fearful of him pulling her?"

"Nope because I'm always on my A game especially with my woman if I had one."

"I hear what you are saying Akeem, but will you respect my wishes?" she asked staring up into his eyes.

"Of course, I will Ashanti" he suddenly smile at her then stared over at him and slightly harden his eyes. "I've been watching you the entire second half while you was watching me. You don't have the vaguest idea the type of woman that you have, but I do. I know your dumb ass is going to blow it. I only wish I could be there" he slightly smiled at him while still glaring at him. "Fate had initially both, us together three years ago just like it did today" he smiled down on her. "We will see one another again. Have an enjoyable day, ladies and you too paper soldier" he wish them while staring in his eyes then left through the door with his partners.

"That nigger just don't know" he barked twisting his face.

"Oh, he knows" J corrected him watching him walking out the main door. "Don't start talking about a man behind his back or I might start believing that you are a paper soldier like he describe" she told him. "Let's bounce ladies."

"Where are you going?"

"To mind my business" she replied stepping outside the community center and witnessing ATM getting ready to climb on the number 57 bus. As she stood there wondering why she just didn't accept his number as a friend, he suddenly turned flashing his radiant smile then blew her a kiss before climbing aboard.

"J, I don't get you girl" Lisa said shaking her head.

"You don't have to" she replied smiling up into her eyes. "I think he does" she sign as she stare at the back of the bus going around the bend.

"I hope another three years don't elapse until you see one another again."

"I don't care how long it might be Lisa" she said taking her eyes off the bus and staring in her eyes. "We will still be in one another's hearts" she smiled.

39

When school started back up, she was excited as usual. She had caught the train with her girls with the knowledge that three years from now she would be free of school and completed her obligations to her parents. Although her father had aspirations of her continuing her education and become the first person in their immediate family to acquire a college degree, she would not cosign his wish. Maybe later but not right now. She had more than enough time to seriously consider college, but for right now, she wanted to enjoy her high school years. When the train came to a stop, seventy-perfect of the people exiting were students. As they follow the crowd out the station and up the escalator up to ground level, they stood on Northern Parkway. With the morning drivers trying to get to work and those with road rage over the simplest traffic infraction, students had to be mindful crossing this busy street. Crossing this parkway was an adventure to say the least. How more students didn't get hit crossing the three lanes street was a mystery.

As Northwestern came into view, J stared in amazement at the well manicure grass and the absence of trash and debris. Although her girlfriends wanted to attend Woodlawn High, she wanted a more challenging academic and Northwestern would provide that plus it gives her time away from Lamont. He never showed any concern or disappointment about her not attending Woodlawn High with him. Although she had her suspicion about him seeing other girls, she haven't caught him yet. In the weeks that has elapse since his run-in with Akeem, he tried to be more attentive, but a zebra can't change its stripes. Time away from one another will give them the opportunity to spread their wings and interact with new people. If they truly were going to have a relationship, this time alone will reveal it.

As she got acclimated to her pristine environment, she was constantly meeting new people, especially guys. T-Bone was a junior and one of the best athletics at the school. Playing varsity basketball and football, he had aspiration of obtaining a scholarship from one of the major universities or colleges in the country. His preference was a team from the A.C.C so he could remain close to home, but he wasn't limiting himself too just them. The Big East was right up 95 heading North. Rumor has it that he's the father of a little girl by some girl that attend a Catholic school. Although they talked all the time, he never mention her in their conversations. Although J was feeling him so were a lot of other young ladies and she wasn't going to compete for his attention. If he was hoping to persuade her into his bed, he needed to adjust his thinking. Although Lisa had to kick out that hundred dollars to them because she lost her virginity before graduating high school, she had no intentions of following suit. Chi was hanging in there, but she keep boasting about how she allow Murk to get to third base before cutting him off. It's only a matter of time before he hits that home run. The erotic feelings he induces in her causes her to have multi orgasm too many times before his fingers are replaced with his dick.

"J, are you going to the pet rally after school?"

"Na, Lisa. I'm bouncing. I'm going to Woodlawn Library to get started on my book report."

"Aahhh, come on" whined Chi. "We have so much more fun when you are there."

"I would love to go but I'm going to jump on this report. The grade makes up a big part of our average."

"You can start it this weekend" suggested Lisa.

"You are the procrastinator not me" she smiled at her. "I'm not fooling with yawl. When this weekend come, yawl will have something else to distract me. I'm getting this thing started."

"Party pooper" claim Lisa.

"Call me what you want but I'm not biting yawl hype" she smiled placing her books in her locker then closing the door.

"T-Bone is gonna be there" Chi mention trying to entice her.

"Ans so will his many fans, nice try" she smiled at her. "I'll holla at yawl later."

"Alright, go then" Lisa stated acting like she had an attitude.

"That used to work when we were in elementary school" she giggled. "I think it's so cute when you use that little ploy" she said waving her hand at them as she headed for a side door exit.

As she walked across the grass, she met up with several other students heading towards the speedline also. In about ten minutes, she was standing on the platform waiting for the train. When it finally arrived, she took a seat in the middle of the car staring out the window. Getting off at Rogers Station, the 57 bus was waiting. She ran with several other people to assure that they caught it. Climbing aboard, she walked towards the back and took a seat. As she drove pass her street, she peeked at her house. Her mother was sitting on the porch with Ms. Hattie. A coy smile came across her lips. Turning onto Woodlawn Drive, she admired the swans with their babies in the little reservoir. They would remain in the area until the winter months and she always enjoyed just watching them. Coming up on the 7-11 Store, she gather her bookbag then proceeded towards the back door to exit. Several students were going to the library also, but they weren't going to study. There would be four different high schools being drop off behind the library on Woodlawn High parking lot. With so many high schoolers congregating in one area, you are going to have a lot of different personalities and dispositions. Alpha males from one school trying to show their dominance over other alpha males. The testosterone in the air was always thick then you have the young ladies. Each trying to grab the spot light from the others while shaking their asses. The whole scene was like "The Young and the Restless."

As she cross the street, she spoke to several people who were acquaintance and from her community. Entering the library, the two-armed security guards were interacting with some students while the marijuana dealer was conducting business inside the boys bathroom. She went to the sign-in table to reserve herself one of the computers. She was assigned the perfect location over by the videos. From her location, she could see everything in front of her including the front door and the rear exit over by the daycare center. Sitting naturally low in her chair, she would have to lift her head just to see over the computer screen. She was deep into her book report when she heard Lamont's name being called by a girl. Lifting her head, she watch a board smile come to his face as he approached a high yellow girl with four of his friends. They exchanged hugs then he forced a guy with his little crew out of the table they were occupying then took a seat. She watched them for almost a half hour. The way they would whisper so no one could hear made her suspicious of their relationship. When she reached under the table and grip the front of his jeans, he didn't jump but continue to stare into her eyes smiling. She had seen enough. She down loaded the material that she needed into her flash drive then gather her stuff and got to her feet to get the fuck out of there. She maneuver through the aisles of video tapes then resurface at the back wall with a direct view of them. He was so engross in what he was doing one of his partners had to put him on point. Looking up and focusing on the direction that he was staring, the expression that engulf caused the girl to turn and look also.

"Who is this bitch heading this way?" she asked forcing everybody at the table to turn and look.

"Chill, Stacy" he advised smiling at her.

As J came closer, she shoot him a stare that took the smile off his face. She never said a word as she walked pass and never acknowledge the girl. She was heading straight for the front entrance and would have made it if....

"Oh, I thought that bitch didn't want no action!" she stated giggling staring at J's back. When she suddenly stop, there was a slight pause in the action going on around them. When she turned and headed back towards the table, Stacy got to her feet. "What bitch!?"

SLAM! One vicious right to the face and Stacy disappeared flipping over the table behind her revealing her stain yellow panties. She never returned. She stared at the other girls but none of them said a word or came to her aide. She gave Lamont the middle finger as she continued towards the front door. By the time security responded to the commotion, Stacy girlfriends were assisting her to her feet. She actually had to take a seat or might have fallen on flat on her face again.

"What the fuck happen?" she asked still dazed and confused.

"You got knock the fuck out!" a group of guys chime together then burst out laughing.

Lamont sat there looking like a fool. He never move or went after J because he knew he had blew it. He didn't give a fuck about Stacy. All she was to him and every guy that paid her a little attention was a sure nut. Her body was banging, and her head was vicious, but her face was fuck up. Old acme scares left black spots consuming her face. Catching her when the sun went down, she was down for just about everything including a threesome. She's definitely not the type of girl you introduce to your mother, but to your partners, definitely.

J stood under the tree waiting on the bus to take her home. She should have been furious, but she wasn't. She had heard many stories from women concerning men always thinking with their lower head. They all shared stories about losing their virginity to their unworthy first boyfriends and finding out they were a piece of shit. All their words of admiration was nothing but a ploy in their conquest. Once their conquest was over, they move to their next conquest. The hurt and shame they felt marinate from them even today. The ordeal left a scar on many of young girls hearts that some never recovered. Most have harden their hearts and don't appreciate a good man when he comes into their lives. J told herself that she would never join that woman club.

She would take her licks from life, but she would never allow a man to take away her joy and definitely not darken her heart.

Later that night, Chi called wanting to see if she wanted to hang out for a couple of hours. She declined her offer stating that she needed to organize the notes that she took earlier today. As she sat at the table that she use as a desk in her bedroom, the story she wanted to share slowly took form.

"Besides outside influences, the destruction of the black family happen from within. Throughout history, the black man was the most destructive force that plagued their family. A true strong black woman will support and motivate her man especially when he's subjected to a form of institutional racism by denying him the opportunity of employment. She would remain as strong and defiant as a mountain by him. The problem is when he's the bread winner. The focus of the family gradually become second in their lives. The alleged strain of keeping the rent paid, keeping the lights on, providing food for the table and other financial obligations is his reasoning for his self-destruction. He envision a life free from family obligations and the materialistic things he could acquire if he didn't have the burden of a family. With his steady income, he starts stealing from Peter to pay Paul. Taking a minimum of a hundred dollars out of the house so he could spurge on the weekends, he slips into a world as a big spender. Women witnessing him freely spending his money seek to link up with him. He find himself flatter by the attention that a single life have to offer so he try to play the role. He has an affair on the woman that had held him down when he was down. Assuming that he got away with something, he has another affair then another. Eventually, he's not concern about what time he gets home from work nor the faint scent of a woman's perfume. When she finally challenge him, he brushes off her words as a simple distraction. He continues on his destructive path he's on not concerning himself about his own children. When things finally come to an end, she tells him to take his shit and go. He eagerly accept her offer. Now, he can do whatever he desire and not worry about who might see him. His responsibilities of being a father and male image to his sons are abandon. In less than two years, he realize the fun that he thought he, desire had dissipated like the morning dew on grass. Trying to reconnect with the family that he previously abandon, his presence is no longer needed or wanted. The once dependent family is now being supported by a reconstructed and self-providing woman. She refuse to ever experience the feeling of hopelessness by depending on a man acting like a little boy. Force to play the role of both parents, a role she secretly despise, she didn't realize her own self-worth until put into this situation. Today, we see these "Super Women" walking among us, and I marvel at them. Why? Because men are afraid of them and know that their bullshit flattering words don't mean shit, they want to know, what have you done for me lately? Stay at home house wives are gone. Mistake of their past have force them to image a life without a man or husband. Men need to readjust their psychology. If they don't change their old ideologies of manhood, they will be left behind."

"Ashanti, you wrote a highly informative paper. How do you think we can correct this historical flaw in our black families?"

"Women have been asking this question long before I was born, Mrs. Taylor" she said slightly pausing. "If men continue to fantasize about a life absent of responsibilities as a father, use a condom. I have seen how men will walk away from their children simply because the woman doesn't want any interaction with him personally. This slight by her to his manhood or ego is the reason men abandon their children. Just because their relationship fail doesn't mean he have to fail as a father. His presence is vital to the development of his children especially little girls. To eliminate the high pregnancy rate of teenage girls, his presence is mandatory."

"Explain yourself, please."

"Personally, my father strokes my ego everyday" she shared slightly smiling. "He constantly tell me how beautiful I am even though sometimes I don't feel beautiful. I'm extremely fortunate to have him in my life. With his reinforcement, I don't allow the alluring words of a guy to think he's telling me something that I already know. If I had any form of self-esteem issues, I would twist their words to meaning love when it's really lust."

"Well put, Ms. Anderson" she smiled at her. "How can boys change this character flaw?" she inquired with a coy smile.

"Boys can be taught at an incredibly early age by watching how their fathers interact with their mothers. Speaking respectfully to her even while having a disagreement and displaying that chivalry isn't dead goes a long way in influencing the psychology of treating a woman or girl as he mature. When I hear guys using the B word as a descriptive of some girl, I'm not foolish enough to exclude me from that derogatory descriptive. They don't have enough respect to understand their mothers, aunts and sisters are affiliated with the same fraternity. If they doesn't respect what they are and who they represents, how I expect them to respect me? What chance does a stranger have with their perspective of us as girls and women?" she asked slightly smiling at her.

"Don't stop now. I can see you have something else to share. Do ahead, please" she insisted.

"You know, Mrs. Taylor" she began in a soft tone. "I don't appreciate seeing our young men on the corners selling drugs. Do they think that makes them a man?" she asked staring at her but not expecting an answer. "If a male child grow up witnessing his father grinding every day, I got them emulating what they see. Changing the mind set of males at an early age could be all it takes for them to become a responsible man."

"Very receptive of you, Ms. Anderson" she smiled marking her book. "Thank you."

"You're welcome" she replied reclaiming her seat.

Things in the city was as it is every day. Addicts scamming to acquire the money they needed to appease their addictions, especially the women. She don't have the usual problems that exist for her male counterpart because of the money maker she possess between her thighs. As long as she keeps her appearance and hygiene up, men will always be perceive as tricks to them or an uncomplicated way to obtain money. During their sexual business transaction, she's plotting to her fingers on a few extra dollars. With his pants usually on the floor, she will make her move. The majority of the times she is successful. He isn't aware that he was the product of a scam until much later. When he see her again and she tries smiling at him, his eyes hold vindictiveness in them. The only option he has is to never give her stinky fingers, scandalous ass another copper penny. A day in the life of the city.

Akeem had just taken his morning shower then got dress. He checked his room before heading down the hallway when he notice his mother staring at him.

"Morning" he greeted receiving her usual no response. "What is it now?" he asked grabbing himself a large bowl, spoon then retrieving the Corn Flakes off the refrigerator and the milk from inside before taking his seat.

"We need to talk" she said coming to stand in front of him then leaning against the sink while smoking a cigarette.

"About what now?" he asked shoving a spoon full of cereal into his mouth while up into her eyes.

"You need to up your responsibilities for your uncle."

"I'm a mule for him now. I'm walking around with almost a half-million dollars in heroin. What more do he need?"

"He wants you to join his crew" she blurted out.

"Na, that's not happening" he said slightly hardening his eyes.

"With your reputation around the city playing basketball."

"Basketball? You have never seen me play a single game so don't use that" he told her slightly snarling.

"No, I haven't but with your street savvy you can help establish his business up in the Heights."

"Not going to happen" he reiterated with more conviction.

"As one of his lieutenants, you can make a hell of a lot more money than you're making now. There are things that his family need."

"Everything in this house I brought. From that fifty-inch on the wall and modern furniture that your worthless friends sit on, I brought it. I buy my brothers clothes and still have to give you half of what I earn. I'm already being exploited by you and I'm not going to be exploited anymore."

"You aren't being exploited."

"Yes, I am and you or nobody else can convince me otherwise" he snarled staring in her eyes.

"You are doing what a man supposed to do for his family."

"I'm not a man!" he replied adamantly. "I'm a teenager and this isn't my family, it's my father's. I'm going to be the first male in our family to graduate high school and not get incarcerated. My brothers will following my lead" he informed her while continuing to snarl at her. "You can tell him, or I'll tell him myself that I'm not doing no more than what I'm already doing for him. If he's unhappy with my performance, he can find somebody to be him damn mule" he informed her getting to his feet and grabbing his bowl. He pour what he had remaining in it into the trash receptacle. "Excuse me" he requested so he could get to the sink.

"Just leave it and I'll wash it" she said looking up into his eyes.

"No, I'll wash it myself" he insisted as she reluctantly move. He wash the bowl then place it in the rack with his spoon and starting to turn.

"Where are you going?"

"To one of my places of tranquility" he said grabbing his net bag that contained his basketball and a dry shirt. "Is there anything else you wish to disgust with me?"

"No, Akeem."

He slung his bag over his shoulder then step out the front door closing it behind himself. He stood for a minute staring down on the complex. From the nineth floor, the city look completely different. Visitors to the Inner Harbor didn't have the vaguest ideal just how violent that the city have become. With over three hundred murders for ten straight years, you are talking about over ten-thousand men and women being murder because of the drug game predominately and most of them were black men. Looking down into the court yard, he saw his two brothers down on the basketball court. Khalil (sincere friend) can be better than he was at his age while Amiri (leader) played the game for the fun of it. He was going to make sure that they creep through the cracks and not get caught up. Whatever it took to make sure that they didn't contribute another link to the chain of incarceration that plagued their family he was going to do it. Much too often he was thinking about his father and what he was doing. He insisted that none of his sons come to visit him, or their mother and they haven't.

He turned and headed towards the stairway. With the temperature hitting the high seventies and it wasn't even ten o'clock, he didn't feel like riding down the nine flights in a musky urine smelling elevator. As he started descending the stairs, he could hear the music being played on the sixth floor. The acoustic always made the music sound so much better. Some nights he would grab a chair from the kitchen and sit at the stairway door to listen.

"Who's that!?"

"Akeem!" he replied from the seventh floor. Turning the corner, they would relax their hands after seeing that it was him.

"What's up ATM!?" they all chime together.

"What's up fellas?" he replied tapping their knuckles as he walked pass.

"Where are you playing?"

"Don't know yet Money."

"I heard some niggers from the East Side is supposed to be bringing over a squad. They supposed to play at the Dome on Biddle Street. Niggers are talking about laying some big money down" he informed him.

"Damn, sound serious" he replied slightly hardening his eyes.

"They are not disgusting cheap change that's for sure."

"Let me know when the game is going down. I don't want to miss that" he admitted smiling.

"Shit, you don't have to worry about that" he told him snickering. "Your squad is the main players that are pencil in" he informed him.

"Who pencil us in?"

"That I don't know but yawl are in" he assured him returning his stare. "Go get your game ready and I'll holla at you later."

"Alright, Money. Yawl be safe" he wish them walking out the fire exit door. He wave to hi brothers then proceeded out the court yard. He was just about to cut through the path when he heard his name being called. He turn and saw Sunshine holding the back door ajar and he casually walked over towards her. He admired the white shorts that she had on. Over the years, she had mature physically into one of the phatest young ladies in the complex. With her maturity, her beauty had evolved also. The little mole at the corner of her nose that he used to tease her about looking like a boogie made her look even sexier. The large doe like eyes she possesses was highlighted by eyeliner. Her medium lips were always glossy. They were never found champ or dry, She was definitely desirable. "Yeah, what's up?" he asked staring down into her light brown eyes.

"Are we close friends?"

"What?" he asked confused by her statement.

"Are we close friends?" she reiterated.

"Of course, we are" he replied lightly laughing. "You know as much about me as I know about you" he smiled. "What's up?"

"Are you still a virgin?"

"What?" he asked, perplex by her question. "You know the answer to that."

"I thought I did but Naomi (sweet) said she fucked you last weekend" she shared her discomfort.

"And what, you believe that?"

"I didn't want to" she admitted embarrass.

"Well, don't. She is just trying to get under your skin" he smiled down at her. "Is there anything else? I have some place to be."

"Yes, there is" she said staring at him extremely unusually.

"What?" he replied confuse by her expression.

"Come here" she requested opening the door wider for him to enter then closing it. With the dim lights, she press her body against his forcing him against the wall. She reach for the back of his neck and gently pulled him down to her. She gently kiss him then back away. They stood staring at one another for a moment before he reach out and grip her around her waist then pulled her back into his arms. The kiss they exchanged were filled with passion and lust. Both bodies became alive from the touch of the others hand exploring their bodies. With their breathing being spasmodic, they release their embrace and exchanged stares.

"I have been wanting to do that for years" she admitted smiling up at him.

"Are you sure we should be venturing down this path Sunshine?"

"Did you know that Biggie had a little girl?" she blurted out.

"Yeah" he replied slightly lowering his head then staring up the hallway.

"Why didn't you tell me?"

"To protect you" he replied. "I didn't want to see the pain that easing in your eyes right now. I knew one of those envious guys would snitch on him and one did, right?"

"Yeah, Mookie" she shared. She knew if anybody would tell her the truth that he would. Since meeting in elementary school, he had never told her a lie. "Come to my house tonight around nine o'clock."

"For what?"

"You will see when I see you" she replied with a coy smile.

"I'll try to make it."

"No, Akeem" she replied stepping into his personal space. "Don't try to make it. I got something for you to see, okay?"

"Alright, I'll be there."

She turned then proceeded back up the stairs as he push open the door and step outside. Reaching Pennsylvania Avenue, he wave for a hack and caught one almost immediately.

"How much to Dru Hill Park?"

"A nickel will get you there" the junkie slurred.

"Good" he replied opening the passenger's door and climbing inside then fastening his seatbelt. As he drove pass Chadwick, the courts was already filled with players. As they swung into the park, children were running around everywhere while joggers and bikers tour the reservoir. Pulling up next to the basketball courts, both courts were filled but that was expected. Players usually start arriving by seven-thirty in the morning. "Here you go" he said extending the five dollars to him then climbing out.

"Have a good game soldier" he wish him pulling off.

He watch him hooking U-turn then cross the street and headed to a group of guys sitting on a table. He took a sit on the grass using his basketball as a pillow. Both games were competitive, but the real game was about to commence.

"Yo, ATM! Are you running?"

"Na, Twist. I'm just watching" he heard himself say. There was something that's been creeping into my mind lately and he found himself unconsciously mapping out a plan. His situation at his house has become unbearable for him. The thought of leaving home was becoming more alluring to him. His main concern was for his brothers. He wouldn't be able to monitor them as closely as he have. Although everyday he talks to them about the traps and perils in the streets waiting for kids wanting to grow up too soon, he believe his teaching haven't been wasted. Khalil has his head on straight and neither of them are followers. Amiri playful disposition could get him trip up. He had to check him on several occasions for playing too much even though he said he was just having fun. Trying to make him more serious although he was only eight is a daily challenge especially while he's living in Murphy Homes. The small beefs with Lexington Terrence and Gilmore Homes shouldn't touch them but bullets doesn't have specific names on them. He didn't want to stifle his childhood, but children from the high rises don't have the traditional childhoods. If something were to happen to either of them, he would blame himself even though it was impossible for him to be everywhere that they go.

It was almost two o'clock when he finally got to his feet and started walking out the park, he admired all the expensive cars as he walked. A 300 Chrysler club rolled into the park with most of them cruising on twenty-two-inch chrome wheels. With slightly tinted windows and special grills brought off of E-Bay, several of them were funky as hell. As he headed towards McCullen Street, his body instead took him towards Chadwick. Entering the park where he earned his nickname, he received great praise from other players. Taking a seat by the building, the boom box was playing dirty south music and the ladies was feeling their groove as they dance seductively with the teenage guys. He was there a good hour enjoying the scene when someone rubbed the back of his head. He turned around to see Naomi wearing a white spandex outfit and wearing it damn good.

"Hi, Akeem" she greeted coming around the bleachers and coming to sit next to him. The perfume she was wearing smell so exotic on her.

"What's up Naomi?" he asked staring in her eyes.

"Not too much" she replied admiring his eyes. "Do you have a girlfriend?"

"Na, why?"

"Who is giving you kisses if you don't have one?" she inquired with an impish grin.

"You don't have a have a girlfriend just to get a kiss" he replied grinning.

"No, you don't but wouldn't it be nice to be able to get one when you desire one?"

"I can get that now if I present myself right" he replied still grinning into her eyes.

"From whom?" she inquired with a coy smile.

"Just about anyone if I present myself right" he reiterated.

"Yeah, sure you can" she lightly giggled.

"I can" he repeated smiling.

"Show me" she dared him.

He look around for a brief minute then said, "Pick someone."

She stared up into his eyes smiling. "How about me?"

He suddenly chuckle while staring in her eyes. "That wouldn't prove my point. Pick someone and if she doesn't have a boyfriend, I'll try to allure a kiss from her" he said with an impish smile.

"Okay" she replied accepting his challenge. Scanning the court, her eyes focus on a group of girls. "You see that prissy ass light skin girl putting on lip gloss?'

"Yeah, I see her."

"Get her to give you a kiss" she said giggling.

"I'll be right back" he said getting to his feet. As he move in the direction of the group of girls, he could feel her eyes following him and other people also. As he came closer to the group girl, their eyes focus on him. "Excuse me, ladies" he apologized. "I don't mean to be intrusive, but I have some burning questions that I need you to answer" he said staring directly at the light skin girl and causing her to slightly blush.

"Sure, what is it?" she replied admiring his smooth deep mocha complexion and pencil mustache. His shoulders and arms were extremely muscular for someone his age.

"What is your name first?" he asked staring into her grayish eyes.

"My friends call me Entice" she replied slightly smiling.

"I'm not five-o but I would love to know your government name" he requested still staring in her eyes.

"Fari" she replied.

"Yes, you are a queen."

"You know the meaning" she replied flashing her smile.

"Fari, I have a very unorthodox question that I wanted you to answer but first, do you have a boyfriend because I wouldn't want to disrespect him or you" he said perking her interest even more.

"No" she replied returning his stare.

"I know every guy out her" he said staring around then focusing back on her. "Find you extremely attractive as do I but I was wondering would you put to rest the burning question on my mind?"

"And what is that" she asked slightly blushing again.

"Are your lips filled with bliss?" he asked causing her girlfriends to start giggling and leaning on one another.

"Huh?" she asked fully smiling at his question.

"Are they, Fari?" he asked in a seductive voice.

"I don't know" she replied.

"Will you be adventurous this afternoon and allow me to find out.

One thing for sure, when the next guy ask you can answer the question" he told her smiling down into her slightly evasive blushing eyes.

"But I don't know you" she said staring up into his eyes.

"He's ATM, girl" her girl chanted his name. "Give him a kiss."

She pause staring over at them urging her then up at him. "Okay."

He lean down and his lips melted into hers Ass their tongues started entwining, praise from the spectators caught their ears causing them to stop and smile at one another. "Don't ever allow a guy to tell you that your kisses aren't filled with bliss. I assure you that they truly are Fari. I deeply appreciate the short adventure with you" he smiled at her before turning and walking away heading back to Naomi. He heard her girlfriends giggling and praising her for having heart. "See" he said taking his seat.

"Alright, you have a little game" she complimented him staring at the girl staring over at them. "What did you say to her?"

"A man never kiss and tell. A woman shouldn't either" he included.

"I don't" she replied not realizing that he caught her in a lie. "You have any plans tonight?"

"Why?"

"I want to invite you over to my house" she replied staring into his eyes.

"To do what?"

"I'm sure a boy and girl having a house to themselves can find something to do" she replied while staring deep into his eyes.

"Where do you live?"

"1247" he plied smiling.

"What time are you talking about?"

"At nine o'clock, my mother is going to a party tonight" she informed him.

"I just might be able to make that" he lied watching the delight coming into her eyes.

"I'll make it worth your while" she replied getting to her feet.

"If I'm not there by nine, I won't be coming."

"I can wait if you want me to."

"Na don't waste your night waiting on me" he advised her.

"You really should come and see what I have for you" she said rubbing his face then climbing down then walking towards the gate. His eyes follow the natural shake of her ass as she headed down Dru Hill Street. All he could do was shake his head at her then lean back and enjoy the games that were being played. It was almost seven o'clock when Fari and her girls walked pass, he wave to them while throwing her a two-finger kiss like L.L Cool J.

"Play on player" he heard Chubby voice say.

"Better to play than be played" he counter smiling at him.

"No doubt" he cosigned coming around and taking a seat next to him. "I see you doing a lot of thinking lately. Is everything cool?

"Yeah, I'm good."

"Have you heard about the big game jumping off next weekend?"

"I got wind of it this morning" he admitted.

"We have some heavy hitters getting ready to drop some heavy money on the game" he informed him staring into his eyes. I want you on the squad that I'm coaching. If we win, you get a piece of the profit."

"How old these guys that we are going to play?"

"Under eighteen."

"They could slip in some guys that are older" he shared his opinion.

"Na, the price for doing that would be too extreme" he informed him revealing his menacing eyes from under his Cartier sunshades.

"Well, you know I'm down for you" he assured him.

"Good" he replied slightly smiling. "I need you here Wednesday at five to meet everybody."

"No problem."

"Do you have any other sneakers?" he asked with a faint smile.

"There is nothing wrong with these And 1" he replied looking down at them.

"We want everybody uniform" he replied.

"Tell them to wear And 1's" he replied with a coy smile.

"We want everybody in black and white Jordans."

"You know that sneakers don't make the player."

"Apparently not" he replied staring at his sneakers smiling. "What size do you wear?"

"Ass kickers" he replied causing him to chuckle.

"Na, really" he insisted.

"Twelves."

"Okay, I'll have them for you by Wednesday" he said getting to his feet. "Are you plan on hitting Naomi?"

"Na, she lied on my dick" he shared.

He burst out laughing. "What she said she fucked you?"

"Yeah. If she hadn't, she could have gotten me later tonight."

"If I, was you, I would still hit it" he gave his opinion.

"Na, I have someone special that want to see me tonight" he shared.

"Alright, I'll holla at you later."

"Later Chubby" he replied watching him walking away. Rumor has it that Chubby used to be the man. Pushing heavy weight in the city back in the day. Two of his previous lieutenants had aspirations beyond their abilities and hit him up with eight bullets. He ate them like they were twenty-twos. Once he recuperated, he extracted his revenge on them. He never got back in the business, but he had a knot that could choke a giraffe. Living the good life just outside of the city with his family, he returns every day to stay connected and have the streets remember his name. Looking at his watch, it was almost eight o'clock, he grabbed his net bag then started out the gate.

"Yo, ATM. I'm heading your way."

"Thanks Smurf" he said heading towards his black Volkswagen Jetta.

It was nine o'clock when Ms. Mable knock on the door to pick up his mother. He was sitting at the kitchen table while his brothers were in the front room watching L.A playing the Bulls. He waited few seconds after they left then got to his feet and walked out the door. He stood on the balcony staring down at the street when they exit and climbed into a car then pulled away. He went back inside.

"I'll be back" he announced grabbing his door key.

"Where are you creeping to" inquired Khalil with a smirk.

"To mind my business" he replied then went back out the door. He took the elevator to the fourth floor and exit then walked to the stairway further down. He descended the stairs a floor and peek down the balcony to make sure it was clear then step out and lightly tap on her door. The door open almost instantly as she stood behind the door and closed it once he was inside. Walking towards the front room as he usually did, he took a seat and waited on Sunshine. When she walked in and stood in front of him butterball naked, his eyes became the size of fifty cent pieces as his swallowing suddenly became difficult. Her body seem to glow in the diminish light. He took in every contour of her body especially her newly acquired naval ring. Her breast was much larger than he thought with a light brown circle around her nibbles. Her flat stomach lead down to her close shaven garden of love with his name engraved inside. His eyes didn't wonder any further until they reverse admiring the same sights again until their eyes met.

"I want to see your body. Get naked" she said going to the love seat and taking a seat then pulling her legs under her while wearing an impish smile.

He was naked in less than a minute. His semi-hard dick had her full attention. She have never witness a dick as big as his except in the porn that she saw with her girlfriends. Her eyes and breathing revealed that she was immensely excited by what she was staring at. She didn't say a word as she suddenly got to her feet and walked towards her bedroom. She peeked over her shoulder to make sure he was trailing her. The movement of her ass had gotten him fully erected. She actually thought he would be a little shy to reveal his body to her but what the hell did he have to be shy about? As she crawled up on her bed, there was a picture of them when they were ten years old on her night stand. He climbed on the bed and laid down next to her admiring her eyes. The scent of her body appeared to be an aphrodisiac to him as he pulled her close inhaling the bio-scent then started kissing her very passionately.

Minutes faded into a memory as she felt their perspiration trying to cool their passion. As he laid holding her in his arms afterward, she was so delighted that he wanted to cuddle with her. Once Biggie had burst his nut, he was usually looking for an excuse to leave but not Akeem. She don't know if it was their earlier relationship and continuous friendship, but she did do something that she always desire to explore. Suck a man's dick. Biggie was constantly trying to get her to do him, but she flatly refused. With Akeem, she caress and kiss it like it was catnip. She never experience such an erotic night filled with pleasurable pain and tears of ecstasy. It was this night that she fell in love with him permanently. At one o'clock in the morning, he was gripping her fingers like he used to do when they were younger heading to the front door. She told him that he could have her any time that he desire, but she warned him that she will ration it to him. They kissed again at the door before he peeked outside then dip back into the stairway.

J-Lo and Chi got dress at Lisa house for the party at the community center, they stared at their reflections in the full-length mirror and broad smiles consumed their faces.

"Oh, we have got to take a picture" Chi stated still smiling.

"We can take one at the party" suggested J.

"Yeah" cosigned Lisa. "Let's get out of here" she said leading the way out of the room as J turned off the lights and closing her door before joining them descending the stairs. Her mother was on the porch waiting on them. The ride to the community was less than five minutes.

As they climbed out her mother said, "If yawl need a ride home just call me."

"We will probably walk home" she told her.

"Okay but be careful."

"We will" she assured her as they headed towards the community center. Cars were everywhere. With the police station less than a block away, they didn't anticipate anything jumping off but when you have fools intermingling and alcohol mixing, you can't assume anything. How did people from the city hear about the party would be a senseless question. With the creation of social media, nothing is a secret, nothing. Spotting the guys from the city was easy. With their style, brash disposition and with a look in their eyes announcing that they were here motherfuckers. Guys in the county that tried to emulate them became soft like cotton candy in their presence. The last thing they wanted to experience is the true aggression that city living produce in them for survival. Watching them walking around in small packs and grabbing girls to the dance floor was their style. Not asking for a dance but demanding one. Although most of the county girls found their threatening demeanor intriguing and sexy, others didn't want nothing to do with their thuggish dispositions, especially Lisa. She welcome their whole disposition.

"Come on and dance" a guy said grabbing J's wrist.

"No, thank you" she replied snatching her hand from him.

"No!" he said revealing his intoxication. "What you too good to dance with me?" he asked snarling in her eyes.

"Yup" she heard herself say returning his stare but not his snarl.

"Oh, you're Ms. Fancy Pants, huh?"

"Whatever you think. Excuse me" she said turning and walking away from him.

"Stuck up bitch!"

She never turned away just put as much distance between them as she could. She wasn't going to allow some ignorant motherfucker like him spoil her night. This was her first big party that she was allowed to attend. Both of her parents had stress that if anything jump off, they will come and pick her up. If something were to jump off, she wouldn't have called them and give them the ammunition to decline her next wish to attend a party. While her girlfriend filled their night with the city guys, she filled her dance card with guys from the county. It was close to midnight when her girls hunted her down.

"Yo, J-Lo. Come outside with us" Chi said snatching her by her arm and leading her towards the front door.

"Are you going outside with those guys from the city?" she asked stopping in her tracks.

"Yeah, why?"

"I'm not feeling them" she admitted slightly snarling.

"You don't have to" she replied. "You're coming to us."

"Alright but if any of them start being disrespectful, I'm bouncing."

"Girl, Ain't nobody going to mess with you" Lisa said laughing.

"You can laugh but I'm serious" she told her, and her eyes held her conviction.

As they walked outside, Lisa started looking around. She tapped Chi then nodded her head towards a small group. They proceeded towards them when the scent of marijuana floated on the air in their direction.

"Na, I'm not feeling this" she said stopping in her tracks. "Yawl can go ahead."

"Ah, come on J" insisted Lisa.

"I don't know what yawl are trying to do or impress but I'm not impress. I'm never going to judge yawl for the things that yawl do. So, stop insisting that I accept shit that I won't accept."

"Damn, Lo" said Chi staring in her eyes. "It's only marijuana."

"Do you think that the junkies we see every day started out shooting heroin?" she asked staring in their eyes and not expecting an answer. "I doubt it very seriously. They probably started out smoking weed then gradually venture to a harder drug by those claiming to be their friends. Yawl can do yawl but I'm out of here" she said turning and running straight into the guy she ran into previously.

"Well, well, well" he stated smiling. "What are you doing out here Ms. Stuck Up?"

"Leaving" she replied.

"Leaving, why?" he laugh. "You think you're too good to socialize with us."

"No just you" she replied exchanging his stare.

"You have a wicked tongue."

"Excuse me" she said ignoring his words.

"Listen."

"No, I'm out of here" she said stepping around him.

"Go on with your worthless ass" he snarled.

"Worthless!" she snap turning to face him then looking him up and down. "Who are you calling worthless you bum looking ass?"

"Who the fuck you talking to?" he barked.

"You" she replied. "The same bum that couldn't take no for a simple dance."

"You need to check yourself."

"No, you need to check yourself" she counter. "Why do you hate women so much that you feel comfortable calling us bitches?"

"I call a bitch a bitch when she acts like one" he replied.

"So, any woman that don't want to socialize or get to know an ignorant motherfucker like you are bitches, huh? She slightly snarled at him.

"Fuck you bitch!"

"Whoa, stop calling out girl a bitch!" insisted Chi hardening her eyes with Lisa.

"Fuck this little boy" J snarled at him. "I know a boy like you could never have a real girlfriend. A real woman wouldn't give your dusty ass the time of day, but a true bitch would take you calling her a bitch as a form of endearment. Silly low self-esteem girls" she laugh at him.

"Let me tell you something you black bitch!" he stated getting snatch up by one of his boys.

"Do you know who that is?" he asked staring over at J then focus back on him. "Well, do you fool?"

"She's just another snobby bitch!" he said with venom and his boy snatch him up.

"Her name is J-Lo."

"So, and why are you snatching a nigger up?"

"To protect your dumb ass dummy" he replied staring in his eyes before releasing him. "Her name is J-Lo and not bitch. Think about the last time we were out here. Think before you speak" he advised him.

He thought back to that first time and the things that occurred. The longer he stared at her the more the haze left his eyes until recognition finally hit him. "Oh, shit! Damn girl" he said staring at her then back at his friends. "J, I apologize for being disrespectful."

"No, you're not" she denounced his apology. "You only express how you truly feel about any women that don't accept your bullshit. I don't understand what just happen, but you meant every word you said."

"J, he's a little intoxicated and."

"And that is supposed to give him a pass because he's intoxicated?" she asked staring in his eyes. "Na, soldier. Liquor let a person express what's in their heart when they couldn't say it while sober. If a person disrespect you while he's intoxicated, will you forgive him like a good Christian?" she asked flipping the question.

"I'm not a Christian and I'm not giving nobody a pass for the shit that comes out of their mouths" he admitted honestly.

"And neither will I" she stated turning and walking away. What the fuck just happen and how do they know her name? What did he mean the last time they were out here? The last time she was here she ran into ATM. What did he have to do with this? She hasn't seen him in almost two years. What in the fuck caused him to flip his script like a county boy meeting a city guy? He actually was afraid, and his eyes revealed that fact. She found herself sitting on a bench trying to make sense of the whole scenario.

"Hey, J" called Lisa coming to sit next to her. "Are you alright girl?"

"Yeah, I'm just trying to make sense out of this bullshit."

"Don't" Lisa said. "Here's the 4-1-1" she said taking a deep breath. "ATM isn't a gangster, thug or drug dealer but he has a big reputation around the city. Do, you remember the day yawl exchanged words here."

"Yeah."

"Nobody have ever witness that side of him before. He was actually very attentive to the things you was saying. A lot of girls are on his heels but he's on your heels and a lot of bitches were jealous as hell" she shared giggling. "Word have been circulating since then that people know your name but not your face."

"Are you serious?" she asked openly flatter.

"Girl you might not want the attention or recognition, but you, damn sure have it" Chi cosigned snickering.

"That's crazy."

"You know what even crazier?" Lisa asked with a smirk.

"What?"

"He got a big game Saturday at Chadwick and guess who is making a surprise appearance?" she asked with a smirk on her face.

"Us" she replied smiling.

"Damn, right" she burst out laughing.

Saturday morning around twelve o'clock, Chadwick was pack with spectators. On Dru Hill, there was five cones reserving spaces for the arrival of the VIP's. Even if you was naïve to the game, a square or just coming off the steps, the people sitting around in the lounge chairs weren't your usual spectators especially the women they were escorting. Money and status just ooze from them and the immaculately dress men standing behind them were their chauffeurs either. When Chubby got some of the teenagers working for him to remove the cones, four luxury vehicles and a van pulled up. As the some of the crowd looked towards the street, the player were the first to get out displaying their purple and gold uniforms then went inside the building. From the back seat of a silver and black Bugatti with suicide doors, an immaculately dress OG stepped out with his two bodyguards surrounding him. He extended his hand back inside and pulled out the sexiest chocolate woman ever seen in Baltimore.

Getting off the bus, J and her girls have never witness such a massive congregation of people or the expensive cars lining the street. Spectators had actually surrounded the outer perimeter also. As they cross the streets, people stared at her with recognition.

"Hey, J-Lo. Hi, ladies. I'm Sunshine" she introduced herself. "I've been a close friend with Akeem since elementary school."

"Glad to make your acquaintance" she replied smiling at her.

"You have to excuse me while I use your status to get inside and get a seat" she apologized smiling. "Come with me ladies" she said gripping her arm and leading her towards the gate.

"Hey, J-Lo" a group of guys greeted her smiling.

"What's up J?" a girl greeted her smiling warmly.

"J, what's going on baby girl?" an OG asked slightly smiling.

She have never seen these people before but the love and respect being shown made her feel a little awkward. What the fuck was going on? She wasn't a gangster bitch or someone that spent a lot of time in the city making noise. She was semi-shy young lady from Gwynn Oaks. All she could do was wonder who was ATM really?

As the crowd open like the Reed Sea, she walked through the entrance with her girlfriends.

"J-Lo!" a dark skin guy that was definitely in the drug game called to her from the bleachers. "I have seats for you and your girls" he informed her getting to his feet with two other guys surrendering their seats then descended the steps.

"Thank you" she said as they exchanged warm smiles as they walked pass then took their seats with people staring and whispering about her.

"Damn, J" Lisa said taking her seat snickering. "The city got mad love for you."

"But why?"

"Don't ask why but wow" Chi said giggling while leaning on her.

People around her started introducing themselves and some of the ladies with gold ropes that indicated that they were about something also greeted her warmly. Only later did she find out that they were true gangster bitches and are always strap. J actually felt like a celebrity.

"Damn she is beautiful" J stated watching her closely coming out of the building with her man and escorts. The Bantu hairstyle she wore complimented her small round face and full lips. There was a hidden hardness in her doe like eyes. Wearing a white silk satin pant suit by Dolce and Gabbana with matching six-inch stain stilettos, she moved with elegance. Smiling at certain young ladies that were in the game with their men, she was being escorted to a shady area where her chair was located.

After they took their seats, both teams sprinted to the courts. The East Siders wore L.A colors while the West Side wore black uniforms with white numbers and their names on the back. Although none of the player were older than seventeen, some of the players was exceedingly tall while others appears older than they look. The anticipated excitement could be cut with a knife. There was also a tension that was obvious as East Siders stared over at West Siders. Little chants slowly started materialized praising their side of town while shooting down the other side of town started while both teams were warming up.

Chubby step out on the courts carrying his blow horn and getting everybody's attention. "Ladies and gentlemen, welcome to Chadwick. Before we get started today, I have just one thing to say. Don't respect my house" he stated with conviction in his voice and eyes as he stared at both sides of the courts. "We have several children here to see a highly competitive game and I want them safe. So, I repeat. Don't disrespect my house. If you do, I can't say what my family will do to you and those that you love. I advising you now to leave Baltimore immediately if you disrespect my house. If you can't control yourself, get the hell out and now!" he demanded snarling at both sides of the courts as he left. There was no mistaking that he was serious and wasn't making threats but promises.

"Yawl motherfucker hear him, right!" a tall thick guy asked glaring at a group of guys specifically on the west side and most of them averted their eyes from his menacing stare.

After talking to the ref about what style of game they were going to play, the ball was toss up and Byrd controlled the tap to Cross. With a back pick on Ice man at the foul line from Byrd, Cross threw him an alley-oop and he caught it slamming it through for the first points. The crowd erupted. For the next five minutes, both centers and power forward played a controlled physical game. With a limited hand checking, it wasn't unusual for both point guards to slap the others hand off of them as they started their move. The Big East style of game is physical both teams knew the limits. When Cross would shake his man and force ATM man to come over, he would hit him with a perfect pass.

"Count it!" the West Sider shouted.

"Yet, once again, ATM missed seven of the ten shots he attempted. The West side was shock. Was the stage too big for him? Have he made an over-draft? Where the fuck was his perfect jumper? By half time, the West Siders were down by eight. As they congregated in the shade drinking Gator Aide, Chubby didn't approach them with a rah-rah speech to try to motivate them. He knew they would eventually figure it out on their own.

"Damn, ATM. Where is your jumper?" inquired Cross taking a big gulp from his Gator Aide.

"If you did something to her, you really need to apologize" Ice said.

"If you won't, let me" request Dink.

"If that bitch on vacation on the other side of town, send a hack to pick her up" suggested Byrd.

As the crowd peeked over at them, they couldn't understand how they could be genuinely laughing. Chubby like what he was witnessing, but he needed an ace in the hole and he knew actually where he could find one. Walking back towards the sidelines and scanning the place, a coy smile came to his face after spotting it.

"Yo, J-Lo" he called out getting everybody's attention around her.

"Yes."

"Let me holla at you."

"Sure" she replied getting to his feet as people made a path for her while he peeked over his shoulder at ATM who was being distracted. Walking towards her, she everybody eyes following her including those in the VIP section. "Yes, may I help you?"

"Do you know me?"

"No, sir but I know that everybody calls you Chubby."

"Yes, they do" he replied slightly smiling then becoming serious. "I need you to do something for me."

"Sure, if I'm able" she replied apprehensively.

"Oh, you're able" he slightly smiled at her. "I need you to step out of character for me."

"Step out of character" she repeated confused by his statement.

"Yes" he suddenly smiled. "I need you to walk on the basketball court just before the second half is about to start. I need ATM to know that you are here."

"What?" she asked surprised his request.

"If you don't, they will lose this game. Do you want that?"

"No, sir" she replied adamantly.

"Then jump out of character" he said then suddenly walking away leaving her dumbfounded.

The confused expression on her face had everybody puzzle as she returned to her seat.

"Are you okay?" inquired Lisa never witnessing the expression on her face.

"Yeah" she replied, absence of all feelings.

The horn sounding snap her out of her trance as both teams returned to the court for their three minutes warm up. J sat there a few seconds before suddenly getting to her feet and excusing herself so she could get down. She walked straight on the basketball court causing a pause in the action. As both teams stared at her, a ref approached her.

"Don't touch me" she informed him hardening her eyes and stopping him in his tracks. A broad smile came to ATM face seeing her as he walked towards her. "What's your problem, young man?" she asked placing one of her hands on her hips.

"Huh, what do you mean?" he asked smiling down on her.

"You need to step up your game" she insisted stepping into his personal space. "Do you hear me?"

"I hear you Ashanti" he smiled down into her eyes.

"This is to make sure that you do" she said suddenly snatching him by his shirt and pulling him down to her then kissing him. He was more surprised than she was, as slapped him on the ass and casually walked away.

"Get him girl!" a girl shouted an eruption that she didn't expect happen causing her to blush.

"Ah, shit! It's on and popping now!" a group of guys stood up shouted across the court at the East Siders while laughing.

The second half was a straight up nightmare for the East Siders. ATM jumper arrive back from its mini vacation and there wasn't anything that anybody could do to stop the onslaught. He hit his next ten shots and with a simple up fake his man would leave his feet or lean and he would take off. The six-foot-seven center coming over to protect the rim got posturized. SLAM! He went back down court blowing J a two-finger kiss.

"Damn" she said getting to her feet applauding him as he went pass.

When the horn sounded, they had a fifteen-point victory. As the west side went to congratulate their team, J got just as praise by the guys and ladies around her.

"Damn, J" giggled Sunshine. "You are a ghetto celebrity. I have to bounce" she said. "It really been nice talking to you, later ladies" she wave to then allowing the crowd to consume her.

"J-Lo!" shouted Chubby waving her over.

"Yes" she replied with a coy smile.

"Nice touch with the kiss" he complimented her.

"For motivation" she replied slightly blushing.

"This is for you" he said placing a thousand dollars in her hand.

"I can't accept this!"

"Refusing a gift is a form of disrespect. Are you trying to disrespect and embarrass me?" he asked slightly hardening his eyes.

"No, sir."

"I didn't think so" he replied suddenly laughing and turning then walking away leaving her grinning.

"What did he give you?" inquired Lisa staring at her hand.

"A thousand dollars" she replied revealing it to them.

"What?" said Chi staring at the money. "Damn!"

"Girl, I don't know what you said to ATM, but that fool came alive" mention Lisa giggling. "And when have you started kissing strange guys, Ms. Virgin?"

"Shut up, Lisa" she replied nudging her. Before she could clear her head, ATM was heading in their direction. "Nice game" she complimented realizing that everybody was watching them.

"I had a good motivator" he replied slightly blushing.

"Blushing? You?" she said snickering.

"You are so beautiful, Ashanti" he replied staring deep into her eyes. "Now look who's blushing" he smiled at her. "Will you call me?" he asked extending his number to her.

"What do you think" she replied accepting the number and placing it in her back pocket.

"We are having a celebration over in Dru Hill Park. Will you attend?"

Although she wanted to say hell yeah, she knew the rules that they establish when they were in elementary school. "Ladies?" she asked never averting her eyes from him.

"We'll be there" they chime together.

"You have your answer" she replied smiling up at him.

"I'm heading home to take a shower and change. I'll be back within the hour" he assure her.

"I'll be waiting" she replied slightly blushing while staring in his eyes.

"Cool" he replied. "Ladies" he acknowledge then disappeared in the crowd.

"Damn, J. After all these years, yawl are finally going to get together" Chi said smiling.

"Slow your roll, Chi" she insisted. "We just might not click."

"Yeah, right" they chime together grabbing her arms and escorting her towards the entrance.

"Young lady" the chocolate woman called to her.

"Yes, ma'am" she replied admiring her smooth complexion and highlighted eyes.

"What is your government name J-Lo?" she asked surprising her by knowing her name.

"Ashanti."

"I'm Trinity."

"Glad to meet you, madame."

"You're not from the city, are you?"

"No, ma'am."

"I thought not" she replied slightly smiling. "You're too polite and your style of dress reveal you know you are sexy, but you dress conservative."

"Thank you" she smile up at her.

"Who does your hair?"

"I style my own."

"You do your own hair" she said uncharacteristically reaching and touching her hair.

"Yes, ma'am. I also did my girlfriend" she said peeking over at Chi.

"I might reach out to you one day. I hope we can talk."

"Yes, ma'am" she assured her.

"Your Juliet antic caused us dearly today" she smiled at her. "Bye, Ashanti" she said wiggling her manicure fingers.

"Bye, Ms. Trinity" she replied watching being escorted back to her vehicle. He open the door for her to climb inside then closed the door. He walked around and climb in the front passenger seat then lead the entourage down Dru Hill towards the east side.

"What did she want?" inquired Lisa.

"To introduce herself" she replied keeping the rest of their conversation to herself.

"Come on, girl. Snap out of your daydream" Chi requested smiling at her. "Everybody is heading towards the park."

At the party, she was approached and introduce to so many people that it was crazy. Several thuggish and drug dealers tip their hats to her as they walked pass. They eventually found a nice shady spot under a tree and took a seat. With the DJ mixing old school music with the latest hip-hop, people were dancing and enjoying themselves. With food, drinks and alcohol freely being given, nobody will leave there hungry but maybe a little intoxicated. It was a little after three o'clock when ATM arrived with his squad, he wasn't dress as she expected. He wore a two-piece gray leisure set with soft black bottom shoes.

"Enjoying yawl selves" he asked smiling down at them.

"Definitely" they replied together.

"Yawl hang together too much" he said grinning at them. "Anytime yawl know actually what to say, yawl hang too much."

"We've been girls since elementary school" she shared.

"It shows" he replied still grinning. "Come, take a walk with me" he requested extending his hand down to her.

"Okay" she said gripping his finger then being assisted to her feet.

As they were exchanging small talk among themselves, they were constantly being interrupted.

"I see that we won't be able to have a decent conversation today.

"It don't seem like it." she agreed. "What do you do on your spare time?"

He paused and smile at her.

"What?" she asked trying to understand the coy expression on his face.

"I spend my spare time at the library" he shared grinning.

"Are you embarrass?" she asked smiling.

"Embarrass, heck no. Do I appear to care what people think about me?"

"Not really" she admitted.

"Good because I don't."

"Where are you from with that hidden brash disposition that you possess?" she asked snickering.

"Very receptive of you" he had to admit grinning. "I'm from Murphy."

"Murphy Homes?"

"Yes, does that bother you?"

"Not at all because I'll never walk in that war zone."

"It's not that bad" he counter grinning. "We have less violence that Lexington Terrance."

"Lexington does have its problem but so does Murphy."

"I can't dispute that" he agreed.

"Can I ask you something?" he inquired staring in his eyes.

"Only if you can accept my answer" he replied returning her stare.

"I'll keep that in mind when I'm ready to ask you a personal question" she told him smiling them allowing it to slowly leave her lips. "I met a woman name Trinity after the game" she mention.

"You met Trinity. I'm extremely impress" he said flashing all thirty-two teeth. "She usually stay in her lane."

"She said something very unusual to me."

"She did. What?"

"That I cost them dearly today, do you know what she is referring to?"

He stared into her eyes then scan who was around them then said,

"There was a wager on who will win the game" he shared. "Didn't you see all the big rollers around you?"

"Yeah" she admitted.

"Do you really think they are the type of individuals to come sit around at Chadwick watching a regular basketball game?" he asked with slight grin.

"No" she had to admit. "How much was the bet for?"

"A half a million."

"Are you serious!?" shew asked clamping her hands over her mouth at being so loud.

"That is what I heard" he shared. "If you hear a half of a million, I'm more incline to believe it was a million dollars."

"Supposed yawl have lost."

"Somebody would have to pay, and this party wouldn't have been as festive" he said grinning.

"Supposed the person didn't pay up?"

"That option is not on the table" he told her allowing her to understand the subtle message he was saying.

"Oh?" she said understanding.

"How about us patching up this week?"

"Sure, where?"

"Since you live in Gwynn Oaks, how about the Woodlawn Library" he suggested then watching her eyes become evasive. "What's wrong?"

"Woodlawn Library?" she asked with apprehension in her eyes.

"Yeah, is there a problem" he asked seeing concern in her eyes.

"My ex hang out there" she shared.

"And what does that have to do with us?" he inquired slightly smiling.

"I just don't want nothing to jump off" she replied staring up into his eyes.

"Nothing will" he replied trying to assured her. "How about this" he said staring in her eyes. "We will bounce before something can jump off" he said with a coy smile on his face causing her to raise her eyebrows suspiciously at him.

"That smile isn't very convincing Akeem" she told him grinning. "I don't know you, but what I came to understand is that you won't bounce if things jump off."

"Hopefully, nothing will jump off."

When they returned to the others, Ice was getting to know Chi and whatever he was throwing, she was sucking it up like a straw in a soda bottle. Lisa was getting double team by Cross and Dink. The way they were operating on her, they have definitely done it before. They had her stumbling over her answers to questions they were throwing at her. They were definitely working on a profile of her, and I honestly don't think she realizes it. All in all, the day they spent in the park wasn't just enjoyable but also highly informative. It was almost eight o'clock when they decided to leave the park and walk the ladies to Mondawmin so they can catch the train to Rogers Station. As they said their goodbyes at the top of the escalators, the fellas watched them descending.

"Very interesting young ladies" mention Cross smiling.

"Man, Chi got that intellectual shit down to an art" complimented Ice snickering.

"I'm going to Woodlawn library Wednesday to patch up with Ashanti" he shared flashing his smile.

"You need backup?" inquired Cross slightly hardening his eyes.

"Na, I'm coo" he replied smiling. "If something does jump off, we will return Thursday and shut the place down."

"And keep it shut down until we let them have their peace again" cosigned Ice.

After a wonderful weekend, Monday morning brought nothing but drama to Akeem. From the moment he open his eyes and took his morning shower, life in Murphy Homes reminded him where he live.

"Akeem! Akeem!" shouted Kahlil to him.

"Yeah" he replied from behind his bedroom door.

"I need you to back me up outside" he informed him.

"Give me a minute" he replied finishing getting dress then opening the doors. He was standing there with a bloody nose. "Somebody got with you, huh?" he smiled at the anger in his eyes.

"Only because they jump me" he snarled wiping his nose again.

"Where is your brother?"

"At the library" he replied already heading towards the front door.

"Slow your roll" he said but he was already heading out the door. He had a purpose in every step he took, and Akeem couldn't contain his smile.

He peeked at his mother before closing the door behind himself. As they descended the stairs, Khalil was several steps ahead of him. He informed the drug dealers down below him who coming pass and they spoke as they went pass. They could see by Khalil action that something was about to jump off. By the time Akeem walked out the front door, his brother was already turning the corner heading towards the court yard. Just as he reached the corn, Khalil was snatching up a guy off the bench by his collar then slamming a vicious right into his mouth.

"Get up, tough guy" he shouted then stared at another guy. "And you, don't you go too far because you are next" he informed him snarling at him.

The guy eventually got to his feet to defend himself, but he was over match.

"Khalil" called Akeem as he stood over the ground snarling down at him.

"No, Akeem" he replied snarling at him also. "They aren't nothing but punk ass bullies. They think that it's funny jumping somebody" he described them then focus back on the guy.

"Watch your language" he told him. "You can see that he doesn't want any more action. Are you going to be the bully now?" he asked him not expecting an answer. "Look at his friend, he's already getting ready to take flight after witnessing what you did."

"Let him take flight, I'll see him again" he snarled over at the guy.

"What have I always told you?"

"No, Akeem. They need to understand that what they are doing isn't cool."

"They know. Look at them" he said.

He stared at the bloody guy then over at his friend. They both had, fear in their eyes for everybody to witness. He could tell that they will never consider messing with him again, but he wanted restitution for all those that they had bank and thought was funny.

"You know what is going to happen to them one day" he said staring at them individually. "If they continue on the path that they are choosing, fate will be their final judge" he told him staring in his eyes. Khalil didn't say a word just suddenly turned and walked away. "Fellas, if yawl don't flip your script, somebody is going to hurt yawl really bad" he warned them walking away. He caught up with Khalil at the front door and they took the elevator up together. They walked into the house and ran smack into their mother.

"I need to discuss something with you" she stated turning and heading towards the front room.

"Keep your cool, man" he whisper.

"I'm not for her stuff today" he replied as he continued to his bedroom. "So, what's up?" he asked coming into the room.

"Your boys up on Edmondson got jack last night. If you don't handle this, T.C is threatening to send a squad through there."

"What am I now a peace keeper?" he asked staring at her.

"You better be" she replied staring at him closely. He was resembling his father every year, especially his eyes. The look that he was giving her right now was the same look that his father would give her when he caught her wrong. "From my understanding, you have a connection with those little niggers on Pulaski.

"Those boys down at Pulaski didn't have a hand in that and you don't want to go through there spraying the corner like they did" he told her. "I'll make an inquiry" he told her walking away.

He left the house a little after six p.m. to head towards Edmondson Avenue. He was positive that Beanie didn't have anything to do with the stick-up. For the past couple of months, they had been flowing as expected and very peacefully. All he could do is see if he could or would provide him with any information as to who might have set it up. The last they needed was blood in the streets. If it does, Monk and Twin blood will be included in the cleaning of corners. Exiting his hack at the top of Fulton, he climbed out and walked into the store to buy himself a jumbo half and half then proceeded down to Pulaski Street. At the bar, he saw several junkies patching up to get themselves a blast.

"Can you spare a few coins brother?" one of them asked.

"I only have forty cents."

"Beats a blank little brother" he smiled revealing spaces where teeth once reside.

Reaching Pulaski, several corner boys was watching him approaching.

"Yeah, how many!" someone shouted to him.

"Chill Tick" a light skin guy told him stepping up. "What's up ATM?"

"I'm trying to reach Beanie. Tell him I'll be posted up until he gets here."

"I'll get that message to him" he said. Terrific game Saturday."

"Thanks man" he replied staring in his eyes so he could remember him. "I'll leave you to your business" he said crossing the street and taking a seat at the bus stop. He watched how they operated, and he didn't like the way their system was hook up. The money and drugs are too close. Besides being distracted by the adventurous flirting teenage girls, some relish in getting their dicks suck by specific junkies. If the stick-up boys study their operation, they could catch them sleeping easily. It was almost nine o'clock when a white 750 Beamer creep up on the block with its lights off and park near Gentle Ten. With the interior lights turned off, the driver open the door and step out, it was Beanie. As he stared over at his corner as he walked down, one of his men spotted him and they tried to straighten up, but it was much too late. As they chase the little hookers in training away, they took on a more alert disposition. He walked straight towards them, and they was openly nervous as they gradually surrounded him.

"Let me catch yawl sleeping again" he warned them hardening his eyes then turned and walked. He cross the street to greet ATM. "What's up brother?" he asked tapping his knuckles.

"Have you heard anything about what went on up the street?"

"I knew you would be coming" he said returning his stare. "I hope that T.C don't think my people had anything to do with that."

"What he thinks don't mean anything to me. I assured him people that yawl didn't have anything to do with it" he told him.

"I appreciate that."

"I still need to know who did do this."

"Answering that would be like snitching" he told him.

"Actually, answering it be good business and will eliminate a hit squad coming through spraying the corner" he informed him.

"It's like that?"

"How would you carry it Beanie?" he asked returning his stare but not his slight snarl. "If the script were flip, wouldn't you come to me not as a competitor but as a friend. Wouldn't you expect me to assist you?"

"You would probably already be out there hunting them down for me" he replied smiling. "The boys that hit you are from out of the Village. The two names that I have is Lucky and Maceo."

"I appreciate the love man" he said tapping his knuckles then heading back up the street. Once he reached Fulton, he waved down a hack and went home. Stepping out the hack on Pennsylvania Avenue, he went to a pay phone and made a call. He relayed the information that he had obtained then hung up. Late Tuesday afternoon near Frederick Avenue, two bodies were discovered several beaten before their lives were extinguish by a single shot to the head by a large caliber handgun.

As Akeem step off the number 57 bus in front of the 7-11 Store, he stared across the street at the library. There were two armed guards monitoring the traffic and socializing with the Woodlawn students. He heard there was always something jumping off with the other students from other schools, but that didn't have anything to do with him. Once it was clear for him to cross the street, he join the group as they cross together. As he walked pass the security guards, they gave him a brief peek before continuing their conversation. Entering, he notice that they actually had an entertainment center for arcades and videos. A little further inside most of the students were playing some game name Uno. What the hell is an Uno? Is there any place where students can actually study? The place resemble a social media spot than a library. He found a table in rear with windows that reveal Woodlawn High parking lot. Instead of security spending so much time at the front door, they need to peek at their back door. Students were having secret rendezvous. Looking towards the glass study rooms, male and female students were more interested in studying the others anatomy.

"Been waiting long?"

The voice took him out of his meditation. "Na, not too long" he replied admiring her attire. He was concentrating so hard on the front door that she slip in the side door on him. "You look very attractive."

"Thanks" she replied taking a seat across from him then placing her bookbag down next to her. "Do you always dress like this?"

"Yeah, why?"

"How many guys you our age dress like you?"

"None" he admitted slightly smiling. "My friends are always trying to call me GQ. I don't have that kind of money" he lied grinning.

"But that is my point, you aren't into "saggin" like most guys. I don't see the flattery in the style that most girls see."

"In don't either especially with the history behind it" he mention.

"They know the history and still think it's cute. I find it ridiculous" she shared her opinion then flip the questioning. "So, tell me something about yourself."

"I'm a boy" he replied smiling.

"Funny" she replied slightly giggling then catching the eyes of two girls walking pass to get a better look at him. "Tell me about yourself Akeem."

"I live with my mother and two little brothers Khalil and Amiri."

"What about your father?"

"He's doing time."

"Oh, I'm sorry to hear that."

"So, am I but if he wasn't incarcerated, he might have been killed before his 30th birthday" he admitted. "So, what was that all about Saturday?"

"Chubby" she admitted surprising him. "He said he need me to motivate you, or yawl might lose the game" she shared.

"Was the kiss his suggestion also?"

"No, that was me enjoying the role I force to play" she replied smiling. "I would have never jump that far out of character in a million years" she admitted giggling.

"Well, I'm glad you did" he replied ignoring the glare of two guys walking pass. As he scan the area, he notice the three guys he saw earlier pointing in his direction. He could see who they were talking to until they disburse. Coming towards them was Lamont and a couple of his boys with two girls tagging behind him.

"Is everything, okay?"

"Yeah, everything is cool Ashanti" he replied with a coy smile, but his eyes stayed fixed on something, and it was coming their way.

She tried to stay focus on his face to see if it was a threat or something, but he didn't give any indication off of his expression and this caused her curiosity to overwhelm and force her to turned around.

"Hey, J. How have you been?"

"I've been okay, Lamont" she replied staring up at his phony smile as Akeem thumb through the book he was studying.

"I haven't seen you around."

"Why should you?" she asked with sarcasm in her voice.

"We were good once."

"Excellent word was and that wasn't shit" she stated surprising him with her language. "What do you want?"

"Let me holla at you for a minute" he requested staring down at her then peeking over at Akeem thumbing his book.

"Ask him if you can have a few minutes of his time" she replied with a smirk.

"I thought you said you wanted me to stay out of trouble, Ashanti" he replied never averting his eyes from his book. "The decision is yours" he replied flipping the script back to her.

"No, it's yours. I'm here with you Akeem."

"See, J-Lo. He don't mind" he smiled at him as his boys smiled also. "Come holla at me."

"Leave me alone Lamont. There is nothing that we need to discuss" she reiterated hardening her eyes.

"Come on, J" he said starting to reach for her.

"Don't touch her" Akeem stated never lifting his eyes off his book, but he didn't touch her.

"What?" he asked staring down on him.

"Take you and your friends then step off" he said peeking up at him before returning his eyes to his book.

"What?"

"You can play your weak ass tough guy role with these fools out here, but I'm truly not impress" he told him peeking up from his book. "If you don't get out of my personal space, things will go downhill fast" he warned him.

"I don't know who the fuck you think you are" he snarled down at him.

"I'm Akeem motherfucker, but I know that doesn't mean shit to a bitch ass paper soldier like you" he replied getting to his feet and walking around the table then staring down into his eyes. "Do you want to get to know me?"

"What you need to do is chill" he lightly chuckled. "My boys might think that you are threatening me."

"You are being threaten bitch. I thought I was making that clear" he smiled at him then peeked over at his boys. "As far as your boys are concern, don't include them in something between two men. I would hate for my crew to come through here like the Gotti Boys and reveal how true soldiers actually carry it" he informed him. "Don't allow your weak ass game get you and your little crew annihilated because we don't so drama, we do nightmares" he informed him. "I'm going to advise you one last time. Step off."

He pause exchanging stares then tap one of his partners arms. "Let's bounce yawl. I'll see you outside J-Lo" he said over his shoulder.

"No, you won't" Akeem corrected him.

"Yeah, right" he chuckled never looking back.

Before he knew what was happening, two of his boys were shoved aside and Akeem was snatching him by the back of his collar. He forcibly spun him around and slam a vicious right-hook to his jaw that flip him backward over a table. Daze from the blow, he stared up at

Akeem as he slowly gained his balance. Both security guards responded almost instantly looking at the group then focus in on Lamont's bloody mouth and nose.

"What happen Lamont" the female guard asked staring at him then at Akeem's body language.

"I stumble" he lied returning her stare then peeked at Akeem gathering his books.

"Let's bounce, Ashanti" he said slinging his bookbag over his shoulder peeking at Lamont while J-Lo collected her bookbag. He took her bookbag then casually walked pass the security guards staring each guy with Lamont in their eyes before heading towards the front door. Walking out the door under the scrutiny of those that knew what had just transpired, they walked down to the bus stop near the tree then took a seat. When Lamont finally walked out with his little entourage, he spotted them sitting at the bus stop, but he never thought about approaching. "Does he usually take the bus?" he asked staring over at him.

"Usually" she replied.

"I'll think about letting him catch the next bus" he informed her then turned around and stared up over the slight hill.

"Here it comes now" she announced getting to her feet.

"No, Ashanti. Not this one" he said lightly gripping her arm while peeking back at Lamont as she reclaimed her seat.

"You are so bad, Akeem" she smiled up at him then over at Lamont sitting up on the handrail in front of the library.

"No, I'm not" he corrected her. "Isn't he supposed to be the tough guy?" he asked not expecting an answer as he peek back at him.

Minutes before the next bus arrival, two of his associated walked over and got in line. They peeked over at Akeem before stepping up on the bus then it pulled away from the curb. When the next bus appeared over the horizon, he announced that they could leave as they got to their feet. As the bus stop in front of her and she climbed aboard, he stared back at Lamont before climbing aboard. Swiping his all-day pass, he located J sitting near the back door. Their conversation was at a whisper, but her constant outburst of laughter and giggling had people peeking back at her. By the time they had reached her stop, he actually had her in tears from laughing so much. She actually caught his intellectual humor, and it was like a breath of fresh air to him. Most girls get lost when he uses naturally words like inquisitive or daunting in his conversations instead of nosy and scare. She reached up and pulled the cord to indicate she wanted the next stop. Getting to her feet with her bookbag, she step off the bus but not before wiggling her fingers goodbye and flashing her board smile.

For the next couple of weeks, J-Lo and Akeem would hook up on some weekends, but his weekdays were filled with obligations. While J hung out at the library or with her girlfriends, he personally had things that demanded his attention like his brothers, being a mule for T.C who was subtly increasing his load by telling him to collect the money from his stash houses. He did it but he was charging him extra also. Although his uncle repeatedly tried to convince him to carry a weapon for his protection and the money, he adamantly refused. Their relationship has never been strong and constantly bumping heads with him over how he should make his pick-ups was putting a strain on their already fragile relationship. With his mother cosigning his bullshit, things finally exploded between them.

"Are you a Superman?" she asked staring down at him while he was eating breakfast with his brothers.

"No but I'm still not going to carry around an illegal gun. I don't know if it has bodies on it or not and don't care" he said snarling at her. "I'm not carrying no damn illegal weapon for him or you" he stress.

"If you are taken off, who is going to be responsible for replacing the drugs or money you lose?"

"That's part of the game" he reminded her. "Does he or you for that matter concern yawl selves with me possibly getting pop or killed with all those drugs on me? Would you still expect me to refinance the lost?"

"If you think you are going to get a pass if you lose the money or product, you're sadly mistaken Akeem" he said staring in his eyes. Restitution in some form must be paid especially if the situation could have been avoided."

"You are something else" he lightly snicker. "If your brother ever try putting his hands on me, he won't be putting them nobody else" he informed her returning her stare.

"Oh, you're a gangster now."

"No, I'm not nut I damn sure can be a nigger" he snarled at her.

"All I am saying is that with bigger responsibilities you need to be more diligent."

"I have never seek the responsibilities but you and him, are constantly loading my plate."

"That's because you are ready for more responsibilities" she kept reiterating. "If I got to push you to show you your full protentional, I will" she glared over at him. "When I'm in the streets, I heard the love that people have for you. Our name have always induce fear and respect in the streets."

"Yeah, I've been hearing that story since you first started exploiting me" he slightly smiled. "The question that been plaguing my mind is this. How many Anderson women been incarcerated or killed on those streets? How many, lady?" he asked refusing to call her mother or any other words that describe a mother. "Here is an easier question, how many have graduated high school or attended college? Well, I'm going to acquire both and so will my brothers" he said with conviction. "A mother would never boast about getting incarcerated like it's a badge of honor as you do. What kind of mother tells their son to step up and get into such a dangerous game except one that don't have to experience it?

As a mother, you don't have any morals or self-respect that's why it's so easy for you to send your child out there to do what you don't have the heart to do or your punk ass brother" he express shocking his brothers with candidness. "A true mother would protect and educate their child, not throw them to the wolves like you did me. I'm done with you lady. Finish. D.U.N. Done" he stared into her eyes menacing. "Khalil and Amiri know I will break my foot in their asses if I ever hear about them handling, transport or messing with drugs. I am extremely comfortable with them and that's why I'm making arrangements to get out of your house" he announced dropping a bomb on her. "I'm done with you lady" he said getting to his feet then heading towards the front door.

"Where are you heading?" she heard herself asked.

"Why? You never concern yourself before so don't start now."

"How are you going to take care of yourself?" she foolishly asked.

"Are you serious?" he asked snickering. "I've been taking care of me and my brothers since I was ten including your begging ass. I'm sure I can still provide for me and my brothers. As far as you are concern, you are no longer a concern of mine" he informed her walking out the door.

He found himself walking up Pennsylvania Avenue. His instinct took him to the Billie Holiday monument at Fayette Street and took a seat. He never understood why this location have always eased his mind and formulate things that wasn't organized in his mind, but it always did. Staring at the old Royal Theater and imaging the old black jazz musicians that used to flood Baltimore since the thirties as part of the Chicken Circuit, heroin has always been the number one drug in the city. He needed to escape this city even if it's just to the Woodlawn section of the county. He had a little more than thirty-thousand dollars stash and that was more than enough to sustain his simple life, but what they are asking for rent, he would have to manage his money even more consciously that he have been unless he could get a deal somewhere and that was when a coy smile came to his face. He needed to talk to

Chubby. He got to his feet and stood on the corner searching for a hack. Less than two-minutes later, a late model Acura pulled over.

"Where you going?" the dusty looking white boy asked. The only reason why he was in Baltimore was to get their drugs and damn sure not to cruise the streets.

"Do you know where Chadwick is located?"

"No but you can direct me. How much do they usually charge?"

"It's a five-dollar ride, it's across the street from the park."

"I know where you are talking about" he suddenly smiled. "They have basketball courts there, right?"

"Yup."

"Hop in" he said accepting the five dollars then pulling into traffic.

He was climbing out of the smelly car and proceeded towards the building. He spoke to several people as he made his way inside the building. As he stood by the office door, he could hear the usual jazz being played and voices mixing with laughter. He lightly tap on the door and waited.

"Yeah, come in!"

He turned the nob then push the door open. Chubby was socializing with several high-profile distributors from around the city.

"ATM!" they chime together smiling and raising their glasses.

"Hey, fellas" he replied smiling at them. "Can we talk?" he asked staring Chubby in his eyes.

"Sure, spit it out" he replied leaning back in his chair with his glass of Hennessey.

He looked around the table at the gentlemen sitting around individually then took a deep breath and said, "I need some place to live."

"What's going on at your mother's house?" he inquired surprise by his request.

"That isn't important" he replied, exchanging stares with him. "Do you or anybody you know have an apartment or house they want to rent?"

"As a matter of fact, I do" he replied. "How much can you afford?"

"Since it's yours" he slightly smiled causing a strange expression to cross his face. "Are you alright Chubby?"

"Yeah" he replied but he wasn't and those sitting at the table knew it also.

"Well, I can afford five-hundred a month" he replied.

"Where are you getting five-hundred a month?" he inquired staring at him suspiciously.

"Men don't ask men their personal business" he replied returning his stare.

"Where are you trying to live?"

"Nowhere near the west side" he replied.

"What, you done lost your love for the west side?"

"You're a funny guy when you want to be" he said smiling over at him.

"I have a place near Woodlawn I can let you inspect."

"I don't need to inspect it" he assured him smiling.

"The house is furnish, but the place need to be air out. An extremely good friend of mine own it but he's away" he said opening his desk draw and searching for the keys. "You can move in anytime you're ready."

"Do I have to pay a month in the hole?" he asked grinning.

"Na, that won't be necessary" he assured him closing that draw and opening another.

"I'll get that money to you later today."

"You don't have to rush. I'm only glad to have somebody in there."

"Chubby" he said in a concern tone. "I'm going to be there until I graduate high school. I hope that's not a problem."

"None" he assured him finally finding the keys and pulling them out. "Here you go" he said extending them to him.

He paused staring at them like they were venomous snakes.

"Hey, are you alright?"

"Yeah, Chubby" he replied taking the keys and holding them in his hands. "Thanks for your assistance and gentlemen, excuse my intrusion" he apologized turning and walking out the office. He lean against the wall exhaling and smiling before opening the door then stepping out.

"What's wrong Chubby?"

"Dice, there is something about that boy that feels so familiar" he replied staring at the door. "From the moment I first saw him four years ago, he has traits that made me shake my head."

"What do you mean Chubby?"

"Like tonight, he gave a coy smile Ricco like he knew something that I didn't" he replied.

"Who is he?"

"I honestly don't know Mousey. Besides his name, he's a mystery."

"Well, one thing for sure, he's not in the game" Dice assure him. "Where do his people live?"

"Murphy Homes."

"That's my region" Mousey replied. "If you want, I can send some people through there trying to gain some information."

"No" he replied instantly returning his stare. "The last thing I need is your people snooping around in his personal life. How do you think he would react finding out and you know he will? The streets have mad love for him. Besides, I might admire his basketball abilities, but I like the person he is. Semi-quiet with an assassin mentality" he described grinning.

As he was walking down Dru Hill, he was floating on a cloud because the unseen weight he was carrying was suddenly lifted from his shoulders. The thought of catching a hack never enter his thought process. When he finally reached his mother's house, she was entertaining her usual leeches, especially Ms. Mable. They exchanged quick stares but that was it. He walked straight to his brothers room and lightly tap on the door.

"Come in" replied Khalil.

He push the door open then step inside and closed the door. "Put that on pause" he instructed and Amiri follow them instantly. "Listen fellas, I wasn't blowing smoke signals at your mother earlier."

"She's your mother too" replied Amiri.

"How many times do I have to tell you that I was born in test tube and not through her like you and Khalil?" he asked staring at him seriously.

"That crap worked when I was naïve but I'm not anymore" he told him causing them to burst out laughing. "Do you know I actually believe that and I'm eight years old until I finally had the nerve to asked Mom earlier this year" he shared to their snickers.

"Well, it was a good lie while it work" he replied as him and Khalil burst out laughing again as he harden his eyes at their deception. "Brothers" he called getting their full attention. "I would never abandon yawl if I thought yawl wouldn't do the right things, but I'm certain that yawl will. I've acquired a place already."

"When are you leaving, Akeem?" Khalil asked staring in his eyes.

"Today" he replied returning his stare.

"Can I have your room?" inquired Amiri smiling.

"Na, it's Khalil room now" he replied then focus back on Khalil.

"When will we see this place?"

"I'll be picking yawl up every Friday after school and yawl will stay with me until late Sunday, Khalil."

"How will we be able to reach out to you?"

"I'll get yawl, a cell phone at the end of the month. Are we good?"

"Yeah" they chime together then tap his knuckles before he left the room.

Inside his room, he started putting his few suites in his garment bag while folding his leisure sets and placing certain pairs of shoes inside his duffle bag. In his over-size gym bag, he stuff his gym attire including his one pair of And 1 and those black and white Jordans. He tap on his wall and his brothers came to his room. Extending certain garments to them, he walked pass his mother without looking at her, but he felt her eyes on him and his brothers as they help him with his clothes as they walked out together. Reaching Pennsylvania Avenue, he got a hack and loaded everything inside on the back seat. He gave the address to the house on Silver Hill Avenue. He didn't know what to expect, but he didn't care. Any place was better than where he came from. Cruising down Silver Hill, a broad smile suddenly engulfed his face. A single-family home. Who could ask for anything better? As he gather his bags, some of his neighbors were sitting on their porch observing him closely. As he climbed the steps, he place his gym bag down and inserted the key into the lock then unlocking the door. He push the door slightly ajar as he picked up his bag then enter the house closing the door behind him.

As he stared around, a broad smile came to his face staring at the open concept and four-seat island at the kitchen. He started to go inspect the stainless-steel appliances, but he climbed the stairs and headed towards the front bedroom. Pullin off the sheet that was covering the bed, the queen size bed look like a twin in the massive room. The love seat and table was a nice sitting area to watch the fifty-inch flat screen mounted to the wall. He had a four-piece on suite with double vanities with a walk-in closet. He turned the stereo system on, and Miles Davis trumpet filled the quietness. After hanging up his clothes, he took a tour of the other two bedrooms. They both had forty-inch flat screens and stereo systems. Descending the steps, he started pulling the sheets off of all of the furniture then he took it all in. Whoever lived here previously had terrific taste and invested well into the property. Descending the basement steps, he was blown away again. Surrounding the fifty-inch flat screen was a collection of jazz CD's that any DJ would be elated, to add to their collection. There were pictures of numerous black jazz singers and musicians that he never heard of before. Towards the far left was a workout area with a heavy bag and a reddish oak bar with six stools. He wanted to sit down and take it all in, but he still had several things that needed to be accomplish including cleaning material and hygienic products. He decided to go to the super market on Northern Parkway to kill three birds with one stone. Climbing out of the hack, they loaded everything on the porch then he paid the man. After getting everything inside, he open the windows then turned on the stereo system. Roy Ayers "Everybody Loves The Sunshine" filter out the Bose speakers then he started putting the food away first. Once that was completed, he spray wash the entire wooden floors throughout the house except down in the basement. He will tackle that tomorrow. For right now, he just wanted to be thankful for his blessing.

College recruits had started attending their games last year to check out the schools seniors. While they were checking them out, they took notice of the team sixth man. As soon as he got into the game, he was instantly an impact. Scoring or assisting on their next ten baskets, he brought a confidence to the team that was previously lacking. He was going into the eleventh grade in September and numerous coaches was trying to lock down his summer by attending some prestigious high school basketball camp being sponsor by Nike, but he had to decline. He simply told them that his family couldn't afford to send him anywhere for a month. They mention something to him about financial assistance and he shot that down immediately. He knew they naturally assume that he was too proud to accept their assistance and if they thought that, he was okay with it. If he wanted to test his game against top competitors, he can always go up to Philly and play in the Sonny Hill League or up on W.155th Street in New York at the prominent Rucker Park, he wasn't going anywhere having anybody inspecting and scrutinizing his game freely. Place a basketball scholarship in his hand and tinker all you want with his game but not his shot.

Although he's been making a thousand dollars a week being a mule for his uncle the last two years, he was still the broke ass kid from Murphy Homes who just so happen to be a bookworm. If he could acquire a scholarship on his academic, he really would have accomplish something. Although he was able to spend some time with J during the months, she always attended his basketball games. He had started to reveal his hand to her twice, but he wasn't ready to share where he was living with anybody not even Sunshine. The conversations that she would initiate always seem to implode in her face. Granted, he have always respected her wishes to retain her virginity until she graduate high school, but he never consider it. Never. With an abundance of young ladies desiring to communicate with him, he wanted to explore their intellect more than their anatomy. The woman body has remained the same since the first woman. So, he never consider them a smorgasbord. A place he could venture to have a little taste this and a little taste of that. No, he was never a sailor of love. A person that docks in strange and erotic ports because it present itself. He admire the mysteries and contradictions in their thinking especially about men. So, when J wanted to display affection to him in public, he never shut he down. He accept her passionate kisses and admiring rubs of his face while others looked on. He knew he could use his position with her and his silvery tongue to coheres her out of her panties, but he kept that little devil in him, in check. In fact, beside Sunshine, she was the only girl fingers that he would hold as they walk. Na, he would never play on Ashanti's emotions. He was a better person than that.

With his driver's license in his hand, he decided to buy himself a birthday present. He had a hack take him up Rt.29 to a car dealership near Columbia. He had foolishly told the hack that he could leave before being certain this was the right dealership. Walking around the lot, he would periodically stare in the office at the white people peeking out at him. He was standing around a good half hour when a middle age white guy pulled up a high-performance car. Instead of going inside, he came directly towards him.

"Excuse me, is everything okay?" he asked staring up at him.

"I was just finish contemplating walking my butt up out of here" he replied honestly while staring in his greenish eyes. "I foolishly allowed my ride to leave."

"How long have you been out here?"

"I've been standing here for a half hour, but I've been on this damn lot forty-five minutes" he replied unable to hide his displeasure.

"I apologize for their non-professionalism" he said staring up at him.

"With all due respect sir, no man can apologize for the actions of another man. I see their character for what it is" he slightly snarled.

"Let me make it up to you" he requested staring up at him.

"How? Can you fire everybody inside?" he asked.

"Would that please you?"

"No, sir" he replied honestly. "Everybody needs to eat including those racist motherfuckers. Excuse my language" he apologized snarling at the window. "What suggestion do you have, sir?"

"You see anything that you like?"

"Yes, sir" he slightly smiled. "That gray metallic 750."

"Although she is two years old, she has less than ten-thousand miles. I can let you have her for thirty-seven."

"Supposed I wanted to spend straight cash?"

Hearing straight cash caused him to stare at Akeem closer, he didn't possess a bash disposition and wasn't dress like a drug dealer with baggy clothing, excess jewelry, and an entourage. "I will consider thirty-two."

"Go and talk it over with your boss. If he agree to the price, we have a deal."

"He'll agree" he assured him slightly smiling. "Do you want full insurance also?"

"Yes, sir" he replied pulling out his license and extending it to him.

"Follow me" he said accepting his license then leading the way towards the front door. Pushing it open, he allowed Akeem to walk in first.

"Good morning, Mr. Stevenson!" the staff greeted him.

"Yawl allowed this gentleman to stand on my lot for almost an hour and not one of yawl tried to assist him, why!?" he demanded staring around the entire Caucasian staff. "Nobody have an answer" he snarled. "I have an answer. He's black but do any of yawl know who he is? Well, I do. His name is Akeem Anderson a highly recruited basketball player. I asked him if he had the power to fire yawl would he and he had the audacity to say no. Although he was directly disrespected because of the color of his skin and not his character, he still consider that yawl have families to feed. I personally would have come in here and fire everyone of yawl. If I ever hear of another customer being racially profile on my lot, your ass will be fire. If you don't like what the fuck I am saying, you can collect your shit and get the fuck out. Now get yawl sorry asses back to work and you really need to make your quota for this quarter" he informed them. He have been carrying much of them much too long and not assisting a customer to help make their quota, is not acceptable. His generosity ends today. "Follow me, Akeem" he said leading him into his private office.

Twenty minutes later, he was signing his name and accepting the keys. He escorted him back to the front door then shook his hand. As he approached the car, he press the automatic starter and the car came to life as he open the door and step inside. He inserted a various jazz musician CD he brought with him, and Buddy Rich "Time Check" filter out the Alpine speakers. He adjusted the seat and mirrors before placing her in gear then pulling off the parking lot. Checking the gas gage, he had a full tank of gas. As he cruise back down Rt.29 to Rt. 40, Edmondson Avenue, he was glad that the vehicle had manufactory tinted window, somebody would thought that he had a mental problem driving alone with a broad smile on his face. As he was approaching Penn-North, he spotted Khalil and Amiri coming out of the library. When the light change, he blew his horn to get their attention then pulled over and lower his window. A broad smile consumed their faces as they waited for the light to change.

"Whose car?" asked Khalil jumping in the front seat.

"Mine" he replied peeking in his side view-mirror before pulling away from the curb.

"This is yours, dag" he replied admiring the navigational system. "When did you get her?"

"About an hour ago."

"I know you are taking us for a ride" he said smiling over at him.

"Definitely" he replied.

"Put this in, please" requested Amiri extending a CD to him. "When did you start listening to jazz?"

"Since moving in at the new house" he replied inserting the CD and Dirty South music replace the jazz to which he was listening. Turning left, he was cruising through Dru Hill Park doing fifteen miles an hour with the windows down and the music wailing. Before long, they were cruising through Cherry Hill before heading out to the lake in Columbia. Although he saw them every weekend, he still missed hearing their bickering and laughter. It was almost four o'clock when he pulled up behind his building, he gave them a hundred dollars apiece then hugged them and told them that he loved them. As he was cruising back up Pennsylvania Avenue, he spotted Sunshine in a pair of white stretch jeans, a black playboy T-shirt with her black and white Jordan. She hasn't reach out to him since their last union and he wonder why?

"Hey" he called out the passenger's window grabbing her attention.

"Akeem?" she smiled looking at him then at the car. "What's up?"

"Nothing much" she replied coming closer to the car.

"Where are you headed?"

"I was going home, why?"

"I need to talk to you, hop in."

"Sure" she replied opening the door and climbing inside then admiring the interior. "Yours?"

"Yeah" he replied hooking a U-turn and heading back towards Murphy Homes.

"Where are you staying?" she asked fastening her seatbelt.

"Near Woodlawn."

"With whom?"

"By myself" he smiled pulling into their court yard then placing the car in park.

"When are you going to invite me over?"

"Any time you want" he replied smiling in her hazel eyes.

"Well, I'm not doing anything now" she said smiling at the surprise expression that came to his face. "Let's ride."

"You got it" he replied placing the car back in gear then retracing his previous route. They drove pass Mondawmin Mall heading up Liberty Street. He stared over at her near B.C.C.C.

"What?" she smiled at his expression. There were certain expressions that she understood, and this was one of them.

"Why haven't you gotten back with me?" he blurted out causing her to giggle.

"I tried but your ass was gone. When I asked Khalil about you, you would have thought I was five-o. He was very evasive. I foolishly thought that since you got from me what I desire, you moved on" she replied honestly. "I forgot that I seduced you" she giggled again.

"Na, Sunshine" he replied slightly hardening his eyes indicating that he was serious. "We are much better than that young lady."

"Yeah, I know" she giggled. "I saw you one evening hanging with J-Lo when I was with Biggie. Yawl seem extremely tight. Is she your girlfriend?"

"No, we just flow" he replied returning her stare.

"By yawl body language, it appears that yawl are more than just friends."

"She like displaying affection in public. You and a lot of people are assuming that we are more than simply good friends. She intends on keeping her virginity until she graduate high school and I'm not going to violate her intensions" he shared with her.

"That's very respectable of you" she complimented smiling. "She definitely made a name for herself in the city and whole lot of young ladies are jealous as hell including me."

"No need to be Sunshine" he insisted peeking at her as they cross Garrison Avenue. "Our roots are extremely deep" he said turning right onto Rogers Avenue. A couple of lefts and rights and he was pulling up in front of the house. "Here we go" he said pulling over in front of the house. His neighbors stared at them curiously. When he left this morning, he caught a hack. Now, he was returning driving a new car and clutching the fingers of an extremely attractive young lady with him. She was the first young lady that came to visit him since he moved in. As they climbed the steps, he unlocked the door for her to enter first.

"Wow!" she declared walking inside. She spotted two pictures of them in the front room when they were about ten years old with Khalil and Amiri in front of the building. The second picture was of them when they were about fourteen down in the Inner Harbor. "This is taken on Valentine Day. Boy was Biggie mad not seeing me until later that day" she shared giggling.

"You want anything?" he asked heading towards the kitchen.

"Na, not now" she replied still take a tour of the house. She climbed the steps to the second floor while he sat in the family room listening to jazz. he sat there almost fifteen minutes before realizing that she haven't returned. He got to his feet and ascended the stairs. He heard Jill Scott singing "The Way" filtering through the slightly ajar door. Pushing the door further open, Sunshine was sitting butter ball naked up on the bed staring over at him with an impish grin. With the evening sun caressing her golden body, her naval ring, her close shaven garden of love revealing slightly swelling lips and just the contour of her body was so erotic to him.

"It's about time that you miss me" she replied giggling.

As he got unrobed, his eyes never waver from her body. Her breast were firm and didn't need a bra to keep them elevated. She looked so damn beautiful. As he walked over to her with his dick slinging, she giggled like a school girl.

"Bring that Mandingo dick over here" her voice was low and slightly cracking.

Climbing up on the bed and lying beside her, they exchanged a long passionate kiss filled with lust and desire. As her small hand massage and stroked his dick, she gently squeezed it causing a low moan to escape him.

"Where is your glove?"

"I got one" he said rolling over and opening the night stand then retrieving a condom.

The4 act itself was a complete blur to her. Between her pleads and tears, she fell back in love with him even more. She had forgotten how he had dominated her the previously, but she remember now. She wasn't sure if she fainted from the immense pleasure, he had induce in her, but when she focus back on his face, he was staring down into her eyes with genuine concern.

"Are you alright?"

"Huh?" she asked looking at him confused.

"You pass out Sunshine" he informed her as his perspiration fell on her chest.

"I did what?" she smiled up at him waving off her hand.

"You pass out, girl" he said rolling over, but still staring in her eyes with concern. "Are you alright?"

"Yes, Akeem. I'm fine baby" she tried to assure him while rubbing his face.

"You scared the shit out of me" he confess slightly softening his eyes.

"I'm sorry sweetheart" she smiled at him lightly kissing his lip while touching herself. "Biggie won't be getting any of this for a couple of days" she giggled staring in his eyes. "I truly love your eyes."

"And I love you" he heard himself say.

"You what?" she said surprise by his statement.

"Nothing" he replied grinning then laid beside her.

They laid talking and laughing for hours. She adamantly refused another section of love making with him. She didn't want to walk around for a week like she had been riding a horse even though his dick appears to be like one. They eventually got their feet and went into his the on-suit to take a shower. As alluring as he was in the shower, she wouldn't submit to his intoxicating and alluring Venus flytrap words of seduction. She wasn't going to be devour by him again. Observing the other getting dress, they eventually left the bedroom and descended the stairs. They walked out the front door then clutch fingers as they usually did when walking. On their ride home, she had the audacity to request some curry chicken, but she wanted it from their spot up on 33rd and Greenmount. Without protesting, he diverted his route. Arriving twenty-minutes later, he brought her the curry while he brought himself some goat with mix rice. Cruising pass Melba Place, the club was just starting to fill. Tonight, was ladies night and they were arriving in packs. Pulling into their court yard, he have her his cell number. He watch as she gingerly walked across the court yard. A board smile came to his face knowing that he had just confess his hidden affection and love to her.

T.C was sitting on the balcony in his apartment in Cedonia reflecting on the past couple of years. He have come a long way since jumping in the game as a corner boy. When his big sister suggested him using the money he won on a settlement from the M.T.A to buy his first couple of bricks of heroin and be his own man, he hesitated but listen to the plan she had map out. With all the I's dotted and T's cross, he reluctantly agreed. She can be so scandalous and didn't care who it affected even her first-born son. He knew the things that he have accomplish wasn't because of him or his reputation, but because of the love and reputation of his nephew in the streets. He was heavy into his thoughts when the doorbell rang. He nodded to one of the men in the room to answer it. Seeing who was walking in, he got to his feet.

"Hey, big Sis" he greeted opening his arms.

"Keep that sentimental bullshit to yourself" she snarled pushing him away. "What is so important that you couldn't come to me?" she asked taking a seat and staring out at his scenery.

"I need you to talk to Akeem."

"Akeem?" she said pulling out a cigarette and light it. "I haven't seen him since he left home."

"What!?" he replied surprise not by her lack of concern but the nonchalant way she informed him. "When?"

"Almost a year now" she revealed.

"A year! Where the fuck is he living?"

"I don't have the vaguest ideal and those two sons of mine aren't saying shit even Amiri."

"Why didn't you say something?"

"Say what?' she asked hardening her eyes. "That little nigger can't stand me, and he made that clear the last time we spoke."

"Woman, you are imaging that" he snicker waving off her comment.

"Boy, I know when somebody isn't feeling me" she snapped staring at him. "He shot me the exact same stare that his father gave me when he said he was through with me" she shared.

"You want me to talk to him?"

"And say what?"

"To take his ass home" he said hardening his eyes.

"You will be wasting your time" she lightly chuckled. "He's still working for you right?"

"Yeah, five-o will stare hard at him, but never step to him because they recognize him as a prominent basketball player. If they knew he was my nephew, they would flip him upside down trying to catch him dirty."

"So, what do you need him to do now?"

"I am trying to cut myself a small piece of turf up in Park Heights, but I can't place none of my men to do recon. They would definitely get step to and that's why I need him. With his recognition and reputation, he could see whose running things and maybe set up a meeting."

"What are you willing to pay those guys?"

"Pay them?" he asked snickering. "I'm not paying them shit."

"Do you really think you can infiltrate another another's turf and not pay taxes?" she asked staring at him like he lost his damn mind.

"Hell yeah" he replied defiantly returning her stare. "Word on their streets is that motherfuckers aren't happy with the quality of the product they are selling."

"What does that have to do with you? If those fools aren't happy with the product, nobody have a gun to their heads forcing them to purchase their weak ass shit" she replied inhaling from her cigarettes. "Besides, they could simply catch a bus down to Penn-North and get anything that they desire."

"You know those fools are scared to come down that far."

"Not even for some good ass dope?" she mention slightly grinning.

"I don't see it happening" he said pulling from his blunt. "If they won't come to me and if I don't pay taxes, the streets will be cover in blood. How profitable is that?"

"It's not" she agreed staring out in the distance thinking. All of the hotspots were occupied and uprooting any of those clicks won't be easy. They might unify against a common enemy. As she scan the areas in her third eye, a coy smile finally came to her face.

"What is it Sis?"

"Since they definitely won't come to us, I'm suggestion a medium point" she said still grinning.

"Where?"

"At Park Circle" she replied smiling.

He ponder her suggestion viewing the place with his third eye. They could set up shop behind the gas station and monitor everything in the area. "Not a bad suggestion Sis" he admitted smiling.

"Yeah, I know" she replied grinning.

"We still have to get Akeem to put his imprint on the spot. He has to be the one to open the spot to establish who was running shit. He could go up to Belvedere and Park Heights to pass out the testers while informing them where they could make a connection with him."

"How long do you think you will need him?" she inquired.

"A minimum of a month then he could go back to transporting full time and collecting from my stash houses."

"All that is fine and dandy, but you will have to lay something sweet on the table before he agree."

"With the possible money I could pull in from those unhappy customers as that spot alone, I can very easily pay him ten-thousand a week."

"Ten G's, damn. You make a bitch like me want to get into the game" she admitted smiling.

"Yeah, right. Women of our clan don't deal drugs" he reminded her. "When can you get with him?"

"Friday" she replied crushing out her cigarette. "He pick up his brothers every Friday like clockwork."

"How are my nephews anyway?"

"Following behind Akeem, academically. Both of those boys stay on the honor roll, and I wouldn't have known it if not for Amiri.

"Make you proud, huh?" he smiled over at her.

"If I was a true mother, I would be" she said lighting up another cigarette and pulling from it deeply. "Everything that those boys have accomplish and gonna accomplish has nothing to do with me and everything to do with him" she stress returning his stare. "If Killa was on the streets, he would snatch Khalil and Amiri from me."

"How is he doing?"

"How the fuck do you think he's doing?" she snap with venom in her eyes. "He wouldn't be there if not for me. He will never forgive me, and I don't blame him."

"Do you think he will get out early?"

"I hope so" she admitted. "He's been locked down ten years already and I keep track by Amiri age. I send him a picture of the boys with a letter. He accepted the picture then burned my letter and returned it to me."

"Do you fear for your life if he comes home?"

"No, silly. He would want to be responsible for the murder of his sons mother. If we didn't have children together, I would have gotten the fuck out of Baltimore a month before his release date" she shared slightly smiling then allowing it to dissipate.

"If he tried to touch you, I would stretch his ass out" he boasted.

"Big talk from a little man" she counter. "Don't forget who the fuck Killa is and what he is capable. He would take you and anybody you send at him out. You can talk like you don't know how notorious he was if you want, but you know. I personally know of twelve people that he took out trying to reach out and touch him. Na, T.C it would truly be an asinine move leading to a self-induce implosion."

He didn't say anything as she stared in his sister cold street harden eyes. Her husband was one motherfucker that you didn't want searching for you. The smart man would make themselves available to him and his possible wrath. Rumor has it that he has well over a million-dollar stash somewhere. Wherever he stash it he knew for certain that no form of development would be taking place. Some people have speculated that it was buried in Dru Hill Park or Lincoln Park.

"I got to go" she announce interrupting his thoughts as she got to her feet. "I need a ride home."

"No problem" he replied snapping his fingers to one of his men. "Get with Akeem ASAP, Sis."

"Friday like I said" she reiterated walking back into the apartment then being escorted out. As she was being driven home, she was trying to decide how to approach him. If he was anything like his father, the direct approach was the best approach. When she walked inside her house, she called out to Khalil.

"Yes!?"

"Come here!"

"Just a moment!" he shouted back. A few seconds later he found her in the front room smoking a cigarette. "Yes?"

Call your brother, I need to talk to him" she informed him staring in his eyes.

He hesitated slightly then reached for the house phone and called him.

"Hello?"

"Akeem, mom want to talk to you."

"Put her on."

He extended the phone to her then turned and walked away. "Akeem."

"What do you want?"

"I have ten G's a week on the table for a month of work. Do you want it?"

"What do I have to do?"

"Set up shop for your uncle at Park Circle."

"And what else?"

"You have to up to Belvedere and Park Heights to give out testers."

He never responded just thought to himself.

"Hello?"

"I'm still here" he replied. "When do you need me to get started?"

"When-ever you are ready" she replied unable to contain her jubilation.

"I'll need a couple of days to get a crew together, but I won't be doing it for a month. I will be doing it for three months. Is that okay?"

"Sure" she assured him privately smiling.

"By the way, if he wants me to continue picking up the money at his stash houses then he need to continue paying me."

"That won't be a problem sweetheart" she assured him.

"I'm not your sweetheart" he replied then the line went dead.

"That went better than anticipated" she said to no one in particular with a coy smile. She wonder how T.C would take his new modified arrangement if he wanted him to set up shop at the Circle? One thing she knew he would do is cry like a little bitch but will eventually concede to his wishes especially if he wanted the money that could be obtained at the Circle. He know he couldn't put no other squad up there and not expect some form of complication except Akeem. With all her subtle snooping, she still wasn't able to understand how he obtained the status he acquired in the streets. No juvenile record or even being detained is unheard of in the drug game, but he haven't experience either. How fortunate for a black teenager.

A week later he was walking in his mother's house to retrieve the fifty vials he wanted distributed. He didn't spend no more time in her presence than he needed to. Accepting the vials, he didn't have any intentions of distributing fifty vials in someone else turf. If he could get rid of twenty before he is approached, he would be content. Those that he had left over will be his. As he walked out the door and took the elevator down, it of course stop at a floor below his then Sunshine and a couple of her girls climbed aboard.

"Hey, Akeem" she greeted smiling up at him. "I thought that was your car that I saw." She wanted to lightly kiss him on his lips but knew she couldn't because of her company. Besides, they were part time secret lovers and she wanted it to remain their secret.

"What's up?" he replied admiring her eyes as usual.

"Are you busy?"

"Never too busy for you. What do you need?"

"A ride to Mondawmin."

"Of course," he replied as the elevator struggle to descend. The door slowly open and they step off heading toward the main entrance. Exiting through the main entrance, they walked towards the courtyard clutching fingers. "There's Biggie" he mention. He was sitting around socializing and smoking blunts.

"Yeah, I see him and the bitch he's flirting with" she included staring over at them.

Somebody point him on point as he suddenly got to his feet staring over at her. "Yo, Sunshine!"

"Yeah, what's up?" she shouted back never breaking her stride.

"Where are you going!?"

"Mondawmin, why?" she asked pausing but not releasing his fingers.

"I might have wanted to hang out!"

"Na, it's just me and my girls!"

"Akeem isn't no girl!"

"That I am certain of" she replied slightly squeezing his fingers while smiling over at him. "He's dropping us off. I'll holla at you later!" she informed him turning suddenly and walking away. "The nerve of that motherfucker" she said opening the front passenger's door and climbing inside.

"You sound like you need some Anita Baker" he smiled over at the tension in beautiful eyes while backing up and searching his five-disc navigational system then "Sweet Love" filled the interior. "What side do you want?"

"You can let us off on the burger King side" she replied leaning back and humming Anita's tune. As they drove up Pennsylvania Avenue still clutching fingers, he whisper nothing but Illicit and erotic word softly into her ears causing her to giggle and poke him in the ribs. In less than ten minutes, their erotic ride was over as he was pulling up in front of Burger King.

"Thanks for the ride, Casanova" she said rubbing his face while smiling at him and opening her door.

"You are my aphrodisiac my alluring Venus Flytrap" he replied causing her to burst out laughing as her girlfriends climbed out and closed their doors. "It's been four months since we last got together."

"I know how long it's been, and it would have been longer if I haven't run into your handsome ass" she admitted returning his stare. "I'll call you soon."

"Alright" he casually replied grinning.

Leaning inside the car, she said "I mean real soon Akeem."

"Alright" he replied again laughing at the seriousness in her eyes as she closed the door and proceeded towards then entrance. He sat their admiring her sexy and natural erotic walk smiling before placing the car in gear and pulling away.

"Girl, what's up with him?" Coco inquired staring in her eyes.

"You would have to ask him" she replied pulling the door open and walking through.

"Yawl been friends since grade school?"

"Yeah, Diamond."

"Why haven't you press up on his fine ass?"

"Our friendship never waver that way Diamond" she lied.

"Do he have a girlfriend?"

"I honestly don't know Coco" she replied sincerely.

"I thought that J-Lo was his girl?" mention Diamond.

"You know J-Lo?"

"No but they hang out together like they are in a relationship."

"That's just him, girl" she light giggled. "He's very affectionate and don't have a problem displaying his affection in the streets either" she shared smiling.

"Like him holding your fingers in front of Biggie" Coco mention smiling.

"Biggie knows he have always held my fingers since we were kids and knowing him, unless it's my husband, he will continue to hold them. Now, Biggie can step up if he wants to, but he know better" she shared giggling.

Riding up Park Heights Avenue, he drove pass four separate drug spots before he reached his destination and they all appeared to be making money. The young soldiers were suspicious of every car that drove pass because any of them could hold five-o. With the quality of heroin that T.C put on the block, other dealers knew they had to match his quality or lose their customers to him. So, coming close to the Heights could be very profitable if the rumors were true about dissatisfied customers. As he near Garrison Avenue, he pulled over closer to the corner. After stepping out and securing the car, he cross the street to walk in the shade. Although it was barely one o'clock, the pool was over-flowing with children that took the opportunity to escape the smothering heat or take a bath while teenage girls wearing bikinis were subtly flirting with the older teenagers standing along the fence trying to get certain girls attention. Scanning up the street as he cross Garrison, he spotted a police cruiser but as usual, nobody was inside, and the drug dealers didn't miss a beat in their absence. Half way up the block, he paused to stare into a clothing store window. Minutes later, he spotted two junkies in the glass reflection heading towards the drug corner. He allowed them to purchase their drug then intercepted them on their way back and gave them a tester. He informed each junkie that he was able to hit off that he probably won't be standing here later but he could be found on the corner of Coldspring and selling what I have left until three o'clock. He told them where he would be opening shop on Wednesday at six to midnight. He was there about a good half hour before he was finally approached.

"What's up with you?" a guy in his mid-twenties asked him with two other guys.

"Nothing" he lied exchanging stares.

"Oh, it's something" he said looking him up and down. "What are you doing?" he inquired again.

"After your customers get hit off, I hit them off with a tester" he admitted.

"Testers? Where is your crew?" he asked peeking around.

"They aren't here" he slightly smiled at him. "We will be at Park Circle."

"Park Circle?"

"Yes, as far away from your business as possible."

"Give me one of those testers" he said staring in his eyes.

"Pardon me" he replied returning his stare and slight snarl.

"You heard me. Kick one out."

"Look into my eyes tough guy" he advised him. "You can make

demands as much as you want with your people but I'm not one of your peoples. Respect is due to every man. So, the disposition you are taking won't get you nothing especially with me" he informed him never averting his eyes or diminishing his snarl.

"Little nigger, you are giving them away anyway so give me one."

"First thing first. I am not or ever will be a filter uneducated nigger, but I do possess one inside of me and I assure you" he said stepping into his personal space. "You couldn't handle him" he informed him staring down into his eyes.

"Did yawl hear him?" he asked slightly backing up laughing.

"I don't need them to hear me just you" he said staring over at him.

"Who the fuck do you think you're talking to?"

"Apparently, you" he informed him. "If you think your soldiers are intimidating to me, you honestly don't know me" he slightly smiled. "Catching a beat down won't be my first, but as sure as I am there is a God, the wrath I will bring upon your bitch ass getting my restitution won't be merciful. I'm smart enough to know that you don't ever threaten a man. What I am saying isn't a threat but a promise" he told him watching the smirk he had on his face slowly dissipate.

"What's your name?"

"Now you want to introduce yourself. My friends call me ATM."

"ATM?" he repeated surprised by the revelation. "You are a baller."

"Do you have children?"

"Yeah, why?"

"That mean you have two images, a providing father beside being a drug dealer. So, why can't I have two images also?" he asked staring in his eyes.

"I thought you was one of Chubby's boys."

"I'm nobody boy" he corrected him slightly hardening his eyes while returning his stare. "I only play basketball for him like I do for my high school, but I'm nobody's boy" he reiterated.

"Does he know what you are about to do?"

"No, do you have intentions of snitching to him?"

"I'm no motherfucker snitch."

"The way that word offends you. The word nigger offends me" he informed him slightly grinning. "So, what a man do is his business, right?"

"Yeah" he replied suddenly turning and walking back up the street.

He decide it was time to leave the area. He had gave away about twenty testers, but he wouldn't have the ones he have left once he reached Coldspring Lane. He retraced his steps back to his car then hooked a U-turn. He pulled up on the corner of Coldspring five minutes later then climbed out. He didn't expect to be bum rush by addicts wishing to buy his last few vials. He was out of the area in less than ten minutes with new clients anticipating him opening in two days. He climbed in his car with all intentions of heading home and changing his clothes when he spotted J-Lo sitting across the street on the bus stop. He blew his horn to get her attention then pulled over lowering his window.

"Ashanti!"

Her broad smile came to her face seeing Akeem. She tap her girlfriend on her shoulder as she got to her feet. They cross the street then she pulled open the passengers door and climbed inside while girl climbed in behind her. "Hey, Akeem. How have you been?"

"Just fine and you?" he asked peeking in his side view mirror before pulling out in traffic.

"Just chilling, where have you been?"

"Taking care of business" he replied peeking over at her.

"Whose car?" she asked admiring the wood grain console.

"Mines."

"Yours?"

"Yeah, mines" he replied smiling.

"Nice" she replied. "Any plans for today?"

"Got something that I have to do in a couple hours" he replied.

"How about dropping me and my girl off at the Plaza?"

"I can do that" he said averting his direction.

"When are we going to hang out again?"

"In about two months" he replied grinning.

"Dag" she replied staring at him. "You telling me that your schedule is filled the next two months."

"I'm surprise that yours not" he replied still grinning.

"I wish it would be, but the quality of conversation is lame as hell."

"I am so sorry to hear that" he replied smiling over at her.

She became slightly silence then looked over at him. "I need to ask you a personal question."

"Ask but be sure you're ready to accept my answer" he warned her.

"I think I can handle it" he replied with a little apprehension.

"You think?" he said peeking back at her. "You really need to know that you can Ashanti."

She heard the warning in his voice and slightly in his eyes when he peeked at her. Now, she didn't know if she really wanted to know and continue to speculate or be intrusively inquisitive as most women can't resist. Now was one of those times that she needed to step up as Lisa constantly told her. So, she took a deep breath and asked. "Who is Sunshine?"

"Sunshine?" he repeated as an uncontrollable smile came to his face because he was surprised as hell to hear her name coming out of her pretty mouth. "She is an extremely close friend of mine. How did you hear about her?"

"She introduced herself at Chadwick when you had that big game" she informed him.

"She never mention that to me" he replied with a coy smile.

"What is yawl relationship?"

"Her and I have been rolling since first grade" he suddenly smiled again. "This guy name Fat Boy was trying to strong arm her chocolate milk, but she wasn't having it. When he got physical with her, I whip his ass and we have been friends ever since."

"Are yawl lovers?"

"When she desire me" he confess.

"Is she your girlfriend?"

"Listen to what I just said Ashanti" he said peeking at her again. "When she desires me" he reiterated.

"Does she have a boyfriend?"

"You would have to ask her that" he replied.

"You are something else" she lightly giggled. "Why are you so respectful to women when I see them damn near throwing their panties at you?"

"Just because they might be disrespecting themselves doesn't mean I have to do the same Ashanti."

"Did you mother teach you that?"

"The things she taught me isn't worth mentioning" he shared unable to contain his slight snarl. "I was self-taught."

"Most guys are just out there hunting but I'm not prey. I'll know Mr. Right when he comes along" she said smiling as he pulled up on the Plaza parking lot.

"Don't set your standards too high" he advised her coming to a stop at the main entrance.

"What I am expecting can easily be ascertained" she said unfastening her seatbelt and opening the door then stepping out. She lean back inside and said, "You fit my criteria Akeem especially after you finish sowing your oats" she shared smiling then closing the door.

He watched her with her friend walking through the main entrance and a broad smile came to his face. "She is so damn cute" he admitted to himself for the thousandth time.

On Wednesday, he was getting dress in unconventional attire. He was dress in black baggy jeans; a long black sleeve pull over with black Tims. Very unconventional attire for him. Around five-thirty, he was hooking U-turn on Towanda Street and parking. He was there for about ten minutes when a late model Caprice and Toyota pulled up behind him then the occupants step out. He met then on the corner.

"Hey, Akeem" a thick dark skin guy called to him while extending his hand. "I'm Nookie and this is my squad. My cousin Smurf said that if I fuck this up, he will cut me off permanently."

"We can't fuck this up" he assured him shaking his hand.

"How do you want us set up?"

"I need a guy up on that corner as a look out. You can rotate your men every hour, so he won't get complacent. Who is hold the weapons?"

"Me and my right-hand man Boogie" he informed him.

"Take them off you and wipe them down for finger prints. You won't have them on you but easy access if necessary. If five-o roll up on us unexpectedly, none of our prints will be on those weapons. Alright?"

"Yeah" Nookie replied. "Are you sure this is a good spot. I mean, we are out of sight."

"And that's the way I want to keep it, I did my recon Nookie" he slightly smiled. "Watch how this money come to us."

"I don't know man."

"You don't have to Nookie. I know" he informed him. "From six to midnight gentlemen. So, let's get started" and they fanned out. A six o'clock their first customers started arriving. After seeing ATM, the first customer requested five vials. Every time the bus stop in front of the gas station junkies were stepping off and walking up pass the Chicken Shack towards them. By eight o'clock, they were walking or riding bikes to their location. He had to send one of Nookies boys to the room he rented on Fulton to retrieve more heroin. The feedback he was getting from the junkies was all about the high quality of his product. As they were leaving for the night, several junkies were trying to convince him to sell then a couple of vials, he reminded them of the time he open and closed. He didn't serve any of them. After collecting the money from T.C stash houses, he hooked up with him a little before two o'clock in the morning.

"So, how was it?" he asked seeing him walking into the room.

"Good" he replied while dumping tonight's money on the table and watching him.

"Damn!" he declared staring over at him. "What is the count?"

"A little over ten bundles" he replied. "But we are leaving money on the table" he informed him. "You need to consider a midnight to seven crew."

"It might take a minute to establish one."

"The longer you wait the more money you are losing" he told him. "I got to go" he said heading towards the door.

It took a good three weeks before they finally established a good routine, they would close shop around eight-thirty for a half hour to eat and get better acquainted. Nookie confided that he fucked up royally three years ago and was thankful that Smurf was his cousin because he surely would have blew his brain out of the back of his cranium. Although he kept him feeding his family, the trust he lost wasn't as easy to regain until this opportunity. He had done a lot of listening to the things that Akeem was advising him about especially how to keep a low profile and never share your business with nobody that isn't in your squad. The half hour sessions have produce several unexpected opportunities. One were when customers suggested that they stay open an additional hour for those wishing to buy at least a hundred dollars of their product. What good business man could refuse such a lucrative offer?

T.C finally brought a late-night crew to their secluded spot. Akeem didn't recognize none of the guys and he didn't like that along with their brash disposition. He pulled T.C aside and spoke frankly that he didn't like their vibes. He wave off his opinion and kept it moving. Not even after a week on the job, bullshit raised its ugly head.

"Excuse me, young blood" an OG junkie excused himself. "Do you recognize my face?"

"Yeah, OG" he replied while exchanging stares.

"I remember when you was passing out testers up in the Heights and I have been a steady customer since you open shop."

"Yeah, I know OG. You are dropping easily a hundred dollars a day with us."

"Yes, I am" he cosigned. "I haven't tasted good shit like what you put out consistently in years."

"O.G what is this about because I know you're not being sociable" he smiled at him.

"No, I'm not young blood" he admitted. "Those boys that come on after yawl are so got damn disrespectful" he snarled. "I had to check several of my associates inside a shooting gallery because they were being emotional and about to put five-o on yawl, but I wasn't having that. So, to keep this heroin flowing our way and the money flowing in your way, I'm hoping you can rectify this situation immediately, young blood."

"I assure you O.G this will be handle immediately" he told him slightly snarling.

"Why are you working with motherfuckers from out of Cherry Hill?"

"I have no answer O.G" he replied then peeking at Nookie. "Take these as a form of appreciation for sharing what was happening" he said dropping five vials into his hand.

"Damn, young blood" he smiled up into his eyes. "I'll let my associates know that you will be handling this matter."

"Immediately, O.G" he replied slightly smiling with him as he retrace his steps. "So now we know where he found those guys at" he said staring at Nookie.

"Nobody fuck with niggers from Cherry Hill" he snorted.

"These motherfuckers are about to put the spotlight on us and I'm not having some dumb motherfuckers to fuck this lucrative shit up. I got to make a call" he said pulling out his cell and walking slightly away. He talked to T.C for about two minutes and Nookie watched him getting very adamant. When he returned, he was quiet for about an hour before slowly getting back into form. One thing he knew about T.C was that he was greedy motherfucker. He wasn't about to allow anybody to fuck up his money and will send a message that they don't want to receive, but he will send one. When they were relieved later that night, there was a noticeable difference in all of them. Besides, the obvious bruises and swollen facial area; their main man had a broken arm and look like a broken person. The brash and thuggish disposition that they usually displayed was noticeably absent. They exchanged stares as they went in separate directions. When Akeem arrived the next day, O.G had a broad smile on his face and brought two-hundred dollars of his product.

His two months were almost over and he almost volunteer to work an additional month because the money was so sweet, but he wouldn't allow himself to get further out of character. In the middle of the week, he got word that Chubby wanted to see him. After completing their duties, he checked the count and money then gave it to Nookie to deliver to T.C. He had told T.C that Nookie will be running things after he leave, and he accepted his suggestion. He tap their knuckles then climbed in his car. While "Sex Machine" by Sly Stone played, he hit Reistertown Road then took that until he bare left to go near Dru Hill Park. Pulling up in front of Chadwick five minutes later, both courts were being occupied. Since getting the lights fixed five years ago, guys had something to do than walking around the streets or hanging on corners. Violence around the area have ceased to exist and real soldiers stood by to assure that it stay that way. Although Whitelock Street and the violence associated with the street was one New York block away, the guys down there didn't want no action with Chubby, so they kept their business out of his house. Crossing the street, he was greeted by several ballers as though he was some kind of celebrity. Pushing open the door, he headed towards Chubby's office. He lightly tapped on his door and waited.

"Come in!"

He push open the steel frame door and step inside. "Hey, Chubby. What's up?"

"Have a seat" he offer pushing aside what he was doing. "Who is this?" he asked turning a picture over and sliding it in front of him.

He picked the picture up and stared at it intensely then up into his eyes. "This is me, you and my father. You knew my father?"

"Why didn't you mention who your father was?" he asked ignoring his question.

"I didn't think you knew him. Plus, it wasn't important."

"Oh, I know your father extremely well. We met back at Walbrook. He was one of the top basketball players in the state before he got his calling."

"I didn't know that about him" he admitted.

"The man was bad Akeem. I should have recognized your name since I name you" he informed him.

"Are you serious?"

"Yeah, man" he suddenly smiled. "Your father and I are extremely tight. When he caught that double murder charge, he took my charges."

"What!?" he said staring at him confused and in disbelief.

"He took those charges for me" he reiterated. "He transformed into an elite street soldier and was making damn good money. Taking care of his three sons meant the world to him, yawl always came first. There were rumors starting to float around about your mother that eventually got on the grapevine. When the rumors finally reached his ears, he was rightfully embarrassed" he shared staring over at him. "He always kept his emotions in check just like you do when a guy is talking shit to you" he slightly smiled again.

"How come he took that rap for you?"

"Not how but why?" he corrected him. "I caught your mother with two guys that couldn't stand the ground your father walk on, and Pinky knew that" he slightly snarled at the memory. "The best way to belittle any man is through his woman. He had confided in me that he suspected that Pinky was fucking with that raw but wasn't sure. Your father was very naïve about the effects of certain drugs because all he ever did was smoke weed, but I knew the signs. Your father never mess with that alcohol. He never wanted to be caught with his equal Librium off balance. When I saw her with Monkey and Cheese, I follow them to Monkey's play pen on Coldspring Apartment. Once they were inside, I contacted your father. Was I wrong for that?" he asked not expecting an answer as he took a hit from his Brandy. "When he arrived, we walked up to the apartment door, and he kicked it in. That was how he always knock" he shared with a faint smile that quickly dissipated. On the front room floor was your mother naked, you father just stared at her with disgust in his eyes. Touching those guys were never a part of his intentions but fear make dumb motherfuckers do dumb things. While he was staring down at her, they were reaching for their guns thinking he had intentions of reaching out and touching them. If I hadn't reacted as I did, they would have taken Killa out Akeem. So, I drop them both out just before Monkey shot your father. Five-o was at the house almost immediately. Somebody must have called five-o after hearing the door kicked in. He told me to drop the weapon and take the fire exit before collapsing on the floor. Like a motherfucker coward, I followed his order and bounce. I left my partner holding the bag" he confessed staring over at him. Your mother testified for the prosecution to escape all charges."

"Bullshit!" he declared knowing that he wasn't lying to him as a tear swell up in his eyes but couldn't accept his mother being the reason why his father was incarcerated.

"I sat there listening to the prosecutors defaming your father character and wanted to beat the shit out of him. Your father didn't have a criminal record. So, the prosecutor charged him with manslaughter charges because what they were seeking wouldn't have been smart, so they charged him with the lesser charge. The prosecutor describe him as man that lost control after witnessing him wife in a very uncompromising position. Bullshit. Killa never loses his cool. Never Akeem" he tried to assure him. "There were a lot of circumstantial evidence and that's all a prosecutor need to manufacture a guys' alleged character to an all-white jury. With all the bullshit evidence, I hired an investigative team and put them work. From their persistence, they have gotten a review of your father's case and a court date."

"What?"

"Your father could be coming home Akeem."

"Do anybody else know this?"

"No and it must remain that way. Do you understand?" he asked staring in his hardening eyes.

"Yes."

"There are certain people that must not know he might be hitting the streets again."

"I understand Chubby. When is his new trial date?"

"In a couple of months."

"I got to be there" he insisted returning his stare.

"You don't have to worry about that" he assured him getting to his feet and walking around the desk. "One more thing before you do."

"Yeah, what is it?"

"I need you to stop slinging for T.C. up at Park Circle."

"How did you find out?"

"People know you Akeem. They were shocked to see you creating the most profitable spot in the city" he slightly smiled at him. "Your uncle is doing something that I'm not able to discuss with you. When you was a mule for him, I stayed in my lane. I piece together how you got into the game and why? You have done a terrific job raising Khalil and Amiri" he informed him revealing that he knew their names also. "You are in an excellent position to graduate high school and obtain a college scholarship. I don't need you getting caught up in your uncle's bullshit."

"I'm out next week."

"He's not going to let you go that simple."

"He really don't have choice" he told him.

"All I can say is watch out for his scandalous ass. The only people that can bring us down is family Akeem."

"I know" he replied returning his stare.

"By the way, you have a rematch in two weeks on the East Side under the Dome."

"What time?"

"At one o'clock" he replied reaching inside his breast pocket and bringing out an envelope then extending it to him. "How can I charge you to stay in your father's house? Now, go find that jumper of yours. You haven't been seen on the courts in weeks."

"I'll be ready" he assured him placing the envelop in his back pocket. "later Chubby and thanks for the revelation" he said shaking his hand then turning and walking out. As he retrace his steps to his car, he climbed inside and started up the engine. He sat there for a minute filtering the things that Chubby just shared with him. His mother had turned state's witness against his father while knowing that he was innocent, but why? The scandalous bitch. Everything that she told him was a complete lie to cover up her freakish disposition. Boy won't she be surprised to see them walking into her house together. He open his sunroof to allow Donald Byrd's "Flight Time" to escape then place the car in gear and pull away. As he cruised down Dru Hill Avenue, all he could say to himself was, "His father was coming home."

Friday came quicker than anticipated. As he was closing up, he got a call from T.C for him to deliver the money to him and not Nookie. He started to decline but thought better of it. He could kill two birds with one stone. He could collect his money tonight instead of Saturday and informed him he needed to find another mule. He told Nookie it was a pleasure to have met him and his crew then they went in separate directions. Climbing in his car, he headed to one T.C pleasure apartments. Pulling up, he spotted his Audi parked in its usual spot. He pulled up next to it then climbed out. He grabbed the leather bag off the passenger's seat then open the door and climbed out. He walked to the building and climbed to the second floor then tap on the door. Seconds later, the door swung open.

"Hey, Akeem."

"What's up Doc?" he asked tapping his knuckles as he walked in.

"They are on the balcony" he informed him giving him a heads up.

As he proceeded towards the balcony, he wonder who they are? Pulling back the screen, he was surprised to see his mother. He haven't laid eyes on her in over a year and now that streak was broken.

"Hey Akeem" he greeted flashing that two-dollar smile when he had a plot he wanted to initiate.

"Unc" he replied.

"You gonna speak to your mother?"

"Here are your receipts" he replied ignoring his question and his mother while extending the bag to him then he pass it to one of his men to check the count like he have ever shorten him. When it comes to his money, he don't trust anyone.

"I need you to keep up the excellent work" he said pulling from blunt while staring up at him.

"You may need me to, but I'm done" he informed him.

"Na, you have to make sure that everything keep flowing steady" he informed him accepting some money from his man and passing it over to Akeem.

"Nookie got it cover" he said stuffing his money in his pant pockets.

"But I want you to run it an additional month" he insisted.

"Not gonna happen, I kept my part of the contract we set."

"Baby" his mother voice caused him to stare at her coldly.

"I'm not your baby" he corrected her.

"You gonna walk away from twenty G's?"

"Just as easy as walking away from you" he replied suddenly turning and opening the screen.

"Akeem, I need you to do this for your uncle" she insisted.

"I needed my father to be here to raise me" he said surprising them with his statement. He have never mention his father's name to either one of them. "But we can't always get what we want, can we?" he said walking off the balcony and heading inside.

"Wait a minute!" shouted T.C. "You still gonna make those deliveries for me right!?" he asked but he never broke his stride.

"Did you see that look he gave me?" his mother asked looking frantic.

"What's wrong with you?" he asked staring at the expression on her face. "What look are you talking about?"

"The look Killa gives me when he's certain about something" she explained adamantly.

"What in the hell are you talking about Pinky?" he asked still staring perplex by her.

"T.C" he called lighting up a cigarette and pulling from it deeply. "Have you ever heard him mentioning Killa name before?"

"No."

"And neither have I" she cosigned. "But his eyes know something."

"Woman, you are tripping" he lightly snicker.

"No, T.C. I'm telling you he know something damn it!"

"Impossible" he said hearing the urgency in her voice.

"I hear he's been playing for Chubby for over a year. If Chubby knew who he was, he would shower him and his brothers with gifts. Akeem eyes is actually like Killa. Before he pulled the trigger, his eyes were certain of a person guilt. Akeem stared in my eyes as he was saying his father's name. Oh, he knows something but just like his father, he won't reveal his hand until he is ready."

"Nobody know what happen?"

"Well, he know something" she replied as a cold chill ran down her spine. "He know something" she repeated softly.

For the next two weeks, he was hitting the basketball court twice a day playing against Khalil and Amiri or just shooting for a minimum of two hours. The first three days his jumper wouldn't comply no matter how good it felt rolling off his fingertips. By the end of the first week, she was at least in town and slowly finding her place back home. By the middle of the second week, she was back and looking as pretty as ever, but demanded that he never neglect her again and he wouldn't since he was free of his previous obligations. He reached out to Cross and told him that he will meet them by Lexington Terrance at noon. Cross, Dink and Byrd was standing on the corner of Argyle and Hoffman Street jiving around. When he pulled up on them, they naturally didn't recognize him.

Lowering the passenger's window, he asked. "Are yawl jumping in or what?"

"Whose car you done stole?" inquired Byrd smiling while jumping in the copilot seat.

"Funny" he replied tapping their knuckles then pulling away from the curb.

"Is this yours ATM?" inquired Cross peeking at him in the rear-view mirror while admiring the interior.

"Yeah."

"How long have you had her?" Dink asked.

"For a minute now."

"Are the rumors about you true?" Byrd asked looking over at him.

"It all depends on what rumors" he slightly smiled at him while peeking at them in the back seat through his rear-view mirror.

"Are you in the game?" Cross bluntly asked.

"I'm not standing on no corner slinging if that's what you mean" he replied staring in the mirror at him.

"You're not."

"No, Dink. I'm not" he replied turning on MLK Boulevard.

"Man, nobody seen you hooping in over a month" mention Byrd. "Have you been hooping somewhere?"

"Na but my jumper is in town" he assured him slightly smiling.

"I hope so because your shit was fucked up the first half of the previous game" Cross reminded him.

"She's on the East Side waiting for me" he replied, causing Dink and Byrd to burst out laughing as he cruised pass the symphony hall then turned right on E. Biddle Street.

As they near the Dome, the area was pack with spectators and expensive cars. They circle the twice before finally finding a parking spot on a small street called N. Spring Street. They filed out then reach out to Ice to meet them on the Caroline Street side of the Dome. They hooked up then posted up in the little park area to monitor the squad that they were playing. They basically had the same guys, but they added more rebounding. They sat on this rail dissecting each player.

"You see how their big man always turn left Byrd?" Ice asked.

"Yeah, we are going to start a fast break every time he tries that weak ass move" he replied grinning.

"If that's true, I got an alley-oop to Ice or ATM" Cross replied smiling.

"That boy is banging out that jumper ATM" Dink observed.

"Yeah, but what have two things have you notice?" he replied.

"You're not defending him, and his left-hand dribble is weak as hell" Byrd answer causing them to burst out laughing.

"If they tried picking so he can pull up, we are going to double him" suggested Ice. "Okay?"

"Yeah" they replied watching him closely.

As they stood studying them, Chubby came out to the sidewalk looking for them. It took him a few minutes to finally spot them, he didn't shout to them or wave them over. He knew what they were doing and all he could do was smile then head back inside. With five minutes before game time, they casually walked inside the Dome and the West Side roar to life causing the East Siders to stare at the entrance. Cross waved the squad over and gave them the game plan on each player including who they were going to double if they start setting picks for him. As they congregated, J-Lo suddenly appeared and the west side crowd let her presence be known.

"Get him J!" a girl shouted, and everybody burst out laughing.

"Where have you been Mister?" she asked invading his personal space.

"Taking care of business, Ashanti" he replied smiling down on her.

"What, you are too busy to let a girl know that your black butt was, okay?"

"Na, Ashanti" he replied admiring her the movement of her lips.

"But you did" she corrected him. "Do some girl got you twisted?"

"You're funny" he replied lightly snickering.

"Do you see me smiling?" she asked snatching him by his shirt and he raised his hands surrendering.

"No, Ashanti" he replied containing his smile but grinning.

"Drop twenty in the first half. I don't want sixteen or eighteen but twenty. Do you hear me?" she asked pulling him closer.

He peeked over at his partners who was snickering and laughing at J checking him again. "I hear you, Ashanti."

"Okay, now go out there and bust their asses" she instructed before pulling him down and lightly kissing him then casually walking away to the laughter of the West Side.

An OG walked out to center court with a mic in his hands. "Welcome ladies and gentlemen to the Terror Dome. My instructions are simples. Do not disrespect my house and I better not hear about any of my guest getting assaulted on their way home either. I will find you" he told the East Siders staring directly in their stands. We have five-o in here thinking that they are undercover, and yawl know who they are" he smiled directly at a guy putting a spotlight on him. Enjoy this game because we need this one. I refuse to go down two-o to Chubby" he shared staring that the players as he walked off the court.

"Damn, ATM. J is like your private wifey" mention Cross as they burst out laughing again as they headed to the jump circle. He stood there listening to their laughter shaking his head before finally joining them. When the ball was toss up, all hell broke out. The first three jumpers were taken by ATM, and he hit all three. Six straight points.

"Ah shit! It's on and popping!" shouted the west side then burst out laughing.

After the nervousness subsided and they settle in, his defender was kept off balance. A slight upward head fake and he would slightly lean forward, and he was slapping his hand off while taking off towards the rim. Staring at their center as he attacked the middle, he would give Ice or Byrd an alley-oop depending on who came over and they would slam the ball through the rim causing a roar from the west siders. Once he had them on his string and afraid to leave their man, he would take flight on them. Their six-foot eight center didn't have enough elevation from keeping him from slamming the ball home and posturizing him. By half time, he had put up twenty-three points. As he smiled at J-Lo as he headed towards the bench, she shouted.

"Do it again!"

As they sat on the bench drinking Gator Aide while enjoying a fifteen-point lead, they stared across court at their competitors. Their coach was trying to motivate them, but they had become mute to his voice. When an immaculately dress OG walked over to their bench, he got deep in their asses. His demeanor wasn't one of motivation but of anger and they were listening to him like he was E.F Hutton. When he was finish with them, he stared directly at ATM before reclaiming his seat.

"I know you seen that, right?" asked Byrd staring at ATM.

"I'm not Stevie Wonder" he replied slightly hardening his eyes. "He put a target on my back."

"Exactually" Ice cosigned.

"No matter what happens. I need yawl to keep yawl cool" he told them staring in their eyes individually. "Alright?"

"We'll try" replied Ice staring over at the guy.

"But we won't promise" Dink included staring at the guy also.

"Well, it won't be the first time I had a target on me brothers" he replied getting to his feet. Instead of going down court to play offense to start the second half, he walked straight over to the OG and stared him in his eyes as the east Siders stared at him. No words were exchanged between them, but no words were needed as they both stared at the other with a slight snarl and malice in their eyes. He never went down court on offense for five straight possessions. He only played defense and he shut the guy with the jumper completely down. When he finally joined them on offense, he shot their lights out. Seven straight buckets and every time he scored or assisted on a basket; he stared the guy straight in his eyes. With five minutes to go, ATM was taking flight towards the basket when the power forward tried wrapping him around the support pole. The dirty play caused the West Siders to get to their feet shouting their disapproval. His inner right knee took the blunt of the force as he collapse to the ground. Chubby instantly called for a time out. He didn't try to hide his anger as he stared at the OG as his teammates assisted him to the bench.

"Are you alright man?" inquired Byrd staring at the power forward.

"Yeah, man. I'm cool" he replied extending his leg.

"I got him" Ice said snarling at the guy.

"No, Ice" he insisted staring in his eyes. "Bring him to me on the second time down."

On the second time down, Dink rubbed his man off on him. The small guard didn't stand a chance, and everybody knew it, but instead of taking him, he pass the ball out to Dink. Ice was just taking his man up to the foul line then suddenly spun on him. His defended ran smack into a back pick that stretched him out as ATM stared down at him grinning. Without them talking on defense, he never saw the pick coming.

"Hey motherfucker!" he shouted getting to his feet. "What kind of shit was that?"

"Pay back" he replied slightly smiling at him.

"Supposed I knock you the fuck out" he threaten.

"That couldn't happen even in your dreams" he replied openly smiling at him. "Please, make my day" he invited still smiling at him.

"I'm going to put my foot so far up your ass when you open your mouth you will see the tip of my toes" he boasted.

SLAP! "Stop talking shit like a bitch" ATM told him slightly hardening his eyes. When he leap, he ran smack into a double stiff jam and vicious right-hand straight down the pike connecting. The force of the blow caused him to stagger backward and fall.

"DAMN!" shouted the West Sider before bursting out laughing.

"Oh, shit! Did you see that!?"

"Somebody better go chill him out before he gets knocked the fuck out!"

"I didn't know ATM was sweet with his hands" an OG mention admiring his tactics.

When he scurried to his feet and rush ATM, he ran straight into another stiff jab follow by a five-piece combination with two biscuits. The force of each blow felt like he was being hit with a set of brass knuckles. The combination rocked him to his knees almost knocking him out. He stared over at the OG as he reluctantly got to his feet. When he came back at him again, ATM hit him with a Superman punch rocking his world again as laughter and shouts erupted from the West Siders. His head was almost decapitated from his shoulder by a vicious right-hand follow by a left hook. As he step around him, they guy fell like a tree. His hands never came up to protect his face from the black top. He was knocked the fuck out.

"Oh, shit! He got knocked the fuck out!" chanted the West Siders then burst out laughing.

ATM stared over at the OG before casually walking back towards his bench. There were two minutes left in the game as they assisted him back to his bench and slowly revived him with an ice pack place at the back of his neck. The game was decided over ten minutes ago. ATM finish with thirty-five points and ten assists. They blew them out my thirty-one points.

"Damn, ATM. I didn't know your hands was that good" complimented Ice staring at him amazed by his skills.

"Nobody should have known" he replied staring over at the OG who was getting his ass chew out by some high-ranking distributors.

He walked away like a little boy that was caught doing something that he shouldn't."

"Well, it's out there now" Cross replied snickering. "I thought he was going to snap your little as apart."

"You're little" he corrected him. "With your smurf ass" he counter causing them to burst out laughing as they changed into dry shirts.

"Damn, Akeem" J said coming to stand next to him. "Are you okay?"

"Yeah, I cool Ashanti."

"I have never witness that side of your before" she said inspecting his face closely.

"I hope that you never do again" he shared getting to his feet then gripping her fingers and heading towards the main entrance. "How have you been?"

"Keeping myself entertained" she shared.

"Yeah, so I have heard and seen."

"What?" she replied staring up at him. "You did?"

"Of course, Ashanti" he suddenly smiled. "You are well known around the city as my girlfriend" he informed her grinning.

"So, I have heard" she openly admitted. "I wonder how everybody is perceiving me after being seen with other guys?"

"Probably the same way they are peeking, at me" he replied smiling. "I know guys are wondering how I could be cheating on a fine ass young lady like you while the ladies are wondering how you could play me" he replied smiling.

"I can see those jealous and envious girls thinking like that" she shared.

"What should we do about it?"

"Nothing" she replied grinning. "It's nobody business about our relationship. As long as you and I know the content of our relationship, that's all that matter to me, okay?"

"Gotcha" he replied looking around and catching Chubby's eyes. "Excuse me, I'll be right back" he apologized walking across the court towards Chubby.

She took a seat in the bleacher admiring and smiling at the swag in his walk. She knew that he would eventually hear about her dating several guys while Ice and Dink was entertaining her girls. Since they were his partners, she expected them to tell him, but she never considered that he might see her for himself. How foolish and negligence of her? Watching Ice and Lisa interacting of the weeks, they made a lovely pair. Lisa with her brash disposition blend excellently with Ice nonchalant disposition. She tried to ruffle his feathers, but he was always too cool to bite her hype and she secretly adored it. When some of her old flirts came sniffing around, he ignored them. He would allowed her to entertain herself, but he wasn't sitting around waiting on her to return. He would spike up a conversation with anyone. Ladies just making is acquaintance found him extremely charming. Most of the time, Lisa would have to come retrieve him from the giggling women. Once and only once, she tried to get out the gate on him. He told her he was representing a mirror. His words forced her to see herself and she didn't appreciate the reverse psychology.

As far as Dink and Chi is concern, they are a pure riot. With Chi's prissy disposition, Dink constantly kept her on edge. They were sitting at a table for two one evening when she regress around him and paid the price for her indiscretion. He had warned her on numerous occasions to drop that prissy persona. Well, on this particular night, he excused himself to go to the bathroom. When he came out, he stood by the men door and stared over at her. When she finally saw him, he waved her over but there was something in his eyes that caused her intuition to start ringing. So, she remained seated ignoring his insistence to come to him. As he shook his head at her as he was approaching, he suddenly diverted his route. The look of shock on her face was priceless.

"Where is Dink going?" inquired Lisa watching him closely from her table then stare over at Chi.

"Oh, he's leaving" answer Ice nonchalantly while wiping his lips with a napkin.

"But he didn't pay the bill" she said astounded.

"Yeah, I know" he replied lightly snickering.

Once he was by the door, he waved her over again but this time, he was slightly hardening his eyes. He got to her feet grabbing her purse then nervously proceeded towards him. As they casually walked pass the hostess, Chi was sweating bullets while Dink stared over at them smiling. Once outside, they took off running. From that moment until today, she has not displayed that prissy disposition around him. He didn't have any problem in bringing her back to earth. In fact, he seem to relish the opportunities. When I say they are hilarious together, I mean tear to your eyes hilarious. He was likely to pull her into any of his antics being like a mirror, so she was very attentive about herself around him.

"Hey, J-Lo" a woman's voice interrupted her thoughts.

Turning, she was surprised to see who it was. "Hi Ms. Trinity" she greeted flashing her broad smile. "How are you?"

"I'm fine, young lady" she replied dress in a black Versace skirt set. "Your hair, do you mind?"

"Na, ma'am" she replied allowing her to touch and feel the texture.

"Our last conversation, you said you do your own hair, correct?"

"Yes, ma'am."

"Where do you get your styles from?"

"The internet" she replied smiling.

"Are you presently working?"

"Yes, ma'am. Part-time."

"Doing hair?"

"No, ma'am."

"Excellent" she replied suddenly smiling. "I would like to hire you to work in one of my hair salons."

"But I don't have the credentials" she mention staring in her eyes.

"Your knowledge and creativity is your credential, young lady" she smiled. "I have some very prestigious clients in dire need of a stylist, and you instantly came to my mind. If you drop that part-time job and give me those hours, I can guarantee you that you will be tip generously for your professionalism" she shared with a coy on her lips.

"Where is your shop located?"

"The one closest to you is at Rogers and Registers."

"Exquisite?" she asked.

"Yes" she replied smiling. "The shop opens from nine to five but most of the ladies either come earlier or stay later to get that money" she shared grinning. "The job is your if you want it."

"Oh, I want it" she replied revealing her jubilation.

"So, when do you want to start?" she asked handing her a card.

"Monday if possible" she answer accepting the black card while staring in her eyes.

"It's possible, J" she assured her. "I deeply appreciate you doing this for me. If you bank your money right, you might be able to open your shop in a couple of years."

"That would be a pure dream come true" she admitted smiling.

"I have to go" she mention looking over her shoulder at someone. "When you arrive Monday, Honey will probably greet if I'm not there."

"Yes, ma'am" she replied watching her turning and gracefully walking away. She was suddenly riding on cloud nine. She couldn't believe her good fortune. She stared at the black card with gold lettering with the word Exquisite. The first thing she had to do was make a portfolio of the assorted styles that she will offer.

"You alright?" inquired Akeem staring at her unusually. "You look like the cat that ate the rat" he slightly smiled at her.

"I just got a job" she boasted smiling.

"On a Saturday?" he replied grinning.

"Yeah, how about that" she snicker. "Ms. Trinity offer me a job at her salon at Reistertown and Rogers" she shared smiling.

"Congratulations" he complimented her.

"Thanks" she replied flashing all thirty-two of her teeth again. "Are you going to the after party in Dru Hill again?"

"Na, I got something better I can show you" he replied with a coy smile.

"There goes that damn impish smile again" she informed him slightly shaking her head at him while grinning. He chirp getting his partners attention then started heading towards the main entrance. They were standing outside on the sidewalk waiting for them to exit.

"Yeah, what's up?" asked Ice staring around.

"Na, nothing like that" he smiled at him. "I know yawl might want to go to the after party, but I have a better offer" he told them unable to contained his impish smile.

"Oh, I like that smile" mention Byrd smiling. "Family, this is Sexy" he introduced his newest quest. She had on a pair of white spandexes that should have been illegal. The girl was phat as hell. "Can she hang too?"

"Of course," replied Akeem smiling over at her. "Whose driving ladies?" he asked staring at them.

"I am" Lisa replied.

"Get your ride and we'll meet on the corner of Caroline, okay?"

"Sure" she replied then Ice and Dink walked with Lisa and Chi while J gripped his fingers and allowed him to direct her towards his car.

They retrieved his car then pulled over on Caroline Street. Minutes later, Lisa pulled up behind them blowing her horn then proceeded to follow him down until he turned right onto Madison Street. They jump on Rt. 83 then taking the Dru Park exit and staying on it until it dropped them off onto Reistertown Road. Five minutes later, they were pulling up in front of his house and all of his security were sitting out on their porches. As the group piled out of the vehicles, his neighbors didn't care that they were gawking at them. In the almost two years of living here, this was the first time he actually brought a group of people to his house. As they climbed upon the porch, he inserted his key then push the door open and led the way inside.

"Damn, ATM. Whose house is this?"

"Mine" he replied casually heading towards the kitchen. "Make yourself at home."

"Wait a minute" insisted J staring at his back as he stood staring inn the stainless-steel refrigerator. "Did you say that this house was yours?"

"Yes" he replied grabbing the bowl of fruit and several bottles of water then sitting at the five-stool island.

"Look" insisted Chi smiling from ear to ear.

"Aaahhhh" the ladies chime.

"Look at us" J said giggling.

"Look Byrd!" insisted Cross extending the picture to him. He show him slamming on a guy up in New York.

"Damn, ATM. How did you get such a nice picture?" he asked studying it closely grinning.

"That's my secret" he replied watching them inspecting every picture on the first floor.

"Who is this?" Cross asked holding up a picture.

"That's Sunshine" answer J admiring the expression on their faces. She didn't want to admit that they look extremely sexy together. "How long have you been living here?"

"A little over a year."

"I told yawl I saw him last year" mention Lisa smiling.

"Yes, you did" admitted J. "Why didn't you tell me?"

"Because I didn't and still don't trust myself with you, Ashanti" he admitted.

"What?" she slightly smiled. "You don't think I can restrain my emotions?"

"I wasn't ready to take that chance."

"Aahhh, that's so sweet" mention Chi grinning.

"Excuse me" interjected Dink staring over at the pair. "Am I understanding what is being suggested?" he asked staring at them curiously.

"It all depends on what you are suggesting" replied Akeem grinning. "Ashanti and I are just very good friends not lovers."

"Well, I'll be damn" replied Ice staring over at them very perplex. "You couldn't have convince me that yawl wasn't lovers."

"You and a whole lot of other people."

"Why do you think I was dating so many guys?" J asked staring over at them. "If me and Akeem were an item, we would have been double dating with yawl."

"She damn sure wouldn't be flaunting other guys around yawl two" Akeem assured them still grinning at their deception.

"I didn't know what to think" admitted Dink.

"And neither do other people" he assured him.

"Well, personally. I'm glad to finally have some damn clarity" admitted Ice shaking his head at their deception.

"Grab that tray Cross and let's go down into the basement" he said leading the way and descending the stairs. "Hey fellas, let us have this."

"No, problem" replied Khalil turning the X-Box off.

"Family, this is brothers Khalil and Amiri."

"Hi, fellas" they chime together.

"Hi, yawl" they replied.

"You look more beautiful in real life than your picture, J-Lo" mention Amiri smiling at her.

"Thank you, Amiri" she replied admiring his smooth mocha complexion and eyes similar to Akeem.

"We will be upstairs" Khalil said leading the way. "Come on knucklehead."

"On your heels" he replied grabbing their bowl of fruits.

The money that Chubby had kicked back to him is how he refurnish the basement. With four paper rice lamps on the floor providing the light, the atmosphere was very tranquil. Other pictures of places they have played basketball and taken with the ladies were also displayed. It was about midnight when they walked back out on the porch, he allowed Byrd to use his car to take Sexy home. He didn't know what time he returned but one thing they knew about him, he wasn't about to leave her without breaking her back. All night the fellas were subtly peeking on her and would share impish grins.

Monday morning around eight-forty-five, J-Lo was stepping of the number 44 bus at the corner of Reistertown and Northern Parkway. She walked back up towards Exquisite when she caught her reflection. The hipster jeans she wore revealed her naval ring and part of her tramp stamp on her lower back. She looked so mature although she was only seventeen. She took a deep breathe before climbing the steps and pushing the door open. 95.9 was playing.

"Good morning" a light skin woman in her late twenties or early thirties greeted her. "May I help you?"

"Morning, ma'am. I'm J-Lo. I'm..."

"Morning J. I'm Honey. Lady T is on her way. Over there will be your work station" she pointed. "If there is anything that you need, just ask" she said. "Welcome to the family."

"Thank you, Ms. Honey" she replied smiling at her then walking over to her station. She stared at the numerous curlers and supplies. She had seen several of them on the internet. Unbelievably expensive and with excellent revues. She placed her cross-body bag on a hook that was used for their styling coats with Exquisite embroiled then took her seat. There were eight women working methodically in the place. Speaking polite and professional to their clients. It was almost nine-fifteen when a white convertible Porsche pulled up in front and parked on its private parking pad. Lady T stepped out wearing a white Jennie jean and a black silk shirt by Milano with a pair of black and white six-inch stilettoes and carrying a Valextra mini purse. Removing her Maybach sunglasses, she stood on the sidewalk smiling at somebody. Moments later, she walked in with J's first client and made the introductions.

"So, you are going to be my new stylist, huh?" the early forty, woman asked.

"Hopefully" she replied slightly smiling.

"Who did your locs?" she asked admiring them.

"I did ma'am."

"She will definitely do, T" she smiled over at her. "Can we get started?"

"Yes, ma'am" she replied accepting her purse and placing in the bottom draw.

"Well, I'm going to let yawl get acquainted."

"Alright, T. I'll holla at you later baby girl."

"Excuse me, Lady T. May I have a word with you please?"

"Sure, J. What's up?"

She walked over to her then asked, "How much am I supposed to charge?"

"Nothing for any of your clients" she informed her. "Everything you receive from them is yours. Later" she said smiling at her then greeting the other women before exiting the salon.

"Do you want the full service, Mrs. Jackson?"

"Every time, J-Lo" she replied.

"Do you know what style you are seeking?"

"The option is yours" she replied smiling.

"Yes, ma'am" she replied taking a deep breath then slowly exhaling. She escorted her to one of the sinks while putting on an apron. One she was seated, she loosen her locs allowing them to hang. She check the water temperature then began shampooing her hair with a coconut base shampoo. Thoroughly was them, she placed her under the hair drier for ten minutes then kept checking it every few minutes until desire dampness then applied a healthy portion of loc oil and rubbed it gently into her scalp allowing her hands to roll down her locs. Another minute of two, she escorted her back to her station. She decided to pick a style that will compliment her oval face. In about an hour and a half, she was finish. She spun the chair around for her to inspect the final result. As she stared into the mirror, she methodically got to her feet unemotionally and stared at the image staring back at her. A broad smile consumed her face as she admired the final result.

"Damn, J-Lo. This is beautiful, young lady" she declared unable to contain her enjoyment. "Where in the hell have you been all my life?" she asked turning and staring in her eyes causing J to slightly blush.

"Thank you, Mrs. Bee-Bee."

"No, thank you."

"Have a seat please so I can remove the two front clips. The two in the back can be removed in about fifteen minutes for the best results" she advised her as she took her seat.

"I'll follow your advice" she replied unable to contain her smile. "You are definitely heaven sent" she lightly giggled.

"Okay, there you are" he said smiling while backing up so she can get to her feet. She retrieved her purse from the draw and extended it to her. "This style can easily last a month."

"A month?" she giggled again while searching through her purse. "No, young lady I will be seeing you every two weeks to always look fresh" she informed her extending five Franklins to her.

"Ma'am, that, is way too much" she informed her looking like she was scared.

"Chubby said you had a problem with people showing you the love that you deserve. Don't let me step to you" she warned her slightly hardening her eyes and causing J to burst out laughing.

"Don't" she replied extending her hand to her and accepting the money. "Thank you, Mrs. Bee-Bee."

"You are welcome, dear" she smiled at her then turned and walked out. J walked over to the window and watched her climbed into a metallic gray G-90 then pulled away and get caught by the light.

"Damn, J!" Honey said coming over and surprising her with a hug. "You did a beautiful job on her locs. She usually never reveal how she feel, but you have her flashing all thirty-two teeth" she giggled then returned to her station.

"Thanks Honey" she replied over her shoulder watching a black Escalade pulling up next to her then they both turned left on Rogers. She returned to her station and took a seat. She was riding on cloud nine. She held the money in her hand a little longer than expected before placing the money in her front pocket. Around eleven o'clock another client came in looking for her. At one o'clock, another client came in. Lady T called her close to three o'clock to see if she wanted to do another hair or bounce? She told her to send the client and she was very appreciative that choose to stay. Twenty-minutes later, a woman walked in that she see regularly on television. She requested one of the Bantu styles that she has to offer. She showed her the styles and she choose one that was perfect for the shape of her head. Just as she was finishing up, Lady T walked in.

"Hey, Vicky."

"Girl, where did you find her?" she asked getting to her feet and admiring her job.

"At the basketball court."

"No, seriously" she insisted turning and facing her.

"At the basketball court, a simple kiss from her to him and my people lost a lot of money" she informed her.

"I don't know when you're bullshitting me or not, but I like her. Not very talkative and all about her business."

"So, I have heard all day" she shared staring at J smiling.

"Here you go, young lady" she said extending five hundred dollars to her.

"Thank you, I hope you come back again."

"Oh, you don't have to worry about that" she answer giving Lady T a kiss on the cheek before she walked out the door.

"My friends been complimenting you all day J and I deeply appreciate you attending to Vicky. She has an important show tonight and came through for her and me. How much did you make today?"

"Almost two thousand dollars" she said extending it to her.

"Give me a G and everything else is yours."

"Are you sure, Lady T?"

"How can you ask your boss such a question?" she asked giggling.

"Excuse me" she replied extending ten Franklins to her.

"Thank you" she said putting the money in her purse.

"I did a lot of thinking today concerning you" she shared staring deeply into her eyes. "I figure I'll have your services for about five years before you open your own shop" she smiled at her. "Until that time baby girl, let's get that money" she giggled turning and walking out the door.

J stared over at Honey who was snickering her ass off. "So, I'll have you at least five years, huh?" she giggled then continued to corn roll the woman's hair.

Weeks later, Akeem was staring at his reflection. He choose to wear a light gray suit with a dark gray round collar shirt with Franck cuff and black Johnston shoes. A gray silk tie and handkerchief completed his hook up. He checked his watch then proceeded down the stairs. He grabbed his car keys then headed out the door. He had an hour before he had to be at his destination, so he decided to finally accept J-Lo's invitation to come see her at her job. As cruised down Rogers Avenue listening to Jelly Roll Martin, he turned left on Reistertown Road and parked. He climbed out the car then proceeded down the street. As he cross the street, he felt eyes watching his movement. As he enter Exquisite, a hush fell upon the place. As J turned to see who everybody was staring at, a broad smile came to her face.

"Hey, Akeem" she greeted excusing herself from her client. She gave him their usual light kiss. "Boy, you're looking handsome."

"Thanks."

"Where are you going if you don't mind me asking?" she said staring up into his eyes still smiling.

"I'll tell you later if I'm able" he said. "I just drop in to see you."

"Well, I'm glad you finally accepted my invitation" she said slightly blushing from what his eyes were saying about her attire.

"I'll holla at you later" he said ignoring the flirting eyes of her coworkers.

"Okay" she replied watching him turning and walking towards the door then stepping out. She stared out the window at him as he walked pass.

"Damn, J!" mention Honey fanning herself. "Is that your man?"

"Na but he has his application on top" she replied smiling then returning to her client.

Entering the Mitchell Court House on the Lexington Street side, he cleared the scanners then took the elevator up to the third floor then proceeded to room 303. Entering the court room, he took a seat in the rear. Chubby and a couple of OG's were having a conversation with a Jewish lawyer before taking their seat. Five minutes later, his father was escorted into the court room by two CO's wearing a dark blue Armani.

Staring at him, he didn't know how much he looked like his father until that moment. He was just a younger version of him.

"Are we ready?" the judge asked staring over at both lawyers.

"Mr. Smith for the prosecutor's office is ready, your Honor."

"Mr. Solomon for the defense is ready also, your Honor."

"Take your seats, gentlemen" he said staring at his notes then staring curiously at the prosecutor. "Mr. Smith, after reviewing the evidence or should I say, lack of substantial evidence against Mr. Anderson, how did your office obtain a conviction? Did Mr. Anderson confess?"

"No, sir."

"Did any of the fire arms found at the scene contain his finger prints?"

"No, sir."

"Was there any forensic taken to see if he even fired a weapon?"

"Yes, sir."

"Oh, you're not going to elaborate. What did it reveal Mr. Smith?" he inquired slightly hardening his eyes at him.

"It came back inconclusive, your Honor."

"Inconclusive?" he repeated staring down on him. "If someone is alleged to have murder two individuals, forensic shouldn't come back inconclusive, Mr. Smith. Wouldn't you agree?" he asked flipping his paper.

"Yes, your honor."

"I'm glad you agree because now I don't have to ask about the clothing he was wearing on that fateful night" he said. "According to what I read from the homicide detectives reports, there was a substantial quality of drugs found in the apartment. Is this true?"

"Yes, your Honor."

"Did Mr. Anderson have any drugs or alcohol in his system?"

"We didn't conduct that test, your Honor."

"Well, thank God that his defense attorney demanded the test a day after being arrested. Do you want to know the results of that test, or do you already know?"

"I'm aware of the negative results, your Honor" he admitted returning his stare.

"I guess that's why you didn't use a drug deal gone bad, huh?" he asked not expecting an answer. "According to the only witness, is this Monica Anderson related to him?"

"His wife, your Honor."

"His wife turned state witness against him" he repeated staring at him then over at Mr. Anderson. "According to the report, she witness him murdering two guys that she was found naked and in a very uncompromising position. Is this true?"

"Yes, your Honor."

"I wonder how any man would react catching their wife and mother to his three sons having sex with two men at once. Did your office make a deal with her to testify against him?"

"Yes, your Honor" he admitted.

"So, the drug charges would disappear if she agreed to testify, huh?"

"Yes, your Honor" he replied solemnly.

"I'm not going to inquire about the make-up of the jurors or the plead offer your office tried to offer just to have it thrown back in your face. I read he said. "If you are going to fuck me, he wasn't going to assist you." Do you have any new evidence to present, Mr. Smith?"

"No, your Honor."

"Mr. Anderson, will you please stand sir" he requested staring over at him. "I can't retrieve the twelve years that you were taken from your sons, but I can give you the justice that have been eluding you all these years. You are free to go sir and this unfortunate incident will be permanently erased from your record."

"Thank you, your Honor" he replied returning is stare.

"Is there anything that you wish to say Mr. Solomon?"

"Yes, your Honor to the prosecutor" he replied then stared over at him. "Unless you want me to start filing Civil Court papers tomorrow, you need to contact my office before noon, Steve."

"We will Abdullah" he assured him.

"If there isn't anything else gentlemen, this court is adjourned" he said hitting his anvil then getting to his feet and walking out his door.

When Killa turned around to face his partners, he walked around the divider and held Chubby tightly then extended their arms while staring in one another eyes then burst out laughing. He then greeted the other four immaculately dress men giving them a hug and broad smile also. As the group headed for the door, Akeem got to his feet staring at him. As they were approaching, his father looked at the stranger very curiously. There was something that about his eyes that were awfully familiar; and he couldn't shake the feeling of knowing him. The harder he stared it became apparent that this person had his eyes.

"Akeem?"

"Yes, sir" he replied slightly grinning.

He rushed to him and pulled him into his arms then held her extremely tight. He hasn't felt his embrace or stared into his eye since his incarceration eleven years ago. He extended his arms admiring him from head to toe while smiling. "I see you have grown" he finally said smiling down on him.

"Just a little bit" he replied smiling up at him.

"How did you know about my court appearance?"

"Chubby" he replied. "He had me promise to keep it a secret and I have" he assured him slightly hardening his eyes.

"So, you heard everything huh?"

"Yes, sir" he slightly snarled.

"I'm sorry that you had to hear about it like this, but at least you know I didn't live you and your brothers because I wanted to" he shared staring deep into his eyes. "I genuinely miss yawl" he said as the prosecutor walked pass. "Come on, let's get out of here" he said leading the way out of the court room with him at his side. As the group walked through the hall, their presence demanded attention. Exiting at Lexington Street, they congregated on the sidewalk. "Where are you staying?"

"At your house" he replied.

"The house is yours now" he told him. "Chubby, meet me over there at noon."

"We'll be there" he said tapping his knuckles then stepping off heading towards Charles Street.

"How are you getting around?"

"I got car Pop."

"Which way?"

"Around the corner" he replied as they headed towards Calvert Street. They enter the garage then took the elevator to the third floor and exit. He hit the remote to his 750 and she came alive. They climbed inside. Playing was Ella singing "Take The A Train."

"What do you know about jazz?" he asked fastening his seatbelt while smiling over at him.

"Since living at your house and finding them in the basement, the majority of music that I listen to is jazz."

"How long have you been living there?"

"Almost two years Pop" he admitted.

"I'm sorry to hear that son."

"Na, Pop" he smiled over at him. "Getting away from her was the best thing that happen to me" he tried to assure him turning on Saratoga Street and climbing the slight hill.

"How is Khalil and Amiri?"

"Honor roll students Pop's. I get them every Friday after school and keep them until seven o'clock Sunday night."

"Good" he smiled at him. "You are doing a terrific job son."

"Thanks, Pop."

They rode in silence as his father took in the sights and view how the city have changed. Driving pass Mondawmin Mall, a coy smile creep across his lips as they proceeded up Liberty Road. As they pulled up in front of the house, his neighbors were sitting outside enjoying the cool fresh air. Seeing them walking up together, most got to their feet to greet him as Akeem continued into the house. When he finally enter the house, he took off his suit jacket and told him to follow him. Descending the stairs, he stared around smiling.

"Nice hookup" he complimented the contemporary furniture while heading towards the bar. "Help me with this" he said unlocking a hidden lock. They lifted the heavy red oak bar about three feet to the left. In a cement square hole was a metal box, he wiggle it loose before suddenly lifting it and placing it on the floor. Turning the tumblers on the lock, it pop open then he open the lid. Akeem eyes became the size of quarters. "Place the money on the bar" he instructed him as he grabbed his two Glocks and several eighteen round clips and placed them on the bar also. "Let's put this back" he said placing the empty metal box back inside hole then they lifted the bar and place it where it was originally. You could hear him securing the bar down again. "That's a million dollar there" he informed him heading towards the tool board and unlocking a hidden lock then pulling out a role up cloth. He placed it on the bar and unravel it revealing his cleaning supplies for his weapon. He disassemble both weapons like they were a puzzle then thoroughly clean them.

"I need you to keep my presence home on the down low. I have some extremely important business to conduct. If certain people know that I'm home, they will get low on me and I might not be able to get my clutches on them, understand?"

"Yes, sir" he replied watching him racking both Glocks.

He open the envelop from the box and pulled out a document. "The deed to the house is there. All you have to do is sign it. If something were to happen to me, I need you and your bothers to be taken care of just in case."

"Pop's."

"No, Akeem. I don't plan on anything happening to me, but I still have to have things in order."

"Where are you going to stay?"

"You don't need to know that" he replied opening the combination lock on a wooden crate. He pulled out a double shoulder holster and put it on then place his Glocks in them. "Come on" he said heading back up the stairs. He reached behind the stove and retrieved a key. "That is to the safe deposit box at the National Bank down town. The code numbers are yawl birth day, understand?" he said grabbing his jacket and putting it on. You couldn't tell that he had the weapons on him.

"Yes, sir."

Checking his watch, he said. "Let's sit outside."

They sat out on the porch, but no words were exchanged between them. His father was dealing with his personal thoughts. His eyes would take on the appearance of his when he was about to shot a guys light out on the basketball court for talking a little too much shit, but his play ground wasn't the courts; it was the streets of Baltimore. Just before noon, a white Bentley with smoke windows pulled up and parked.

"I got to go" he said staring at the car while getting to his feet. "You need to go to Home Deport to get a safe. Spend as needed."

"Na, Pop's. We are good" he assured him. "I'll get that safe immediately."

"I'll holla but not too soon" he replied with a coy smile then stared down into his eyes. "I love you son."

"I love you too, Pop's" he replied as they hugged then he step off. He open the back door that open like one of those old-time gangster cars. Slick as hell. The legs of a woman wearing black stocking was evident as he climbed inside and closed the door then the car pulled away.

In a city that consistently have three hundred or more murders annually, those that wasn't in the game wouldn't have piece together was transpiring in the past couple of weeks. High-level distributors and their bodyguards were being hit and hit hard by a quiet assassin. He couldn't help but wonder if his father was taking revenge on people. He decided to drive down to Chadwick to get an eye on Chubby, but he's been M.I.A. Missing In Action. On Friday as he usually did, he picked up his brothers from their mother's house. When he enter the house, the vibe was eerie different. The television wasn't on, and she didn't have any guest that she was entertaining. She was sitting damn near in the dark listening to 95.9 while change smoking her cigarettes. She gave him an unusual stare but didn't say anything. When he went to pick up his usual delivery, T.C was noticeably missing. Something was going on.

"Hey, Akeem" greeted Khalil coming out his bedroom.

"What's up? Are you ready?"

"Yeah" he said going back into his bedroom to grab his bag.

"Where is your brother?"

"Right here" replied Amiri coming out of his bedroom carrying his bag over his shoulder.

"Let's bounce yawl" he said leading the way back towards the front door. He peeked at their mother but kept it moving.

"Bye, Mom" they chime together string in at her.

"Bye, babies" she said with a faint smile.

Akeem was already at the elevator when they caught up with him. When the door open, they all climbed aboard then felt the elevator descending. "What's wrong with her?"

"Don't know" replied Khalil. "She's been acting strange for a minute now."

"Since when?"

"We were eating breakfast almost two weeks ago when uncle T.C came over and they had a private conversation in the front room. Since their conversation, she told her usual associates and friends that she needed some space."

"I haven't witness her leaving the house since their conversation" mention Amiri.

"I haven't even seen her creep out to get her daily blast" cosigned Khalil.

"Do you know what might be troubling her Akeem?" inquired Amiri staring up at him.

"I would like to say her conscious, but she doesn't possess one" he replied as the elevator doors open and they step out.

"Will you ever show forgiveness for Mom?" Amiri asked as they walked out eh main entrance.

"I'm not a Christian, so I don't have to forgive her for the things she have done over the years" he replied slightly hardening his eyes as they walked across the court yard. Have his father been spotted? Is he the reason that T.C had suddenly gotten low? Bringing his money to his mother's house instead of their usual location brought all kinds of thoughts to his mind.

He was sitting out on the porch around ten o'clock that night when a dark color SUV pulled up and turned the engine off. When the unknown driver open his door, there was no inside light to illuminate his identity. The stranger walk is what got him to his feet smiling. "Hey, Pop's" he greeted giving him a hug.

"How you been son?"

"I've been good Pop" he replied staring at him closely. "Khalil and Amiri is here" he informed him.

"Good" he replied smiling. "Can they keep a secret?"

"Yes, sir."

"Take me to them" he said.

Akeem open the front door and step inside follow closely by their father then proceeded towards the basement steps. Descending the steps, Khalil and Amiri was playing Call of Duty on their X-Box.

"Do you have winners?" asked Khalil never averting his eyes from the television.

"Put that on pause for me" he instructed and Amiri instantly followed his instruction. Turning around, they realized that he wasn't alone. They methodically got to their feet staring at the shadowy figure coming further into the light causing them to stare at her curiously.

"Who is this Akeem?" inquired Khalil staring at her unusually.

"Who does he look like?" he replied.

"You" admitted Amiri slightly stepping forward.

"Right" he cosigned. "So, who can he be?"

They stood there looking very perplex before Khalil asked, "Is this Pop's?"

"Yeah" he replied grinning.

They methodically started walking slowly towards him. Khalil extended his hand for him to shake, but he snatched him into his arms then lifting him and squeezing him tightly. Placing him back on the floor, he extended his other arm to Amiri and held him just as tight.

"Fellas, no one is to know he's home" he told them as they stared up into their father's eyes still confused.

"Nobody will" they chime together still staring at him.

"Yawl really look good" he flash his smile at them. "Fellas, I still have some business to conduct. So, keep my presence on the down low."

"We will" they assured returning his stare.

"I'm tire and need to get some relaxing sleep. Will yawl go get my bags out the vehicle?" he asked extending the keys to Khalil.

"Yes, sir" he replied, and they headed up the steps.

"Place the bags in my room" Akeem told them as they disappeared.

"Well manner also" he shared smiling.

"Or get knocked down" he informed him smiling.

"You have anything up there to eat?"

"Yes, sir. I made some barbecue turkey wings and sides" he informed him leading him back up stares.

"You cook" he replied snickering.

"I'm very domesticated" he replied causing him to laugh for the second time since he's been home. He told him to have a seat and he would hook him up. After taking his bags upstairs, Khalil and Amiri sat next to him smiling at how much their brother looked like him. Placing four wings and steam broccoli on his plate, he lean back listening to their father talking to them and sharing uncomfortable laughter. After finishing his meal, he excused himself and climbed the stairs. They heard the shower running then the sound of jazz filtering from the vents. When they woke up around ten o'clock the next morning, they climbed the stairs together. Akeem stared out the front window and his vehicle was gone.

"He left huh?' asked Khalil.

"Yeah" he replied starting to prepare breakfast.

"How did Pop get out?" inquired Amiri.

"Yeah, how and when?" asked Khalil knowing that he had the answers.

"The when part I will answer. Pop's been home almost two months now. I was at his court appointment to hear how he got him, and yawl will too when he's ready to share it with yawl" he shared.

"So, our father isn't a murderer?" asked Amiri.

"Not those two guys" he replied with a coy smile causing Khalil to snicker, but Amiri was still slightly confused.

"When will he be back?"

"I don't know Amiri, but rest assure, he will come back for us" he replied placing two wheat pancakes on their plates and scrabble eggs.

Two weeks later, another high-profile distributor was taken out with his four bodyguards in Park Heights. Two hired guns from Cherry Hill also got hit up one night with no suspects. Chubby reappeared at Chadwick but in quick spurts then got low again. When he exchanged stares with Akeem, his eyes have gotten harder since his father's reappearance. He would acknowledge him, but he always kept it moving. Sitting waiting for the next game to begin, his cell phone rang, and he didn't recognize the strange number.

"Hello?"

"Come pick me up at Pennsylvania and Fulton."

"On my way Pop's" he said ending their conversation and grabbing his gear.

"Yo, ATM. Where are you going?"

"Got to bounce man" he replied tapping their knuckles then heading out the game and jumping into his ride. In matter of minutes, he was pulling up in front of the Red Fox. His father step out of the fast-food store then walked across the street and climbed inside.

"Where to Pop's?" he asked staring over at him.

"To your mother's house" he replied fastening his seatbelt. "Is your brothers there?"

"They should be" he replied hooking a U-turn then proceeding down the Pennsylvania Avenue. He stared out at the city that he once knew but could barely recognized now. At Penn-North, he slightly snarled at the open drug market and the young addicts. A vacant police cruiser sat with its lights on. "You mother and I went there almost every Friday and Saturday night" he shared as they cruise pass the Arch Social Club. Minutes later, he was pulling up in their court yard and both gentlemen step out approaching the building.

"ATM!" his name was shouted by the drug dealers and young teenage girls.

"Got yourself a little rep, huh?' he smiled down on him as they climbed the steps.

"Not intentionally" he replied entering the pissy smelling building and heading towards the elevator.

As the door open up, Ms. Mable step out. "Hi, Akeem" she greeted.

"Hi, Ms. Mable" he replied stepping around her and entering the elevator. She stared in at the man with him. Just as the door was closing, recognition and shock consumed her eyes as they door closed.

They exit on their floor and Akeem turned the doorknob then walked inside. His mother was still sitting in the semi darkness change smoking. She took a brief glance at Akeem then returned to what she was doing. As he went to the bedroom to get his brothers, she felt someone else presences. As she turned her head and stared at the silhouette of another person, she methodically got to her feet and appeared to float towards the stranger as her sons returned. Akeem held them up to witness what was about to transpire. Both of them were very confused watching the scene unfold. Their mother suddenly stop and collapse to her knees crying.

"I'm sorry Killa" she apologized from her knees crying. "I'm so sorry baby" she pleaded from the floor.

"The only reason why you are still breathing is because I would never want my sons to know I murder their worthless ass mother" he snarled down on her.

"I am so sorry, baby. Will you ever forgive me?" she asked staring in his cold eyes.

"Not in this life time" he replied honestly. "Boys, gather your stuff. Yawl are moving in with your brother" he informed them.

They never said a word but follow his instructions.

"How long have you been home?"

"None of your got damn business" he replied still snarling down on her.

"If you take my boys, what do I do?"

"Keep breathing" he replied with a callous stare. "Tell your bitch ass brother I'm looking for him. He can reach me through Chubby" he told her as his sons returned with a duffle bag with their most of their clothes inside. "Tell him he don't want me hunting him down" he warned her. "You hear me?"

"Yes" she replied almost inaudible.

"Come on boys" he said starting to turn.

"Yawl knew he was home?" she asked surprised by the revelation.

"Yeah, Mom" replied Amiri staring into her eyes.

"Come on boys."

"Wait a minute Pop" insisted Khalil staring at him then down at their mother. "What is this about?"

"Tell them or I will" interjected Akeem staring down at her, but she refused to admit what she had done.

"Pop never murder those two guys and she knew it because she was caught naked with two of Pop's enemies" she revealed to them. "What got Pop incarcerated is our mother turning state's witness against him."

"No, she didn't" Amiri denounced what his brother was saying. "Mom isn't no snitch."

"Did you really do that?" asked Khalil staring at her as his eyes started to harden, but she never responded. "After all the times you talk about being a soldier to Akeem and stepping up, you snitch on Pop. Why?"

"To beat a simple possession charge" Akeem replied.

"How do you know this Akeem?" inquired Amiri.

"I was there to hear the judge describe everything that transpired" he told them. "Come on" he said heading towards the front door where their father was waiting on them. Khalil looked down on their mother contempt while Amiri still refused to accept the truth until it come directly out of her mouth.

"Did you really do that Mom" he asked with hurt in his eyes. "Did you?"

"Yes" she finally admitted staring into his hurt and innocent eyes. "I'm sorry baby."

"How could you do this to us?" he asked.

"I was scare baby."

"You was scared" he repeated snorting at her. "All these years you boasted about our family reputation, and you turn out to be a snitch. I guess no female in your clan never went to jail because yawl are quick to snitch to save your own butt" he stared at her coldly then turning to join his brothers.

"Come give me a hug before you go Amiri" she requested.

"Na, you might snitch" he replied walking away from her pleading and crying eyes then closed the door behind himself. As they waited for the elevator, they could hear her cries of anguish until they climbed aboard, and the door closed.

For the next couple of weeks, they better acquainted with their father. Although they still didn't know where he lived, one thing became apparent to Akeem, he was making late night visits to the house. He found himself constantly checking the position of the bar and the toothpick he had set-up. It took two people to move the bar and he knew who the second person was, Chubby. Two weeks before school was to start, he took them to Philly for the first time to do some school shopping around eight-thirty, one morning. The black Cadillac Escalade was like a cruise ship floating up 95 North. With his E-Z pass, he didn't have to stop to pay the tolls just cruise through. They arrived in Philly close to ten o'clock. They were like big kids visiting their first big city. He drove down to 3rd and market then occupied two spaces with his cruise ship and they bailed out. Standing on the corner, he pointed out the Suit corner, shoe corner and fashion corner all owned allegedly by the mob. He told them that he would he inside 3rd Street

Jazz whenever they completed their shopping but insisted that they take their time. He gave Akeem the key then headed towards his destination down 3rd Street.

"Let's get it in fellas" he said pulling out an envelope and extending it to them. They stared inside then up into his eyes. "There is five G's in there. Watch each other's back" he told them then they disburse. Khalil and Amiri walked into shirt corner while Akeem went towards suit corner and walked inside. Buy two and get three free. A broad smile acme to his face. Across the street at shirt corner, they were offering unbelievable deals also. Forty-minutes later, Amiri walked in needing through the door needing the keys. Ten minutes later, he was exiting carrying well over twenty suits and place them inside the Escalade. They went inside Shoe Corner together. From lizards to gator to ostrich boots, they had it all and at a very reasonable price. They were in there a good thirty-five minutes before exiting and finding a place for their shoes inside the SUV. The things that they just brought probably won't reach Baltimore until late next year. They walked up 3rd Street and walked inside the jazz place. They scanned the first floor but didn't see their father, so they climbed the steps to the second floor. He was at the counter talking to an old Italian guy.

"Al, these are my sons" he proudly introduced.

"Akeem, the last time I saw you, you was about three" he smiled at him. "Glad to meet yawl Khalil and Amiri" he smiled over at them. "Abdullah, you need to get with me."

"I will after I'm finish with my personal business" he assured him.

"I'll hold you to that" he said shaking his hand.

"Grab those crates fellas" he said leading the way back down the stairs. He shot the deuce sign to two younger men down stairs before holding the door for them to exit. Less than five-minutes later, they were climbing the ramp to 95S.

"Do you think you can find your way back up here?" he asked merging into the fourth lane.

"Yes, sir. It's basically a straight shot" Akeem replied.

"Come back next weekend to get yawl winter attire, okay?"

"Yes, sir" he said leaning back and listening to Cannonball Adderley's "Mercy, Mercy, Mercy" as he stared out at the scenery smiling. When they come back up next weekend, they were going to tour this alleged city of brotherly love with its high murder rate.

T.C was sitting out on his balcony at his apartment in Columbia. Since acquiring the place almost six months ago, his sister was the only one that knew of its location. Nobody else from the city know it existed. They only knew of his apartment on Coldspring Lane. Only the prissy ass county girls that he met at Columbia Mall knew of the fashionable bachelor pad. They found his brash disposition intriguing. He knew they were attracted to his looks because he wasn't somebody that causes a woman's panties to become moist. The expensive things that he wore and the Audi he possess was his Venus flytrap. As he stared out at the pond hitting lines of coke and dope, he knew his life was in danger. One of his people claim to have seen Killa but he discarded his words. If it were Killa that he thought he saw, he would have gotten with his sister by now, but he hadn't. When she initially said that Akeem knew something weeks ago, he had foolishly discarded her words too and what happen, he appeared like the morning dew on grass. Since then, motherfuckers that was indirectly involved was getting stretch out and homicide couldn't connect the dots. Trying to pay restitution to him wasn't desire just their blood, but he did take their offers afterward anyway. His sister would get a pass only because she was the mother of his children, but will he get the same blessing? He knew he should have gotten with him weeks ago when she first called him, but his addiction had him paranoid and doing dumb shit. He knew that hiding out only complicated his situation, but what other choices did a shit talking punk ass motherfucker like him have to do?

Ring! Ring! Ring!

"Hello?"

"Hey, Akeem."

"What's up Ashanti?"

"Are you busy?"

"Mmmm" he said staring over at the young lady he recently met. "I'm having a very interesting conversation with a very attractive young lady" he said staring over into her grayish eyes.

"Get rid of that hooker and come pick me up at my job" she said hanging up.

"What? Hello? Hello? Well, I'll be damn" he said staring at his phone before putting it away.

"You have to go?"

"Regrettably, yeah" he said getting to his feet.

"You have my number" she said smiling up at him adjusting his hat. "Is there any way I can convince you to stay?" she asked in a very seductive voice while revealing her impish smile.

"She is one of two close friends that I will answer their call" he informed her. "I'll hit you up later."

"You better."

"Later, Shy" replied turning and walking off. He had met her two weeks ago when she had a flat tire. He had gotten a junky to change her tire while they got acquainted. During that time, they actually vibe. She was recently divorce from her high school sweetheart. She obtained his beloved 750 and the house for their two children. Although she was only twenty-five, she could easily pass for someone that had just turned twenty-one. With her medium mocha complexion frame with slightly flaring hips and full lips, how could a man foolishly cheat on her? He could understand for money, but not for another piece of pussy. As he drove up Park Heights, he turned left onto Rogers Avenue and took that down to Reistertown Road and parked on the corner. He climbed out and walked around the corner then push open the door.

"Okay, ladies. Kick it out" J said giggling at them as she collected twenty dollars from them except Honey. "See yawl tomorrow" she said fanning herself with their money while smiling.

"See you tomorrow, J."

"Later Honey. You ready Akeem?"

"Yeah" he replied tipping his hat to the ladies as they walked out. "You betting on me?"

"Betting implies gambling" she said clutching his arm. "That was a sure shot" she replied smiling.

"Where do you need a ride to?' he asked unlocking the door for her and opening it.

"I want to put a down payment on a car I saw" she said taking her seat and closing the door herself.

He climbed in and asked, "What kind of car are you considering?"

"A Dodge Charger" she replied as they fasten their seatbelts.

"Why such a high-performance car?"

"To get away from these fools" she replied giggling as he pulled away from the curb.

"How much are you putting down?"

"I have seventy-five hundred. It's costing twenty-seven."

"With your monthly note, you do know your insurance will be outrages especially being under twenty-one."

"I think I can manage it" she said still smiling.

"Okay, so where do you want to go?"

"Out Rt. 40 to that Dodge place" she replied.

"I know where it at but first I have to make a stop."

"Okay" she replied leaning back and getting into the jazz.

He drove down Rogers until he connected to Woodlawn Drive

then took that to Security Boulevard. He pulled up on the State Credit Union parking lot then parked. "I'll be right back" he said climbing out the car while leaving it running for J. He was in and out in less than three minutes. He drove down Rolling Road turning right instead of left towards her destination.

"Where are you taking me?"

"To a more appropriate dealership" he informed her ignoring her slight pouting. Fifteen minutes later, they were pulling off of Rt.29 onto a Chrysler dealership. He pulled into a visitors parking spot, and they climbed out. "See if there is anything that you like, and I'll be back" he said walking towards the entrance. He spotted who he wanted to see ignoring the stares of the white people. Just as he was almost upon him, his peripheral vison caught his movement. Looking up, a board smile suddenly came to his face.

"Akeem" he greeted getting to his feet and shaking his hand.

"How are you sir?"

"Just fine, young man" he assured him smiling. "What can I do for you?"

"I have a friend searching your lot" he told him.

"Well, let's go see if there is anything that she is interested in" said escorting him outside.

"You see anything that you like?" Akeem asked her.

"Several" she admitted smiling. "How much for that Jeep Cherokee?"

"Twenty-four" he replied.

"Would you take a seventy-five hundred down payment?"

"Yes, of course" he assured her.

"So, what will you charge her if she wanted to pay cash?"

"Didn't you and I meet like this" he replied smiling. "I'll let her go for twenty" he replied.

"Write it up for her Mr. Smith and included a year insurance please."

"No, problem Akeem. May I have your license young lady."

J reached into her cross-body bag and retrieved it then pass it to him.

"I'll be ready in about fifteen minutes" he said turning and walking away.

"You are paying it off?" she asked staring over at him.

"No, you are. I am just your lender" he informed her smiling.

"Are you going to charge me interest?" she asked flirting with her eyes while giving him an impish smile

"We can negotiate that later" he said returning her coy smile.

After she sat and played with her new toy for about ten minutes, he dragged her out and went into the office. He had her signed several sheets of paper then ownership was hers including her insurance. With the keys in her hand, she climbed back inside the Cherokee and started up the engine. She set the music to 92Q then adjusted her seat and mirrors.

"I see you need gas" he mention.

"I have a quarter tank."

"If you ever run out of gas, call anybody you want but never call me" he warned her.

"Let's stop by a gas station before we head home."

"Now, you are think" he said turning and walking away towards his car. Pressing the remote, the car came alive, and he climbed inside then lead her off the lot. They drove about a quarter mile before they were able to do a U-turn. They were cruising back up Rt.29 when he spotted a gas station and pulled in. She pulled near a pump then sat waiting until he pulled up next to her. "Ashanti, are you suggesting that I pimp ass in your pimp for you?"

"I was hoping that you would" she admitted smiling.

"Young lady, I'm not even going to give you the money that you might need. So, you might as well get your fine ass out of that seat and pay for your gas. Hopefully, you will be the first person to pump gas in your vehicle unless you think you can get one of these law-abiding white people out here to do it for you" he teased snickering.

"Na, I got this" she replied stepping out and walking around.

"I see you trust them too, huh?" he asked out his passenger window as she hit her locks causing him to burst out laughing. He backed into a parking spot staring out Rt.29 and houses hidden behind the forestry. J finally came out and stuck her tongue at him as she walked pass. He laugh at her then looked up in time to see T.C Audi cruising pass. He placed his car his gear then rolled up on J. "Stay here until I get back" he told her pressing on his accelerator then jumping on Rt.29. He could see T.C about two miles ahead. He closed the distance to a mile then pace him. He watched him pulled off then went into a small community. Minutes later, he was pulling up into Columbia Apartments. From the street, he watched which complex he went into while pulling out his cell phone and pressing a pre-set number.

"Hey, son. What's up?"

"I just stumble upon T.C. he's hibernating pout here in the Columbia Apartments."

"Did he see you?"

"I kept my distance but with him, I honestly don't know. If he knew I was following him, he still would have brought me here."

"True" he admitted because he would have done the same thing. Lead his prey to him. "You can bounce. I got it from here."

"Alright, Pop. I'll holla at you later" he said ending their conversation then rerouting himself back to the gas station and pulling up next to J.

"Is everything okay?" she asked with concern in her eyes.

"Yeah, everything is okay. Do you know how to use that navigational system?"

"No but I'll study the manual later. Right now, I'm going to catch up with my girls and flaunt my gift" she admitted giggling.

"Okay, follow me back into the city and I'll try to holla at you later."

"Okay and thanks Akeem" she smiled at him as he took the lead. Once she knew where she was, she press on the accelerator and the V-8 came to life then cruised right pass him. All he could see was her broad smile at the jubilation of the powerful jeep climbing the hill and disappearing. He caught up with her three miles up the road. She was receiving her first speeding ticket. He blew his horn at her when he cruised pass laughing his ass off.

Killa had two of his associates posted up on T.C. for a whole week, but he was nowhere to be found. Asking a friendly white guy about him, he informed him that he had suddenly moved late one night. He must have peek Akeem trailing him but that was okay. Sooner or later, he will lift his ugly junky head again and he will be right there to rip it from his shoulder.

School finally started and Akeem couldn't be happier to start his junior year. He had numerous of basketball scholarships on the table including from Morgan State and Coppin State even though they knew that he would take his talent out of state. Byrd had graduated and accepted a full scholarship up in New York playing for Syracuse. Whenever he had a home game or was in the region, they always made their presence known. He wasn't starting but during the crucial moments in a game, he was always on the floor. Although he will be miss, Ice was representing him extremely well.

Since they played ball all summer together in leagues like the Sonny Hill league up in Philly and making noise up in Rucker's Park in New York, they were very aware of each other's game and tendencies when people were defending them a certain way. Coach G didn't have to do anything except show up and enjoy the show. Although they appeared to be playing street ball with their perceived antics, they were slicing teams apart with easy back door plays from the opposite side of the court. College coaches were drooling over their performance mid-way through the season and feel in love with their dedication to sitting down on D. Constantly talking to one another, teams never caught them sleeping. They had a big game coming against their cross-town rival, Dunbar High. Most of their players have been served up during summer games outside in different parks or recreational league games around the city. One guy in particular got a rare taste of Akeem's physical play and whatever he had whisper to him, they knew he wish he could take it back, but once words filter pass your lips, you can't take them back and have to deal with the circumstances. With April showers, the team was twenty-three and 0.

Saturday afternoon, Akeem was heading to Northwood Shopping Center for an outside jazz concert with his two brothers. As they drove up the Alameda, they spotted their father's Escalade parked two blocks from their destination on Argonne Drive. He circle the block fortunate to catch a driver pulling out and swung into his spot. As they climbed out and closed their doors, he pop the trunk for them to grab their lawn chairs then proceeded towards the sound of the music. The place was pack with individuals. They eventually found a nice cool spot near the wall. As they stared out at the numerous flavors of young ladies, their laugher and snicker could be heard.

"Hi, Khalil" a teenage girl called to him with three of her girlfriends.

"Hey, Baby Girl" he smiled up at her. "What are you doing here?"

"I could ask you the same thing" she counter smiling down at him and openly revealing that she was attracted to him.

"I'm here with my brothers Akeem and Amiri" he introduced them.

"So, you are Amiri, huh?" a bronze complexion girl asked staring over at him.

"Yes, I am" he replied grinning. "What is your name?"

"I'm Ebony. Baby Girl little sister" she replied grinning.

"We're heading over to Mickey D's. You want to hang?"

"Sure" he replied starting to get to his feet.

"Aren't you coming too Amiri?"

"Are you inviting me Ebony?" he asked with a copy smile.

"Yes" she replied smiling down at him and he instantly got to his feet.

Akeem watched them until they melted into the crowd. They were definitely growing up. As he waved to several people he knew and those that knew him from the basketball courts around the city, he spotted then wave to J and her girls being escorted by Dink and Ice. He didn't know the guy that was escorting J. She seem to be slightly embarrassed especially after seeing that he was there alone. As they gradually disappeared in the crowd, two guys grabbed his attention. As he watched them, he could tell that they were searching for someone. Good luck finding them in this cluster. When one of them suddenly pointed in a specific direction, he allowed his eyes to search in that direction, but he couldn't see anything. When he got to his feet and stared again, he spotted his father. His male intuition started banging like when five-o was almost upon him. As he started moving towards his father, he took an angle while they slowly fanned out but stayed close to one another. They were going to hit his father and he was almost certain as he picked up his pace. Twenty feet from his father, their hands disappeared under their shirts and when they rested their hands again along their thighs, it was clutching something. When they fanned out, he knew they were plotting to hit his father. As he aggressively started pushing people aside to get to him, he started shouting.

"Pop! Pop!" he shouted but the music was drowning his words. Just as one of the guys started to elevate his hand, he called out again. "Pop! Pop!" he screamed at the top of his lungs. His father vaguely heard him but stared around until their eyes met. The fear in them told him that something was about to jump off and he started reaching for his weapon. Just as one of the guys raised his hand to fire, Akeem slammed his fist to the back of his head causing him to stumble forward, but he didn't stop; he continued towards him with his eyes on a second assailant just as his father hit the first guy twice center mass. Hysteria consumed the once festive environment. Suddenly, two rounds sounded and struck Akeem twice as his father zero in then squeezed his weapon twice catching him and forcing hm off his feet. One round splinter off his left collar bone, but the second bullet struck him in the abdomen. He was on the ground in a fetal position groaning when Khalil and Amiri suddenly appeared. Tears instantly consumed their eyes staring at the blood escaping their brother.

"Khalil, take this" he said extending his keys to him. "Go get Pop gun and get low with your brother."

"No!" he denounced his suggestion snarling at what he wanted.

"What did I say?" he asked slightly hardening his eyes.

"But I want to stay Akeem."

"I know but you have to bounce. Go get Pop gun" he told him watching the father whispering to the guy.

"Who put up the contract?" he asked kneeling while staring down into his eyes.

"Fuck you!" he said trying to smile.

"Fuck me. No, fuck you" he said forcing the barrel of the weapon into is chest wound.

"Aaggghhh, shit! Motherfucker!"

"Who paid you?" he whisper starting to force the barrel again into his open wound.

"No! Wait!" he insisted trying to gain his breath while staring up into his menacing eyes.

"Who motherfucker" he insisted hearing the police siren in the distance then shoved the barrel into the wound deeper.

"Okay! Okay!" he replied in excruciating pain. "T.C" he snitched forcing his father to shove the barrel even deeper.

"Pop, I need that" insisted Khalil staring down on him.

When he stared up into his son eyes, he forced him to slightly repel. "What?"

"I need that Pop" he said reaching down for his Glock and taking it from his hand as the police sirens were getting closer. "Akeem need you" he told him being the focus on his wounded son and not the revenge he wanted to take. "Amiri, come on!" he insisted as they walked through a small opening and cross the street just as five-o were turning the corner.

News of the incident consumed the six o'clock news. "A prominent and highly recruited high school basketball player for Lake Clifton High was caught in the cross fire of individuals at an outside jazz festival being given up at Northwood Shopping Center. Witnesses implied that the two deceased individuals were attempting to assassinate somebody, and Akeem "ATM" Anderson appeared to cross their line of fire resulting in him being struck twice. The person they were trying to assassinate couldn't be identified, but Akeem's father just so happen to be attending the festivities also. He was still clutching his son in his arms when the paramedic arrived to take him to Good Samaritan Hospital. His condition was not readily available."

Killa remained by his son's side after surgery and didn't never consider leaving his side until the doctor assured him that he will make a full recovery then he went on the hunt. Three days later around ten o'clock in the morning, he finally open his eyes and the first person his eyes focus on was Sunshine. She was fast asleep in a chair with her math book in her lap. As flowers and cards filled his room, Khalil and Amiri spent every moment after school in his room. They would complete any homework that needed to be attended or book reports that needed to be started or completed. Sunshine made it her personal mission to be his damn nanny and make sure he got all of his class assignments. During his recovery, he had to constantly reinforce in Sunshine that he was okay, but she wouldn't relax until she saw him on the basketball courts again. As far as J was concern, she would come through periodically.

Word on the grapevine, two immaculately dress silver backs climbed out of a black Suburban in Lexington courtyard and casually walked through then enter the building. Security never consider impeding these two gentlemen from their assignment. They took the elevator to the nineth floor then exit. Staring up from the court yard, people watched them entering Akeem's mother's house without being announced. Seconds later, all of her guest were filing out quickly. They stayed and talked to her for about twenty-minutes before leaving. As they walked back towards their Suburban, they were scanning the area closely before they climbed back into the Suburban and pulling away.

She sat on the couch shock at the information that they just brought her. They wanted her to know what happen to Akeem and who was responsible before the news blast the information around the city. The news literally fucked her up psychologically especially because her little brother initiated a contract on Killa. How dumb of his stupid ass. Motherfuckers have been trying to reap the rewards of contracts on Killa before he was incarcerated and every person who initiated it paid for their indiscretion with their lives. Motherfuckers couldn't seem to touch him like he was a Teflon Don especially if he pull out Dick and Harry. If he does, you're dead. He's extremely prolific with them in his hands. He purposely allowed one person to live so he could extract the information that he desire and then send people from his previous life to make a house call. She grabbed her cell phone and called him.

"Hey, Sis. How are you on this lovely day?"

"What the fuck have you done!?" she snapped.

"Whoa! Easy!" he insisted. "What are you talking about?"

"What the fuck have you gotten your dumb ass in now?"

"Melody, I don't know what the fuck you are talking about?"

"Killa, you dumb motherfucker. They miss their intended target and hit Akeem instead."

"What?"

"You heard me. You stupid motherfucker. Two of Killa's enforcers were just here and who do you think they were looking for?"

"I don't have anything to do with what you are saying" he tried to convince her.

"I can hear your lie through this phone motherfucker. So, stop lying to me or I'll leave your ass hanging" she threaten. "Do you hear me!?"

"Yes, Sis" he replied solemnly.

"I have to find out what's the condition of my child from the six o'clock news because Killa nor his people will be telling me shit, but you better pray that he recover, or your dumb ass is on barrow time and no amount of pleading from me will do shit" she informed him ending their conversation.

As he sat there listening the pieces that the news reporter was say, Akeem got hit because he saw what was about to happen and put himself in harm's way. He never consider that he might take his nephews with him to the festival. Now, Akeem is on the operating table with no current information coming out about his status. Now, Killa had his street soldiers on the streets looking for him. They will never find him out in Joppa town. His concern wasn't about his present hiding spot now just the desire to continue to breath. Sis has always been able to bail his dumb ass out of the stupid shit he have gotten himself involved in, but this time it's completely different and the victims were also. They are supposed to be family. Whatever it takes to not be subjected to the medieval shit that Killa were alleged to do to motherfucker, he was willing to pay. Anything.

Miraculously, Akeem was released from Good Samaritan two weeks after being rolled in unconscious. Sunshine had gotten his keys from the house to bring Khalil and Amiri with her. The ride home was like when they were children filled with laughter. They could barely remember the ride home. Pulling up in front of his house, he was surprised to see the banners welcoming him home and the flood of close friends. Getting out of the car, Cross was all over him asking questions after questions until Khalil shut him down. As his neighbors stared on, he led his entourage into the house then the latest R&B and hip-hop filter out the windows. Around eight o'clock, Sunshine was forcing everybody out of the house including J while sending him upstairs to get comfortable. She assisted Khalil and Amiri cleaning up. They were finish a little after nine o'clock. While they went down stairs to play on their X-Box, she crept upstairs to see if he was asleep. She could hear Miles Davis "So What" filtering out the ajar door. Pushing it open, she stared in on him. She was lightly snoring. She bend down and kissed him lightly on the lips stirring him awake.

"Stay with me" he whisper.

"When you are stronger, my beloved" she smiled down on him watching his eyes slowly closed then exit the room. She went down stairs to call a cab and sat on the porch with Khalil and Amiri quietly talking until the cab pulled up. She kiss them lightly on the cheek then walked down the path and climbed inside. They watched the taillights until they turned a slight curve.

With the doctor's recommendation that he stay home the remainder of the school year, he took the time to lift his weights and hit his heavy bag twice a day. As his strength and flexibility gradually returned, Sunshine continued to pick up his class assignments while returning those that he had completed. She had spent more time with him as he got body strong than she have in years. Reconnecting with him always build her confidence like her desire to attend college. He said he would help pay her tuition it if the scholarships didn't cover it. As he stayed connected to his partners mainly by reading the newspaper, they had a share of the conference title with a record of thirty and two, but in the regional, a very controversy called with time expiring gave their opponent two free throws. The guy hit both giving them a one-point victory. They lost in the state semi-final by twenty-five indicting that they shouldn't have won their previous game because Karma is a motherfucker.

He started going to the basketball court around his way with his brothers. They would play certain shooting games like around the world and twenty-one. When Akeem finally made his debut back at Chadwick in mid-June, he left no doubt that he was back and better than ever. He had increased his jumper by three feet and his leaping ability also increased. He left no doubt that he was back and better than ever if that was even possible. He was sitting on bleachers talking when Sunshine walked up.

"Hey, birthday girl" he greeted smiling while getting to his feet and kissing her lightly on her lips.

"I thought that you might have forgotten" she confess staring up into his eyes smiling.

"Yeah, right" he lightly laugh. "I knew you would hunt me down eventually because I damn sure wasn't going to try to figure out where you were. Can you take a ride with me?"

"Sure, can my girls hang?"

"Sure" he smiled over at them. "Fellas, I have to bounce but I will be back" he told them grabbing his net-bag and changing into a dry shirt. He clutch Sunshine's finger as they walked out. He unlocked his car doors then they climbed inside. Starting the engine, George Coleman's "Amsterdam After Dark" filled the interior.

"Can I hear Machito "Congo Mulence" please."

"Who?" her girlfriends asked from the back seat.

"Nobody that yawl will know" she smiled at him as they drove down McCullen Street until they reached MLK Boulevard and turned right. They merge onto the new highway coming out near Edmondson Avenue then taking that straight out.

"Where are we headed?" she asked as they were cruising up the Baltimore National Pike.

"Does it matter?" he asked peeking over at her.

"No."

"I didn't think so" he smiled over at her as they turned on Rt.29 then he pulled out his cell phone. "Hey, Rob. I'm five minutes away" he informed him ending their conversation. He pulled up on the Chrysler dealership parking lot then found a parking space in one of the slots available for visitors then they all climbed out. A smiling white man stood outside as they approached.

"Hey, brother from another mother" he greeted Akeem smiling.

"What's up Rob" he greeted shaking his hand. "This Sunshine" he introduced her.

"When you said she was gorgeous, you wasn't lying" he confess admiring her golden complexion and enchanting eyes. "That right there is your birthday present" he pointed at a white Chrysler fully loaded.

"What?" she said staring at him then over at Akeem.

"My birthday gift to you baby" he informed her as she leap in his arms giving him butterflies kisses all over his face.

"Will have some class and get your crazy ass off of me" he smiled slowly allowing her feet to touch the ground.

"All I need is your driver's license and your signature, young lady" Rob told her smiling.

She was still stun by her birthday present as she extended her license to him. He filled in a couple of blank spots then requested her signature and pass her a set of keys with the ownership paper.

"I'll holla at you later Sunshine" he said starting to turn.

"Where are you going?" she asked grabbing his arm.

"Back to the courts" he replied.

"I'll see you tonight" she said releasing his arm.

"No, you won't" he replied over his shoulder.

"Yes, I will" she replied adamantly.

"No, you won't Ayanna (beautiful flower)."

"Ayanna?" she repeated staring over at him slightly hardening her eyes. "Oh, you are using my government name now."

"Only because I know you have good intentions, but I won't see you tonight, sweetheart."

"You must have a previous engagement" she suggested staring at him as he open his car door.

"No, I don't have any plans Sunshine" he smiled over at her.

"Then tell me why I won't see you?"

"Because you will be stroking Biggie's ego and soothing his jealousy" he replied as he burst out laughing at her and the anger that leap into her eyes.

"Come give me a kiss before you leave, my love" she requested in a seductive voice while smiling over at him.

"Said the very alluring words from the Venus Flytrap" he burst out laughing again as he climbed inside. He started up the engine then place the car in gear and gently pulled pass her giving her the deuce sign, but now snickering at her expression.

She stood there watching his car going down the road while shaking her head at him.

"Sunshine, he actually brought you a car" her girlfriend stared over at her amazed.

"Yeah, Dee-Dee" she replied unlocking the door for them to climb inside.

"How come yawl just don't hook up?"

"Because he's sowing his oats, Tiny" she replied smiling as they climbed inside. "He would never want to disrespect or hurt me. So, we stay away from one another" she shared.

"Girl, I would drop Biggie in an instant to get with him."

"So would I but like I said, he's sowing his oats" she smiled adjusting the mirrors as 92Q filled the interior.

"Open the sunroof" requested Dee-Dee.

"Nope" she replied opening the arm rest and finding a card with her name on it. She pulled out the card and ten Franklins fell into her lap. "Ching! Ching!" she said smiling from ear to ear. "Time to go shopping ladies" she said giving them two-hundred dollars apiece.

"Sunshine, how can ATM afford to buy you a car?"

"Now, you are being a woman and very intrusive Tiny" Sunshine replied staring over at her. "Whatever he might be about has nothing to do with me and definitely not you" she informed her shutting her down. Bitches have been signifying about him for years and she have shut every one of their signifying asses down. Yeah, she knew what he have been doing for years because of her snitching ass mother. When he took care of his brothers, he always gave her money to buy clothes even though she was with Biggie. So, she was very protective of him when it came to signifying bitches.

All summer he was snatching up his squad from the arms of lovely young ladies around ten o'clock in the morning and hitting basketball courts outside of the city. They would patch up with Steve from Boys Latin in Columbia and started calling him "Vanilla Chocolate." Four brothers and one white guy was bringing a horror show to the courts that they visited. It was during this time that universities started rescinding their scholarship and he took it personal as he should. When that impish smile came to his face, his partners knew he had something special waiting to displayed during their season year and he did. He had all of the colleges name monogram on several black T-shirts that he wore to remind him of their decisions.

Starting his senior year, he was on a personal mission. Earlier that morning while eating breakfast with his brothers, they were listening to Sports Center when a question concerning him was mentioned. "Did Akeem "ATM" Anderson retain his skills or did the tragedy that touched him permanently affected him physically and psychologically?" he stared over at his brothers who were trying to contain their snickers but failing miserably. They wanted to know. Well, he can show them better than telling them. From the moment basketball season commenced, he showed his ass. A triple double with twenty-seven points, fourteen rebounds and twelve assists. By the tenth game, sports announcers were already rescinding what they said. He was better than before and that was scary. College coaches started reemerging and wearing three dollars smile, but he never returned their smiles. He was known to keep his emotions in check so they couldn't read what was in his eyes. Those that tried to impede him, he would point to their university name on his T-shirt and ignore them. Although they weren't allowed to approach him or try to make amends for their previous decision, he told his coaches that if any of them try relating a message from any of the college scouts that he would quit the team immediately, he wasn't threatening them. He was promising them. When they won their conference, there mission wasn't over.

At the Washington Wizard home court in D.C, the Capital Center was the host of the regionals. He met several players that heard of his incidents and were elated for his recovery while others were coming to take a peek at him, but they didn't see this alleged quite assassin. His friendly personality didn't fit the descriptive. He was easy to talk to and seem to extend himself to get acquainted to his opponents. Only when the ball was toss up did his eyes become a little serious and the smile leave.

The first team they played didn't bring their away game with them. Coach mainly used their second-string players to get acquainted with the big show and displayed their talent. By the time they reached the regional finals, ATM had unwanted attention upon himself especially from the sports reporters. Mandatory interviews, they asked about the black T-shirt he started wearing during the year with numerous of colleges name on it. He advised them to ask the colleges. When they wanted to know how and where he rehab, he always became evasive like it was a great secret. When the obvious question came about which colleges had the inside track, he replied they all do. They are offering me a free education for my talent and only a fool wouldn't take it, but he never gave them what they desired, a definitive answer.

"Coach!"

"Yeah, ATM."

"I got Robinson" he announced causing Cross and Ice to start snickering.

"He has three inches on you" he reminded him.

"He got him Coach" Cross and Ice assured him still snickering.

And he did, he was studied Robinson game and he was much too comfortable on the court. He had all intentions of making him extremely uncomfortable. From the moment the game got started, he was Robinson shadow. Sitting down on D and standing tall when on the blocks, by all standards, ATM shut him the fuck down. The alleged best swing man in the state was being shut down in the biggest game. When they tried to rub ATM off of him, they always hit him with a strong double team. Although he scored fifteen points, he shot an icy five for twenty-two while ATM was busting his ass and anybody else that called themselves defending him. He finish with thirty-two points, fifteen rebounds and eight assists. He was awarded the MVP of the tournament, but he gave more praise to his teammates and what they contributed than his personal achievement.

With the basketball season over, he was glad to get home at a more reasonable time and so was his brothers. He had been talking to them recently about the transition that was about to take place in their lives. He knew he was placing a tremendous amount, of responsibilities on their young shoulder but they did have options. If they thought they couldn't do what was asked of them, they would have to return to their mother's house. They were adamant about staying where they were. They constantly kept reinforcing in him that they would never abuse his trust and Khalil especially didn't want to return to the house of a snitch.

Weeks zip pass before he knew it, he was getting a hint from J about the prom. Sunshine would have been his date, but she foolishly thought that J had already scoop him up weeks ago. So just last week, she invited Biggie. Hearing that, Akeem got up in her beautiful ass and she rightfully deserved it. He had constantly told her to not assume anything about his personal like, but once again she had and this time, it cost her dearly. The love of her life will be escorting another woman to his prom and whispering romantic illicit words in her ears while she was taking the man that she knew wasn't going to show her the romantic evening that she desperately desired.

Akeem had rented a black limo for him and his partners. They picked them up at eight-thirty and arrived at Lake Clifton a little after nine o'clock. The first thing the ladies wanted to do was get the pictures out of the way. With three camera people getting their grind on, they completed that aspect of the night in five minutes. Waiting for the development of the pictures took longer. He had seen J's broad smile often over the years, but tonight, her smile seem to illuminate their entire gym. Once her name filter on the grapevine by those that recognized her, east side girls were constantly pulling her up and introducing themselves to her. Her ghetto fame had guys very curious about her. They eventually settle on which after party they were going to attend. The driver will drop the ladies off at Lisa house to get changed while the fellas will go to Akeem's house then hook up at a designated spot and follow the other over to the party.

They arrived at the party a little before midnight. The spacious house near Rosedale had a massive backyard. With a portable dance floor, the DJ kept the dance floor pack. With alcohol in everybody cups and the scent of blunts floating on the air, the festive environment was genuinely exciting. Between Byrd's stories and Cross picking with Dink, tears stayed in their eyes. As the DJ slowed the beat for The Whispers to ask, "Are You Going My Way?" J gripped his fingers and escorted him to the dance floor.

"Look at the time" she suggested.

"Three o'clock? I didn't think it was that late" he admitted smiling down into her eyes.

"You really made it an enjoyable and memorable night" she said staring up into his eyes. "I want to spend the night with you."

"Now, you know I would accept that invitation, but are you sure?"

"No but I don't think any girl is sure when they are considering if they are ready to lose their virginity" she replied from her perspective.

"I can respect that" he replied returning her stare.

"Come on, let's bounce" she said walking to the table where they had left their friends. "Here, Lisa" she said extending her keys to her. "Make sure everybody get home."

"What? Yawl are leaving?"

"I'm giving you my keys, aren't I?" she replied sarcastically while hugging Chi then giving her a hug then gripping Akeem's fingers.

"Later, family" he smiled as they step off. They waved to several people as they made their exit. He hit the remote starting the engine and unlocking the doors. He open her door then closed it once she was inside. He climbed inside then place the car in gear then proceeded towards 695. He took the Security Square exit then proceeded up Woodlawn Drive. Minutes later, they were climbing the porch and walking inside. She proceeded straight up the stairs towards the bedrooms while pulling her shirt over her locs. His rice paper lamps had the room dimly lit as she stepped out of her white stretch jeans displaying Victoria's latest secret in boy shorts and matching lace bra. She walked over to his discs

185

and found Angie Stone then put it into the disc player. He sat on the love seat to removed his shoes and shirt then got to his feet to remove his pants. His eyes remained fixed on her body. Feeling his eyes on her, she turned and stared over at him. Her eyes instinctively went towards his dick for a quick glance before staring in his eyes. She unhooked her bra revealing her slightly spike 36B nibbles the freedom they craved. Slowing pulling down her panties, she stood in front of him revealing all she had to offer. He pulled down his stretch Gildan's then stood erect in front of her.

As she focus in on what was swinging between his thighs, her knees openly buckle once he step further into the light. "I can't handle that!" she confess staring at it. "I've only seen something big in the porn."

"We can take our time, Ashanti" he whisper closing the distance between them.

"You are much too large, Akeem" she insisted feeling his arms around her and his dick pressing against her thighs. "I'm scare."

"Do you think I would purposely hurt you?"

"No" she replied escaping his arms. "But that is going to hurt" she said backing up until her legs hit the bed. "If I wasn't a virgin, I might try it, but I can't Akeem."

"Okay, Ashanti" he slightly smiled at her then back away. He grabbed his shorts and slip them back on.

"You want me to go home?" she asked putting her panties and bra back on.

"Don't even try it. I still want to know how you look with crust in your eyes in the morning" he replied walking over and gripping her fingers and climbing up in bed.

"I'm sorry Akeem" she said holding his arm tighter as they spoon.

"No apology needed Ashanti. Our relationship is more than us having sex. So, go asleep and if you snore, I'm kicking your ass out my bed" he said snickering while inhaling her biochemistry.

In less than fifteen minutes, her breathing change and light snoring could be heard. It was the morning sun creeping through his bedroom that eventually woke him. He stared into her lightly snoring face smiling then climbed out of bed. He put on a pair of shorts and a wife beater then started to leave the room until she rolled over. With her legs wide open and revealing light public hair from around her camel toe, an impish smile came across his lips before shaking off the erotic thought and getting the hell out of the room. Ascending the stairs, he turned on the CD player in the family room and Dexter Gordon's "Cheese Cake" filled the house. He pause to stare at the picture that he and J had taken at the prom. He got to his feet to start breakfast. He had just completed making the wheat pancakes and omelets when Khalil and Amiri materialized wearing smiles.

"Morning" they chime together getting plates and forks.

"What's up fellas?" he replied. "Set another plate."

"We need to talk" Khalil informed him while getting glasses form the picture of orange juice.

"What is it?" he asked placing the turkey bacon on the serving dish.

"We talked to Mom last night" he mention getting his attention.

"And?" he replied peeking over at them.

"If Pop kills Uncle T.C, he could go back to jail" mention Amiri.

"Yeah, that's a possibility" he replied placing the turkey bacon and wheat pancakes on the table.

"We don't want him to go back to jail" Khalil said staring at him.

"Neither does he" he nonchalantly replied.

"If he goes back, I don't think I can forgive him" Khalil said in a tone that made him around and stare at him. "I honestly don't know why he's trying to touch him, and I normally would cosign such a move, but you are always advocating increasing the peace. Well, you need to tell Pop that so he can stay here and watch over us."

"That is not your job Akeem" interjected Amiri. "For as long as I can remember you have taken care of us. Pop has life lessons that only he can share with us. I want him to see me graduate also. I don't want to send him pictures of me as I mature and the grandchildren that God might bless him. I need him to step-up and be the parent I need him to be."

"I've heard subtle stories about Pop over the years, but he don't have to relive that guy of his past. Just talking to him over the past couple of months, he's a very educated person so why regress? He's no longer a nigger but a black man. So, we need you to talk to him, okay?"

He didn't answer right away as he stared in the eyes of his younger brothers. They have follow the path that he had coordinated for them and without too much, objections. Now, he see something in their eyes he don't usually see even when they were in the streets. The only times he see it is when they were watching a horror movie. Fear. They were fearful for their father. "Okay, fellas. I'll holla at him but there is something that yawl need to understand."

"What is that?" they chime together.

"T.C is the reason why I got shot. He put a contract out on Pop, and I was just fortunate to peek it."

"Are you serious?" inquired Khalil hardening his eyes.

"Ask our mother" he replied staring in their eyes individually. "I'll relate yawl concerns, but you must understand his anger. Pop have been trying to reach out to him since he got home but T.C got low on him. Now, he send a hit squad at him. So, now you know."

"I'm gonna call Mom" insisted Amiri.

"I hope that you do" he replied slightly grinning. He will always love their mother even though she doesn't deserve their love.

"So, who is the extra plate for?" inquired Khalil changing the subject.

"Wait and see" he replied turning and heading for the stairs. As he approached his bedroom, he heard D'Angelo's "You're My Lady" coming from the ajar door. Opening the door further, he leaned against the door frame watching her gyrating and doing a two-step while in her panties and bra. He stood there almost a minute enjoying the scene before she spotted him from the full-length mirror.

"Morning Akeem" she greeted turning slightly blushing and grabbing her white stretch jeans then sliding them on.

"Morning" he replied with a coy smile.

"Was you standing there long?' she asked putting on her shirt.

"Na, not too long" he smiled.

"I'm glad" she replied grinning. "The scent of breakfast is what woke me up."

"I'm surprise your snoring didn't wake you."

"I don't snore!" she counter.

"Ask your girls" he suggested. "Are you ready to eat?"

"Definitely" she replied grabbing her stilettoes and following him out of the room. "For future reference, if you're the last out of bed, you have to make it up" he said over his shoulder as they descended the stairs.

"I'll keep that in mind" she replied. "At least I know I can still spend the night" she replied grinning at his back as they turned the corner. "Morning fellas" she smiled over at them.

"Morning, J-Lo" they chime together returning her smile.

She paused in the family room to admire the pictures they took at the prom. She became mesmerized by their image. They really look good together. He hope that last night wouldn't change their relationship even though he assured her that it wouldn't. She had waited so long to make love to him then she make off. She didn't know what to expect but she damn sure didn't expect his dick to be so damn large. The guys that she had been allowing to get around her bases didn't possess anything like the anaconda that was swinging between his thighs. If he had a more appropriate size, she would have tried him, but she wasn't fucking with what he was slinging. How was the other girls able to handle and please him? Wasn't they scare like her when they first saw his size? She could understand why so many young ladies were vying for his attention. They wanted to experience what she wasn't ready to experience. How could they keep up their image of lovers when girls probably caught her with other guys around the city? There wouldn't be a need for other guys if they were actually lovers. This revelation seem to have caught her off-guard as she stared over at him slightly shaking her head.

After sharing laughs and breakfast, Akeem went upstairs to take his shower and get dress while Khalil and Amiri clean up. J sat at the island watching them moving methodically through their chores. They just about finish when Akeem reappeared.

"Dag, player" Khalil snicker causing everybody to stare towards the stairs. "Where are you going?"

"To mind my business" he replied wearing a blue Armani with his little gangster hat. "You ready, Ashanti?"

"Yeah" she replied admiring his attire from head to toe. There is the gangster image he portray when he wear a suit. Although still handsome as hell, there was also a revelation of a darker side of him. His eyes were exactually like his father's when she first stared into them at the hospital. Soft and intriguing but death reside there also.

Pulling away from the cub and hooking a U-turn, he asked "Are you heading home?"

"No, take me to Lisa house to pick up my car" she replied as they drove through Woodlawn and arriving sat her house ten minutes later. "I got this month's payment at my house."

"Kick it to me later" he replied.

"How much later?" she asked unfastening her seatbelt. When you say later, you won't show up until a week or two later."

"I'll try to get with you tonight" he replied.

"Okay but I only have three heads today. I will be done by two o'clock. You can come through and pick it up."

"Na, I'm not feeling that" he admitted grinning. "Those freaks in there are always disrobing me with their eyes."

"Yeah, I know" she admitted giggling while opening the door and stepping out. "I get a kick at them lusting after you" she said closing the door then walking up the path towards the front door. She didn't push the doorbell to make people aware of her presence. She walked straight inside the unlocked door without hesitating. "Lisa!"

"Up here!" she shouted back.

She climbed the steps then walked inside her bedroom and flop down on her bed.

"So, you finally lost your virginity, huh?" she teased giggling while not looking at her but closing her book. "Tell me every sordid detail" she insisted sitting up then staring over at her. "What's wrong?"

"There is nothing to share" she replied solemnly.

"Bullshit!" she waved off her comment. "Give me the 4-1-1 J."

"I punk out" she confessed.

"Punk out. Why?" she asked surprised by her statement. All she boast about was wanting to make love to him after graduating school but when the opportunity presented itself, she punk out. Why? "What happen J?"

"Girl" she stated taking a deep breath then slowly exhaling. She slightly turned her body to stare in her eyes. "Do you remember that porn guy name Mandingo?"

"Hell. yeah" she admitted smiling. "His dick look like it will rip a bitch apart" she replied giggling.

"Well, Akeem is packing like him" she shared still staring in her eyes.

"What? Are you serious?" she asked unable to contain her excitement. "So, the stories we heard are true, huh?"

191

"Yeah" she replied getting to her feet and walking over to her window then staring out. "I was too afraid to even try it."

"Girl, I would have" she replied showing her jubilation. "My shit is starting to twitch just thinking about it."

"Not cool, Lisa" she said turning and staring at her with harden eyes. "How would you like it if I said something like that about Cross?"

"Shit, if Cross dick was the size of Akeem. I would offer you a try" she said giggling

"Where is my keys?"

"Aahhh, J. I'm just fooling with you" she said seeing the anger in her eyes.

"Where is my keys, Lisa?" she reiterated with her eyes still harden.

"On the dresser" she replied watching her grabbing her keys and understanding that she had jump over boundaries with her Illicit statement. "I'm sorry J."

"Apology not accepted" she said walking out the room and descending the steps. She open the front door and damn near rip it from its frame slamming it shut. She climbed in her car then readjusted her seat and mirrors. She changed the CD to some soothing jazz then place her car in gear. She press on the accelerator spinning her wheels as she pulled away from the curb. She instinctively drove home. She didn't remember anything about the ride home. She knew that Lisa wouldn't fuck Akeem but just her saying that she would infuriated her. Saying it wasn't cool. She didn't know if she over reacted or what, but she didn't care. She had told her repeatedly to have her brain in gear before her mouth get to running. Once shit left it, you can't snatch it back. One of many lessons she have learned from Akeem.

She had more than enough time to take a shower and get dress for her eleven o'clock appointment. As she stared at her image in the full-length mirror, she realized that eyes were still slightly hard. "Fuck it" she heard herself whisper and hearing herself using profanity caused her to lightly snicker. As she climbed back into her car, she knew she needed to get her emotions under control. Was she mad at Lisa because she confess that she would have tried him while she admitted to being a straight up punk? She was lucky to spot a parking spot across Reistertown Road on Rogers. She hooked a U-turn then swung into the vacant spot. After securing her car, she turned the corner and walked inside the salon.

"Hey, are you alright?" inquired Honey because she was used to seeing her radiant smile when she came in.

"Yes, ma'am" she replied walking towards her work station and taking a seat. "I just got some stuff on my mind."

"Well, hurry up and work it out" she said smiled over at her. "We have been waiting all morning to laugh."

"Yes, ma'am" she replied smiling back at her. Being the youngest in the shop, she never intended to reveal her problem to them and definitely wasn't going to elaborate on them either. As with most women, they are going to naturally assume that Akeem is causing this distress and they would be so wrong. How can she tell them that she ran away from a good piece of dick like a little girl? How could she explain it to them after them thinking that they were already lovers? How? She couldn't.

Three weeks later, Akeem was jumping up on 95 heading South. The navigational system said he was about twenty miles from his destination as he press on the accelerator. He took the Scaggsville exit wearing an impish smile. Is he going to where all the scags live? As he followed the instructions, he couldn't ignore the massive expensive houses separated by at least two football fields. Pulling up on the parking pad, there were numerous of expensive cars with names he didn't recognize and those that he did recognize were the top brand like the Genesis 90. He found a parking spot next to a lip-stick red Porsche with Michigan tags. As he casually strolled pass the cars admiring them and the out of state tags, he spotted Chubby's GMC. He press the doorbell then waited. He could hear the faint sounds of music. Who live here? Seconds later, the front door swung open.

"Akeem, welcome godson" Chubby greeted him tapping his knuckles.

"What's up Chubby?" he asked as he step aside to allow him to enter.

"Have any problem finding the place?"

"Na, I just followed the instructions. I don't know how yawl got around back in the day."

"Maps to get there then get with people" he replied smiling. "Right this way" he said. As they walked through, he spotted a massive portrait of him and his family. Amiri wasn't even one years old. His mother didn't look like the woman she is today. She was actually extremely attractive. Hearing The Temptations singing "I Wish It Would Rain" caught his attention, he remember as a child his father constantly singing their tunes with heart felt emotions. "Man, you look so much like your father it's funny" he lightly chuckled as they enter the family room. A portrait of his father and his crew filled the wall. Chubby was easily a hundred and fifty pounds lighter but staring at his father, he thought he was staring at his twin. Walking through the French doors onto lime color stones that comprise the massive patio, his father was sitting at an over-sized table with six immaculately dress gentlemen with moderate, but extremely expensive jewelry like Cartier Maillon Panthere and Iced out Rolex watches. Call these gentlemen Rocky. The women they were escorting were gorgeous as they sat around the pool about twenty yards away.

"Hey son!" he called snatching his eyes off the women.

"Hey, Pop's" he replied wearing an impish grin while exchanging hugs. "Haven't seen you since our last conversation."

"Your brothers had some powerful words that I had to consider" he replied slightly grinning. "Looking good" he replied adjusting his tie.

"Thanks, Pop" replied smiling.

"Do you recognize anyone?" he asked placing his arm around his shoulder and smiling over at them.

"Yeah, I remember them vaguely" he replied slightly smiling while studying their faces closely. "I remember him especially" he said staring at a mocha complexion guy. "He told me to get money from the ladies that wanted to kiss me" he shared smiling at him. "His name is Big Money."

"Kick that shit out!" he demanded laughing as they kicked out a hundred dollars each except his father.

"You was even corrupting him at six years of age. Damn, Money."

"Can you image what we could have done if he was back in the day with his father" he asked causing them to burst out laughing.

"They were already shitting themselves with one of him. If we had two, I dare to imagine what we could have accomplish."

"That's why Killa made me his godfather and not yawl corrupting ass Detroit" Chubby reminded him shaking his head at them. "So, where are you going to school?"

"I'm going to Morehouse."

"Morehouse? They don't have a basketball program."

"I'm not going there on a basketball scholarship" he informed him slightly smiling. "I acquired a full academic scholarship."

"Academic scholarship?"

"Yes, Chubby" he replied smiling over at him. "I'm going to study micro-engineering."

"A lot of coaches are going to be surprised by your decision" he said surprised as hell over his decision.

"I hope that they are" he replied. "They are paying for me to attend a basketball camp out in Cali to see if I have really healed and I'm going to accept their two-week vacation. Afterward, they can kiss my butt" he said with conviction in his eyes although his voice didn't display it.

"What brought about this change?"

"They took their scholarships off the table and now they are sniffing around trying to amend what they initiated. I'm not built like that. Hypocrites have to keep their distance from me."

"But you are back and even better than before" he replied.

"Yeah, I know" he replied smiling. "Instead of them pimping my talent, I'm flipping the script. I'm using my intellect instead of my ability. I'm going to show my butt when I get there so that they can witness why they call me the quiet assassin" he slightly snarled.

"Look!" Money insisted laughing. "He got the same stare when he's going to tare shit up" he continued to laugh.

"You know most charts have you as the best shooting forward coming out of high school in America."

"According to who?" he replied with a smirk.

"Academic scholarship?"

"Yeah, Pop's" he replied grinning.

"Your father is the geekish guy I have ever met" an OG shared causing them to burst out laughing again.

"No doubt about that" two more OG's cosigned laughing.

"Pop's, can I speak freely around your family?"

"Always son" he replied returning his stare.

"Why don't you seek restitution from T.C. he's not worthless as you claim. He has a multi-million-dollar enterprise."

"An enterprise that you initiated from what I gather making my rounds."

"Yes, sir" he replied. "So, he will pay your price to keep breathing. You must also take into consideration that I put myself in harms' way, alright?"

"I'll consider it."

"I can't ask for anything more" he said. "I got to go but gentlemen, I hope seeing yawl won't be as long."

"It won't" they assured him.

"I'll walk him out Chubby" he said getting to his feet then leading him back to the front door. "You know you and your brothers mean the world to me."

"Prove it" he replied returning his stare then giving him a hug before heading back to his car. He climbed inside then gently pulled away. He saw his father watching him until he disappeared over a slight decline.

Akeem was on a flight to Cali the following week. He haven't seen nor heard from J since dropping her off at Lisa's house. The money he keep neglecting to pick up from the salon shop will be there when he return. He could only smile thinking about what she was thinking. No form of communication must have her wondering if he really cut her off. A light chuckle escaped him feeling the plane starting to descend. As the plane touched down at Santa Monica Airport, he grabbed his bag from in the over-head compartment then joined the others leaving the plane. Gathering his suit case, he spotted a white guy holding a sign welcoming them to the NCAA minicamp. He directed him to a bus that will take him and the other players to UCLA. As the bus climbed the ramp to Rt.10 then transfer over to the 405, he spotted the signs to Long Beach and Compton. Two places he had all intentions of visiting. As the bus maneuver through the streets, he spotted UCLA in the distance. He thought about the many legendary players that once attended the university. Driving on the campus, his head was constantly on a swivel admiring the sway in the hips of the California ladies. Pulling up in front of the dorms that they will be spending the next two weeks, he got off the bus with the other players and grabbed his suitcase then followed one of the assistant coaches inside the dorm. He was bunking with a six-ten red hair white boy from Indiana. Coming out the gate, he let it be known that he wasn't like Larry Bird. He didn't let it be known in front of the coach, but as soon as he left, he made it clear that he wasn't happy bunking with a black player. Instead of Akeem whipping his ass, he was going to make him is special assignment. The first practice was tomorrow at eight o'clock with a second practice at four o'clock.

Six-thirty the next morning, a light knocking at the door indicated it was time to get up, take your shower then go to the cafeteria to eat breakfast or you could lay in your bed until seven-thirty then walking over to the gym. There was a total of a hundred players that were invited. For the first three days, they tested your endurance and strength while doing suicides full court. Reds, as he started calling his roommate on the first day wasn't just out of shape and weak, he was just plain lazy. Guys six-nine had a better vertigo than he possess. A waste of good height.

From the moment they initiated scrimmage, he introduce them to ATM. He was making withdrawal out of every defender that they put on him. If his defenders were taller, he would use his speed against them. If they were his height, he love coming from the opposite side and posting the person up then busting their asses with various inside moves. Utilizing his six-foot ten center, you would have thought that they had played together for years. He just was in tune with the guy from North Carolina. His unselfish play got the admiration of his teammates. Even with the coaches insisting that he shoot more, he never waver from his game. After the first week, everybody was calling him ATM including his coaches.

"ATM, where are you from man?"

"Baltimore" he replied as they sat on the bleachers watching a second team take the court. "You're from Carolina, right Big Mack?"

"Yeah" he replied taking a big gulp from his Gator Aide. "Man, you have these coaches salivating over you" he snicker. "Me and a couple of the fellas are hanging out tonight. You want to hang?"

"Sure, I'm down" he replied.

"Man, how did you perfect that bank shot?"

"Repetition, that's all, Big Mack."

"If you keep feeding me the ball as you're doing, my stock to going to go up" he smiled at him. "I'm hoping to make it to Chapel Hill" he shared.

"If I have anything to do with it, you will make it" he told him returning his stare.

"The coaches are giving you the green light. How come you don't shoot more?"

"This thing isn't about them or what they want brother. They can honestly kiss my ass" he informed him. The expression that came to his face caused Akeem to burst out laughing. "I'm here to help others not myself."

"What?"

"If everybody play for number one, they are playing selfishly, and I honestly don't want any part of that mentality. I need the game to remain fun. So, I'm going to make it fun for every squad they put me on."

"Cuz, you are rare find" he complimented shaking his head smiling.

"Yeah, I know" he replied grinning. "Can I ask you something?"

"Sure, what is it?"

"Suppose and I use the word suppose" he repeated still grinning. "That Carolina don't give you the nod, do you have a second choice?"

"Actually, yeah" he replied smiling. "I'm starting to feel Louisville and N.C State."

"Then consider them, man. Why put unnecessary stress on yourself when the dream is play college ball. You feel me?"

"Yeah, man. I feel you" he replied smiling like the weight of the world was suddenly lifted off his shoulder. "If you ever get to Carolina, you have to look me up."

"Southern hospitality, huh?" he smiled at him. "Kick me your number and address."

"You will stay in touch?"

"Yeah, man. Definitely" he replied tapping his knuckles.

"What's up with you and Reds?"

"He showed his racist hand the first day and I became his personal nightmare" he replied snarling at him as his lazy ass tried to hustle back on defense. He had slammed in his face so many times during practice that the image that the coaches thought he had was a mirage. His stock fell like a crack head trying to sell her pussy. Coaches were reconsidering their previous offers while those that never heard of Akeem "ATM" Anderson were in awe of him. He had them salivating at the possibility of acquiring him to join their program. He could easily score twenty points a game not even trying while making those around him better.

The last two days consisted of talking to prospective coaches. Every coach that had taken back their scholarship offer when he was shot over a year and a half ago was now trying to suck his dick without a condom. The bullshit reasons that materialized in their mind and filter out of their mouths should have been thought thoroughly through especially while displaying their three-dollar smiles. He didn't commit to none of them. He was standing outside of the bus with other players that he became acquainted when Reds approached. He had ostracized himself because of his racist antics that even his peers gave him distance. He tried to connect with several of them, but he was like the black plague. As he started to climb aboard the bus, he paused to say something to Akeem, but nothing came out and everybody burst out laughing as he climbed aboard the bus.

Landing at Thurgood Marshall International around one o'clock, there was no place like home.

"Taxi, young man?"

"No, thank you" he said heading for the trolley. Minutes later, he was taking a seat in the back and enjoying the scenery heading back into the city. He exit near Lexington Market then walked to Saratoga Street to catch a hack. Fifteen minutes later, he was arriving at his house and gathering his bags then headed towards the house. Ignoring his neighbors as he usually did, he inserted his key and unlocked the door then walked inside. He went straight up the stairs to discard his dirty clothes in the hamster and took a quick shower then got dress in a brown casual walking set with a matching hat and shoes. He went back down stairs and drop his bills on the table in the family room as he went to the kitchen to get a couple pieces of fruit then returned to the family room. He was sorting through the mail when he notice a letter from Sunshine. He started to read it but decided against it. He wanted to be relaxed when he read her words. As he got to his feet, he grabbed his keys and headed out the front door.

Walking through the salon door, a hush filled the place forcing J to stare into the mirror. A broad smile came to her face as she turned around. "How was California? She asked walking over and getting a light kiss from him.

"Hot" replied exchanging smiles.

"When did you get back in town?"

"A little over an hour ago."

"And you made this your first stop?"

"Yeah, for my money" he replied grinning at her expression.

"Funny" she replied poking him in his ribs. "I got it right here" she informed him turning and grabbing an envelope out of her cross-body bag then extending it to him. "So, what are your plans?"

"Taking you out" he replied. "What time do you get off?"

"Now" she replied smiling up at him and pulling out her cell phone.

"What are you getting ready to do?"

"Cancelling my three o'clock appointment" she shared peeking over at him.

"Na, slow your roll young lady" he told her. "You have a previous obligation, and you shouldn't cancel especially when it come to a woman's hair."

"I can get with her tomorrow morning Akeem" she counter.

"Yeah, if God bless you" he replied staring down into her eyes.

"Okay, Akeem" she replied signing.

"I'll holla at you later" he told her. "Ladies" he replied tipping his hat.

"Bye Akeem" they chimed together watching him turning then burst out laughing as he walked out.

He climbed back into his car then headed for the city. As he approached Penn-North, he spotted his brothers exiting the speedline. He blew his horn to get their attention then pulled over.

"Hey, big brother" they greeted as Khalil got in the front seat then tapping his knuckles before fastening his seatbelt.

"What's up fellas?" he asked watching Amiri getting in the back seat. "I see yawl kept the house clean."

"Nobody want you jumping down their throat" replied Amiri.

"How was Cali?" inquired Khalil.

"As cool as the other side of the pillow" he replied pulling away from the curb.

"I know you showed your butt because Sports Center revealed it" shared Amiri giggling. "Have you decided which college you are going to attend?"

"I knew which college before I took their free vacation" he shared grinning at them. "I'm going down to Atlanta to attend Morehouse."

"Morehouse? I never heard of it" admitted Amiri.

"A prominent black university with a high academic demand, Amiri" replied Khalil. "Having a prominent female college right next door is a motivating factor."

"An all-girl college?"

"Yeah, Amiri. Spelman" he smiled over at him.

"Dag, I wanted to see you on television" Amiri shared his disappointment.

"Not in my cards, little brother" he told him peeking in the reaview mirror.

"It can be if you want it to be."

"True but would I be happy" he replied pulling up in their old court yard and climbing out. "Why are yawl coming down here?"

"To see uncle T.C" revealed Khalil.

"T.C?" he replied stopping in his tracks.

"Yeah, are you coming up?"

"I wasn't initially and damn sure not going up now" he replied slightly snarling.

"Alright, we won't be long" he told him as he and Amiri continued towards the building.

So, he reappeared from the whole he was hiding inside. He took a seat on the bench staring up to the nineth floor. He watched them open their mother's door then step inside and closed the door. Rumor has it that his father knew exactually where to find him. A shun girl peeked him at a farmer's market and followed his car to his location then made the call to put him on blast. The five G's she received could have been a motivating factor, but a woman scorn can be a motherfucker. When he heard that they knew where he was from his sister and how long they knew blew his mind. Not knowing when he have witness his last sun rise or rising moon could be a more psychologically frightening than any form of physical abuse. When he finish with his cat and mouse game, Killa had an incredibly attractive young lady from the streets of Baltimore to knock on his door one evening. Peeking in his peep hole, he couldn't ignore the white micro-mini that she wearing and eagerly foolishly open the door. Expecting to see her, he instead stared up into Killa's menacing eyes. He damn near fell backward as Killa and two of his old street soldiers walked in and closed the door. He could only imagine how he was looking when he saw his father face. He agreed to spare his life with a heathy restitution fee, and he happily agreed to pay it. How much was unknown.

"Hey, stranger" a voice interrupted his thoughts.

"Damn" he smiled getting to his feet. "How are you, Sunshine?" he asked kissing lightly on the lips while staring in her grayish eyes.

"Why can't you keep in touch with a sister?"

"I've been extremely busy."

"Too busy to get with this?" she asked profiling.

"As inviting as you are, I honestly was Sunshine" he replied admiring her hour glass body.

"Apparently" she replied staring up at him. "What are you plans for later?"

"I'm supposed to be taking J out to an early dinner" he shared.

"Oh, she's not going to let you get out of her arms" she replied smiling while trying to hide her rejection.

"We aren't on that type of time. How many times do I have to say this to you, baby?"

"I know, my love but things can change Akeem."

"Yes, they can but not between her and I, Ayanna. Her and I will always be friends baby but I'm not what she desire in her life."

"Yeah, right" she waved off his suggestion smiling. "What woman would want you?"

"Not everybody is interested in me or even desiring me" he replied lightly chuckling.

"Bullshit! I see full grown women disrobing you with their eyes. Oh, you are definitely desirable."

"I appreciate your confidence" he replied snickering as she poke him in the ribs smiling up at him. "How about this proposition?"

"I'm listening."

"If I'm not being distracted, I'll hit you up at nine tonight."

"Hit me up even if you are being distracted so I can say goodnight."

"You got that but I'm hoping to say good morning to you instead of goodnight" he replied smiling down on her.

"Now, that is what I want to hear" she replied smiling then pulling him down for a light kiss. "I have to go and catch up with my girls."

"Alright, I'll holla at you later" he replied admiring her very natural but provocative walk. As they piled into her car and turned the corner, he focus his attention back at his mother's front door. The front door suddenly open and they appeared with their uncle. He wave down to him, but he didn't return his greeting. Just because he told their father to choose them over him didn't mean they would be on good grace. He is still the guy that tried to assassinate his father and exploited him with him mother as a child. He said something to Khalil before going back into the house. They looked down at him then proceeded towards the elevators. Coming out the front entrance, they were trying to decide which one should deliver the message that was being sent, but he would handle it for them. "Whatever message he asked yawl to deliver keep it" he told then hardening his eyes. "Jump in, let's go home.

Killa have been doing a lot of reflecting in the past month. With Akeem getting ready to attend college and Khalil and Amiri in high school, he needed to know what he was going to do with his life. No longer did he have the desire nor stomach to regress back to his previous profession. In order for him to be the man and father that his sons deserve, he need to flip is script or image. Manual labor wasn't happening and sitting under a boss wasn't very promising either. They might say something that might result in a computer key board slapping them in the face. In order for him to progress, he would have to leave certain elements of his past behind like Dick and Harry. They have been a part of his attire since he was sixteen years old. In order for him to see the possibilities of tomorrow, he has to think for tomorrow.

"What's on your mind, man?" Chubby asked staring over at his closest friend.

"My future" he replied solemnly.

"Your future" he replied snickering. "Man, with all the money you have acuminated since coming home, you don't have to do a got damn thing. What you should be deciding is which of these beautiful bitches you are taking home tonight."

"I have all night to contemplate that" he replied watching a mocha complexion woman walking pass in a black bikini. The diamond naval ring attached to defined abs, small doe like eyes and radiant smile made her one of the most attractive women at their exclusive splash party. "I'm thinking about attending Morgan State."

"Morgan State?" he repeated staring over at him. "I know you might be bored but attending college isn't going to satisfy you. I don't see you taking orders from some punk ass white boy" he slightly snarled. "Consider being your own boss. Open your won spot."

"Own my own business, huh?" the thought intrigued him. "Now, that isn't a bad ideal" he slightly smiled as he thought about it more and it wasn't a bad ideal. "Do you still have your connection at the liquor board?"

"Yeah, of course" he replied studying him closely.

"If I am going to open a business, it has to be one that I won't get bored with" he said returning his stare.

"What are you suggesting?"

"A jazz spot" he replied with enthusiasm. "All I got to do is locate a suitable location. I got a hook-up in the Health department to acquire a license to serve food" he shared staring over at slightly smiling at his vision. "My own business. Mmmm, I like the way that sounds."

"I don't know if you did the right thing giving T.C a pass but it does reveal one thing about you?" he said with a coy smile.

"And what is that?"

"You have mellow" he replied grinning.

"I'm still debating that" he replied. "Just because I gave T.C a pass doesn't mean I won't reach out and touch his scandalous ass in a couple months" he replied snarling.

"Remember man, he tried to kill you."

"Never."

"I thought that you might have."

"Never" he reiterated returning his stare.

"Now, that's the man I know" he laugh lifting his glass to him. Before his incarceration, he would have blown T.C scandalous soul out of his body and smile while doing it. The pending compensation wouldn't mean shit to him. Witnessing his brain particle exiting the back of his cranium would only suffice him. His sons pleas is what prevented him from being the killer that he choose to be not some form of sympathy. His killer instinct might be lying dormant, but the slightest form of disrespect will shake him awoke and it won't be easy putting him back to sleep. "So, when will you start your search?"

"Monday morning. I see what they have out there."

"Good that is Monday. Now get your mind back on these beautiful women" he suggested watching two honey complexions women walking pass in matching white tongs bikinis. "Two for the price of one" he smiled lifting his glass as they walked pass giggled at them like school girls.

Being one of the top recruits coming from out of the state of Maryland, everybody especially the sports reports was wondering where he would be attending school. Sports announcers especially on Sports Center were giving their opinion which university would be right for his style of play. When he heard enough of their speculations, he gave the sports reporter at the Sun Papers an exclusive interview up at Chadwick. When the story broke the following morning, every college scout was in shock. He showed the reporter all of the rescinded offers from the colleges and universities after being shot multiple times. He informed him that their selfish act revealed just how malice a coach can be when you can't provide them with what they wanted and need. The incident turned him completely off concerning playing college basketball. Turning pro after college was a possibility but it wasn't in his cards right now no matter what a sports announcer, sports writer or sport agent may suggest. He only went to Cali to show them what they could have possess for four years not what they could get. He took the two-week audition as a form of vacation. He intend to attend Morehouse this coming September on an academic scholarship. The revelation shook the athletic world.

At five o'clock, Akeem was pulling up in front of the salon. J was standing on the sidewalk patiently waiting on him. Her smile came to her face seeing hm as she walked over to the passenger window and told him to follow her home so she can park her car then ride with him. They pulled up in front of her house then she transferred to his car, and they retrace their previous route to Reistertown Road.

"Where are we going to eat?"

"A Caribbean spot I know down by the Inner Harbor" he replied watching her taking off her saddles and wiggling her toes.

"I heard over the news that you are going to attend Morehouse" she stated peeking over at him.

"That information got out that fast" he replied surprise that it did.

"95.9 put it out" she informed him. "Why did you go to the basketball camp?"

"Have you ever been to Cali?" he asked turning on Coldspring Lane.

"No."

"Neither have I" he replied smiling. "So, I took the free ticket and room and board then showed them what they weren't going to get" he told her as they jump on 83S.

"Your mind was already made up before you went?"

"Yup" he replied moving in the fourth lane and pressing on the accelerator. He maneuver through the traffic and was exiting a few minutes later. Once down town, he had to watch out for the dumb ass shit that tourist do as he neared Federal Hill. He eventually found a parking spot then they climbed out the car and clutch fingers as they cross the street. He was glad that there wasn't a line outside. As they enter the establishment, Caribbean music filled the air. Obtaining a table over-looking the dirty water of the Chesapeake, they settle in and gave their orders to the dread loc wearing young lady.

"Exactly where is Morehouse?"

"In Atlanta" he replied studying her eyes.

"In Atlanta, why?" she asked staring in his eyes and revealing her emotions. "You can stay in Baltimore or go down to D.C to play for Georgetown."

"True but an opportunity like this doesn't happen every day, Ashanti."

"Yeah, I know" she sigh. "What about us?"

"We will stay in touch. I promise" he said using the word vaguely.

The waitress bringing their food caused them to pause their conversation. He peeked over at her and seen the disappointment on her face. When they exchanged stares, there appeared to be pain.

"What's wrong?"

"Things are going to change" she said shoving some cabbage into her mouth.

"I hope it change for the better."

"I don't know Akeem" she stated returning his stare. "Don't they have an all-girl college down there also?"

"Yeah, Spelman" he said crewing on some goat.

"Somebody is going to snatch you up, Akeem" she replied sharing her fear.

"Somebody can grab my attention here on the streets of Baltimore" he informed her.

"You know what I mean."

"Predominately all the scholarships that I was offer would have taken me out of Baltimore."

"Take Georgetown offer."

"They don't have my academic."

"Pick another" she insisted.

"Ashanti, you are making this thing about you baby but it's not" he said staring in her eyes. "If we were romantically involved, I would have consider Coach Thompson and Coach Shaka at VCU offers, but we aren't baby and I'm kind of glad we aren't now. I would hate for you to think I played you for your virginity. My main concern was on my brothers and assuring that they will follow my instructions. None of their close friends have ever convince them to do dumb shit in the streets. So, I gave them an option. Follow my instructions or go home to live with our mother. Although we might want to think that we are ready for a relationship, we aren't. There are so much of life we both have to experience and you dating other guys reveals that you know what I'm saying is true, Ashanti."

"Let's have a romantic relationship" she suggested.

"Now, you are being desperate and I'm not feeling that" he said slightly hardening his eyes. "You are ready to surrender your virginity to keep me in town and I'm supposed to accept it, huh?" he asked staring in her eyes, but no response came from her. "Not cool, Ashanti."

"I know" she replied softly. "You are right, Akeem. This isn't about me" she admitted lifting her eyes to his. "I know you would have consider your choice if we made love back in June, but we didn't, and I can't blame anyone but myself" she said revealing watery eyes, but no tears escape them. "I honestly didn't think about this day coming even though I knew it would. You are right about me thinking that you played me if I had surrender my virginity to you. I would have been devastated by your decision."

"Yeah, I know Ashanti" he slightly smiled at her, but she wasn't smiling back. "I don't know what the future will hold for us, but I hope our friendship can endure it. You think you are the only person with hidden fears. Well, I have mines also. Without even looking, you could stumble upon somebody that really perk your interest."

"The same could be said about you" she counter.

"You're funny" he replied lightly snickering. "Yawl are the emotional being not us. We can be sailors of love but not yawl. There have to be some form of emotional attachment for a guy to get anywhere near your most prize possession no matter how much he begs like Keith Sweat or Barry White. Men don't play by the same rules of engagement. We will hit and run like it was nothing" he smiled at her.

"Yes, yawl will" she cosigned.

"Students at Morehouse and Spelman are basically old Southern money with strict traditions. I don't have the resources or traditions" he said smiling. "If we knew what the future hold for us Ashanti, life wouldn't be complicated, and all mystery would be eliminated. Who would desire that?"

"Not me" she admitted. "I don't want to lose what we have Akeem."

"As long as we keep our love for one another in our hearts, we will get through this" he tried to assured her.

"I wish I was as sure as you are" she admitted.

"You don't have to Ashanti. I am" he smiled. "As long as we stay open and honest, no amount of distance can impede our friendship. Let me share something that my father shared with me. Never fear what you are leaving because what you could find could be so much better" he quoted. "We all must leave the comfort of our nests to spread our wings. If we are afraid to take that initial step, we can become prisoner in our own created pandora boxes, understand?"

"Yeah" she replied hearing those same words filtering through her parents lips. "So, when are you leaving?"

"The last week in August."

"That's only two weeks away" she replied. "Are you driving down?"

"Oh, yeah. I damn sure not going to tempt Khalil leaving my ride" he smiled.

"I hope we can get together before you leave."

"Me too. You are the one with the busy schedule" he reminded her off all the time she have cancel on him.

"I'll clear it for you" she said. "I want you to do something with me" she said with an impish grin.

"I don't know if I like that smile or not, but it's definitely intriguing" he admitted smiling.

"You will" she replied still smiling. "How does that goat taste?"

"You tell me" he said putting a piece on his fork then serving her.

"Mmmm, taste like beef" she compared.

They finish their meal then went to the cash register to pay their bill. They step back out-side retracing their route to the car.

"Let's climb Federal Hill" she suggested as they cross the street then proceeded up the hill. They found a bench over-looing the Harbor and the white people playing volleyball. She reached inside her cross-body bag then retrieved a blunt. "Will you smoke this with me?" she asked apprehensively.

"When did you start smoking weed?"

"About three months ago" she admitted returning his stare. "Will you smoke this with me?"

"Girl, peer pressure is a motherfucker" he slightly smiled at her.

"I would like to be the first with something with you."

"There are so many other first you can be, Ashanti" he counter.

"Will you smoke with me or not?" she asked ignoring his statement.

"Reluctantly, yeah."

She lit it up then pass it to him while reaching inside her purse for some tissues. With an impish smile on her face, she watched his virgin lungs pulled deeply from the blunt then held the smoke inside. Seconds later, he was coughing and gaging while accepting the tissues from her. While still trying to obtain some oxygen, all he could hear was her laughter. By the time he regained some control, his eyes were reddish and with his Asiatic type eyes appeared even smaller.

"Damn, Ashanti" he said passing the blunt back to her. "That almost sever my head" he described causing to continue ton giggle while hitting the blunt.

"True but how do you feel?"

"Nice" he admitted seeing the world through inhibited eyes.

"Good" she replied smiling and extending it back to him. "Take it easy this time."

"You should have advised me initially" he said accept it and pulling from it again then resulting in the same effects.

By the time the blunt was gone, he was floating on Cloud 9. The ride back to her house a slow and deliberate. He wasn't in any hurry. This was the first time in his life that he ever mess with any sort of drug, but he couldn't shake the feeling that it wouldn't be the last he smoke weed. Although he still held on to his perception of alcohol, but his perspective of marijuana have now been permanently alter.

The last weekend of the month came upon him quicker than he anticipated. He took his brothers over to their house Saturday afternoon and told them he will be pick them up on Sunday. That night, he invited all of his friends over with their dates, He informed Ashanti that Sunshine will be his guest and she brought one of the guys that he had seen her with previously. They party until almost four o'clock in the morning. Tapping his partners knuckles and hugging their dates, he and Sunshine watched them from the porch as they eventually pulled off then they went back inside to clean up. It was almost five o'clock when they finish taking their shower and crawling in between the sheets, sounds of erotic bliss consumed their ears throughout the night. They never closed their eyes just talked and shared their eternal love for one another. He drove her home clutching fingers around eleven o'clock. His brothers were waiting in the court yard for him. They hugged Sunshine as she climbed out the car leaving the front door open for Khalil.

"I have a stop to make before we go home" he informed them jumping on MLK then connecting to 395 and transferring to 95S. Taking Scaggsville, he was pulling up in front of their father's house.

"Who live here?" inquired Khalil unfastening his seatbelt and climbing out.

"Pop's" he replied.

"Pop" they chimed together.

"Yup."

"This is humongous" described Amiri walking up to the front door then pushing the doorbell. Second later, the door swung open.

"Hi, fellas" a deep mocha complexion smiled at them. "I'm Chubby sister Monica" she introduced herself. She had the most intriguing eyes and beautiful smile.

"Glad to meet you" they chime together admiring and smiling at the one-piece form fitting dress that accentuated her anatomy.

"Come on in, your father will be pleasantly surprised to see yawl" she said stepping aside to allow them to enter. She led them through the house, and Khalil and Amiri slightly paused to stare at the portrait of them with their parents. His father was sitting outside with several of his close friends. "Honey" she called.

Turning and seeing his boys, a broad smile engulfed his face as he git to his feet and hugged them individually. "Damn, it's good seeing yawl" she smiled down on them.

"You home is hook, Pop" complimented Khalil staring out towards the two gazebos.

"Thanks, son" he replied. "Make yawl selves at home, I need to talk to your brother" he informed him. "Follow me, Akeem" he said leading him back inside and walking into his study then opening a door and retrieving an over-sized briefcase. "This is for you" he told him placing it on his desk.

He opened it and stared at what was inside like it was a snake as his eyes became large. "How much is this Pop?"

"Two and a half million dollars" he replied.

"What is this for?"

"Restitution from you junky ass Uncle" he replied. "He's lucky I'm leaving his money that's on the streets alone. I came pass last night but all the laughter had me retrace my steps" he revealed smiling.

"Yeah, we got it in until early this morning" he shared smiling.

"So, you are leaving in the morning?"

"Initially" he replied closing the briefcase back up. "I'll be bouncing after I make this deposit. I know this might be a dumb question. but do you need anything?"

"Na, the settlement from my incarceration was almost twelve million" he revealed smiling. "I have a million-dollar account set up for your brothers, they don't know it yet" he shared smiling at him. "Are yawl staying?"

"I couldn't drag them away even if I wanted to" he replied smiling.

He was sitting in front of the Harbor Bank at nine o'clock in the morning. When the door swung open, he was one of the first clients to walk through the door. After depositing the money, he was climbing the ramp to 95S. He had everything that he needed including his new girlfriend, Mary Jane. The trip should take eleven hours and be very memorable as he cruised in the fourth lane. Reaching Virginia, he transfer to I-85. He have never witness so many cows, horses, wooden barns, and houses in his life. He stared out at people in the fields etching out a living. Arriving in Atlanta a little after eight o'clock that night, he found a hotel to sleep in for the night.

The morning sun had been up for hours by the time he open his eyes. Staring at his watch, he couldn't believe it was almost ten-thirty. He swung his feet to the floor then stretch before getting up. He was in and out the shower in five minutes. Ten minutes later, he was grabbing his keys and checking out. His navigational system took his pass Clark University and Spelman's Museum of Arts to Westview Drive NW. With assistance from several students, he located the admission office and obtained his dorm. He knew when he first walked inside that he wasn't going to stay long. The room was much too small. His roommate Dog was from Texas only assured him of his brief stay. Listening to the whining stories of country music, he made preparation for his immediate departure. They had nothing in common. I mean nothing. From politics to social issues plaguing America, they couldn't see eye to eye. Just because you say you are black don't necessary men you are black especially if your ideologies are more in tune to Caucasians. After the first semester ended, he was making his departure for a two-bedroom at the Ashley Apartment he had acquired off of Joseph and Lowery Boulevard. He left three out-fits at his dorm just in case he was hanging out late and didn't feel like driving home.

During his second year, communication with Ashanti had diminish tremendously. With her business at the hair salon booming and her social life, she was terribly busy. He would make his appearance during Kwanzaa and on his brothers birthdays. They would reconnect but once back in Atlanta, their line of communication ceased again. He never took it personal. He was leaving his apartment to go to the laundry mat when he spotted a young lady standing in from of her brown Mercedes GT looking disgusted.

"Is everything alright?" he asked surprising her.

"Oh, shit. You startle me" she replied flashing her beautiful smiling. Her chocolate complexion was smooth and absent of make-up except lip gloss. Her eyes were slightly tilted with medium lips. "I'm constantly riding over nails and glass" she informed him staring at her flat tire.

"Do you have a spare?" he asked placing his dirty clothes down on the ground.

"Yes, but I don't want you to get your clothes dirty."

"I appreciate the concern, but what type of guy would I be not to assist you?"

"Like those guys sitting over there on the bench" she slightly snarled at them.

"Sorry to disappoint you, young lady" he replied grinning. "Let me get my car so I can use my jack."

"I have a jack" she mention.

"I'm sure you do but it's manufactory issued, right?"

"Yes."

"I have one much faster" he assured her. "I'll be right back" he said lifting his bag then walking around the building. He returned less than a minute later then pulled out his hydraulic jack. In less than five minutes, with a minimum of transfer grease and dirt, he was finish and placing her flat in the trunk of her car. "Leave the screw in it so the mechanic know exactually where the hole is located."

"Thank you."

"My pleasure" he replied placing his jack back in his trunk then turning and climbing in his car.

Peep! Peep!

He looked around seeing here lowering her passenger window. "Yes, ma'am."

"I'm Cola. What is your name?"

"Akeem."

"Glad to meet you" she slightly smiled.

"Na, the pleasure is mine" he replied placing his car in gear and pulling off. He was in and out of the laundry mat in an hour and on his way back to his apartment. He spent the next couple of hours pressing off his shirt while preparing dinner his later. He was sitting out on the balcony drinking a glass of Moscato while smoking a blunt. His collection of music have been taken over by jazz including Afro-Cuban jazz. He didn't understand their language, but he knew is when motherfuckers were jamming, and they left no doubt to him that they were definitely jamming. He was sitting out there a good three hours when he spotted Cola car returning. He watch her climb out with two young ladies and a guy. She never looked up or she would have spotted him. It was about eight-thirty when he got the urged to go out, he leap into the shower then grabbed a gray leisure set with his black Stacy Adams and matching gray semi gangster hat as Sunshine and Ashanti called them. He didn't know if he wanted to his to some jazz or get his freak on. He brought the book he has been reading called "Product of My Environment" just in case he decided to listen to some jazz. Sitting back out on the balcony, Cola's car was gone. It was a little after eleven o'clock when he was exiting I-85 towards the city, he had heard of a club alleged upscale called Harlem Nights and decided to see for himself. Driving down John Portman Boulevard NW. He turned right on Courtland Street and slowly drove pass the club while searching for a parking spot and finding a garage then pulled inside. He climbed out then descended the second floor by the stairs. He walked down the street then stood in line admiring the smorgasbord of women heading inside. He eventually walked through the scanners and walked into the foyer staring in at the massive crowd. His attire was very appropriate although a few guys wore suits. He obtain a drink from one of the three bars then lean back getting a feel for the place. With his buzz on, he requested a dance from a honey completion young lady standing almost six feet tall. They remained on the dance floor dancing with energy for a good half hour before perspiration forced them to abandon their marathon. As he was heading back to the bar to get himself another drink, an ebony complexion young lady gripped his fingers and lead him back to the dance floor. Her Southern black eye peas, cornbread eating Southern phat ass made him realized that he haven't had sex since arriving in Atlanta. She was dancing so provocative that a person would have thought that they were awfully familiar instead of strangers considering he wasn't shying away. She left no doubt in his mind that she wanted to explore what she was feeling in his pants as she stared up into his eyes smiling seductively. She slid her card into his hand as she stared into his eyes then seductively walked away. He finally made it back to the bar and order himself another drink. As he stood cooling off, he caught several guys peeking on him in a usual way. As hard as he tried to ignore them, he couldn't, and they were starting to irritate him. Just as he was about to get to his feet and step out of character, a hand tap him on the shoulder.

Turning around, he was pleasantly surprised. "Hey, Cola" he suddenly smiled easing the tension in his eyes.

"Hey, yourself" she replied smiling while walking around in front of him and taking a seat. "You appeared to be ready to initiate something."

"What's up with these guys?" he asked snarling at two guys walking pass.

"They like what they see" she teased giggling.

"Like what they see, what are you talking about?"

"You don't know about Atlanta's reputation, huh?" she asked trying to contain herself but failing miserably.

"What reputation?"

"Where are you from?" she asked with a coy smile.

"Baltimore" he replied catching a guy diverting his eyes.

"Let me buy you a drink" she replied getting the bartender's attention and placing their orders. "A lot of guys in Atlanta are down low brothers."

"What is this down low thing?"

"They are basically bi-sexual."

"No, such person" he denounced her explanation. "If you desire or want to explore another man, you ass is gay" he said with conviction in his eyes.

"You can't tell them that" she replied giggling.

"The hell if I can't" he replied causing her giggle harder.

"According to them, the love women and most of them have a woman at home. Yet, they also enjoy the company of certain men."

"Good that's crazy" he replied shaking his head. "How does these women feel about that?"

"I'm sure that they aren't happy, but what can they do?" she asked smiling at the bartender then paying for their drinks.

"They can be single" he replied giving her the obvious answer.

"Most would rather say they have a man than admit to being single" she revealed staring in his eyes.

"That's crazy and psychotic as hell" he replied looking perplex. "They rather take the chance of contracting HIV than to be safe and alone. I see why HIV have found a home here."

"Yes, we do have a severe problem here" she cosigned taking a sip from her sex on the beach then stared in his eyes. "What are you doing in Atlanta, Akeem?"

"Attending Morehouse."

"Morehouse? I'm impress. I'm attending Spelman."

"Yeah, I walk over sometimes and take in the sights" he admitted smiling.

"Yeah, and we be peeking on yawl too" she shared giggling again. "What year on you in?"

"Going into my sophomore year. I was bless with an academic scholarship."

"Academic?" she quoted staring at him closely. "You honestly don't fit the image."

"Yeah, I know" he admitted grinning at her.

"What are you studying?"

"Micro-Engineering and you?"

"Child psychology. You trying to get that money, huh?"

"Something that my family never had" he lied returning her stare.

"I know your parent are proud of your accomplishment."

"My father is on Cloud 9, but my mother could care one way or another" he shared.

"Do you know somebody at the apartment complex?"

"Na, I live there."

"You live there since when?"

"My freshman year. I saw you returning later in the day from my balcony" he revealed smiling at her.

"I live on the third floor. What floor do you live?"

"The fourth."

"You have a partner living with you?"

"I came here alone, and I live alone. I don't have no partners because I stay in my lane" he replied.

"How do you spend your time?"

"Usually sitting on my balcony reading and listening to jazz."

"Have you ever been to Café 290?"

"Often but I prefer St. James Live. I'll hit Studio 281 when I don't feel like traveling too far" he shared.

"Maybe we can hook up one evening" she suggested grinning.

"My calendar is always open."

"Do you have a girlfriend here or in Baltimore?"

"Na, girlfriends are too expensive" he casually said causing her to burst out laughing again.

"You are naturally funny" she said smiling at him.

"Do you have someone special?"

"I was engage two years ago but our private lifestyles clashes" she replied staring in his eyes deeply wondering did he catch what she was subtly saying.

"That's a shame" he replied returning her stare. "You don't think you are too young to be considering marriage?"

"Why do you think that?"

"You haven't explore or experience the things that life have to offer you yet."

"You sound like my parents."

"Sorry for the comparison but they are just looking out for you" he grinned at her. "We, meaning men, aren't mature enough to seriously consider marriage until we are at least thirty, hopefully. It take some men longer to mature while others never do."

"My father mention the same thing to me" she admitted.

"He's a man so he should know if he's going to be honest.

"You dress and sound very mature for your age?"

"My life experiences forced me to be mature faster than I wanted."

"Do you think you could be a monogamist man?" she blurted out the question never adverting her eyes.

"Definitely" he smiled trying to assure her.

"What make you think so?"

"I don't think I could be Cola I know I could be. I know what I personally like and desire in a woman's disposition. Unless yawl anatomy have changed miraculously, I could be very contempt with one woman."

"You seem to have all the right answers" she replied with a coy smile.

"Not according to the test, I had last week" he counter causing her burst out laughing again.

Before long, he forgot about the down low brothers and found himself being very attentive to the things that she sharing. It was well after two o'clock when they were suddenly interrupted.

"Damn, Cola" a light skin girl said to her while peeking over at him. "What's up with you?"

"I'm sorry Tiny" she apologized smiling over at her. "I got caught up in very enlightening conversation" she explained smiling over at him. "This is my neighbor Akeem" she introduced. "Akeem this is my girl, Tiny."

"Glad to meet you" he replied tipping his hat.

"Hi, yourself Akeem" she replied looking his up and down. "Do you have any more at home that looks like you?"

"Khalil does but he and Amiri is too young for you although Khalil is quick to say age is just a number."

"So, Khalil would be down for an older woman?"

"His adventurous butt, definitely" he admitted snickering.

"After meeting you, I sure he could be" she openly flirted.

"Stop, Tiny" Cola interjected smiling. "Can I continue my conversation please?"

"Why don't you bring him upstairs?" she suggested with a coy smile.

"Nope, I'll holla at you in a few minutes."

"Okay, selfish" she said sticking her tongue out at her. "Nice meet you Akeem."

"You, too Tiny" he smiled at her walking away. Standing barely five-feet tall, she was built like a brick house with her medium frame. Yeah, Khalil would love to try his hand on her thick Southern thighs.

"She so flirtatious" she said smiling at her as she climbed the stairs.

"That's just her personality" he replied.

For the next half hour, they returned to their private conversation. She told him about being raised in home with love and hefty expectations. Coming from old Southern money, she had a spoil and protective life with all of her childhood desires fulfilled. Yet, dating all the guys she have, she never seem to acquire what she desperately desire. A love of her own. Someone that wasn't afraid to show his tender side when they are out socializing while making her feel safe and protected. The things that she express was the same blue print he have heard since he was a juvenile. Numerous of times, women and close female friends express the same desires in their men.

"Akeem, I really have to go" she said getting to her feet. "I sincerely hope we can get together again."

"I'm in 410."

"I don't like just showing up at a person door" she mention returning his stare.

"Here" he said writing his number on a napkin then extending it to her. "Call me."

"I will and enjoy the rest of your night."

"Na, I'm up and out of here. I don't have no bail money for disassembling these alleged bi-sexual guys" he stated causing her to giggle again as she proceeded towards the stairs. He down his drink then adjusted his hat and headed towards the front door. He peeked on the two guys that had been peeking at him earlier posting up at a table by the door.

"If you give me your number, I'll call you."

Akeem stopped in his tracks. "What did you say to me?" he asked staring at both guys because he didn't know which one had said it.

"You heard me" a light skin guy about twenty-five replied smiling up at him.

"Do you know me?" he asked closing the distance between them.

"No but I'm trying to" he flirted while smiling up at him.

"Then let me introduce myself" he replied suddenly snatching him by the back of his head and slamming his face twice into the door frame. He turned the almost unconscious bloody face guy towards him and whisper into his ears, "Now you know me." When he released him, he slid down the wall? Security was about to approach him but seeing what it was probably all about, they didn't try to impede him. "Have a good evening gentleman" he wish them as he walked pass then out the front door.

"Damn! Did you see that Cola?"

"Hard not to Tiny" she replied smiling.

"How do you know him again?"

"I honestly don't know him. I just found out that he live in the same damn building I for over a year."

"Bullshit and we haven't seen him."

"I met him earlier today. He was the guy that changed my flat tire I told you about."

"You didn't mention how handsome he was."

"Was I supposed to?" she asked grinning.

"No" she admitted giggling then they turn to rejoin their entourage.

It was in early June when he caught a flight back to Baltimore, he contacted Ron and informed him that he will be at his location by ten o'clock. Once at Thurgood Marshall, he jump on the trolley to get him into the city. He walked up Lexington Street and turned right on Eutaw. Hacks were standing around conversing waiting for their next fare. He took a thirty-dollar hack to his destination. Climbing out the car, he approached the office and walked inside. Ron was sitting at his desk with his eyes close.

"Working hard I see."

"Yup" he replied swinging his feet down then turning around a getting to his feet. "My brother from another mother. How have you been Akeem?"

"Just fine, sir. How have things been?"

"A lot of customers have been coming from out of the city the past year to buy my cars and only will deal with me. Do you know anything about that?"

"Me, no but Ayaana might have put the word out" he lied smiling.

"Well, thank her."

"Yes, sir."

"All I need is your signature" he said turning some forms around for him to sign.

"And the money, right?" he asked with a coy smile while reaching for an envelope in his inside breast pocket in the black Versace suit, he was wearing.

"That goes without saying" he replied smiling while accepting the envelop. "How is your car running?"

"Purring like a kitten" he replied finishing signing his name.

"I hope you don't stay away too long?"

"I'll drop by every time I come home."

"I'll appreciate that Akeem" he said shaking his hand then walking him to the door.

He climbed inside the new fully loaded metallic gray Acura then proceeded on Rt. 29 towards the city. He had more than enough time to reach his destination. He stared at the new housing across from Edmondson High as he cruised pass. He arrived at City College High ten minutes later. He was lucky to find a parking spot on the school lot. He climbed out then proceeded towards the auditorium. He stood in the back allowing his eyes to adjust to the diminish light then he spotted his father and Amiri with a woman. He took a seat in the back and enjoyed the ceremony. Khalil was actually valedictorian of his class. His speech was dedicated to the importance of a positive older brother laying the path the follow and a father whose love never waver for his sons. A person could tell he took great care in presenting his oratory. As the ceremony ended and people started filing out, he made his presence known.

"Hey son" he asked giving him a hug. "When did you get back in town?"

"Earlier today Pop" he replied then stared over at the woman. "I remember you" he suddenly smiled surprising her. "Your name is Ms. Candice."

"Yes, it is" she admitted smiling.

"You was always bringing me candy" he smiled at her. "That's how remembering your name was so easy" he confessed.

"He look so much like you Jamaal."

"Yeah, a chip off the old block" he smiled down on him.

"He's more than a chip. He's a chunk" she corrected him flashing her radiant smile.

"What's up knuckleheads" he asked giving them a hug.

"What's up with you? You haven't brought us down to Atlanta yet" Khalil said staring up at him.

"And that is cold" cosigned Amiri shaking his head.

"When do yawl want to come down?"

"School is out. So, there isn't no reason why we can't go back with you" Khalil replied staring in his eyes.

A coy smile suddenly came to his face knowing there was no reason that he could muster not to take them back with him. "No problem but bring your own money" he informed them.

"That isn't nothing but a chicken wing" replied Amiri laughing.

"I'll be back" Khalil said tapping Amiri and they were off scouting.

"How is school son?" he asked clutching Candice fingers as they exit the building.

"Maintaining my A" he replied.

"A lot have changed since the last time you been home."

"So, I have notice" he smiled at Candice.

"As you know, we go back a long way. She is Chubby's cousin. She stayed connected while I was away and continued to click once I was home" he shared smiling down into her greenish eyes. "The change I mention wasn't her but the jazz club I now own" he revealed smiling.

"Where?" he asked surprised by the revelation.

"I got so lucky. It's down On Charles Street down town.

"How long have you had her?"

"A year now. We are open only Thursday thru Sunday from two to two with meals being served."

"What did you name her?"

"Strictly Jazz. With the place being down town, I am cleaning up. White folks dominate the place most nights, but more blacks are finding their way after the article that the Sun Paper wrote" he shared flashing all thirty-two teeth.

"We are ready" Khalil said waving to the girls that he and his brother were talking to.

"How tall are you?" inquired Akeem.

"Six-three. Are you going to go and see mother?"

"Na" replied nonchalantly. "I got something for you."

"Yeah, what?" he said watching him reaching into his pocket.

"That" he pointed extending the keys to him.

"Why do you have to play so much" he asked slightly snarling.

"Check the registration before snarling at me" he replied grinning.

"You are serious" he replied staring in his eyes then taking the keys. He rush over to the car unlocking the door. Amiri was right on his heels. He admired the interior before starting her up. 92Q filled the interior. He leap from the car and briskly walked over to Akeem and giving him a tight hug. "Thanks, big brother" he said in his ear.

Extending his arms and staring in his eyes, he smiled and said, "My pleasure man."

"I can't wait to graduate in two years" mention Amiri. "You better kick me out a car too" he preorder his wish smiling.

"Come on, Amiri. Let's bounce."

"Hold your roll" insisted their father smiling. "I have something for you also" he said extending a velvet box to him.

"Thanks Pop" he replied accepting it and opening it. "Damn! Sorry Pop and Ms. Candice" he apologized admiring the diamond studded Rolex.

"I hope you know you can't wear that every day?" his father said.

"And be jacked for it, no sir. Special occasions only" he assured him closing the case then hugging him. "Thanks Pop."

"My pleasure son."

"Where do you want to go Amiri?"

"Straight to Philly and go shopping" he suggested.

"An effective way to see how she handles in the curves" he replied with a sexual under tone smiling.

"Yawl be careful" Akeem said staring at them.

"I'll drive her like a point guard protecting the rock" he replied slightly hardening his eyes.

"Good enough for me" he replied tapping their knuckles as they rush towards the car then climbed inside. You can see him altering something as The Crusaders "Lilies of the Nile" filter out the sunroof as they took off.

"Jazz already" his father said staring over at him grinning.

"Khalil but Amiri is starting to feel it too" he replied smiling. Khalil was transforming in a very handsome guy with numerous of admiring young ladies. With a car and his little brother in tow, they will be like foxes in the chicken coop. Parents will freely open the door for them to gorge themselves because of their calming disposition. He decided to remain in Baltimore and accept the scholarship being offer by the University of Maryland Law School. Two awfully close friends of his were murder last year and it had a profound effect of him. He decided to study law to check the corruption he have witness and become a mentor for young black boys. A motivational speech he heard from Jesse Williams had set a fire under him. You could him after playing a game constantly talking about increasing the peace in the streets. His approach always grabbed their attention when he mention a stray bullet coming down the block and striking a child in their family. A bullet that they themselves had fired.

He got his father to drop him off at the house. He went straight to the wooden bowl on the mantle and retrieved almost two years of payments from J-Lo. He took it upstairs and placed it in his safe with the other money he had stash inside. He came back down stairs and went into the basement then grabbed a pre-rolled blunt. The paper was hard as a brick, but the weed was good as hell. He found himself relaxing for almost two hours before getting to his feet and climbing the stairs. He grabbed his keys then walked out the front door. Buying a Chrysler 300 for when he was in town the last time, he was home was a worthwhile investment. He started up the engine then gently pulled away from the curb. As he drove down Roger Avenue, he wonder how J would react to seeing him after so long. He had tried to reach out to her too many times and not getting an immediate response. A day later was bad enough but when it became three days or longer that wasn't cool, and she had to explain herself. Conversing over a cell wasn't going to happen. He needed to be staring in her eyes when they talk.

Finding a parking spot, he climbed out the car then proceeded around the corner. A sudden hush seem to come over the place. A particularly unusual expression engulfed Honey's face at seeing him also. She looked over at J who was staring in the mirror at him. As he stepped furth inside staring at her, she never turned around just kept staring at him. There wasn't anything in her eyes that warranted him to be apprehensive.

"Hi, Akeem" she greeted him still staring in the mirror.

"Hi, yourself Ashanti" he said staring at her. "What's up Ashanti?"

She took a deep breath then lower her head from his stare. As she turned, she embraced her stomach. She was about eight months pregnant. The look of shock that engulfed his face couldn't be contained. He open his mouth, but nothing filter through his lips. Looking back into her eyes, tears were already falling.

"Hey, hey" he said coming closing and hugging her. "Easy Ashanti."

"I'm so sorry for not telling you" she apologized while holding him tight."

"Hey, that's okay" he tried to assure her. "I need you to relax. Come have a seat please" he requested escorting to the love seat by the window.

"Oh, Akeem. I am such a fool" she said grabbing some tissues and blowing her nose then wipe her eyes.

"You really need to calm down Ashanti" he tried to insist clutching her fingers.

"How? How can I Akeem?" she asked staring in his eyes. "Everywhere I go people naturally assumed that I was pregnant by you until I tell them the truth and they all gave me the same stare you did" she shared shaking her head. "I am such a fool."

"You have never been a fool so stop saying it" he insisted staring in her eyes.

"You don't understand Akeem. I'm pregnant by a guy I can give a damn about."

"Now, I'm supposed to believe that, huh?" he asked staring at her. "You have never carried yourself like some cheap trick so there was something definitely there that convince you to make love to him."

"I honestly don't care about him like that Akeem" she insisted. "He is just someone that I knew from middle school. He have always liked me and spoke very respectful to me. I convince myself to believe

231

making love to him would make it easier for me to make love to you" she confesses staring in his eyes. "I never had any intentions of continuing to make love to him, but as you see, I did. In the heat of an uncontrollable moment of passion, I neglected to protect myself and this is the consequences of my negligence" she said rubbing her stomach. "Will you ever forgive me for keeping you in the dark?" she asked staring in his eyes.

"Woman, you don't need n forgiveness from me."

"Yes, I do" she insisted staring at him closer. "Whatever dreams I had conjured up pertaining to our future together is shot to hell. You should have seen the look of shock then disappointment that came to their eyes. Neither of them have ever liked him from day one, especially my father. He said there was something about his eyes that he didn't like or trust."

"Is he gonna be there for you?"

"Why should he" she suddenly snarled. "He wasn't there for the other three girls he got pregnant. He was actually fucking another girl while he was fucking me. His daughter was born last week and I'm due within the next three to four weeks. If I knew he had three other children out there that he wasn't providing for, I would have never given him the time of day" she snarled at her decision. "When the mother of his first daughter pulled me up, she introduced herself and told me she had seen me at Chadwick with you. She actually tried to pull my coat about him, but I dismiss the things that she was saying as an angry ex. So, yeah Akeem. I'm a fool. Once he knew I was pregnant, he drop me like a bad habit. I didn't deserve that."

"You nor the other women he has a child with" he replied.

"Now look at me" she said staring in his eyes. "I'm left to provide for my daughter alone. Why would any man want to provide for a child that not his?"

"Because he understands that loving you mean loving everything that you bring with you. Men have always done this during our history. They might not be able to raise their own children but will incorporate themselves in the lives of another children. Try to explain that" he smiled at her.

"Would you?"

"I never consider it. I'm just twenty Ashanti" he replied grinning.

"If I were a man, I wouldn't. Why take on the burden of raising another person child?"

"So, if I had a child, you wouldn't assist me in raising him or her?" he asked with a coy smile.

"You know I would" she replied slightly smiling.

"Then don't be so dramatic" he told her smiling. "You have a right to be piss, but you need to get over that hurdle and keep it moving" he advised her.

"This is what I miss about you" she suddenly flash her broad smile. "You know just what to say to get my head back on straight. Thank you."

"My pleasure Ms. Emotional" he teased.

She sat there quiet for a moment unconsciously rubbing her stomach. "How long are you in town?"

"I don't know" he replied returning her stare. "Khalil graduation was today."

"What?" she suddenly flashing her radiant broad smiled. "Tell him I said congratulations."

"Sure will."

"What are your plans?"

"We are going to hook up at my Pop's house and celebrate later. You want to hang out?"

"Na, I want to sit this ass down when I get off" she replied still rubbing her stomach.

"My father also open a jazz club down town."

"He did. Where is it located and what's the name?"

"It's called Strictly Jazz."

"That's your father spot" she said with enthusiasm. "My mother and father are constantly going down there. They said the place is elegant as hell and the food was mouthwatering" she shared smiling.

"I haven't been there yet, but I will before I return to Atlanta."

"Do you have a girlfriend down in Atlanta?" she flip the questioning.

"Na."

"Why not?"

"Because I'm not looking for a relationship yet Ashanti."

"Are you at least dating?"

"Nope. The only thing that I'm dating is my books" he replied grinning.

"This is your junior year coming up, right?"

"Actually, I can say it's my senior year, but I honestly can't. I spent the last two summers in classes."

"Typical geek thing to do" she replied giggling. "Are you planning on returning to Baltimore after graduating?"

"Of course, Baltimore is my home. Unless something drastic occurs, I'm coming home."

The front opening caused them to stare at the door.

"My three o'clock is here" she informed him. "I hope I see you before you leave."

"You will" he said getting to his feet then assisting her to her feet. "How are your girls?"

"They are good" she replied smiling.

"Tell them I said hello."

"I will."

"Hey, I need you to keep your head up" he said lightly kissing her on the lips then heading towards the front door. He tip his hat to Honey then pulled the door open and step out. He took a deep breath then slowly exhaled before stepping off and heading up Reistertown Road.

He jump in his car then headed up Rogers Avenue heading home. Pulling up, he spotted Sunshine's Chrysler parked outside his house. He climbed out his car seeing her getting to her feet as he approached the porch.

"Sunshine" he smiled up at her.

"Yeah, fool."

She couldn't have appeared at a more appropriate time. He needed to feel the warm embrace of a devoted friend arms, especially a woman.

His father had sold the previous house and purchase a house in New Ellicott City off of Chapel View Road. A much closer ride to his place of business and sons. Pulling up on the parking pad around nine o'clock that night, he stared at the five-thousand square feet home in awe while wearing a broad smile. Walking up to the seven-foot-high door with African sculptures engrave into it, he open the door and walked inside. Walking through with his brothers, there were several pictures of them throughout the house, but none containing their mother.

"Akeem" whisper Khalil nudging him. "There goes Ms. Candance daughter" he said nodding towards the French doors. "Her name is Harmony while her little sister is called Storm."

"Yeah, they are cute" he complimented admiring her slightly bow-legs on a petite frame that was dipped in a bronze.

"Cute" he replied. "Those girls are fine as hell" he counter leading them towards where their father was socializing.

"Excuse us, hey Pop's" they chime together.

"What's up fellas?" he greeted them giving them a hug. "Let me finish my conversation and I'll get right with yawl."

"One quick question" she asked stepping into his person zone while Khalil and Amiri stepped off. "Khalil said that Ms. Candice daughters are off limits. Do you have plans of marrying her?"

"Na, Akeem" he replied smiling. "Marriage is not in our cards and as far as her daughters are concern, I needed Khalil to stay focus. Being valedictorian of his class, I think it worked" he shared snickering.

"Apparently so" he replied tapping his knuckles then joining his brothers.

"What was you and Pop discussing?" inquired Amiri.

"You are an inquisitive knucklehead."

"That's the only way to obtain information" he replied. "So, what's up?"

"Pop said that the only reason he told you that Storm was off-limits is because he didn't want you being distracted Khalil."

"Are you serious" he replied staring over at their father who was raising his glass to him smiling.

"Would you have been distracted?"

"Absolutely" he replied flashing all thirty-two teeth. "I damn sure wouldn't have been valedictorian" he admitted snickering. "So, she's not off-limit."

"Nope" he replied.

"See you later" he said heading straight towards Storm with his ears perked up and wearing an impish smile. Apparently, he did care that his horns were showing.

He decided to take a tour of his father house. He found the basement door and descended the stairs. At the bottom of the stairs to his left was a regulation pool table with a couple playing. They both nodded to him the continued their game. Chubby was sitting at the bar with two women flanking him. In the communal area, there were two oversized couches with a six-foot-long coffee table between them. People were sipping on glasses of alcohol or wine while smoking blunts. The Infinity stereo system had six-feet-high Bose speakers with the reel to reel providing the jazz music. His collection doesn't just have CD's but vinyl also and it was ridiculous. He eventually retrace his steps to the first floor then made his way to the second floor. He peeked in all three bedrooms with their fifty-inch television and stereo-system except for his father's bedroom. In the back bedroom, a French door grabbed his attention and walked towards it. Opening it, he was pleasantly surprised to see a balcony. He took a seat over-looking the massive back yard. The lights from the inground pool provided a romantic scenery for the people leisuring around while drinking.

"I was wondering where you disappeared to" a woman's voice interrupted his thoughts.

He turned to see who it was, and a smile came to his face. "How are you doing Harmony?"

"Hi, Akeem" she greeted smiling. "Who told you, my name?"

"My enthusiastic brother Khalil" he replied.

"I kind of figure that" she admitted smiling down on him. "May I join you?"

"By all means, yes" she said sliding his chair further apart.

"Khalil and Storm got a thing going but they think no one knows" she giggled. "How is school?"

"School is good."

"I wanted to attend Spelman myself, but I didn't trust myself" she admitted giggling.

"Trust yourself how?" he asked with a coy smile.

"I would have been too far from home, and I know I would have let my hair down. So, to keep my self-respect, I kept my butt close to home and am attending Georgetown."

"I was considering Georgetown, but they were more interested in my basketball skills than my intellect."

"Is it true what the rumor say about some of Atlanta's men being bi-sexual?"

"You can use that descriptive for what some of them are doing, but that word doesn't exist for me" he explained.

"I personally feel you" she cosigned giggling while searching in her purse. "Do you mind?" she asked displaying a blunt.

"Not at all."

"My Mom said you brought Khalil a car?" she mention pulling from the blunt and holding the smoke in her lungs.

"It's two-years old but he's thankful."

"I would be too" she said extending the bunt to him. "So, how long are you staying in town?"

"I'm leaving Friday."

"No!" she replied louder than intended.

"No?" he smiled over at her. "What's happening Harmony?"

"You can't leave Akeem. I'm having my twenty-first birthday at Identity on Saturday" she explained. "Do you know where that is located?"

"Yeah, up near Reistertown."

"So, please attend" she requested studying his face closely. "You are so much more handsome that your pictures."

"You do know that flattery will get you the world" he replied trying not to get hypnotize by her alluring and flirtatious eyes while extending the blunt back to her. Yeah, if she had went down South to Spelman, she just might have lost some self-respect. "How could I deny those eyes?" he asked smiling at her.

"Oh, thank you" she flash her smile at him while pulling from the blunt. "According to Uncle Chubby, you could have been a professional basketball player."

"Yeah, that was the rumor, but I chose a different path."

"I'm impress that you chose to reveal your intellect over your basketball abilities."

"Yeah, most geeks make such decisions" he replied causing her snicker.

"Most little boys grow up with that aspiration."

"So, did I" he admitted smiling.

Since receiving his graduation present, Khalil decided to postpone their visit to him. They have an expanded territories that they could explore like the Columbia Mall or the county streets outside of D.C. So, he was catching his flight out mid-day on Sunday. He had more than enough things to reflect on during his flight. First, Ashanti pregnancy. Playing sexual baseball, ladies will always lose. Once achieving second base, curiosity always prevail and before you know it, you are snarled in the trap. The sensation is like a junky thinking they can experiment with heroin one time and walk away. That dick can be an extremely powerful tool. Just as addictive as hitting a main line with a syringe filled with dope, very euphoric. Secondly, Sunshine. Although she forced herself away from him after three hours, the sexual explorations they took can only be classified as freaky. She allowed herself to try all of her sexual fantasies. She was the only woman that he make love to that demanded the pain his dick induces. Tears would be flowing freely from her eyes, but never surrendering to the painful pleasure. She insisted that he understand just how much she was in love with him and tried to explain it in words but never satisfied. There was another level of sexual pleasure and love that she didn't know existed until they became lovers, and he always took her there. All she requested was he come home to break her back for her birthday. How could he refuse such a request? Last, there was Harmony. When he arrived at Identity close to midnight, he presented her with a birthday present. A Largo gemstone bracelet.

"This is beautiful Akeem."

"I'm glad you like it."

"Come on, let's dance" she insisted gripping his fingers and taking him to the dance floor. They click too well for two individual that had just met. The erotic way that they dance on the was ridiculous; not even lovers dance the way they were dancing in a vertical position.

She actually was massaging his dick on the dance floor while staring seductively up into his eyes. Why they didn't fuck that night was a mystery that they discuss before his flight. Something that they need to ratify on his next return trip home.

On the 3rd of July, Akeem and Cola was landing at Savannah-Hilton International. As they left the terminal carrying their suitcases, a gray limo was sitting in the arrival parking area with a black chauffeur standing on the sidewalk smiling.

"Hi, Marshall" she greeted him warming while smiling.

"Mistress Cola" he smiled accepting her briefcase then peeked over at her guest.

"This is my close friend Akeem."

"Glad to make your acquaintance" he replied reaching for the suitcase.

"No, sir. I have this but thank you anyway" replied walking with him then placing his suitcase in the trunk. He climbed inside after Cola then lean back as Marshall closed the door then hurried around and climbed inside then pulled away.

"So, it's like this Cola?"

"I told you I come from old money" she said pulling out the bar. "Would you like a glass of Moscato?"

"Sure" he replied accepting a glass then leaning back.

As they left the terminal, the limo felt like they were floating. She pulled out a blunt from her bra and lit after opening the sunroof for ventilation. They jump on I-95 to 516 into Savannah. As they shared the blunt, she tried to prepare him for what he was about to experience over the next two days, he told her he will take everything in stride. Making light jokes of what could transpire, this caused her to relax along with the blunt. She was glad to have him for assurance. Ever since they have met, she have found a new confidence within herself. She had been secretly waiting for another side of him to materialize, but it never did after two years. They have spent numerous of romantic dinners together that he had prepared, hung out socializing in jazz clubs or the latest hip-hop spots he never changed. When I feel like just chilling and watch a good movie, he would allow me to lay across his lap even if he were doing a research paper. He have never displayed any form of dissatisfaction with her constant intrusions. If he were extremely busy, he would give her the remote and go to his bedroom. He has seen her intoxicate but never used her intoxicated state to press up on her sexually. One night, she was out of character and gotten extremely intoxicated then passed out. He carried her into his spare bedroom and gently laid her down then threw a sheet over her. Not a stich of her clothing was out of place. During her freshman year, a guy that she thought she could trust made her pay dearly. She had awoken partially naked and sexually assaulted. She wanted to file charges against him, but his defense lawyer would have tried to flip the script on her. Using how she got intoxicated after she arrival against her. She might not could file charges against his scandalous ass, but she could put him on blast and three other young ladies came out of the closet on his ass.

"You have got to be kidding me!" Akeem stated taking her out of her thoughts. "Is this the house of the rich and famous?"

"Don't start Akeem" she insisted. She haven't been home in over three years

"Oh, it's on and popping" he informed her ignoring her rolling her eyes while he kept smiling at the castle, damn near look like one. Pulling up in front of the house, a late fiftyish man was washing a white Bentley with four more expensive cars waiting. Opening the back door for them, they step out and the mansion appeared even larger.

"This way" she informed him opening the eight-foot-high front door and walking in.

"Cola" he whisper admiring the double staircase.

"Stop Akeem. Come on" she insisted leading hm from one massive room to another.

"How do you furnish such a massive place?" he asked staring up at the cathedral ceilings.

"Stop Akeem" she repeated looking over her shoulder at him staring at a massive family portrait. They eventually walked through some French doors to a spectacular patio and an Olympic size swimming pool with lounge chair on both sides. The largest gazebo he have ever seen was about fifty yards away.

"Jasmine!" a woman announced leaping to her feet.

"Hi, mother."

"Oh, you look so beautiful" she replied giving her baby a hug and kiss on the cheek.

"Hi, darling."

"Father" she replied flatly.

"Aren't you going to give me a hug?"

"No" she replied flatly.

"How many times do I have to apologize for what I said?"

"I'll never accept it so stop requesting" she told him slightly hardening her eyes.

"Who is this?" her mother interjected trying to change the subject.

"This is my extremely good friend Akeem" she suddenly smile at him. "Akeem, this is Harold and Deloris."

"Ma'am, sir" he greeted tipping his hat.

"Do you attend college?" she asked admiring his attire.

"Yes, ma'am. I'm attending Morehouse."

"Impressive, what are you studying?"

"Micro-engineering."

"What year are you in if you don't mind me asking?"

"No, ma'am. I'm entering my senior year in January."

"Kind of young to be graduating next year."

"Not when you formulate a plan" he slightly smiled at her.

"Well, I want to welcome you to our home."

"Thank you, ma'am" he smiled down on her.

"Do you have a place to stay?" her father asked staring up at him.

"He was going to stay in one of the guest rooms in the east wing" interjected Cola slightly hardening her eyes at him. "Why would you want to embarrass me like this?"

"I don't" he lying ass insisted. "I was just asking, darling."

"I'm not your darling like I told you years ago" she reminded him slightly snarling. "You have never asked before."

"I knew the guest that came into my home" he replied staring in her eyes.

"No, you didn't" she slightly chuckle. "You are so full of..."

"Cola!" interjected Akeem forcing her to cut her last word off. Easy young lady" he smiled over at her. "Take me to a hotel."

"I didn't say that you couldn't stay Akeem" he said trying to clean up what he said. "I was just..."

"I know what you was doing and saying, sir" he interrupted him. "I've seen individual just like you on campus" he snarled at him until he diverted his eyes. "Ma'am, it's been nice meeting you."

"Akeem, we have plenty of rooms. Please stay" she insisted.

"I apologize but I honestly can't" he said smiling down at her.

"Will you join our party tomorrow?"

"No, ma'am. I must refuse your offer but thank you anyway. Good afternoon" he said suddenly turning and walking away. He was so embarrassed that he didn't realize how fast he was walking.

"Akeem! Slow down please!" she called out to him. He slowed his pace. She caught up and grip his arm. "I truly apologize for that. You see why I don't come home" she said signing.

"Yeah" he replied never breaking his stride.

"My mother will be very disappointed if you didn't stay at her home" she informed him. "Knowing her as I do, I know she is deep up in his ass right about now. She can't stand when he leap up on his high horse. A horse that she provide for him financially. This was her parents' home before they moved to California. He don't own a damn thing in this house. Nothing. The position that he works was created to give the image of him doing something positive. Why she would even entertain marrying an ass hole like him is still baffling to my mind. She is such an intellectual and refine woman while he is the complete opposite, an absolute ignorant motherfucker" she snarled while sharing their family secret. "She forced him to get a GED. He didn't initiate it on his own. So, hearing how successful you are going to be only heighten his jealousy over certain black men."

"Wow" he smiled at her.

"Never allow an apron holding guy like him to get under your skin" she described him causing to slightly smile. "So, you have to attend the party tomorrow, Akeem. My mother would internally hold that embarrassment inside of her, understand?" she asked staring in his eyes.

"Yeah" he replied with his impish smile.

"I usually don't like that little impish grin on your face, but I eagerly await what transpires" she giggled. "Come on" she insisted as they walked out the front door and headed towards the garage. "This is my high school graduation present" she informed him unlocking the door then climbing inside. The metallic gray Corvette roared to life. Her mother had brought it for her because she never wanted to flaunt her wealth among her friends like her siblings do on the regularity. A twenty-dollar pair of jeans fit just like as good as a pair of jeans from Valentino or Dolce & Gabba, but a hell of a lot cheaper. This caused unwarranted friction between her and her mother wanting her to appease her. Once she graduated high school and received part of her initial inheritance, she was gone from her parents' home. Her mother had pleaded with her to return home to take her graduation present, but she kept it moving. This was the first time they had laid eyes on her since she left three years ago, but there was a new found strength in her eyes and in her voice. As they drove on the highway, she called the prestigious hotel to make a reservation. Pulling up fifteen minutes later, she gave the valet her keys while accepting a ticket then gripping his fingers and strolling casually towards the receptionist desk. After acquiring his electronic key, they took the elevator to the twentieth floor then follow the arrow to his suite. The elegance of the place made him flash all thirty-two teeth. He walked over to the patio balcony then open the door and step out while Cola turned on the radio then came out to join him. "This scenery was gorgeous" he replied staring out at Lake Savannah.

"Yeah, I used to go swimming in that lake with my girlfriends when I was younger. I wouldn't dare swim in it now."

"Can you hook me up with some weed?"

"Here" she said reaching back into her bra and bringing out two more blunts then extending them to him. "I'll get with some friends later and buy us an ounce."

"Sound like a good plan to me" he cosigned grinning.

"I'm gonna head back home, but I'll see you around nine o'clock. We can go out to a club or just chill here watching T.V."

"I rather chill."

"So, would I" she admitted grabbing his fingers and leading him back inside. "I'll see you later and stay out of trouble."

"How much trouble can I get into being here by myself?"

"I don't know but trouble always seem to find you" she mention wiggling her fingers as she walked out the door.

It was a little after eight o'clock when Cola light tapping could be heard, he open the door and step aside for her to enter. Wearing a pair of white silk shorts with a white silk blouse revealing her red bra, she was carrying a bamboo lunch container, several CD's, two bottles of

Moscato and an ounce of weed called Hydro. After eating the meal filled with seafood, they went out on the balcony to digest their food and get their buzz on. It was a little after one o'clock when they went back inside to watch one of the videos that she brought with her, they decided on "Red Tails." A half hour into the movie, she laid her head into his lap then sleep crept up on her. Her light snoring is what alerted him. He allowed her to sleep until the movie was over. He was lifting her into his arms then carrying into the second bedroom when she stirred awoke.

"Are you trying to seduce me, sir?" she asked in a hoarse whisper.

"I always love your humor" he replied grinning into her eyes.

"I have to go home Akeem."

"Oh" he replied lowering her to the floor. "If I had known that I would have woke you up when you first went to sleep."

"I'm glad you didn't" she replied heading back towards the communal area. "That little cat nap did wonders" she said sitting down on the couch and putting on her stilettos then getting up. "Come on and drive me home" she stated already heading towards the door.

"You can't drive yourself home?" he asked staring over at her but not moving.

"Of course, I can" she replied turning and seeing him staring over at her. "Come on, Akeem. I want you to drive me home. I really want to see what you wear tomorrow" she smiled at him.

"Alright but only because I can use your car to get around tomorrow" he informed her grabbing his electronic key and the bamboo basket then following her out the door.

The party got started around three o'clock, but he didn't arrive until almost eight o'clock. He wanted the humidity to be down. When he pulled up in front of the house, cars were everywhere. As he drove towards the garage, one of the people caring for their cars directed him towards a specific space then accepted the keys from him. Hearing the music, laughter and people talking, he headed in the direction of the backyard. Did he just step into a time zone? Khakis, penny loafers and Polo shirts dominated the dress code. No jeans, Tims or flannel shirts accepted. As he walked around almost unnoticed, he grabbed a plate then filled it with a piece of catfish, potato salad, cabbage and two-pieces of cornbread then found a nice spot to devour the food. While he was eating, his eyes were scanning the place. He eventually found Cola sitting at table with a group of people. He could tell by their interact that they were extremely close. Laughing and touching one another while their body language converse just how much they missed one another. She would look periodically at the French doors to see who else was arriving, but it wasn't Akeem and the slight disappointment that came into her eyes made him smile. After finishing his meal and disposing of his trash, he returned to his perch.

When four pretty boys arrived, they were welcome with open arms by her father but not her mother especially one of them. She was truly standoffish and didn't care if he realize it. Her father pointed in the direction of Cola then smack him on the shoulder as he made his way towards her smiling. With her back slightly towards him, the atmosphere of their little reunion changed instantly as a couple of them stared at him approaching. Forcing Cola to turn around. The pleasant smile and joyful eyes dissipated almost instantly. He study the guys sitting with her and they had pure dislike for him.

"Damn, Jasmine" he smiled down on her. "You look fine as hell girl."

"I haven't been a girl since my eighteenth birthday" she informed him staring into his greenish eyes from an interracial marriage. "I am a woman now Derrick."

"You aren't lying" replied smiling down at her while nudging one of his friends. "When I heard that you was home, I must admit I got excited" he said staring in her eyes.

"Well, get unexcited" she advised him staring at him with cold eyes.

"How about you and I taking a walk so we can talk?" he asked extending his hand to her.

"Negro, we don't have anything to discuss" she lightly giggled.

"Come on, Jasmine. I make a mistake over three years ago. Are you going to hold that against me forever?"

"Na, when the stars from the sky or the mountain crumble into the see will be when I forgive your punk ass" she called him slightly smiling.

"We were good together back then."

"No, we weren't Derrick" she corrected him slightly snarling. "Or your punk ass wouldn't have cheated on me."

"I was immature back then Cola, but I have matured since then. I really miss you."

"No, you don't" she waved off his comment giggling. "You miss this good pussy and that's all" she corrected him shocking all of her friends with her vulgarity. Since meeting Akeem, he forces and demand that she speak her mind to him or how will he truly get to know you? So, expressing herself was as easy as tying her sneakers especially to a motherfucker that took her virginity then broke her heart.

"Where in the hell did that word come from?" he asked staring at her confused.

"From the mouth of a woman and not the fragile young lady that left here with her heart shatter" she replied returning his stare. "Why don't you take you and your goonies and go harassed somebody else. As a matter of fact, where is Trina tricking ass?"

He just stood there staring down at her. She was definitely not the same naïve girl that left here. There was an awareness in her eyes that wasn't present previously. As a matter of fact, where is this guy that she brought home with her. "I heard you brought somebody home with you" he stated ignoring her question.

She stared at him unusually then stared over at her father. "Oh" she lightly snicker. "My father told you that huh?"

"Yeah" he admitted returning her stare. "He knew we were good together."

"Then go fuck him" she suggested smiling at him as her friends were unable to contain their giggles and chuckles causing him to stare over at them with a slight snarl.

"Where did you get that mouth of yours from?" he inquired again slightly smiling.

"Don't worry about it" she replied. "And as far as my friend is concern, you really don't want to meet him using the disposition that you are."

"What makes you think that?"

"I don't think so, I know Derrick" she corrected him.

"Where is he now?"

"Knowing him" she suddenly smiled up at him. "He's probably sitting in some shadow enjoying this whole scene" she giggled staring around searching the shadows.

"What kind of guy would allow such a beautiful woman to be alone?"

"Not the type that cheats, that's for sure, but a noticeably confident person. My friends are dying to meet him" she replied still staring in the shadows then spotting him and a broad smile came to her face.

"What are you smiling at?" he asked staring in the direction that she was staring then seeing a guy getting to his feet. He watch the guy elevate to six-five while wearing a gray leisure set with his patent gangster hat. The swag in his walk couldn't be denied by the women watching him approaching. His eyes were focus on Jasmine.

"Hey family" he greeted placing his hand over his heart and slightly bowing his head at her friends sitting at the table. "What's up Cola?" he asked ignoring the other three guys staring over at him.

"How long have you been sitting in the shadows?" she asked getting to her feet and lightly kissing him on the lips.

"Long enough to eat, dispose of any evidence and lay back enjoying the show" he admitted grinning. "I was enjoying myself until you snitch me out and started searching the shadows" he mention causing her to burst out giggle.

"Oh, you saw that huh?" she snicker.

"You made it so obvious" he smiled at down on her.

"Are you going to introduce us Jasmine?" Derrick asked staring him up and down.

"No" she replied staring over at him.

"I'm Derrick. Jasmine old boyfriend" he said extending his hand to him smiling.

"So, you are the dummy that broke my girls heart" he smiled at him slightly shaking his head and watching him slowly lowering his hand. "Yeah, you need to put your hand down. Why would I want to shake the dummy hand that cheated on my girl?" he asked staring over at.

"Yeah, I was dumb but I'm not a dummy" he counter returning his stare.

"Yes, you are. Even I would try to make amend of some dumb shit I might have done to get back with her, look at her boy" he invited him then returned his eyes back to him. "You couldn't see that she is gorgeous. I would have valued her from the start so I wouldn't be coming back later begging. So, yeah. You are a dummy Derrick" he corrected him grinning causing her friends to burst out laughing.

"You got me twisted with someone else partner" he replied.

"No, I don't" he assured him. "Negroes like you I see every day at school. Yawl are all full of shit. I wish I could be a fly on the wall when you hear one of your white friends remind you that you are a nigger in their eyes."

"I'm not no nigger!" he snapped instantly.

"I never called you a nigger, Negro. I understand the difference. Do you? You probably think that being a house nigger is better than being a field nigger, but you don't understand that both are still classified as a nigger" he asked smiling but not expecting an answer. "Watching you rolling up in here with your paper soldiers was hilarious. Where I'm from yawl would be somebody bitch" he smiled at his three friends.

"Well, you aren't where you're from. You are in Savannah now" he boasted.

"Na, I'm not but a dummy like you would think so. Baltimore goes wherever I go, but I wouldn't be boasting about here. This place is more like Disney World, and you are one of the main characters" he informed him grinning.

"We aren't no thug" he snarled.

"Are you calling me a thug?" he asked hardening his eyes for the first time and stepping into his personal space causing him to slightly rock backward. "Be very careful with your answer Negro" he advised him staring down into his eyes.

"Be careful Negro" Cola advised him grinning from ear to ear.

"No" he finally replied taking the edge off the situation.

"I didn't think so. You and your friends need to step off" he told him staring in his eyes. "Why the fuck are you looking at her? This is supposed to a conversation between two men" he informed him with harden eyes.

Derrick didn't say a word nor stared in Akeem's eyes. He nudged one of his boys then they turned and away.

"Damn" one of her male friends stated snickering. "Where was that tough guy that he always portray?"

"Probably sitting on a toilet like a little bitch" a chubby guy replied causing them to burst out laughing as Derrick stood next to Cola's father. "One thing I know from this point, he better watch himself around me" he said staring at his back. "I'm ready to surrender some ass to get to his ass" he said with conviction in his eyes and voice.

"The next time he step to me I'm going to see if he's really ready to put up or shut up" the first guy cosigned.

"Everybody, this is Akeem" she introduced him while clutching to his arm smiling down at them.

"Hi, Akeem" they greeted him.

"Family" he replied slightly bowing is head.

"I was wondering when you would get here" she said with an impish smile. She had tried to prepare her friends about him and the pictures that she showed them hanging out didn't corelate with the stories she had shared earlier in the day. She had witness many of so-called tough guys shitting in their pants fucking with Akeem intellectual ass. She didn't know how brutal he could be until the night she called for him to come to Ecstasy. His attire was completely out of norm. Jeans and sneakers. The way he dismember those two guys was like he was a pro and didn't show them any mercy. He watch when she called him after that displayed. She told her friends that when Derrick come with his partners with their bullshit antics. You will see how a paper soldier reacts to a genuine soldier.

"I really didn't have a choice considering I was driving your car" he replied staring at Derrick and Cola's father staring at him then going inside the house. "So, that's the guy that your father want for you, huh?" he asked grinning.

"You can take that grin off your face but yeah" she replied.

"I see that they mirror themselves" he mention grinning.

"Absolutely, they are both full of shit" she replied. "So, you want to get out of here?"

"Sure, where do you wanna go?"

"To your suite" she replied.

"Can't refuse that offer" he replied watching her. "What is that coy smile about?"

"I was just thinking. How about you and I cashing in our return flight tickets and drive back to Atlanta?"

"I'm cool that."

"Good" she suddenly flash her radiant smile. "I'm going to grab my clothes and tell my mother goodbye while my father is soothing Derrick punk ass. I'll meet you out front."

"No, problem. Family" he slightly smiled bowing his head then turned and retraced his steps.

"Damn, Jasmine. You didn't mention how handsome he is?"

"You think he look handsome T.T?"

"Hell, yeah" another one of her friends cosigned. "Are you getting with him Jasmine?"

"No, Michelle. We are simply good friends."

"Does he have a girlfriend?"

"Na, Mona. He's single" she admitted.

"Why?"

"I guess he likes his freedom. He would leap at the invitation to attend a jazz club, but I like chilling at his apartment being entertained by him.

Girl, you need to jump on that or better still, invite me down for a weekend" suggested Mona.

"I've been trying to get you and the others to come shout at me, but as soon you see Akeem you are ready to come. Now, that is cold" she said shaking her head at her.

"If I knew the appetizer was like him, I would have rented a room" T.T replied giggling.

"I'm going to make plans to come down there real soon Jasmine" Michelle informed her.

"Well, we will be there" she smiled getting to her feet. "Let me go handle this and I'll holla at yawl" she said giving them a hug.

She walked over to her mother to inform her she was leaving, but she wasn't trying to her it. It has been almost four years since her baby girl came home. She had stumble upon her when her grandmother came into town, or she wouldn't have known she was in even in town. They had sat and talked until four o'clock in the morning. She had mature so much. They shared what have transpired over the years in their lives. She revealed how she met Akeem and how their relationship have blossom over the years. She shared how well he could cook and how secure she felt whenever they were in the streets. Intellectual as hell with roots deeply embedded in the hood. He's the type of guy you introduce to your mother and make arrangements for marriage. She admitted to being extremely attracted to him but neither have explore falling in love. I think he knew that Derrick still had an effect on me, so he stayed in his lane. He's very therapeutic to a shatter heart.

Driving back to Atlanta, she realize just how much she have fallen in love with him. She thought it was a passing infatuation, but she had to admit it was much more. When he requested that she escort him to his brother's graduation, she openly told him a lie. The look that came into his eyes then that little smirk that came to his face let her know that he knew she was lying but accepted her bullshit explanation without seeking any further explanation. But she couldn't tell him, why? How could she tell him that she felt threaten by Sunshine and J-Lo? Two young ladies that she have never met but knew oh so well. He had flown home to be present when her daughter was born and gave him the privilege of being her godfather and naming her Mandisa (sweet). "What kind of man does that? A faithful friend" she had to admit. Although they haven't stayed in close contact over the years, she knew he would look her up because of him being the godfather. Sunshine would also be on his hit list. When she stare at their pictures, both were extremely attractive especially Sunshine with her deep bronze complexion and natural sexy smile. Although she wanted to experience Baltimore streets and party scene, his brothers and father jazz club also intrigued her, but she wasn't woman enough to face Sunshine or J-Lo. She knew she wouldn't keep her composure nor hide her jealousy for the love he have for them.

Just as he had done with Khalil, he instead brought Amiri a used 750 Beemer. With over a million dollars in their personal accounts, Khalil and Amiri didn't have to concern themselves with nothing but concentrating on their books. Coming home for Amiri graduation, Akeem seen how the streets have changed again. Guys that are seven and eight years younger than he was are now on the corners. Monk and Twin used their money wisely to buy a key and now control Edmondson and Fulton after T.C had to bow out. Rumor has it that they are getting high on their own supply. A definite no in the drug game. Girls that they knew growing up were being persuaded to use their houses as stash houses for them while their parents are away at work. The money that they received were appreciated. Fuck the consequences. Other girls that like being drug dealers play toys eventually experiment with the drug that they are selling. Before long, a little monkey forms but you are too naïve to understand its needs until it's too late. After being pass from one drug dealer to another for their daily blast, they rationalize that it's more profitable entering the oldest profession of prostitution. Pulling up in his old court yard, time seem to have stood still. Individuals that were slinging when he was playing basketball were still out there trying to sling. They might have acquired some materialistic thing like a used car but none of them had their own places. They rather impose on their mother in her two-bedroom apartment that has five or six people residing. Tapping on his mother door after exhaling from that pissy smelling elevator, the front door suddenly swung open.

"Is Deloris here?"

"Who the fuck are you?"

"An acquaintance" he replied staring in his eyes.

"An acquaintance?" he repeated rubbing his nose while slightly nodding and rocking. "Nigger, I need a name."

"Look, that's okay" he replied starting to turn.

"T.C! Who the hell is at the door!?"

"An acquaintance" he replied snickering while rocking from the heroin in his system.

"An acquaintance? Move the hell out of the way fool" she insisted pushing him aside then covering her eyes from the morning sun. Shock consumed her face. She never thought she would ever see him again even his brothers have stop coming over. When Amiri stop almost two years ago, she knew she had lost their respect and any love they had for her. After missing Khalil graduation, he step completely off, but missing her baby's graduation was the straw that broke his back too and she didn't have anybody to blame but herself. "Akeem, baby" she stated wanting to reach out and touch him, but he knew she lost that privilege years ago. "Will you come in?"

"Sure" he replied removing is derby as he enter. All the foul smells from his youth invaded his nostrils.

"Come, have a seat" she invited at the kitchen table. "How long have you been in town?"

"Since Amiri graduation."

"I wanted to make it. I really did but I got sick. You can understand that right?"

"Of course, but it never dawn on you to save yourself a gate shot so you could attend your last child graduation."

"Of course, I did but T.C scandalous ass found it" she snarled over at him in the front room nodding.

"You talking about me" T.C asked coming out of his nod and coming into the kitchen. "You talking about me Sis?"

"Yeah, you dumb ass fool" she replied looking up at him. "Do you know who this is?" she asked watching him closely as he stared at the stranger.

"Na, I don't know this motherfucker" he declared snarling.

"Look closer, T.C" she insisted.

"Looking closer isn't going to make me remember" he snap still staring at the stranger.

"It's you nephew Akeem, dummy" she told him shaking her head at him.

"Akeem?" he repeated then stared at her then back at him "Akeem?"

"Uncle T.C."

"Akeem" he smiled revealing spaces where teeth once resided. "Boy it's good seeing you. Man, I was fuck up over your shooting."

"Old water under the bridge" he replied staring up at the shell of the man he once was and that wasn't shit.

"No, Akeem" he said coming closer then pausing. "I lost everything."

"No, you didn't" he replied slightly snarling. "You are still breathing."

"Do you know how much he took me from?"

"So, you can keep breathing. Of course, I do. I received every dollar" he informed him slightly smiling. "From what I heard you was still sitting sweet because he didn't take your uncut keys or the money you had on the streets. So, what are you whining about?"

"Fuck that! Look at me! Look closely!" he insisted.

"I am" he replied returning his snarl. "My father didn't force you to put that spike in your arms. Do you consider how you destroyed families pushing your drugs over the years?"

"No" he admitted.

"So, why should I concern myself with your own conjure dilemma? If you got a problem with what transpired, you know to take your concerns" he said staring in his unfocused eyes. Understanding that he wasn't about to receive the empathy he needed, he turned and walked away.

"What brought you here today, Akeem?" she asked staring in his eyes.

"I was just in the area" he replied.

"I'm glad that you did" she slightly smiled. "You did a terrific job raising your brothers. If not for you, they would have followed those fools in the court yard."

"If you didn't turn them out first" he included. "All you had to do was be a mother to us."

"Easier said than done, Akeem" she replied pulling from her cigarette then exhaling. "How was I supposed to be a mother when I never acquired any parental skills?" she asked staring into hie eyes intensely. "Our entire family is either drug dealers or addicts. You broke the chain and pulled your brothers with you. There was no way that you would be attending college, let alone graduating from high school, if you or your brothers had depended on me. Look at me Akeem" she slightly smiled raising her arms. "I'm nothing more than a crack head with a heroin addiction. A hell of a combination" she slightly snarled at the descriptive she gave of herself. "You are graduating soon, right?"

"Yes, in two weeks."

"My family said that yawl wasn't going to amount to shit, and I initially didn't have any reason not to believe them especially after the scandalous shit I did to your father" she confess staring in his eyes then slightly lowering them. "But look at you and your brothers" she suddenly smiled. "Although I can't accept responsibility for yawl success, I can boast that yawl are my babies and none of them can compare their boys to mine" she stated proudly while hardening her eyes. "Your father even started talking to me again" she lightly chuckled. "I don't know why? In his younger days, he would have discarded me like a pair of old shoes. I don't ever expect him to forgive me. He's not a Christian so he don't have to forgive anybody" she stated lightly chuckling. "He used to tell motherfuckers that before initiating his revenge. I think what Khalil advocating is touching his consciousness. He actually thank me for bringing forth his roots and been giving me a few dollars in the past year. I still can't stare him in his eyes too long just like I can't stare in yours because yawl have the ability to see how dark my soul actually is" she confessed avoiding his stare. "Are you plan on returning to Baltimore after you graduate?"

"That was my initial plans, but things have slightly changed, I'm making damn good money during my internship working part-time."

"Do you have a young lady in your life?"

"You know Sunshine will always be my girl" he replied slightly smiling.

"Yes, she is" she cosigned lightly giggling. She used to watch how he watch over her since they were four years old and still does today.

"Besides her, I don't have anyone."

"What about Khalil?"

"He's been in love for a couple of years with a young lady name Storm."

"And Amiri?"

"A regular Casanova after getting his heart broken" he revealed grinning.

"He better look out for one of those chicken boxes eating girls" she advised.

"I had that conversation with both of them years ago."

"So, where are you headed from here?"

"To hunt down an old friend" he said suddenly getting to his feet then counting out ten Franklins and placing them into her hand. "I got to go."

"Well, it's been nice seeing you. You do know I love you, right?"

"Most mothers do even if they don't know how to display it" he said walking towards the front door. He stop briefly to stare at T.C nodding then open the door and walked out closing it quietly behind himself.

She got to her feet and stared out the window until she saw him walking across the courtyard. He waved to the fellas that he grew up with and the younger brothers of friends that were either incarcerated or have fallen at deaths' door. Watching him pulling out of the courtyard, she couldn't remember the last time he called her mommy or mom. A badge of honor she never deserved. She couldn't help wondering how many more years will elapse until she see him again.

As he cruised up Pennsylvania Avenue, the streets seem the same, but he wasn't that naïve. There were more teenager experimenting with "Perks" and "E-Pills." They hubber across the street from Upton Market as five-o monitor their movements. There was no doubt that somebody was getting paid, but five-o seem to close their eyes as though they are on someone's payroll. At North Avenue, the scene was worse. Zombies shuffling around while others seem to be in a rush like they are running to catch a bus to work. As he waited for the light to change, he spotted Sunshine entering the check cash place. He wanted to pull over and get with her, but if he did, all his plans for the day would be blown to hell. She was the only girl he knew who could pull the right strings to turn him on and out. Na, he need to keep moving. The horn of the driver behind him brought him out of his thoughts as he press on the accelerator and proceeded towards his destination. With all of Baltimore faults, seeing his city steadily declining from the abuse of drug addictions and the violence associate with its sells was disheartening, but children losing their innocence so young is shameful.

A nervousness suddenly consumed him spotting J-Lo's car parked on Reistertown Road in front of the salon. It has been well over two years since he saw or communicated with her, he told her to reach out to him if his goddaughter needed anything. Parking behind her and stepping out of his car, he spotted Mandy's car seat on the back seat of her car. A faint smile creased his lips. He spotted her through the window laughing while doing a client's locs. He turned the doorknob then push the door open and step inside. Instinctively, all eyes stared in his direction.

"Ladies" he greeted tipping his hat then focusing on J-Lo. "What's up woman?"

"Akeem?"

"I haven't changed that much, have I?" he asked smiling over at her. She rush into is arms and squeezed his very tight while resting her head on his chest and inhaling the scent of his body. "How have you been?"

"I've been good" she whisper in his chest then slowly releasing him and smiling up into his eyes. "You look so good" she complimented slightly blushing.

"Damn, becoming a mother have given you the weight that makes you even more sexy and I never thought that was possible" he admitted admiring the new contour of her body.

"You always know what to say to make a person feel so sexy" she complimented rubbing his face lightly.

"How is Mandy?"

"Bad as hell" she replied gripping is fingers. "I'm almost finish. How about you chilling?"

"Sure" he replied removing his hat then taking a seat on the love seat by the window.

"What brought you home in the middle of the week?" she asked peeking over at him.

"Amiri graduation."

"Amiri graduated today?"

"Yeah, from Dunbar" he shared smiling.

"Tell him I said congratulations."

"Sure will" he assured her admiring the weight she have put on and how phat her ass appeared with her slightly flaring hips.

"Did you graduate yet?" she asked removing the curlers from her client's locs.

"In two weeks."

"Are you still planning on coming home?"

"Initially" he replied.

"What caused you to change your mind? Surely not a woman."

"A woman could but money is the determining factor" he replied catching her eyes. "I'm making damn good money working part time for a very prestigious company."

"Don't you want to witness your goddaughter growing up?" she asked removing the gown from her client and spinning the chair around for her to inspect her work.

"That is so foul" he replied shaking his head at her impish smile. "You are going to use Mandisa as a lure."

"I don't know of any better bait" she admitted giggling while accepting money from her client then walking over and taking a seat.

"I have matured so much living down in Atlanta. Do I really want to come back to Baltimore and endure the violence associated with this city?"

"I understand. I really do but those that love you live here" she said gripping his fingers and playing with them. "In the past couple of months, you have really been on my mind. Your absence have caused me to do some self-reflecting" she shared briefly staring in his eyes then slightly lowering hers again. "How come you haven't been home and don't bullshit me, please?" she asked staring in his eyes.

"Shit" he said to himself hesitating as they exchanged stares, but he couldn't continue staring in her eyes. He knew this damn question would filter out of her mouth and now it have. The question he need to ask himself is lie or speak the truth?

"Akeem" she said in a voice that caused him to refocus on her eyes.

"Talk to me please" she insisted not understanding him hesitating and being evasive.

He gave her a nervous grin then took a deep breath and slowly exhaled. "Do you remember how much in love with you I was?"

"Of course, I do" she replied solemnly.

"Although the world thought that you and I was an item, we have never been officially boyfriend and girlfriend, but seeing you pregnant, how do I explain that I felt betrayed?" he got it out for the first time, and he couldn't hide his embarrassment.

"I know I embarrass you but not as much as I embarrass myself" she replied slightly shaking her head. "As hard as you tried to hide your hurt, the pain I administer was too much for you to ignore. I caused a pain in your eyes that I hope I never induce again. I wish I could turn back the hands of time and be the woman I needed to be on that special night, but I can't. Although you said you would be there for me, you was the last person I expect to see when Mandy was born" she admitted smiling. "You accepting to eb her godfather brought immense joy to my aching heart.

"It's an honor Ashanti" he replied slightly smiling.

"Yeah, I heard. I know that if anything were to happen to me that you would take care of her like she was your own" she shared staring in his eyes.

"That goes without saying" he replied sincerely.

"Do you still love me?" she blurted out.

"I will always love you Ashanti, but the question is, could I fall back in love with you."

"Can you?" she found herself asking afraid of his reply.

"I honestly don't know Ashanti" he replied in a soft voice.

She remained quiet taking in the contour of his face. He have become more handsome, and she never thought that was possible. Why didn't he have a girlfriend down in Atlanta made her ponder.

With Spelman just across campus, she assumed some young lady would capture his heart, but she was wrong. Completely wrong. That was the same mind set she had that caused her to start playing baseball sex games with Derrick punk ass until he scored a home run. Her own conjured assumption is what caused her own destruction. Has her deception caused him to stop seeking love? She hope not. She suddenly felt Daisy and the other women eyes on her.

"Can we patch up before you leave? I genuinely want you to see Mandy and take a picture with you."

"Definitely, when?"

"How about tonight?" she suggested with a coy smile.

"Na, I got something that need attentions."

"I get off at two o'clock tomorrow."

"That sound good for me" he replied.

"Will you call me later?" she asked getting to her feet with him.

"No promises" he said staring in her eyes grinning.

"I know" she replied sighing. "I'll be content for tomorrow" she smiled.

"Thank you" he replied adjusting his hat then kissing her lightly on the lips before tipping his hat to the other ladies before walking out.

"J-Lo, girlfriend" called Daisy snapping her out of her trance.

"Huh?" she replied coming out of her daydream and staring over at her.

"Whatever it takes, you need to get that man back" she suggested. "I thought he was attractive when he was younger, but now, damn girl. He is handsome as a motherfucker."

"Isn't he with his chocolate ass self" she giggled walking over and taking a seat in her chair. "That man makes my heart flutter and my panties moist" she shared causing them to burst out laughing.

"Shit my old pussy had the audacity to start fibrillating" she confess causing the ladies to burst out laughing again. "You need to get him back young lady."

"How Daisy?"

"How?" she repeated then burst out laughing. "You are a woman. Seduce him girl."

"That won't work on Akeem. He's too intellectual and desirable to fall into a dumb trap like that" she shared smiling. "Na, I need something much better that using sex to lure him in and I have been contemplating on something" she admitted with a coy smile.

"Well, you have a couple of days to come up with something.

"Indeed, I do" she replied then leaning back contemplating her play. There was a business proposition that have been churning in her head for over a year. There was no guarantees that he will stay in town even he if agree to help finance what she was considering. Tomorrow she will make her pitch.

He was at his house joking and laughing with Khalil and Amiri. Khalil have been making a lot of noise in the city over the past two years with certain politicians reaching out to him. He was considering getting his master's degree once graduating from Morgan State while Amiri wanted to graduate from the University of Maryland and go straight into the work force. Khalil and Storm was eager to start playing house together, but he was adamant that she graduate from Georgetown University for venturing into that realm. Amiri was just enjoying life and the smorgasbord of young ladies that were vying for his attention. They were sitting on the family room floor listening to jazz and smoking blunts when the doorbell rang. Khalil went to answer it.

"Hey, Sunshine" he greeted smiling down on her then giving her a hug.

"Damn, Khalil" she said extending her arms and admiring him. "My girls would be all over you" she shared giggling. "Is your brother home?"

"Yeah, come on in" he said stepping aside to allow her to walk in

Walking through, she admired the portrait of them at Dru Hill Park when they were still young teenagers. "Hey, Amiri" she greeted watching getting to his feet and giving her a hug.

"Hey, Sunshine. You look beautiful" he complimented smiling.

"Yeah, that what I constantly hear" she admitted giggling then focusing on Akeem. "What you thought I didn't see you earlier today?"

"Actually, no" he replied honestly hugging her then kissing her lightly on the lips. "You look like a million bucks" he complimented staring in her hazel eyes.

"Negro, please. I look much better than that" she counter smiling then joining them floor and taking a blunt.

"How is your nursing thing?"

"Very well and thank you again for picking up the tap."

"My pleasure."

"Fellas, get low for me" she requested.

"Later, Sunshine" they chime together gathering their blunts and they instantly got to their feet then headed towards the basement.

"You did a hell of a job with them" she complimented staring seriously into his eyes.

"Yeah, they Have their heads on straight."

"A lot of young ladies would love to get their finger on them. They are both heading places and the last thing they need is a chicken box eating girl to trap them in a trick bag."

"We used to eat chicken boxes" he counter smiling.

"Like you said, used to. I'm a steak and egg type of woman now."

"I hear you" he replied snickering.

"Was you going to call me?"

"The thought ran through my mind a couple of times" he admitted.

"So, you wasn't going to call me."

"Don't put words in my mouth, Ayanna" he replied smiling knowing saying her first name would slightly irritate.

"Well, you know I'm a go getter" she reminded him. "I'm not too proud to go get what I want."

"That's for sure" he cosigned relighting the blunt he held between his fingers. Staring closely at her while she laugh, she had gotten extremely attractive over the past two years. Her honey complexion was still acme free and smooth. The only make-up she wore was eyeliner because he had always complimented the way it highlighted her Asianic like eyes and lip gloss. Her full lips still appears to be as soft as cotton candy. Her silk blouse revealed her black lace bra. Her breast were still firm looking and perky. She appear to be still working out because she look like she was in excellent shape.

"Come with me" she said getting to her feet. The white stretch jeans hugged her slightly flaring hips while accentuating her petite ass. She gripped his fingers then lead him upstairs. She was already removing her blouse by the time they reached the second floor. She toss her blouse on the love seat then step out of her jeans never missing a step and toss them on the love seat also as she walked pass. Victoria's latest secret was revealed. With her back to him, the song she dedicated to their love by Anita Baker "You Bring Me Joy" filled the room. She unhooked her bra and allowed the last strap to roll down her left arm then squeezed her nibbles at the freedom they now enjoyed. She step out of her lace panties then turned to face him and got a surprise.

"Damn, you got naked quickly" she giggled climbing up on the bed and staring back at his naked body. "Mmmmm, that thing look bigger than I remember" she said extending her arms out to him. "I'm spending the night."

"I wouldn't dare put you out until you had breakfast" he assured her walking over and climbing up on the bed.

"I wouldn't advised you" she said feeling his body on hers.

It has been well over two years since they felt one another's embrace, they entwined their bodies like a vine on a tree. They were like an aphrodisiac to the other. The things they revisited and explored that blissful night allowed the morning sun to catch to still embracing. Echoes of moans, groans, and pleads still rung in their ears. Like a feather floating on a gentle breeze, words of love and admiration were shared in a whisper. Since attending elementary school together, their friendship and love have endured the test of time. All words of anger were dismiss and replaced with by an everlasting love. Neither knew what tomorrow will bring, but just knowing they had one another's back would sustain them.

"Will you marry me Akeem?" the question flowed from between her lips.

"Huh?" he replied smiling down into her eyes.

"You heard me" she replied smiling up at him while rubbing his face.

"Are you serious?"

"You know I am" she replied staring deep into his eyes. "I'll give you time to consider my proposition just remember one thing" she smiled up at him. "Nobody know you as well as I do, and you know I would never disrespect you. There is nobody out there better for you than me. If there is someone, introduce me to her so I can kick that bitch ass."

"Yeah, I know you would" he admitted snickering.

"Are you still in love with J-Lo?"

"No, Sunshine" she admitted honestly.

"Then give your heart to me" she suggested grinning.

"Where is this conversation coming from?"

"My heart, Akeem" she admitted. "Men ask me to marry them not the other way around, but it was nice to know that you would consider my proposal instead of giving me a flat no" she admitted giggling.

"Why would you purposely mess with a guy's head like this?"

"I wouldn't but I would do yours if I'm able" she admitted snickering. "If you ever consider marriage, I'm an option for you also my love" she said pulling his head down and kissing him passionately. "Now, het up and fix me that breakfast please."

"I'm up" he replied wrapping his arms from around her and swinging his feet to the floor. He stretch before getting to his feet and walking towards his on suite.

"You got some fries with that shake?" she asked smiling at his firm ass.

"Na, just a foot long" he replied turning and staring at her. "You want some?" he invited allowing his dick to swing from the sway of his hips.

"Na, I'm good" she replied still feeling the blissful aches for an erotic filled night between her thighs.

It was well after one o'clock when he took Sunshine home, she had moved out of her mother's house over two years ago to her disapproval. She was disapproving to keep her only child close to her. She voiced her disapproval over the extra money that she was losing by her moving out. She found a beautiful two-bedroom apartment on Northern Parkway by Wideman Park. After dropping her off, he headed towards Park Heights to look up J-Lo. He was surprised to see her standing on the corner waiting on him. He pulled up next to her and unlocked the door.

"Hey" she greeted leaning over and kissing him lightly on the lips. "You look GQ as usual."

"I don't see you in Aqua blue often. That dress truly look good on you."

"Thank you" she said fastening her seatbelt.

"So, what you want to do?"

"I want to show you something" she replied grinning.

"I'm not sure I like that little grin of yours" he replied returning her grin. "So, in which direction do I go?"

"Head to Fulton and Clifton Street."

"You got it" he replied peeking in his side-view mirror before pulling away from the curb. "What did you do last night?" he casually asked.

"I was thinking about you honestly" she admitted peeking over at him. "Mistakes of the past can't be alter but of course, I wish they could. I wanted my first child to be yours. Instead, I allowed my curiosity to get the best of me and got caught up."

"Isn't Derrick a good father?"

"He's learning to be, but he's not the person I was in love with" she replied slightly smiling. "How can I still make such a statement?"

"You said it I didn't" he replied peeking over at her as they drove pass Mondawmin Mall. As he turned on Fulton Street, he found a parking space near the corner then climbed out. "Okay, what am I looking for?" he asked staring around.

"This" smiled at the building of an abandon beauty salon. "What do you think?"

"Nice" he replied studying the foundation as he walked. He notice a group of guys watching them with one at the mouth of the alley. "You do know this is someone's corner, right?"

"What do you mean?" she asked looking around.

"Somebody is selling drugs from that alley" he informed her.

"Are you serious?" she asked taking a closer look at the guy. She notice several people emerging from the alley and disbursing in several directions. "Damn."

"Yeah" he replied smiling.

"I can get a great price on this building if you cosign with me."

"Be a part owner?" he asked staring at her. "You are serious."

"Yeah, I'm serious" she replied smiling up at him. "I know we can make a lot of money at this location" she said with conviction. "There is no salons in the area. With the recruits I can obtain from meeting people, We can be sitting on a gold mine. I learned the lessons of the business from observing Lady T and Daisy over the years. With your connections in the streets, I know we can pull this off. What do you say?"

"Are they apartments up there?" he asked ignoring her question.

"Yeah, two apartments with two-bedrooms" she replied.

He stood staring up at the building. "How much are they asking?"

"Two-fifty for the building" she replied.

"Two-fifty with an additional two-hundred with everything that is going to be needed like chairs and products, right?"

"Yeah" she replied unable to read his intentions. "I have a whole seller in D.C that I know."

"How much do you need from me?"

"I only saved ten-thousand-dollars" she admitted. The apartments upstairs was an afterthought for her. She wanted the building first.

"I'll put the certified check in the realtor's hand tomorrow after I have a conversation with him."

"Oh, thank you" she said leaping into his arms revealing her jubilation.

"Damn, woman. You have picked up weight" he said lowering her back to the ground. "After him and I have an agreement, I know of a remodel company that I can get under contract to get started on the apartments."

"I didn't consider the money that could be made from them" she admitted smiling.

"Don't trouble yourself about it because all the revenue from the apartments are coming straight to me and we can split what you make in the salon. Is that cool with you?" he informed her smiling.

"Yeah" she replied grinning.

"So, have you thought up a name for your place?"

"Of course," she replied flashing her broad smile. "ATM and J-Lo."

"Of course," he replied smiling then gripping her fingers and leading her back towards the car.

"So, tell me Akeem" she started then pausing before continuing. "What about you and me? Is there a future for us?"

"Besides, this business adventure, our time has crept pass us Ashanti. We must continue on our separate road and see if we ever meet in the fork of the road."

"You know I don't want to hear that Akeem."

"Would you prefer a lie? A lie leading to me taking advantage of you sexually then politely excusing myself. Is that what you want Ashanti?"

"Of course, not Akeem" she replied softly.

"I don't take pleasure in hearing those words being audible and filtering pass my lips. I going to give you truth than give you deception."

"I don't want the truth, sometimes" she replied slightly smiling.

"Maybe not but it's better than a lie J" he said staring in her eyes.

"You are extinguishing my hopes and dreams" she admitted as sadness started creeping into her eyes.

"We are about to commence on a very profitable journey together Ashanti. I remember you always talking about being your own boss. Well, baby. You are about to be the owner of your own salon. So, don't you shed a tear on what could have been and focus on what is about to happen" he advised her staring down into her eyes.

"You're right" she said catching the one tear that had escape her right eye. "I apologize for being so damn emotional" she said with a faint smile.

"No apology needed."

"So, will you be returning to Baltimore?"

"I don't have to be here for our business to flourish" he replied with a coy smile. He knew his response was one that she consider before making her pitch.

"No, you don't but a lot of people would love to see you at the grand opening."

"Oh, I'll be here for that" he assured her. "There are a lot of things that I need to alleviate down in Atlanta. Am I going to take the extreme pay that this very prestigious firm want to offer me after graduating and revisit some previous adventures or return to where my family and loved one resides? This is my dilemma Ashanti" he shared.

Khalil and Amiri came to Atlanta a week ahead of his graduation. Since coming down over a year ago, he had to put them on pause. They were invading his apartment twice a month flyfishing after the Southern girls and scoring big. They would spend two days in a hotel room with the adventurous young corn bread eating slightly naïve to the world young ladies. On Monday morning around ten o'clock, he was surrounded by his loved ones including a surprise visitor, his mother. She had miss all of her sons high school graduations, but she refused to allow her addiction and pride to deny herself of witnessing her oldest son graduating college. Dress in a black dress that hit her at her knees and her long thick hair immaculately done, you would never suspect she was a full blown junky. His father had put a round trip ticket in her hands and waited to see what she would do? Would she cash it in and get low or try to mend the bridge between her children?

Entering the auditorium, he bid them goodbye as he went to the meeting place for the graduating class. As the line seem to move quickly, he took time to reflect on his previous life. The odds were drastically against him from achieving the things that he have. According to Baltimore City Police statistic, he should have dropped out of school either after graduating middle school or before but remaining in high school wasn't consider. He was supposed to be a juvenile delinquent with the path to his incarceration already laid out for him, but he eluded their traps and took both of his brothers with him. With everything that he had accomplish, he still had some serious unfinish business and decisions to make concerning his personal life. Storm mother have come to fall in love with his calm and intellectual wit while her father witness how attentive he was towards his daughter and never allowed his eyes to wonder even when it was obvious that some of their friends has obvious aspirations. She understood why her daughter praise him as she does for forcing her to open her peddles and allow her voice to be heard. He was definitely a rare find. Handsome, strong, educated and with no baby momma drama. If he does return to Baltimore, he won't live in Baltimore but one of the outer counties. His heart will always be in Baltimore, but his body doesn't necessarily have to be. He had kept in contact with very few of his old close friends and most of them were women. Sunshine was the one that knew how to make him laugh with her crazy ass. She was one person that will always reside in his heart. As far as his mother was concern, she was who she was and will be. A lifelong scandalous motherfucker snitch and dedicated junky. End of story.

During the gathering at his apartment, he introduced everybody to Cola. She instantly put Khalil and Amiri on blast with their flirting ways. They both confess to admiring her witty mind and beauty. Witnessing Sunshine snatching her up, he knew they would hit it off even though Cola had a lot of apprehension. During their private conversation on the balcony, Akeem watched them intensely trying to read their body language. They would periodically stare in at him then burst out laughing.

"You know they are talking about you, right?" his father whisper in his ears grinning.

"No doubt about that" he said taking a sip from his glass of Moscato.

"So, she is the woman you are contemplating on staying in Atlanta for, huh?"

"Yes, sir. Contemplating" he reiterated staring up into his eyes.

"She appears to be sweet?"

"She is Pop and she come from old money" he included with an impish grin.

"Stop, you sound like Smooth" he teased snickering. "You know Sunshine will be very disappointed if you stayed down South."

"That goes without saying, I would be closing a very important door of my past Pop" he admitted unconsciously smiling out at her. "Whoever pull her will have a soldier by their side Pop and a woman who have their back, but I won't have any empathy if he is caught cheating. I told her I have bail money for her" he shared snickering. "She is one hell of a good woman. They kind you introduce to your family."

"True but it wouldn't be you son" he reminded him. "She have constantly shared her love and aspiration with your mother over the years. Her love is undeniable" he shared smiling out at them her sharing another laugh with her competitor. "I can't tell you which woman is better considering how your mother turned out" he stated making Akeem to spit out his drink in his hand and rush towards the kitchen laughing with his father in tow laughing also. He didn't mean for it not come out as a joke, it just materialized as a damn good one. He stared back at her talking to their other two sons. "She was a damn good woman back in the day before she started fucking with her bitch ass brother T.C." he shared when their relationship started deteriorating. "That was ions ago" he said suddenly becoming quiet.

"You alright Pop?" he asked seeing a hardness coming to his eyes.

"Yeah" he replied focusing his eyes back on him. "I got something for you. Come on" he said leading him towards the bedrooms. He open the spare bedroom door and step inside with him following then closed it. He went to the dresser then slid it from the wall and retrieved a black briefcase plus a portrait of them when he was the oldest at six.

He thought he had seen what few pictures of them that was taken, but this one was hilarious. He placed the briefcase on the bed then open it for him to see inside.

"Whoa!" he said staring at the money. "What's this Pop?"

"A graduation present from your uncle T.C. He actually thought he could hide this from me" he informed him slightly snarling. "If not for you and your brothers, he would have been took his last breath. My love for yawl is all I need and nothing else."

"That's good to know Pop" he said giving him a hug.

"There is one point three million in there. If you do stay in Atlanta, you do know your brothers will be following you. When will you make your final decision?"

"In about six months or sooner" he replied.

"Well, you waited years for me. I can wait a couple of months for you" he replied grinning. "I have seen the gleam that come to those boys eyes after spending a month with you down here. I want you to come home."

"I know Pop, but I can't sign off on that just yet. I do have a business deal in place with J-Lo" he revealed.

"What business?" he asked looking at him surprise.

"We brought a salon on the corner of Shelton and Fulton. It has two two-bedroom apartments above the establishment with a private entrance, I got a remodel company already at work. So, I will be coming home for the grand opening."

"Alright, I'll leave it alone" he said with a smirk leading back into the front room after he slid the briefcase under the bed.

"So, tell me Sunshine, how Akeem get so smart?"

"He lost a bet and had to go to the library with me for a month. I didn't tell him about the little boys that were messing with me. He found that out later" she shared as they stared in at him and started giggling again.

"Have anybody ever broke his heart?"

"Yeah, his official first girlfriend me" she replied smiling.

"What did you do if you don't me asking?"

"Kiss another boy and didn't see him standing there. Talking about somebody that could have piss their pants, I was guilty" she shared giggling.

"How did yawl become cool again?"

"He gave me a birthday card eight damn months later. He carried me that long as a foster child" she shared staring in at him with slightly harden eyes as they burst out laughing again.

"So, yawl was back on track after the card."

"Girl, he's not conceding like that. I broke his heart Cola" she replied grinning. "He step up to defend my honor. When he did that, I knew his punk ass had forgiven me. The weight of the world and the loneliness of losing my best friend was lifted then I could breathe again. I'm a RN because he picked up the tab and paid for everything I needed. I really fell in love with him during my coldest time. He was always there to keep me warn and kept my heart from becoming dark."

"So, you know this girl name J-Lo?"

"Yeah, one beautiful sister" she replied smiling.

"Why isn't he with her?"

"Why isn't he with we?" she counter then started snickering at her expression. "No, really" she said becoming slightly serious. "Let's just say, she took another path. A path that didn't include him."

"Are they still friends?"

"A person would have to do some scandalous shit to get on his shit list."

"I've only been hanging out with him since his sophomore year. I saw him during his freshman year and watch the girls jockeying for position, but he didn't taste the fruits of ecstasy that was being offer to him too often. As far as we are concern, we have never made love. We have kiss often, but he never cross that line and I know that I am the reason why" she admitted.

"Why not?" she inquired surprised by the revelation.

"I have some personal issues that I've been working through, and he have been extremely therapeutic for me" she smiled staring in at him.

"Do you think he is going to stay in Atlanta?"

"I hope so, but I honestly don't know" she replied while exchanging stares then seeing him walking back in with his father.

"I don't mean to sound selfish, but I hope he comes home. He has a special place in my heart."

"Yours and a lot of other vying young ladies" she replied fully smiling at her. "He is a younger version of his father" she said smiling.

"Yeah, no doubt" she cosigned staring in at them talking. "I told him at least we knew how ugly he was going to be later in life" she mention as they giggled again staring in at him. He waved them off with his hand and they burst out laughing again.

For the next couple of hours, the atmosphere was very festive, but with the setting of the sun, the atmosphere gradually changed. The bewitching hour was creeping up on them. They had an eight o'clock flight to take them back home, but they were still leisuring around until his Pop tap his watch and everybody started grabbing their belongings. As they stood in the parking lot saying their goodbyes and exchanging a kiss with Sunshine, his mother pulled him aside before climbing up into the rented Escalade.

"I'm proud of you. Maybe I can make you proud of me" she said opening her arms to him.

He hesitated briefly before giving her a hug. "Time will tell."

"Yes, time will" she cosigned staring up into his eyes then turning and climbing into the rented Escalade.

While gripping Cola's fingers, he watch them pulling out of the complex and turning left towards the airport before heading back up the steps. They climbed the stair in silence as she turned the doorknob and walked inside.

"You have a lovely family Akeem" she complimented removing her stilettoes again.

"Yes, I do" he replied grinning stepping out of his shoes.

"You want to get your place back in order?" she asked staring around at the glasses in the sink and trays on the counter.

"Not just yet, let's just chill for a few minutes" he said as they walked out on the balcony and took a seat. Darkness haven't consumed his scenery yet, but it was closing in.

"Sunshine is so charming" she complimented.

"If you say so" he replied nonchalantly while lighting up a blunt.

"Yawl go way back she shared."

"I shared that with you" he reminded her.

"Do you love her?"

"Hard not to with a history that we shared" he replied. "It appeared that yawl connected."

"Hard not to with her brutal honesty" she said taking the blunt from between his fingers then pulling from it. She pulled a second time before extending it back to him then slowly exhaling. She stared up at the stars slowing starting to glow in the sky then asked. "Are you staying here or returning to Baltimore?"

"I haven't made up my mind yet."

"You know I want you to stay but I know your family and Sunshine wants you to go home."

"You never mention about wanting me staying" he said stating over at her.

"I thought that was evident" she replied surprised by his reply.

"Why because of all the time we spend together" he asked staring in her eyes. "Na, Shorty. I need a lot more than that young lady. Although I have never been a sailor of love docking in strange and exotic ports, you and I have never been intimate, not the slightest. Why? I naturally assumed that you wanted to remain simply good friends and I accepted it. Are you suggesting that I am wrong?"

"Definitely, Akeem" she replied but avoiding his eyes. "Who couldn't eventually fall in love with you especially after all the time we spent together. I see the admiring stares women give you. I see how they undress you with their eyes also and that's my dilemma."

"What do you mean?"

"Can I endure that" she confessed revealing her vulnerability to him again. "I'm not suggesting that you would act upon it, but my mind will play tricks on me. I would unconsciously imagine something is jumping off if it weren't. false accusations can destroy any relationship and that would be the last thing I would wish for our friendship. Derrick fucked me up psychologically by cheating on me. Trusting a man is extremely hard for me, but I found myself trusting you then my mind would start playing tricks on me again and I would pull back. Although you have never warrant such an apprehension, it still overwhelm me" she confess getting to her feet and leaning on the rail. She unconsciously shook her head knowing that she was about to sabotage the best thing that ever enter her fucked up dysfunctional life. She had set a high standard for any man that desire her heart and trust. Akeem have past every test that she had set with flying colors yet psychologically, she knew she was still fucked up. "Akeem" she whisper turning and facing him. "I've been on medication for delusion" she shared staring down in his eyes. "I've been talking to a psychiatrist for years and told her how fantastic you are. Although she advised me to open up about the love I have stored away, I'm scare. Petrified actually" she confess staring in his eyes as her tears suddenly started falling causing him to get to his feet and hold her tight. "I'm sorry" she whisper allowing her tears to soak his shirt. She embrace him so tight. "If I am afraid to commit to you, why should you stay? I know Sunshine or J-Lo will acquire what I searched so long to acquire, but there is nothing that I can do to prevent it especially if you return to Baltimore. I don't want to grow old and unloved" she sigh slowly gaining control. "Foolish huh?" he smiled up at him.

"No, Jasmine. I understand" he replied wiping the remaining tears from her eyes. "At least your heart isn't darkened to love, you do still desire it and that is a good thing. Remember Cola, love demand you give trust to someone."

"I trust you Akeem" she insisted.

"You probably do Cola, but not as you should especially if you desire their love back. No words filtering pass my lips could force you to love me willingly as I deserve and without trust in our love, how can we build a future for us?"

"I don't know" she replied peeling herself out of his embrace. "Who am I to deny you the love that you deserve?" she asked staring in his eyes then avoiding them. "I'll understand if you decide to return home. Just know you will be taking a big piece of my heart with you. I can only pray that this isn't the last time I see you."

"No matter if I stay here and work this lucrative job or return home our paths will cross again" he told her reclaiming his seat. They sat on the balcony far into the coming morning. The moon appeared so much brighter than usual. It was well past two o'clock in the morning when they started washing the dishes and rearranging his apartment. Hearing Donna Washington's voice, she gripped his fingers and pulled him into her arms to dance. Ever since he introduce her sultry voice to her, she always took her to him, and a smile would crease her lips. Feeling his arms around her and the intoxicating scent of his biochemistry, she hoped that the song would never end. She didn't know when the next time they would share these special moments. With the coming of the morning light, their fairytale journey just might come to a permanent conclusion.

"Are you staying the night?"

She have heard the hidden lust in his words every time he desired her, but she always denied him and why should tonight be different? She had crawled in his bed on numerous of nights to feel his arms, but she couldn't ignore his massive dick pressing eagerly against her ass. She would contemplate until sleep would overwhelm her. The next morning when she is woken by the morning sun everything was as it should be, friendly and without any animosities. He would prepare her a beautiful breakfast then accept a kiss from her and she would drive away feeling like a queen. "Not tonight baby" she said as Dinah sang the final note.

He remained in Atlanta an additional month to map out his plans and do his research. He sold his furniture dirt cheap to members of the Q's while giving his two televisions away to two pre-teen he had met on the basketball court. His tropical fish and fish tank he will be taking back home with him. He have grown very accustomed to them. He would stare at them contemplating many decisions. Searching the internet, he eventually found the house that would become his home just outside of Columbia. With four bedrooms, three bathrooms and little over three-thousand square feet, he will get the renovation started as soon as he meet with the realtor once he get home. The job market was looking up for him also. He had Howard-Packard vying for his skills and offering little perks. Although their initial conversation was pleasant, he wouldn't commit himself to them as they wish. Several engineering firms had little perks that they were offering also, but he was searching for more than just perks. Exactly what he was looking for he didn't know but he would know it when he seen it or heard it.

Driving thought D.C a little after nine o'clock at night, he almost stop to catch a set at Blues Alley but decided to keep it moving. He was anxious to see his knucklehead brothers. As he pulled up in front of their house a little after ten o'clock, he spotted his brothers cars parked on the parking pad. The tree lined street was exactly as he like it, quiet. He parked at the curb then climbed out and grabbed both of his suitcases. He proceeded towards the porch then inserted his key to unlock the door and step inside. He could hear George Duke and laughter from two females down in the basement. The last thing those two young ladies need was a third wheel interrupting their festivities, so he kept it moving up the stairs. He place both suitcases to the left of his door then grabbed the remote from the coffee and press on. As he got undress, Billie Holiday was singing "God Bless The Child That Has His Own." He got undress then flop down on his bed staring up at the ceiling. He started to pick up his cell and call Sunshine but thought better of it. She had to go to work tomorrow and inviting her over for his own pleasure wasn't cool but knowing her, she will jump in his ass for not calling once they finally do talk. He didn't remember hearing the third song on the CD. The morning sun creeping through the window is what eventually woke him up. He stared over at the clock it had eight o'clock. He swung his feet to the floor then went into the bathroom to take his shower. He got dress in a pair of black dress slacks, a blue shirt with a tie. He descended the stairs and went outside to sit on the front porch. Feeling the morning breeze, he stared up and down the quiet street before going back inside to prepare breakfast. The scent of the food floating on the air caused footsteps to be heard and feet descending the stairs.

"When did you get home" Khalil asked giving him a hug then walking to the cabinet to get some plates.

"Last night around eleven o'clock" he said flipping his wheat pancake.

"Why didn't you say something?" inquired Amiri coming around the corner.

"Yawl was entertaining" he replied giving him a hug. "You look more and more like your mother every day" he teased.

"You sound like Pop" he said grabbing some glasses. "Are you home to stay?"

"Yeah, things didn't go as I had hoped" he replied cracking some eggs for his cheese omelet.

"Well, I'm personally glad that you are home. Khalil can't cook for nothing."

"I cook well enough for us to survive, and I don't see you losing any weight" he counter.

"That's because I keep oodles of noodles on standby."

"How is school?"

"Straight A's" mention Khalil grinning over at Amiri causing Akeem to peek over at him.

"You are being quiet. What's up?"

"I got two B's on my last report card" he mention catching is eyes.

"Who is she?" he inquired smiling.

"Philly" he replied suddenly flashing his broad smile. "She flip my game on me and looking for her in the daylight with a damn flash light" he admitted.

"Is it like that?" Akeem asked smiling.

"Just like that" replied Khalil.

"The girl got my nose wide open" he admitted freely. "I finally got myself back in order after cutting back on my visit to her."

"He was hitting 95N like he was driving to Park Heights" Khalil snitched smiling over at him.

"When I brought an EZ Pass, I knew I hitting 95 too much then stop taking her fine ass home every other weekend. I wasn't even charging her for gas. That's how far off my game she has me."

"Are you still seeing her."

"Definitely" he burst out laughing. "She was here last night. Her cousin drove down to meet Khalil like he's going to cheat on Storm" he smiled over at him smiling from ear to ear.

"The girl has my heart" he confessed laughing.

"Do yawl have homework?"

They stared at one another and replied, "Yeah."

"Get on it after breakfast" he instructed them as they took a seat and said grace.

The house he had found on the foreclosure list in Columbia wasn't available. Somebody had jump right on it, but when one door close another one open. He was heading to a community not far from Ellicott City according to the navigational system. Entering the quaint community, he pulled up on the thirty-five-hundred square house and a smile came to his face. Peeking inside the windows, there was natural dense wood floors extending throughout the first floor that resurfacing them will bring them back to life and save him thousands of dollars. The back yard was massive with two full grown trees opposite of one another far away from the house. He will definitely get an inground pool. Peeking in the basement, he could envision a finish product. The roof look good, and the foundation appeared sturdy. With paint on the exterior and flowers to give it a curb appeal, yeah this could be home. He called the number on the for-sale sign and spoke briefly to a Mr. Winker. With the property being on the foreclosure list for two years, the owners were anxious to sell her at a price of four-fifty dollars instead of the six-fifty originally asked. He said he will be at his office within the next hour and a half. He went to the bank to obtain a certified check and presented it to him an hour later if the house pass the inspection from the inspector that waiting for them at the house. He told the guy to bring all necessary paper work that will require his signature with him. He will take over ownership if the house is deem worthy. One hour later, he was signing the deed of ownership and accepting the keys. The contractors that he had on hold were hire that same day with instructions on what he wanted in his four-bedroom, three and half bathroom house he wanted transform into his home.

With a two-hundred-thousand remodeling check in their hands, they got started the very next day.

While he was completing one of his tasks, J-Lo was unable to concentrate all week. All she was able to do was think about Akeem. She knew she was foolishly hoping that they could rekindle what they had since meeting almost eight years ago, but nothing beats a failure but a try. Watching him interacting with Mandy, she had taken some very genuine moments as they laugh at one another. Although she was still tight with her girls, they each had a personal life that didn't included them all the time. Chi had hooked back up with Dink and they were openly feeling one another. There were rumors that they were discussing marriage once they settle into their professions but that is just the rumor. Lisa had stumble upon an old acquaintance that J nor Chi was feeling. They didn't bite their tongues in voicing their opinion about Diamond and it wasn't flattering. Chivalry was dead with this street knowledge knucklehead. The class teaching to holding a simple door for her to enter first as a woman or walking by the curb to protect her from an erratic driver hopping the curb and striking her or getting splash as a car drive through a puddle was classes he skip purposely. He even sometimes forget that she is there with him, and they have pointed out several occasions that he admitted it openly. The truth will set you free and she freed herself from Diamond.

During the two months since he returned home, he kept his head on point and didn't let anybody know he was home especially J-Lo and Sunshine. The only thing he could concern himself with is employment, but for some unknown reason, he wasn't in a hurry. He rationalized that being a millionaire had a lot to do with it. When he got an unsuspected call from the remodeling company about his house, he didn't realize how fast time had flown. He instantly jump up and went to inspect his future home. Walking through the front door for the first time was like entering a dream world. Every specification was completed.

From the five-seat quartz island to his walk-in closet in his on suite, everything looked perfect especially the light grain floors throughout and multicolor patio and Olympic size swimming pool. He contacted the furniture store to start delivering his prepaid furniture. They could start delivering tomorrow at ten o'clock. He left the house to go to Five Below to obtain his bath towels CVS to extract certain pictures from his cell phone and had specific ones made into a portrait. With picture frames in tow, he returned to his house to find his brothers had left for school. He grabbed most of his clothes and took them to his house then sat on the screen-in balcony constructive from his bedroom overlooking his front yard smiling.

Just like clockwork, they started delivering his furniture a little after ten o'clock. By noon, he had everything in their respected places including the African sculptures and figurines. After inspecting the final product, he took a seat on the wicker set on his balcony and lit up a blunt while jazz filter out his bedroom. His neighbors had been wondering who brought the dilapidated monstrosity that transformed into a swan. Seeing it was a young black man, they stared at him like he was an alien. All he would do was stare back at them with an impish grin. The appraisal price of his home was now nine-fifty with the new additions. The highest in the community.

Tuesday morning about ten o'clock while he was sitting out on his balcony smoking a blunt and watching his neighbors leave for work, he received a call from Mr. Washington. The salon was completed, and the apartments were finish to specifications. He thanked him and told him he would be there within the hour to pick up the keys then got to his feet. He got dress in a black suit then walked out is house and climbed inside his car. After obtaining the keys, he inspected both apartments. They appeared larger especially with the thick oak color laminated floors. With double vanities in the bathroom, women will adore it especially with separate shower and porcelain tub.

He was walking out the apartments and setting the alarm then he made a phone call.

"Hey, Akeem" she greeted smiling over at Daisy. "Are you in Baltimore?"

"Yeah" he replied. "I was wondering when will you have little break today."

"Actually, I'm finishing up on a client now hair now. I can be ready in fifteen minutes."

"Alright, I'll be outside" he informed her.

"Okay" she replied then the line went dead. She took a deep breath then a board smile consumed her face.

"He's back in town, huh?" inquired Daisy observing her excitement.

"Oh, it shows huh?"

"You would have to be blind not to see your glow" she replied shaking her head at her closest friend.

"He has that ability to have that effect on me" she giggled waving herself with a magazine."

"So, what's up?"

"I honestly don't know or care" she replied methodically finishing her client hair then cover her chair. She grabbed her purse from out of the bottom draw then waved to Daisy as she walked out the door. The sun felt good on her face coming from out of the air-condition environment. She put on her sunglasses to shield her eyes from the afternoon sun then proceeded down the steps. Seeing is car, her broad smile came tom her face as she open the door and climbed inside. "Hi" she smiled leaning towards him and receiving a kiss.

"When did you get that naval ring?" he asked surprising her.

"You notice that" she giggled. "My girls convince me to get it on my birthday and thank you for the present" she suddenly smiled extending her right wrist to him revealing his bracelet. "How long have you been home?" she nonchalantly asked fastening her seatbelt as he hooked a U-turned.

"Three months" he replied with a coy smile.

"Three months!" she replied shock by the revelation. "What have you been doing?"

"Taking care of business" he replied driving pass Mondawmin Mall.

She didn't know how to respond to his answer. Taking care of business, apparently his business didn't included her. "Are you staying at the house?"

"Na, I have a place outside of Ellicott City" he replied peeking over at her.

"When I can I see it?"

"Whenever you get time" he replied grinning.

"I want to see it today" she said.

"No problem" he replied turning on Shelton Avenue and parking.

She was so engross in their conversation that she didn't realize where they were initially. As she unfasten her seatbelt and climbed out, she hadn't been at this location since she presented her proposition to him. The dark paint job on the building was very subtle but the sign bearing their names brought her broad smile to her face.

"Here" he said extending a set of keys to her as they walked towards the front door. He unlocked the door and turned the lights on then allowed her to enter. She was astounded by the elegance and details. She walked around touching a few of the work stations chairs before heading back to where the driers and her private office was located. She thoroughly tour the place including locating the controls to the stereo system that allowed the music to flow through ceiling speakers. She emerged looking for him, but he was waiting outside. "How Akeem?" she asked staring at him with a perplex expression. "You even filled the stock room with the products I said that we will need. How?"

"There is more Ashanti" he said opening the side door leading to the second floor. He unlocked the door and allowed her to enter first then closed the door behind them while hitting the alarm system.

"An alarm system?"

"You have to know your environment" he replied following her up the steps and admiring the sway of her hips. He unlocked the door and allowed her to enter.

"How was you, able to do all this Akeem?" she asked staring inside the bathroom then looking over her shoulder at him. "This place is gorgeous" she said admiring the kitchen while walking towards the first bedroom.

"Money and time" he replied. "When you give Lady T her two-week notice, you can also put out there that you have two fully remodel apartments for rent at eleven-hundred. I choose who I will live in them, and they will definitely be professional people" he assured her grinning.

"You can a lot more for what you offering Akeem. You have stainless-steel appliances baby with a three-seat granite island."

"Yeah, I know" he simply replied heading back to the door. "You can come through later and check it all out" he said opening the door.

"Alright" she sigh not wanting to leave. "So, what is my part of the remodel" she inquired with an impish smile.

"We have time to discuss that" he said allowing her to exit then setting the alarm at the foot of the stairs before exiting the door.

"Akeem, we are going to get paid" she boasted standing on the sidewalk giggling. "I didn't expect eight chairs and a beautiful chilling sections for the ladies."

"Is Daisy coming with you?"

"She is my mentor. I'm going to show it to her this weekend" she giggled. "I have five excellent stylist on standby also" she informed him smiling at the sign again.

"You finish star gazing?" he asked.

"Yeah, where are you going now?"

"You said you wanted to see my place, right?"

"Definitely."

"Then that is where we are headed" he said opening the door for her to climb inside then closing it.

As they drove up Edmondson Avenue to Rt.29, she was in deep thought. Looking over at him, he actually had gotten more handsome. With his natural pencil mustache, his smile appear broader and sexier. One conversation that they shared three years ago still plagued her mind. He still loved her, but he wasn't in love with her like when they were younger. Although those word cut her heart like a straight razor, she could only admire his brutal honesty that has always been a part of his character. Without them ever making love, they had a connection that most male friends couldn't maintain without incorporating sex into the mix. "Hold your virginity until Mr. Right come along" he had advised her because he knew he wasn't the Mr. Right, she was seeking during that moment in their lives, and she eventually had to admit it to herself. He had left for college in late August, and she turned up two months pregnant in May. She hadn't found her Mr. Right to played baseball with in Turnerstation. "No glove, no love" but she couldn't follow her own advice. To make things worse, Derrick had two other women pregnant. Her embarrassment is what kept her from confessing to Akeem. Daisy keep insisting that she need to step up, but she don't know his personal side. A slight and you're done. She had slighted him in the worse way. Deception.

"Here we are" he announced snatching her out of her daydream.

"O.M.G!" she said opening her door and stepping out. "Damn, Akeem. This house is beautiful" she declared looking up at the screen in balcony from the master bedroom. The seven-foot-high reinforced steel-frame black door had her shaking her head as he unlocked the door and allowed her to enter first. "O.M.G. The floors are beautiful. Did you coordinate or hire somebody?" she asked still in awe.

"Na, I did this myself" he said tossing his keys in the basket by the door.

"Can I take a tour?" she asked staring up the stairs.

"Make yourself at home. I'll be in the basement" he said heading towards the kitchen.

"Okay" she nonchalantly replied while her eyes stayed focus on a poster size picture of them in his front room. Someone had taken two pictures of them at a natural moment. The pictures was taken at the basketball courts in Dru Hill Park. They were so young looking and the expression on her face indicated he had whisper something illicit into her ear again. The two pictures reflect the before look of her blushing and the second look of admiration. She wish she could remember what he had whisper causing an impish grin to come to her face. Studying the one picture closer, there was something in her eyes that she hadn't notice before. The look of love. She pulled out her cell and stare at one of the many pictures she had of them. There it was again. Why did she notice it? Walking through his bedroom, he had a picture of her and her girls up at Chadwick with Sunshine. Standing on his balcony, she took in his neighborhood. Exquisitely manicured lawns and no debris on the street. A very tranquil environment. He could never acquiree the peace he seek out here in the city. She took a deep breath then retraced her steps. Coming through the family room, she stop in her tracks staring up at a poster size picture of him and Sunshine. He was staring in the camera with his little gangster style hat while she seduced the camera with her eyes and devilish smile. They look extremely sexy together. The sound of jazz coming from the basement is what snapped her out of her trance. She descended the stairs and found him sitting on a sofa smoking a blunt while sipping on some Parrot Bay.

"Who is this you are listening to?" she asked taking a seat next to him and pouring herself a glass also.

"Donald Byrd's "Flight Time" he replied. "I thought you got lost" he said pulling from his blunt.

"You have a beautiful home, Akeem. I found myself walking down memories lane on some of the pictures you have displayed like me and my girls up in the Terror Dome. We were so young" she mention giggling then slowly becoming slightly quiet while preparing the next question. "So, what are your intentions?" she finally asked.

"I'm waiting on you to give a grand opening date. Once you put potential renters in my hand, I can't start renting out those two apartments. Let them know that I will continue paying for the security system for a year. If they still desire it, they can either get with another company or pay me for the continuous service."

"I'll get right on it" she assured him. "I have some personal friends that were interested in seeing the place."

"You can show them, but I make the final decision" he reiterated.

"I know" she replied slightly grinning. Her friends would slight occasionally her, but he wasn't going to have it. "Do you have plans for the rest of the day?"

"Yeah" he lied.

"So, when can I see you again Akeem?"

"I honestly can't answer that question right now Ashanti" he replied seeing the feeling of rejection creeping into her eyes. "Let's try to hook up next weekend for a couple of drinks."

"Identity is a nice spot" she recommended.

"I know the spot" he said finishing his drink then pulling from his blunt.

"I can see you want to relax but I have a five o'clock appointment I have to keep" she said taking another sip from het glass then placing it on the table.

"No, problem" he replied putting out his blunt then getting to his feet. He grabbed both glasses then follow her up the steps. He place the glasses in the sink as she stared at a picture of him with his brothers when he was about fifteen. Khalil had that street stare while Amiri had that coy smile he possesses. "You ready?" he asked walking pass and grabbing his keys out of the basket then opening the door for her to exit. He set the alarm then secured the door.

"This is really nice" she complimented again breathing in the fresh air. He open the door for her then walked around and climbed inside. Starting up the engine, Dexter Gordon's "Cheese Cake" filled the interior. He pulled off the horse shoe parking pad and turned left. "When did you get interested in jazz?"

"When I moved into my father's old house when I was fifteen, the collection in the basement is his and I eventually listen to every one of them including the classical music by Baum and Mozart" he admitted smiling over at her.

"Are we through Akeem?" she heard herself asking. She knew she wasn't ready for the answer, but the words had filter pass her lips before she could check them.

He took a quick glance at her then focus back on the road. Where in the hell did that curse ball come from? "Yeah, Ashanti."

"Is there any way I can correct this?"

"No, Ashanti baby" he replied peeking over into her eyes. "As hard as I tried to get around what transpired, I honestly can't" he admitted slightly shaking his head.

"Technically, we weren't going to together" she snap back.

"Pardon me" he replied peeking back at her. "Are you going to used that as an excuse?"

"Well, it's the truth Akeem" she said staring at his face.

"True that" he replied never averting bis eyes from the road then slightly shifted his body. This conversation was over as far as he was concern. The words she was uttering were falling on deaf ears. There was nothing she could say or do to correct the deception she initiated. Of all things to say to him, she choose that. The truth.

After dropping her off, he called Khalil. He was surprised to hear that they were over their mother's house until he informed him that they were celebrating her birthday. The thought of buying her a gift enter his mind then buying her a card. Both ideals quickly left just as fast as they had materialized. Pulling up on his mother's court yard, he spotted his brothers cars then pulled up next to them. Only when he had step out did he notice his father's Escalade. As he casually strolled towards the building, his name was called.

"Akeem! Akeem!" a voice shouted to him.

He stopped and stared in the direction of two guys walking in his direction. Their walk was extremely familiar, but recognition was slowed. As they got closer, broad smiles were on their faces and then it click. "Monk!? Twin!?"

"Yeah, nigger" replied Twin without stretch arms. "Give a nigger a hug, fool" he laughing as they hugged.

"What's up Akeem?" smiled Monk staring in his eyes as they hugged.

"You, brother" he replied staring in his eyes. "How long yawl been back on the street?"

"A little over a year" he shared. "I don't know how you found out about us getting pop, but I appreciate you keeping our commissary account fat."

"My pleasure man, really" he tried to assure him. "Are yawl still in the game?"

"Na" replied Monk rocking while sniffling. "We can't patch on with nobody. If you put your stamp on us, motherfuckers will gladly put us on" he said staring in his eyes.

"Man, I don't hold no weight on these streets except in the basketball circle."

295

"The use that circle to get us patch on with somebody" he insisted staring in his eyes.

"Na, I'm not cosigning anything that might get yawl incarcerated Twin, so you really need to accept that and leave it alone" he told his slightly hardening his eyes to make him understand that he was serious.

"Alright man, damn" he slightly snarled at him.

"You should have finish college by now knowing your geek ass" teased Monk smiling.

"Five months ago," he admitted as they snicker.

"I heard your Pop got the hottest jazz club in the city."

"He's the only jazz club in the city" he replied sharing another laugh.

"Is that how you got your car? Your father brought it for you" inquired Twin staring at him.

"When have it become appropriate to ask a man how he is eating Twin?" he asked staring him in his eyes curiously. He took a closer look at him then he sniffle again, and their secret was out. It was right there in front of him for his eyes to see once he actually took a peek. They had obtained a habit while up in Jessup that he unknowingly was financed. "If you can remember, I got this years ago when I was making Park Circle the hottest spot in the city."

"I heard that rumor while we were up in Jessup, but I couldn't believe it" admitted Monk smiling. "You was making big bank at that location until it got pop."

"I was long gone by then."

"What happen to T.C? That nigger is all fucked up now" inquired Twin.

"Why are you asking me about another man Twin? What's up with you? You know him, go ask him yourself" he told him slightly shaking his head at him.

"Man, fuck that" he replied waving off his comment then said. "We are hungry. Can you help feed a motherfucker?"

He ignored his question. He stared over at Monk who was openly embarrassed. "Yawl been my boys since elementary school Twin. You know if I have it you can get it just like those tasty cakes yawl used to share with me" he said reaching in his pocket and pulling out a small knot then peel off a hundred dollars and extended it to him.

"My nigger!" he replied smiling then looking over at the dealers.

"Thanks, Akeem" Monk replied stuffing the money into his pocket. "If we are here, holla at us before you leave. It's good having you home."

"Yeah, welcome home" Twin said as a second thought already methodically walking towards the drug dealers.

"You got that man" he replied peeking at Twin as he went to a specific guy. "You be careful out here man" he told him staring in his eyes.

"I try to be man."

"If you ever get tired of this, I got a place up in Philly that will put you back on track."

"I'm listening not hearing" he replied quoting what he used to tell him when they were younger.

"I'm here for yawl man. Give me love" he said opening his arms giving him a hug.

"I know man" he told him in his ear. They tapped knuckles then he watched his devoted friend heading towards his mother apartment. A coy smile came to his lips remembering how he and Twin tried in vain to corrupt him, but he never bit their hype. They did little mischievous things together, but stealing was completely off the plate. He never took because he didn't want anybody taking anything from him. When they had come home from the juvenile detention facility, he placed five-hundred dollars in their hands. It was during those days that he told him he needed to cut ties with Twin, or he was going to take him down with him and I be damn, less than a month later, they were getting pop by five-o. Watching him walking into the building, a sadness suddenly filled him. He had invited him to come down to Atlanta to escape the path that he was walking, but he refused. He didn't want to abandon Twin even though the invitation was given to both of them. A mistake that he wish he could correct.

"Yo, Monk! Monk!"

Hearing Twin's voice, he snap out of his trance. "Yeah."

"Come on man" he insisted. "It's time to get on" he smiled revealing spaces where teeth once resided.

"Alright" he replied still staring at the building until he saw Akeem walking to his mother house then turned and headed towards Twin.

"How many do you want Monk?" the drug dealer asked.

"Two."

"Two?" replied Twin staring over at him. "Nigger I just brought five. You better kick that shit out. I'm not supporting your habit."

"Motherfucker, you have never supported no part of me" he counter instantly hardening his eyes and snarling at him.

Twin instantly checked himself. The last time he got out of his lane with Monk in front of people was at Jessup and got the surprise of his life. Monk easily beat the shit out of him. He didn't find out until years later that he used to hook up with Akeem on the down low and learned how to defend himself while hitting his heavy bag. All the time he thought that he was the alpha male Monk was actuality the alpha male. "Damn, man. Chill" he said staring over at him.

"I am chill Twin" he replied cutting his eyes at him. "Two" he reiterated to the teenage drug dealer. He retrieved his products then turned and walked away.

Twin stared at his partner in crime. He have come to understand this switch in character and have never liked it. Something, usually a change was about to occur, and he knew he wouldn't like it.

"What's up with your boy Twin?"

"He got something on his mind" he replied flashing his smile. "He will be alright" he assured him turning. "Yo, Monk! Hold up!" he called rushing to catch up with his best friend. "You alright man?"

"Na, a change need to happen" was all he said as they went towards his mother's house before she got home from work.

Akeem was standing staring down at them from in front of the door. There was nothing he could do for them until they were ready. His hands were tied. He knew Monk was ready, but abandoning his sidekick is preventing him from the future he wanted desperately. Hearing Amiri laughing is what brought him out of his daydream. He always did have an unusual laugh. He turned the doorknob and wasn't surprised to see that after all these years that she still leave her front door unlocked.

"Akeem!" his brothers put him on blast smiling.

"Knuckleheads" he replied tapping their knuckles.

"I thought you was still in Atlanta" Khalil said.

"Na, I've been home a couple of months" he whisper to them peeking around. "I've been dipping in the crib while yawl was at school mainly" he smiled at them.

"What have you been doing?" Amiri asked surprised by the revelation.

"Taking care of business, I'll share it with yawl later" he said with an impish smile.

"Oh, I know this is going to be good" commented Khalil already snickering.

"I saw Pop's SUV outside. Where is he?"

"Pressing up on Uncle T.C" Amari replied with concern in his eyes.

"What's up?"

"Apparently, T.C venomous words about Pop eventually reached his ears from the streets" Khalil shared while peeking at the little crowd.

"That isn't good" he replied staring back towards the bedrooms.

"What he thought his words wouldn't reach Pop's ears then he's dumber than I thought. Where are they now?"

"In your old room" replied Khalil grinning.

"I'll be right back" he said heading towards his room. Their mother was entertaining her old friends and associates. Their eyes vaguely connected as he headed up the narrow hallway. He could hear his uncle pleading before a loud thump. Opening the door, T.C was on the floor staring up at his father with fear in his eyes. His sudden appearance caused his father to cease any further assault. His eyes was menacing as he stared over at him.

"Akeem" his voice was low.

"Hey, Pop" he replied staring down at T.C then back up into his eyes. "Am I disturbing you Pop?" he asked with a coy smile.

"Na, this conversation is over. Right, T.C?" he asked staring down at him.

"Yeah" he replied containing the blood that was trying to seep out of his mouth.

"Come on, son" he said slipping pass him.

He stood there staring down at T.C shaking his head. Oh, how far he have fallen over the years. The drug that he once sold that destroyed many of fragile families was now his mistress. He suddenly turned and followed his father towards the living room. He wish his mother a happy birthday then joined his brothers in the kitchen with their father.

"How you doing son?" he asked giving him a hug.

"I've been good Pop" he replied.

"Did I see you about three weeks ago?"

"You might have" he admitted grinning.

"Are you staying with someone?"

"No, sir. I have my own home" he shared with them.

"What? Where?" insisted Khalil interrupting.

"Calm your monkey butt down and excuse yourself the next time" he said shaking his head. "I'm outside of Ellicott City."

"Ellicott City?" Amiri interjected staring at him confused. "What are you doing out there?"

"Assuring that I have peace of mind. One thing for sure, you can't reach me on public transportation" he assured him smiling.

"So, what is the address?" inquired Khalil already having his cell phone out and waiting.

As he was giving it to them, a knock came at the door then it automatically swung open.

"Akeem?" a sultry voice asked causing him to turn around. Sunshine sprinted into his arms embracing his tightly. "Hi baby" she greeted him kissing him lightly on the lips. "When did you get back home?" she asked admiring his attire while starting up into his alluring eyes.

"Hi, Sunshine" he smiled down into her enchanting eyes then took in the full silhouette of her body. "Woman you are so beautiful."

"Boy, I have always been beautiful. Your eyes were just cloudy from those other women" she corrected him returning his stare. "I ran into Monk and Twin by Shake and Bake. They told me you was home" she informed him. "You haven't answer my question, Akeem."

"A little while Sunshine" he replied slightly grinning. He could never slip anything pass her.

"A little while, huh?" she stated staring up into his eyes.

"Yes, just long enough to get some business taken care of" he admitted. "Who are your friends?" he asked trying to change the subject.

"Misty and Chilly" she introduced them. "So, where are you?"

"Just outside of the city" was all he surrender to her while her girlfriends were present.

"When can I see you?"

"Soon Sunshine."

"Na" she replied waving off his response. "I need something more concrete" she insisted staring up into his eyes. "When can I see you?"

"How about this Saturday?"

"How about tomorrow night?"

"I can't Sunshine" he insisted returning her stare.

"Since when, you can't?" she counter with her hand on her hip staring in his eyes. "A man can do what he wants to do at any time, right?" she quoted his own words back at him with a coy smile.

"Good shot" he admitted grinning.

"Well?" she asked grinning at him.

"I'll pick you up at nine."

"Make it eight o'clock instead I might want to discuss something."

"Okay but I'm not cooking for your greedy butt" he informed her.

"That's okay" she replied getting on her toes to kiss him on the lips. "You are all the substance I need" she whisper. "Bye, Mr. Anderson."

"Bye, Sunshine" he snicker at Aleem.

"What's up Khali? Amiri?"

"Not too much Sunshine" they chimed together still focusing on her girlfriends anatomy.

"Later yawl" she said leading her girlfriends out the door.

"Let me holla at you son" their father requested taking him outside.

"What's up Pop?"

"I'm glad to have you home" he mention pausing.

"But?"

"But I wish you had stayed in Atlanta; these streets are crazy Akeem. If you had stayed, your brothers would have eventually joined you. You know that right?"

"Not necessarily Pop" he corrected him. "Khalil voice is reaching a lot of people and they want him to speak at community functions to curve the violence in the city. Amiri isn't going anywhere without Khalil" he tried to assure him smiling.

"If anything was to happen to you or your brothers, I don't know what I would do and that frighten me" he admitted staring down into his eyes. "Your punk ass uncle is saying his life is the way that it is because of me and not him choosing to stick a needle in his arms" he snarled at the thought."

"If he want to blame somebody, he need to blame his sister" he replied.

"I saw your old friends today. Monk and Twin. They really look bad."

"They will always be my boys" was all he could say.

"Twin is on the East side sticking up the young drug dealers. I don't get these guys. Don't they know that Baltimore isn't New York? You have five different boroughs to get low in, but Murphy Homes is less than fifteen minutes away from the East side and sooner or later they will get his scent."

"I pulled Monk up about him, but they are still boys and there is nothing that I can do about that" he shared. "All I can do is hope that Monk isn't standing too close to him when they do come."

"I hear you" he replied watching him watching Sunshine exiting the building. "SOOO?"

"So, what Pop?" he asked grinning at his coy smile.

"What's up with you and Sunshine?"

"She's my girl" he boasted proudly while smiling.

"And?"

"There is no and Pop" he replied still grinning.

"I hear that yawl been flirting with one another for years."

"Yes, sir but we have never taken it any further" he shared.

"Well, yawl aren't kids anymore Akeem and there is a definite connection between yawl."

"I'm not going to deny that" he cosigned watching her shove one of the drug dealers out of her personal space. She said something to him that cause him and his little click to stare up in his direction. Whatever they thought about doing ceased immediately as she continued on her way.

"So, what are your plans?"

"Getting a J.O.B eventually" he replied slightly smiling. "As far as today is concern, I'm going to ask Khalil and Amiri if they feel like going to Philly."

"I only been up there once since we went together" he admitted. Getting to know those boys, if there are girls presence, they will go."

"And I'm hoping that will be the lure that I need" he replied grinning.

"I'll bring you a house warming present tomorrow."

"Okay, Pop's" he replied as they exchanged hugs then walking back inside and found his brothers still sitting at the kitchen table. "Fellas, I'm heading to Philly. Yawl want to hang?"

"Heck yeah!" they replied jubilantly getting to their feet.

"We just need to make a quick stop at the bank" Khalil informed him.

"No, problem. Let's bounce" he said leading the way pout the door. They paused to hug their father then took the elevator down to the main lobby.

"You don't think we should put some eyes on our cars?" mention Amiri as they walked through the court yard.

Akeem and Khalil stared at one another then burst out laughing.

"We have all the eyes we need on our cars Amiri" Khalil assured him still snickering as they climbed Khalil inside then pulled out of the court yard.

All that day they discuss their personal lives with one another. Khalil shared how Storm had given him a scare a couple of months ago by missing her menstrual. He tried to assure her that he would be right there for her and their unborn child, but there was something in her eyes that he couldn't understand. Her whole disposition flipped on him. Trying to make outlandish demands on him and insisting that they get married, her whole attitude was like a stranger. The way she tried to talk to him made him take a few steps back from her. When she threaten to take him down to child support, he told her he didn't need no white man to tell him how to be responsible for a child of his. The alleged threat wasn't a threat to him only a revelation. When her menstrual arrived a week later, she tried to flip her script back, but Khalil wasn't biting her hype. He gave her back her resume then handed her walking papers. Although she tried in vain to make amends for his attitude and disposition, her words fell on deaf ears. Her mother tried pleading for her at their father, but you know that was a short conversation. Venomous from her at his college didn't make him jump out of character and that embarrass her even more. After accepting her rampage like water on a duck's feather, he calmly walked away and never looked back. He admitted to getting immense pleasure out of escorting several young ladies into his father's club where she works the weekend. He only stop when his father finally asked him to.

Amiri didn't have that type of drama in his simple life. Although the basketball coach and a few players tried to convince him to play ball on a scholarship, he had to refused. He wanted to stay focus on his academics. Although he's been spending a lot of time with Mahogany, a young lady from Philly studying Afro History. She was definitely smitten by him, but she wasn't taking no wooden nickels from his slick talking ass. She was time for him. She kept him intrigued with the knowledge of their history. He was soaking it up like a sponge. No weave, extraordinarily little make-up and a smile that could light up the world. Their cool disposition made them very approachable.

They arrived back in the city a little after eight o'clock.

"So, we will be at your house tomorrow" Khalil informed him.

"No, problem. Now get the hell out."

"You aren't saying anything" replied Amiri opening the back door and stepping out. "We will be over for breakfast."

"You better bring it with you, or Khalil must be cooking for you" he informed him.

"Na, we will bring something" Khalil replied. "Later, big brother."

"Later, yawl be safe."

"We are heading home and put this stuff away then chill" Khalil informed him. "Talk to you tomorrow" he said closing his door. They stood there watching him hooking a U-turn then headed out the court yard. "I'll meet you home" he said carrying his bags towards his car. Once everything was in the trunk, he started up the engine and Quincy Jones filled the interior.

All that night Akeem toured his house. He stop in every room to take it all in. From the personalized pictures to the Afrocentric artifacts, every piece seem to be in its specific place. It was a little after eleven o'clock when he finish putting his clothes away and taking his shower then walking out onto his balcony. With Giant Panda playing "Love U More," he took a seat and lit up a blunt. While sipping on a glass of Parrot Bay coconut, he stared out his community and all he heard was quietness. No gun shots or cops sirens every minute just a feeling of tranquility. Watching a family of deer walking across his neighbor lawn brought a faint smile to his face. He could have never witness this in the hood. Somebody would have taken them all out and have the on the corners trying to sell it. From where he came from to where he was, his journey was one of circumstances. Yet, he couldn't shake the uneasy feeling that more unsuspecting circumstances was still in store for him. Whatever is lurking in the shadows will be dealt with like he did everything else. Diligently.

In two months, a lot have occurred. He acquired a job at a prestigious engineering firm in Columbia. J-Lo had her grand opening with all her girls present including Sunshine. His father had hooked up with one of his connection at the Sun Paper and brought a page revealing the elegance inside. Her services were really for those women that she met at Exquisite, and she always gave Lady T half. She thought that she wouldn't need eight stylists, but she needed to hire two more part-time especially Thursday thru Saturday. The two apartments were rented out to two couples working at the University of Maryland Medical Center. As winter was fast approaching, his communication with Monk increased to the displeasure of Twin. He felt like Akeem was becoming a wedge between him and Monk. Granted, Monk had continuously mention about getting clean, but they both knew it was just jail house talk. Nothing. He will know when he's ready and no amount of conversation can convince him otherwise. Yet, he had to admit that their conversations about getting clean came more often by him. Talking about attending that prominent facility up in Philly with Twin, he said he was one that would never leave Baltimore. Why couldn't they just attend a program here? In his mind, all this bullshit talk about getting clean was a product of Akeem and he wasn't shy about saying it. What he needed to have done was close his mouth and keep his scandalous opinions about their closest friend to himself.

Sitting inside a shooting gallery on Fayette Street, Monk was watching Twin closely. Ever since their conversations, he have been acting strange or stranger than usual. Why was he constantly talking to motherfuckers that were rotten to their core? When he got low on him, he would always returned with that look of "I got over." Although he was trying to get him to shoot up more drugs, he have been weening himself off for weeks. He was down to two vials of dope a day instead of four. Whatever he was patching up with those guys to do wasn't legal and he told him he wasn't never going back to jail. Whatever he was doing time will reveal it. All he knew was he wasn't going to get caught up in whatever he was doing. Akeem's word kept ringing in his head. "You need to step off from Twin, but I'm here for you." And he have been giving him five-hundred dollars to start his recovery by not going to into the streets to steal. His words weren't falling on deaf ears, so he needed to act on it.

"What are you thinking about partner?" Twin voice invaded his thoughts.

"The future" he replied solemnly.

"The future" he chuckled while wiping his slightly snotty nose. "Fuck the future. Now is what is happening" he said slurring his words.

"Now, huh?" he repeated staring in his eyes.

"Hell yeah. Tomorrow isn't promise to anyone."

"That may be true, but we are the determining factors by how our tomorrows are spent" he counter returning his stare while holding the syringe in his hand. "If I continue to shoot this shit up in my arm, my habit will increase until I have an arm like Donkey and I don't want a hundred dollar a day habit. That would be twenty-eight hundred a month, Twin" he stress.

"So, we would simply hustle it up" he replied smiling.

"Yes, we would but there is a better way to spend twenty-eight hundred dollars than on heroin."

"Nigger, you been tripping since Akeem came home" he slightly snarled.

"Akeem doesn't have shit to do with how we are living our lives" he replied returning his stare. Talking to him only make we realize how my life could be. I have my GED because of him trying to watch out for us but you didn't want to take the classes and that's on you. We are still young man and can flip this script" he urged him still staring in his eyes.

"That nigger wouldn't have shit if not for his father" he snarled openly at him.

"Bullshit!" he counter snarling at him. "You can act like you don't remember if you want but don't forget how we got on when we came home broke as hell. Akeem hooked us up. As slick as we thought we were, we were so blind to what he was doing in middle school. Middle school Twin" he slightly smiled shaking his head at the deception. "He knew we weren't ready to get into what he was about, so he protected us instead of manipulating us. You know he created that money making machine down at Park Circle until those fools fucked it up two years later. You heard how T.C tried to hit up his father but hit Akeem instead. For the price to keep breathing, T.C took the second option. He paid restitution. What would have done step to Killer?" he asked snarling at him. "He was making big boy money at the time we were stealing tasty cakes. So, don't go there about how or where he got his money. He earned it the same damn way we once earned it except he didn't fuck up his money like we did."

Twin ceased his attack on Akeem's character because he knew everything that Monk was saying was true. None of his family sent him a dime while he was incarcerated but Akeem did and regularly. He just didn't like the conversation that they been having recently. Getting clean wasn't option for him. He loved the euphoric feeling that heroin induces. He could never divorce his mistress. "Listen, man" he finally said. "Do what you want" he told him with conviction. He didn't want to have this conversation or argue with him again. He refuse to lose the effects that he was starting to experience. "Listen, man. Do what you want" he finally said returning his stare.

"I intend to" he said suddenly getting to his feet then extending the syringe that he was holding to him until he took it staring up into his eyes. The scent of the shooting gallery and the bloody cotton balls on the floor was suddenly making him sick to the stomach.

"Where are you going?" he asked confused by his action.

"To do as I want as you suggested" he replied climbing the stairs to the second floor. "Enough is enough" he heard himself say to himself as the back door open to allow him to exit. Walking through the urine swelling alley, he resurface on Fayette Street then proceeded home. He walked straight to his bedroom and stripe down to take a shower. Something that he realize that he haven't done in days. Reemerging twenty minutes later, he put on some clean clothes and picked up his cell then push a preset number.

"Hey, Monk. What are you doing up this early?" he asked snickering. He usually don't start his day until noon.

"What's up Akeem?" he asked in a solemnly voice.

"Yo, man" he said hearing dread in his voice. "Is everything alright?"

"I'm ready" he simply replied.

He didn't say anything initially. "You know one simple call and the room is your in Philly" he reminded him.

"Make the call man."

"Are you sure?"

"Yeah" he replied.

"I will be there in an hour" then the line went dead. He searched his index then dial the number. A quick conversation and everything was set.

Monk was sitting outside looking at the environment that had took control of his life exceedingly early, but there was more years ahead that could transform him completely. With every journey, you taking the first steps makes your journey shorter. A nervousness consumed him like the first time he went to Jessup. He has spent his entire young life in Baltimore never venturing no further than down to D.C to comp their drugs. He knew that if things got hot for him that his partners would flood Philly and Akeem will be leading them like the Gotti Boys. An hour and a half into their journey, he spotted the old Veteran Stadium and his ears perked up. In the distance, he could see Philly's skyline. Fifteen minutes later, he was pulling up in front of the outreach building on Broad Street.

"Nervous?" Akeem asked smiling over at him.

"I'll be lying if I said no" he replied averting his eyes to the building.

"Good" he replied snickering causing him to lightly snicker. "I got a G on your books for you and a cell phone. If you need anything, call me Majako."

"My government name damn" he replied snickering. "I hear you Akeem. You don't have to get so serious" he replied smiling.

"I just need you to know."

"I've been knowing man" he tried to assure him still smiling.

"You better or I will fuck you up" he threaten slightly hardening his eyes.

"No, you won't" he replied waving off his comment trying to contain his laugh. "You don't start fights, but you can defend yourself very well."

"Yes, I can" he cosigned smiling. "I got you after you complete the six-months program."

"You do?" he replied surprised by his statement.

"Yeah, man. While you are getting your body and mind strong, think about what you want to do as a profession. You always mention getting into HAVC. Think about it."

"I will. Later man" he said tapping his knuckles then exiting the car. He took a deep breath then climbed the steps. Just as he was about to enter, he turned and gave him the deuce sign then walked inside.

In the months that elapsed, Akeem had been establishing a routine. With his job under his arm and the money that he was making from the apartments above the salon, he kept asking himself repeatedly why was he working? She had started acquiring high-profile women and guys from out of D.C as new clients. With his father using his connections, Town Beat came through to do an interview with the owners of the highly sort after salon skills and J-Lo willingly gave it to them. The pictures of the elegance tickle a lot of people curiosity.

Ring! Ring! Ring! "Hello."

"Hello, Akeem" a woman voice greeted him.

"Yes, who is this?"

"My name is Candy. I'm a friend of Sunshine."

"Okay, what's up? Is she alright?"

"She pass me your number. She is being harassed by some guys, up at Melba's Place. She wants you to call her."

"Alright, later" he replied ending their conversation then pressing a preset number.

"I see you got my message" she smiled at the guy. "I need you to have a conversation with someone" she said never averting his eyes from the guys.

"On my way" he replied ending their conversation then hooking a U-turn on Pennsylvania Avenue.

"What's up?" inquired Khalil staring at him.

"Sunshine got some guy sniffing up her ass again" he replied peeking over at him grinning then turning left on North Avenue. "So, I have to go and bail her out again."

"You have always been her shining knight even when she was messing with Biggie."

"Probably always will be" he admitted turning left on to Greenmount Avenue then pressing the accelerator.

"I don't know why yawl just don't hookup" he said slightly shaking his head. "When yawl hang out together, yawl give the impression of two people immensely in love."

"Our love for one another isn't the issue. I don't think I'm ready to be a part of the monogamy crew" he replied smiling.

"Those words might be coming out of your mouth, but your actions are telling people otherwise including me. You are ready especially with Sunshine" he voice his opinion catching his eyes as they drove pass 25th Street. "Are you still pondering over J-Lo?"

"Na, her and I have made peace with our relationship. She is in a relationship with another guy. She informed me recently that this guy name Stokey is requesting her hand in marriage" he smiled over at her.

"Are you serious?" he asked surprised by the revelation. He had secretly hoped that they rekindle their teenage romance.

"Na, man" he said turning left on 32nd Street. "I'm really glad for her man. She deserve somebody to love her."

"I really liked her man."

"I still do" he replied smiling over at him as her pulled up on the parking lot then exiting the car and walking back up 32nd Street. Turning the corner, there was a small line out front but moving quickly. Walking inside, they paid the entry pay then walked towards the back. Walking through the second door, they step inside and allowed their eyes to get adjusted to the diminish light.

"Wow, this place is pack" Khalil stated. This was the first time that he ever been inside the Melba's and the expression on his face indicated that it wouldn't be the last time. He acknowledged several guys and girls that he knew from around the city as they walked through.

"This way" Akeem tapped him walking towards the tables on the right-hand side. Walking around the outer edge of the dance floor, he spotted Sunshine with three of her friends. Standing by the smaller bar, three guys were watching Sunshine so closely that they didn't notice him and Khalil making their way around. He was almost upon her when she spotted him. A broad smile came to her face forcing the three guys to stare in their direction. Their whole demeanor instantly changed. She got to her feet and embraced him then kiss him lightly on the lips.

"Where are they?" he asked staring down into her eyes.

"At the bar" she indicated staring over at the bar. "Hi, Khalil" she smiled over at him.

"Hey, Sunshine" he replied never taking his eyes off the three guys then followed his brother over towards them.

"Evening, gentlemen" he greeted them while staring in their eyes individually.

"What's up?" they chime together starring up at him.

"That is exactually why I'm here" he replied. "What is up?"

"All man, we were just fooling around" the taller of the three responded revealing a slight slur in his speech indicating intoxication.

"If you were just fooling round around as you say, I wouldn't be here" he corrected him slightly hardening his eyes.

"Man, look at her. She is cute as a motherfucker" he replied snickering while staring over at her.

"Brother, you need to focus on me" he replied finally catching the guys eyes.

"Akeem!" a light skin guy interjected while nudging his friend aside. "He might have been a little aggressive."

"You know me?" he asked never taking his eyes off the first guy.

"Na, man. I'm just aware of you" he replied slightly smiling. "I used to watch you up at Chadwick back in the day and witness your other skills un the Terror Dome" he shared still slightly smiling.

"Much love" he replied placing is hand over his heart and slightly bowing then focusing back on the main character. "Do you a sister or daughter?"

"Yeah."

"What would you do if they call you about some guy sexually harassing them?" he asked staring in his eyes.

"I would find out what was happening" he replied.

"Supposed the guy wasn't feeling you?" he inquired still staring in his eyes.

"It would probably get ugly and very quickly" he admitted.

"I feel you" he cosigned. "Thank goodness we are feeling one another. The last thing I would hate to do is fuck you up on a Saturday night because of your refusal to accept an attractive young lady not desiring your unwanted advances. Hopefully, you will consider your own statement when a woman refuse your approach. There are far too many fish in the sea to have to sexually harass one" he said never averting his eyes from his eyes. "Gentlemen, yawl have a nice evening he wished them tapping Khalil on the arm then heading back towards Sunshine. "Well, my duties are complete."

"So, what are you about to do?" she asked and the tone in her voice didn't go unnoticed by him. Something was on her mind. He have heard it often over the past year.

"Gonna drop Khalil off at his car then head home."

"Why don't yawl stay and join us?"

"Na, but I appreciate the offer" he replied smiling down into his eyes.

"You want some company?"

His smile slightly dissipated staring down at her. Since returning home, she have avoided him like the plague. Although they have spent some quality time together, her attraction and love for him kept her out of his bed. He was her aphrodisiac, and he knew it. So, this invitation will not slip through his fingers. "Of, course" he finally replied slightly smiling.

"Yeah, I thought you would" she replied slightly hardening her eyes forcing his broad smile to crease his face. "Ladies, yawl will have to excuse me" she said getting to her feet.

"I'm going to chill" announced Khalil staring at one of Sunshine's friends.

"How are you going to bet home?" inquired Akeem staring at him.

"Oh, I think I can find a ride home" he assured him causing the girl to blush.

"Alright" he replied peeking at the young lady as they hugged. "Holla at me."

"I will."

As they headed towards the front door, Akeem peeked over his shoulder at Khalil. He was escorting the young lady to the dance floor as Keith Sweat began singing "Nobody."

"Who is the young lady that Khalil is sniffing after?"

"That's Ashley" she replied giggling. "I thought you didn't recognize her. She's, my cousin."

"Ashley?" he repeated totally surprise. "Snotty nose Ashley that used to be chasing him?" he asked already snickering.

"Yup" she replied smiling while gripping his arm as they walked out the club. "She's not snotty anymore."

"No doubt. She is incredibly attractive."

"It runs in the family" she replied as they turned down 32nd Street.

As they made their way up Rt.40, Sunshine was unusually silent. She was in a deep thought. He understood from their long relationship not to press up on her, so he laid back enjoying the music. Pulling up on his horse shoe parking pad, Sunshine came out of her thoughts and gazed that house.

"Is this you Akeem?" she asked stepping out the car. She grip his fingers when he came around the car then proceeded towards the front door. Inserting his key, he push the door open for her to enter first. "This floor are ridiculous" she smiled removing her stilettoes and holding them in her hands. She stared at the portrait over the fireplace of him, his brothers, and their father. Walking toward the family room, another portrait size picture of him and her on her fifteenth birthday occupied a wall. How was she to know that would be the last picture they take together until years later? The memory caused a tear to swell in her eyes. He had kept the picture all these years.

"Bring back memories, huh?" he asked standing beside her admiring the picture grinning.

"Yeah, good memories" she acknowledge slipping her arms around his waist. "I was so in love with you then and still am. You aren't just my knight in shining armor, but my best friend."

"Yes, I am and probably always will be" he admitted smiling down on her.

She stared up at him for an unusual long moment with something on her lips before releasing him and took a seat on the couch. "Akeem, I need to share something with you."

"Oh, oh" he replied snickering as he came to take a seat next to her. "The last time I saw that expression on your face I had to beat up Ike."

"It's something more serious than that baby" she admitted returning his stare.

"Baby?" he repeated slightly grinning. "Now I know it's serious."

"I've been keeping something from you for over two years" she admitted becoming emotional.

"Hey, easy Sunshine" he insisted moving closer to her. "Whatever it is we will handle it" he said with conviction in his eyes.

"I know" she replied grabbing some tissue and wiping her eyes then blowing her nose. "I need to show you something" she said opening her purse and pulling out her wallet. She search through it until she came upon what she was looking for then pulled it out and extending it to him.

It was a picture of her hugging a little boy, he study the child's eyes. There was an awareness and familiarity. A slow recognition occurred like he was revisiting his past. "Is this" was all he could say staring at the picture intensely then staring over at her.

"Yes, his name is Akeem Aswad."

Shock, surprise then joy consumed his eyes as he stared over at her.

There was so much emotion in his eyes that he appeared to get ready to cry and that would be a first for her. "How old is he, Ayanna?"

"Two, baby" she revealed catching his eyes again then smiling.

"Why didn't you tell me?" he asked staring back at the picture.

"I wasn't going to influence your decision to return to Baltimore or stay in Atlanta."

"Does my family know about him?"

"No baby not even my mother know that you are the father.

"Where is he now?"

"My aunt is watching him. I don't allow my mother to watch him until she gets clean. I definitely kept him away from your brothers and mother" she giggled. "If she saw him, she would know instantly."

"Damn, Sunshine. I need to see him" he express staring in her eyes.

"It's two o'clock in the morning baby, tomorrow I'll watch you sweat" she replied smiling at him. She was privately ecstatic that he wasn't angry with her for keeping his child out of his life for two whole years. She had wanted to share her secret with him for so long but didn't know how to tell him. When he asked her why she finally cut Biggie off, she replied she didn't need him anymore. He naturally thought because she was financially taking care of herself as a register nurse, and she didn't say otherwise.

"Is he why you don't have a boyfriend?"

"No, silly. I'm not that ugly" she replied giggling. "I can get a man from anywhere, but my son is going to need his father."

"You know he got that" he said hardening his eyes to show his conviction then stare back at the picture.

"I know baby" he replied. "I just didn't want to infiltrate your life or your love life. I just knew I had to share him with you."

"And I'm thankful that you did" he confessed pulling her closer then kissing her passionately. "Thank you for the blessing."

"The pleasure was really all mine" she replied with that adoring impish smile she sometimes possesses.

"Can we go to bed now?" he asked almost in a whisper.

"I thought you would never ask" she allowing him to grip her fingers and assist her to her feet then leading the way up the stairway. Inside his bedroom, under the diminish light and sultry sounds of R&B music, their silhouette undress one another while passionately kissing. For the next three hours, moans, groans, pleads with laughter floated on the air. Only the warm caress of the morning sun caused them to slowly open their eyes.

"You are so nasty Akeem" she whisper staring in his eyes.

"True but what does that say about you allowing me?" he counter as she burst out laughing.

They laid an additional hour talking before peeling themselves from the other's arm and went to take a shower. It was well after eleven o'clock when he was pulling off his parking pad and heading toward the city. Now, he was unusually quiet.

"Where is our son?" he asked coming into the city.

"Park Heights."

Driving down Edmondson Avenue, he became quiet again. He was a father then an uncontrollable smile came to his face. He couldn't wait to reveal him to his grandfather and two knucklehead uncles. What happen to the air suddenly? Was he hyperventilating?

"Damn" she burst out giggling. "You are sweating like a sweat hog. You need to relax" she insisted still giggling while taking some napkins and lightly tapping his perspiring face.

"Woman, I'm nervous as hell" he admitted taking the Hilton Parkway pass Coldspring Avenue and continuing until her got to Belvidere Blvd. then turning right and taking that pass the race track before turning right again. A couple blocks further he turned right again.

"You can park behind my car" she told him. After stopping, she got out and waited for him on the sidewalk then clutched his fingers as they walked towards the house. "Boy, you look like you are about to face the sentencing judge" she compared giggling as they climbed the steps and walked inside.

J-Lo was sitting at her station admiring the environment that she and Akeem have created. Since the interview with Town Beat over a year ago, she had the most desire salon in the tri-state area and in the city with reservations being advised, but walk-ins were welcome. With all the money filtering through her fingers, she would splurge in cities like New York and Philly with her girls once a month on shopping sprees. Akeem finally step to her and brought her snatch her back to earth. Stop wasting your money splurging like an immature young lady and het your priorities in order first. Stop throwing away good money renting. Get my goddaughter a home to be raised in and that message was all she needed to hear to get her priorities back on track. She still goes shopping but obtaining her home off the foreclosure list was her greatest accomplishment after Mandy.

It had shattered her heart when Akeem walked into the salon that Saturday morning with his son, the adorable little boy looked exactly like him. The pride he display in his eyes is the same display that she wish Mandisa father had in his eyes. How could she not embrace him, smell him, or touch him? He could have been hers. When he smiled at her, her heart melted like a hot knife in warm butter. She never live down that she had the opportunity to have him, but faulter. She had foolishly got pregnant again but did the worse thing a mother could do to her unborn child and sorrow still touches her heart sometimes. Although it was the best decision for her, she wouldn't be as careless ever again under no circumstances. They say if you walk theses streets long enough, you will stumble upon Mr. Right and Stokey is doing a hell of job emulating him.

Akeem was at the Amtrack station on St. Paul Street leaning against a gray metallic fully loaded Cadillac STS. A broad smile came to his face seeing his partner walking out wearing a black suit with a small gangster hat. His weight was back and so was his glow.

"Welcome home Monk" he greeted him giving him a hug then extending his arms and taking in the full transformation. "You look good" he confess smiling.

"I feel even better" he replied smiling up at him.

"Let's bounce" he said as thy climbed into the car then pulled off. "Why didn't you call me?"

"Man, you did more than expected for me for the last year. Hooking me up with the HAVC school kept me focus. I can never pay you back for what you did" he said catching his eyes.

"I don't expect you to Monk. We are family man."

"I know" he sigh.

"I do have a job set up for you" he shared turning left on North Avenue.

"With whom?"

"Baltimore HAVC and the entry pay make me wonder why I went to college" he said smiling.

"When is the interview?"

"There isn't any. All you have to do when you are ready is go fill out some paper work and pass the physical."

"No better time that Monday morning. I've been spinning my wheels long enough."

"You still have a couple of dollars?"

"Yeah, Akeem. I'm straight man" he replied smiling at him while slightly shaking his head.

"By the way, I have a son" he shared turning left onto Pennsylvania Avenue.

"What!? By whom?"

"Sunshine."

"I knew it. I just knew it" he burst out laughing. "I stumble upon her one day pushing a baby carriage. When I stared at the little boy, he looked exactly like you. When I asked her was you the father, she said no but I knew she was lying. Damn, congratulations Daddy" he said then burst out laughing again.

"Man, it blew my mind" he admitted.

"Nobody knew that yawl was getting down, but everybody knew you was his knight in shining armor" he said returning his stare as they pulled up on their old court yard then he put the car in park and step out. "I see things haven't change" he said staring over at the young drug dealers.

"Not until they decide to change, man" he replied as they watched Twin emerged walking with Little John. "Hey" he called getting his attention. "This is for you. I brought her a month ago for you" he said dropping the keys in his hand.

"Are you serious?" he asked staring at him then at the car and back at him.

"You always say I am too serious" he replied slightly grinning.

"Thanks man" he said giving him another hug then looked back at Twin. "He look bad."

"It's the life style" he simply replied.

"You know I have to say hello" he said never averting his eyes from him.

"Yeah, I know" he replied. "You don't know that he is going to try to pull you back in, right?" he asked catching his eyes.

"That's how the devil works" he replied slightly hardening is eyes. "He uses those closest to us to do his bidding."

"As long as you know, he can't deceive you. Later man, you know how to reach me" he said tapping his knuckles then walking to his car and climbing inside. Starting up the engine, Wayne Shorter's

"Footprints" filled the interior as he gently pulled off. From his rearview window, he watch Twin admiring his best friend transformation. Seconds later, he witness Monk reaching in his pocket and pulled out some money then extending it to him. He watched Monk shaking his head no. He said something to twin that forced that three-dollar smile to quickly dissipate and slightly repel. Their conversation was abruptly ended before he walked away shaking his head at him.

In the months that followed, life was steadily evolving. Khalil graduated from Morgan State and stumble upon the love of his life with Sunshine cousin Ashley. She graduated from Coppin State Nursing School last week and contemplating sharing a place together somewhere in Woodlawn. When he brought her an Acura as a gift, there was no doubt that he was feeling her. Remembering how she used to chase him down like he was a prey and hope the script have been flip was hilarious. They are truly in love. Now for Amiri, after getting his heart broken, he became another black Casanova. Charming every young lady with his intellectual slick street tongue, he would be on one quest then moving to the next. Although he have always put his cards on the table, for some unknown reason, most of the young ladies for some reason thought they had what it took to change his disposition only to realize that they didn't. Entering his junior year at Morgan State, he started playing fire. Her name was Dee-Dee, and she came straight from out of North Philly. Her mesmerizing eyes, seductive smile and chocolate complexion had Amiri completely off his game. When he brought her to Strictly Jazz and introduced her to the family, she was the first young lady he ever done that with and the broad smile that consumed his face that evening had his brothers teasing him all night. He willingly surrender his players card to dedicate himself to her. As far as Akeem is concern, Sunshine and Aswad fulfilled his life. Spending every free time with his son was his top priority considering, she refuse for them to move in with him and play house.

At the Winchester Apartments in Sand Town, Twin was conducting a meeting with a couple of associates. They had shot dope up together and were complaining about being hungry. So, Twin produced a solution.

"Listen, man. We can pull this off man."

"Twin, what you are suggesting isn't a walk in the park."

"Yes, it is Silk" he insisted.

"No, it's not" he insisted. "Fucking with Akeem shit isn't some walk in the walk. The last thing a conscious motherfucker wants to do is awaken that nigger lying dormant inside of him" he corrected and informing him while staring in his eyes. "Are you willing to pay the restitution his father will demand if Akeem is accidentally killed? If you are, I'm not. I would rather walk-through hell with gasoline strap around my body then to fuck with that family."

"If we do as I said, there is no way that he will find out who robbed him. The ski masks will hide our identities" he tried to convince him.

"That might be true but if he suddenly show up and hear our voices, we are done" he informed him.

"They don't say shit!" he snapped staring at him while revealing his frustration. "The pay is worth the chance Silk."

"There is no doubt that they are clocking big boy money but is it worth my life?"

"I thought you was about getting paid."

"I am but I'm not a desperate fool" he replied returning his stare. "Yawl will have to excuse me" he said suddenly getting to his feet. "I hope none of yawl get hurt and God forbid if they get their clutches in you."

"Man, why don't you step off and allow men to have a discussion on business" he snarled over at him.

"Check your mouth Twin" he warned him staring at him coldly. "I'm not one of your junky friends sitting here. I will fuck your bitch ass up and have you sucking on my Glock like that glass dick you secretly love" he informed him then turned and casually walked out the front door.

"Fuck him!" Twin declared snarling at the door. The money that they bring in all week is worth the chance. They don't deposit the money until Monday morning" he reiterated smiling.

"How do you know this for sure?"

"I got somebody on the inside" he admitted chuckling while taking a sip from his Hennessey.

Naomi was just finishing up a client's hair and place her receipt slip in the metal box. She sat waiting on her next appointment to show up. Looking around, the atmosphere was like a loving family environment. Laughter filled floated on the air and vulgarity was prohibited. Several young ladies were given the maximum of two pardons for their indiscretions but when they persisted, their privileges were permanently cut off. All of their pleads fell on deaf ears. As she sat staring over at J-Lo beautiful smile, remorse filled her consciousness. Why did she tell Twin about the set-up? Granted, they were once lovers, but he treated her like shit. So, why did she give him the information that he requested like some young naïve bitch? All J-Lo ever did was show her love from day one. She ignored the statements from her previous employer and took the word from a mutual friend then what does she do with the blessing? She set her up to be robbed by a worthless motherfucker like Twin. She have more than enough time to avert the situation from acquiring by just confessing but how would J-Lo and the others look at her? Would she even still have a job to provide for her babies?

Monk was hanging out at the 5 Mile House on Reistertown Road with his new love Flo when he spotted Silk with a group of guys sitting back in the VIP section.

"Excuse me, baby but I see an old friend" he told her.

"Go say hello then get your ass back here and whisper some more of your bullshit in my ears" she smiled at him rubbing his face as he got to his feet. They were junior high sweetheart before the streets snatch him from her embrace. Over the years, she watched his gradually descending into a state of degradation. It broke her heart to see him fall as much as he had then eventually got incarcerated. One thing she have always admired about him is that he never asked her for any money even though Twin was constantly trying to convince him to ask her, but his pride wouldn't allow him. When he disappeared for over a year, she thought that he was incarcerated again, and that Twin had somehow escape the long arms of the law. When he suddenly reappeared at her mother's house, she was blown away by the transformation. He had been home and working for six months to obtain the apartment he presently reside in Woodlawn. Ever since that night, they have been inseparable.

"Silk!" he called across to him while standing just outside of the VIP area.

"Monk?" he replied not believing who he was staring at as he methodically got to his feet. "Damn, man. You look great" he complimented showing him some love.

"Thanks man" he smiled at him. "How's things?"

"Still doing me" he said staring in his eyes. "You feel me?"

"Yeah" he admitted smiling while shaking his head him.

"I heard that you had flip your script."

"Yeah, I got clean up in Philly" he proudly announced.

"Yeah, I heard that program was excellent."

"It worked for me because I couldn't run back home" he shared.

"You got it through the courts?"

"Na, Akeem paid for it plus kept money on my book" he revealed.

"Akeem!" he stated surprise

"Yeah" he admitted smiling at him. "He set me up in a HAVC program up there and paid for it all. For a graduation present, he actually brought me an STS" he shared shaking his head smiling.

"Are you serious?"

"Yeah, man. The brother actually saved my life."

"How do you know him?"

"Man, me and Twin have known him since elementary school."

"Twin?" he was surprised to hear his name filtering through his lips.

"Yeah, he gave him the same offer he gave me. Whenever we got locked up, Akeem was right there to keep our books phat when our family wouldn't touch us with a ten-foot pole and rightfully so. I mean every time we got locked up Silk, Akeem never abandon us man. Never" he revealed smiling then studying him closely. "What's up Silk?"

"We need to talk. Excuse me yawl" he apologized directing him towards the bar then taking a seat.

"What's up man?" he asked with concern in his eyes.

He stared into his eyes then blurted out. "He's planning on hitting their salon?"

"What? Who? Twin?"

"Yeah, he's setting it up for a Sunday."

"Sunday? Why on a Sunday?"

"Because they drop their money on Mondays" he shared.

"How do he know that?"

"It's not hard to figure out that he has somebody on the inside" he replied returning his stare.

"Do you know who?"

"Na and I didn't ask either. When we talked Wednesday, I didn't know who we were going to hit but after I found out it was ATM, I bowed out."

"Do you know how many people he will be bringing?"

"Unless he filled my spot, four."

"Man, this is crazy" he expressed stun by the revelation. "Thanks for the info."

"No problem, man. Besides, ATM being as cool as the other side of the pillow, he never fucked with anybody. He offer Twin the same deal he offer you and now, he want to take something from him. Now, that is one lazy scandalous ass motherfucker" he slightly snarled. "I wish a motherfucker would show me some love like that."

"Akeem have always been like that Silk. We didn't know the money he was making being a mule for his uncle T.C in middle school because he wanted to keep us safe" he shared slightly smiling. "I have got to make a call man" he said getting to his feet. They gave one another a hug then Silk stepped off. He pulled out his cell phone and press a preset number then waited.

"Hey, Monk. What's happening on this Saturday night?"

"Listen man" he insisted. "I just got some information that you need to hear."

"I hear the seriousness in your voice. What's happening?" As he related the information that he just obtained, Akeem's eyes got harder. "Thanks for the info."

"Thank Silk when you see him" he offer.

"I will" he replied. "I got to make a call. I'll get back to you later."

"Alright man" he said ending their conversation.

He press J-Lo's number and waited.

"Now, this is a pleasant surprise. What's happening?"

"Call your staff. Tell them a family emergency came up and that the salon will be closed tomorrow."

"What about the clients?"

"Call them but don't open the shop tomorrow. Do we understand one another, Ashanti?

"Yeah, Akeem" she replied solemnly hearing the slight strain in his voice. A cold chill ran down her back hearing that tone he vaguely uses. If he's telling her to shut down tomorrow, she will although her most influential clients like having their locs done a day before Monday. She started cancelling her appointments after notifying the staff of her emergency except Daisy. She told her that something must be going down that Akeem insisted that the shop remained closed tomorrow and she cosigned her intuition.

Ring! Ring! Ring! "Hello?"

"Beanie?"

"Who is this?"

"Akeem."

"Who!?"

"ATM."

"Well, I'll be damn" he suddenly chuckled. "What's happening partner?"

"Sorry I haven't reached out to you over the years, but I need your assistance."

"Shit, you know you have that. What's the deal?"

"I need a couple of your soldiers" he informed him.

"Where and when?"

"Meet me at Appleton and North at noon tomorrow so I can lay out my plan."

"I'll be there."

"Thanks, Beanie."

"My pleasure man really" he replied smiling while ending their conversation. He haven't heard from him in years, but he will always have love for him. When a close friend of theirs suggested that he get with ATM concerning Smokey, he laugh at him because ATM was a hooper not someone that deals with shady motherfuckers especially like a ruthless motherfucker like Smokey, but he did. When he casually walked up to him and introduce himself, Smokey instantly took the same disposition that most motherfuckers took not knowing ATM including himself. When Smokey step to him laughing, he lit fire to his ass like he was a child. As he got to his feet a second time, he reached for the .38 he had tuck in his waist line. ATM allowed him to get it clear from his waist and start to raise his hand when he suddenly struck him three times center mass. He was already turning and walking away before Smokey's lifeless body hit the ground. "Who would have thought?" he lightly laugh picking up his cell and dialing another number.

The set-back didn't deter Twin especially after talking to Naomi. Who could have foretold a family emergency? So, the following Sunday he initiated his plan. Just before closing time, an old model Chevy with four individuals inside pulled off of Fulton Street driving slowly pass the salon with ski masks on their heads. If they weren't concentrating on the salon, they might have notice two guys sitting low in the seat of a Yukon as they initially drove pass. With them sitting lower in their seat, they watch the car go around the block twice surveying the area before finally parking. If they had done their homework, they would have known that the front door was never unsecure. Both owners were very aware of the environment they choose for their business. As they rush into the establishment, they step straight into a trap.

"Don't move Bitches!" demanded Twin staring at the two women with their backs to him as one of his men ran towards the office. "Who else is in here!?" he inquired still pointing his nine-millimeter at them.

"Just death" she replied turning just as three-gun shots erupted from the office area forcing the stick-up crew to stare in that direction. As the would-be robber stagger from the back and collapse to his knees, he had the look of surprise was on his face before falling face first to the floor. When they focus back on the two females, they both were cradling Mossberg shotguns.

"Drop them or get drop!" a voice instructed them from behind. Without much hesitation, they dropped their weapons. "Get the fuck on your knees" he instructed striking one of them in the back on his head then snatching off their ski masks. "Clear Boss!"

From the office area, Beanie and Akeem walked out clutching their Glocks in their hands. The fear that had engross their eyes were replaced with horror. Both men stop in front of Twin and glared down on him. All he could do was lower his head and slightly shake it.

"I guess we weren't boys anymore, huh Twin?"

"Akeem, I'm sorry man" he replied staring up at him.

"No, you're not Twin. You are only sorry that your scandalous ass got caught" he replied staring down into his eyes slightly snarling. "I would have given you anything within my power if you had just accepted my help like Monk did, but instead, you conspire to steal from me and fuck if anybody might have gotten hurt. Na, Twin" he slightly smiled down at him. "You aren't sorry, but you will be" he informed him.

"Take them to the house" Beanie instructed his men as they started binding their hands and placing tape over their mouths.

"Wait! Wait!" he insisted staring up at Akeem with tears starting to form in his eyes. "Please, man. Don't!" he pleaded openly crying. "Give me just one more chance for old time sake. Please, Akeem" he begged.

"Give you another chance to correct your fuck up" he replied lightly snickering. "Na, I don't think so partner" he informed him as one of the guys snatched him up then headed towards the back door where two cars were parked in the alley. As they threw them into the trunk, he and Twin exchanged stared before the trunk closed on him. Tearing were freely flowing from his eyes like a little bitch and the sympathy he was seeking never arrived. He pass Beanie an envelope then shook hands before he left by the front door with the two gangster bitches. For the next hour, he splash bleach wherever blood was located and thoroughly clean the area twice. After he was certain that everything was clean, he turned the video system back on, set the alarm and walked out the front door securing it behind himself. He peeked over at the drug dealers who witness the attempted robbers entering but never exiting. He climbed into his Audi 7 then pulled away from the curb listening to "Rock Creek Park" by the Black Byrd's.

Weeks had elapsed when Twin's name was mentioned. All sorts of rumors started surfacing about him and all of them was a possibility including some East Side guys finally catching up with him for the rash of robbery he was responsible for. Over the years, he had done too many scandalous shits to determine who finally got their clutches in him. One thing became absolutely apparent, he wouldn't be seen walking the streets of Baltimore seeking his next fix or stick-up. The only person that seem to show any interest was his mother but that was expected. A mother's love is unconditional, but the streets aren't.

In three years, J-Lo's life have transformed tremendously. She accepted that a grease monkey for the MTA could be very intellectually stimulated also. While watching his son and Mandy interacting, she realized just how happy her life had turned out. Although she will always have deep affections for Akeem, Theo love her madly and placed her on Cloud 9 with his affection. When they got married, Akeem sent them away for a week to Trinidad while watching over Mandy. With the birth of Malcolm, Mandy now had a little brother to watch over and she relish her role. All of her girls are now married with a child and settle into their domesticated roles, but they still hooked up every weekend to eat crabs and slipping on glasses of Moscato as they children played at one of their houses. Her and Akeem have also establish two more salons while he venture into the realtor game. He brought four two-bedrooms apartments complexes in Gwynn Oak and had tenants paying close to two-thousand dollars a month for all the additions including free HBO.

When Sunshine and Akeem got married, it appeared the whole city tried turning out. All of his basketball friends attended. His father's friend were flying high witnessing their partner's eldest son getting married. Monk and Flo left their two children over his mother's house. Their love glowed almost as bright as Sunshine joy. She appeared from through the French door wearing an Afrocentric gown and hair wrap. Wearing a smile, the size of the Mississippi River. She causally walked down the aisle to the man that fulfills her dreams and love. Little Akeem was the ring bearer while Mandy was one of the three flower girls. Relinquishing their own vows from the heart, their words touch those that knew them since elementary school. The separate journey they took over the years only made their love grow stronger. As they dance as husband and wife, "You Put A Move On My Heart" played. The words seems so perfect for them.

"Listen, motherfucker! If you want to get paid, I know a very profitable job, but you have to do it exactly as I say and no deviating from it. The last motherfuckers I laid my plan down to wanted to do it their way and none of them have been seen or heard from since. You have got to be ready to pull that trigger. Do you understand?" he asked snarling at them coldly as he look them individually in their eyes.

"Yeah, T.C" they replied.

"Okay" he said with a coy grin creasing his lips. "This is how it's going to go down."

Printed in the United States
by Baker & Taylor Publisher Services

Printed in the United States
by Baker & Taylor Publisher Services